Infinity + One

by
Amy Harmon

This is a work of fiction. Names, characters, places, brands, media, and incidents are either the product of the author's imagination or are used fictitiously. The author acknowledges the trademarked status and trademark owners of various products referenced in this work of fiction, which have been used without permission. The publication/use of these trademarks is not authorized, associated with, or sponsored by the trademark owners.

Copyright © 2014 by Amy Harmon
First Paperback Edition: May 2014
Editing by Karey White
Cover design by Rebecca Berto of Berto Designs
Formatting by JT Formatting

All rights reserved. Without limiting the rights under copyright reserved above, no part of this publication may be reproduced, stored in or introduced into a retrieval system, or transmitted, in any form, or by any means (electronic, mechanical, photocopying, recording, or otherwise) without the prior written permission of the above copyright owner of this book.

Printed in the United States of America
Library of Congress Cataloging-in-Publication Data

Harmon, Amy, 1974 -
   Infinity + One / by Amy Harmon.—1st edition
     ISBN-13: 978-1499535396
     ISBN-10: 1499535392

1. Fiction—Romance   2. Fiction—Contemporary Romance
3. Fiction—New Adult   4. Fiction—Contemporary Women

http://www.authoramyharmon.com/

OTHER TITLES BY AMY HARMON:

SLOW DANCE IN PURGATORY
PROM NIGHT IN PURGATORY
RUNNING BAREFOOT
A DIFFERENT BLUE
MAKING FACES

*For my mom,
the mathematician.
Brilliant, blonde, and beautiful.*

Prologue
The Origin

THE TELEVISION WAS on. Blaring. It was tuned in to some entertainment news channel, and the program's hostess sat at a desk as if that made her look smarter and made the show more credible. But her spray tan and her false lashes undermined both the desk and her serious expression, and he reached to turn it off. Then he saw his own face flash across the screen, and his hand fell limply to his side. He stared at a shot of himself smiling down into her upturned face. His arm was wrapped around her waist and one of her hands rested on his chest as she smiled back at him. The image then morphed into an old black and white photo, and he watched, helplessly transfixed, as the hostess of the entertainment show began to lay out her case:

Bonnie Parker met Clyde Barrow in Texas in January of 1930. It was the height of the depression, and people were poor, desperate, and hopeless, and Bonnie Parker and Clyde Barrow were no exception. Clyde was twenty years old, Bonnie, nineteen, and though neither had much to offer the other—Bonnie was already married, her husband long gone, Clyde had nothing but a rap sheet and an ability to survive—they became inseparable. Over the next four years, between stints in prison and life on the run, they would blaze a path through the dusty south, robbing banks, convenience stores, and gas stations, killing police officers and a handful of civilians, and never stopping anywhere for long. A roll of film and a collection of poetry written by Bonnie found at a hideout in Joplin, Missouri, brought the story of the young outlaws to life and cemented their place in the landscape of American history and in the imaginations of a worldwide audience. They were young, wild, and in love, with little regard for anything but each other. They ran from the law, knowing their deaths were inevitable, and in May of 1934, they met their fate. Ambushed on a lonely road in Louisiana, one-hundred-thirty rounds shot into their car, they went down together, their bodies riddled with bullets, their young lives and their crime spree brought to a close. Gone, but not forgotten.

So has history repeated itself? Do we have our own, modern-day version of Bonnie and Clyde? Two lovers, on the run, leaving chaos in their wake? Although not identical, the similarities between the two stories are notable. And one has to wonder if fame and fortune at such an early age aren't partially to blame in this story. Instead of the poverty that was the backdrop for the Bonnie and Clyde of the 1930s, we have the opposite extreme. But in both cases, we have young people who grew up too fast, were exposed to harsh realities at an early age, and ultimately rebelled against the system.

We've seen it time and time again—such a promising career, such a stunning talent. And we're all left asking, what exactly happened to Bonnie Rae Shelby?

1

Angle of Depression

Eleven Days Earlier

"I'VE HEARD EVERYONE screams when they fall—even if they jump."

    The voice came out of nowhere, making me jerk, making my stomach shudder and drop as if I'd actually just let go and was free falling through the fog. I couldn't see anyone. The mist was thick, giving me the perfect opportunity to let myself slip into the velvety white without anyone knowing. The thickness was deceiving, the density lulling me into a false sense of safety, wrapping itself around me as if it would catch me, as if I could just hide in it for a while. It whispered wetly that letting go would be easy, painless, that I would simply be swathed in a cloud, that I wouldn't fall. But part of me wanted to fall. That's why I was here. And I couldn't get that song out of my head.

> *Oh, my darling Minnie Mae, up in heaven, so they say*
> *And they'll never take you from me, anymore*
> *I'm coming, coming, coming, as the angels clear the way*
> *So farewell to the old Kentucky shore*

"Come on down from there." The voice came again. Disembodied. I couldn't even tell which direction it was coming from. It was low, gravelly. A man's voice. If I had to guess from the timbre, it was an older man, maybe my daddy's age. My daddy would have tried to talk someone down from a bridge. Or maybe sing them down. I smiled a little at that. His voice was central to my earliest memories. Rich and folksy, thick with the twang and yodel that had become my signature sound. In the beginning, I always took the melody, Daddy dropped to the tenor, and Gran would chime in with the high harmony. We would sing for hours. That's what we did. That's what we were good at. That's what we lived for. But I didn't want to live for it anymore.

"If you aren't coming down, I'm coming up." I jerked again. I'd forgotten he was there. That quickly, I'd forgotten he was there. My brain was as foggy as the air around me, like I'd breathed it in. He said "aren't" without the 'r' and the 'a' flattened out—like he was saying the word *ant*. I couldn't place the accent. My mind flickered in confusion for a minute. Boston. That's right. I was in Boston. I'd been in New York City last night and Philadelphia two nights before that. Was it Detroit last Monday? I tried to remember all the stops, all the cities, but they blurred together. I rarely saw much of the cities I found myself in. One place just bled into another.

Suddenly, he was beside me, balancing on the railing, his arms braced against the trusses, his posture mimicking mine. He was tall. I took in his size quickly, peering around my own upraised arms clinging to the support beam above my head. My heart dropped and landed with a sickish thud at the bottom of my stomach. It bounced. My stomach was empty. But that was nothing new. I wondered if the man was a rapist or a serial killer. Then I shrugged tiredly. If I was worried about being raped or killed I could just let go. Problem solved.

"Do your parents know where you are?" There it was again. The flattened "are" without the burr of the 'r' at the end. Not the same as my daddy's voice after all. Daddy was born and raised in the hills of Tennessee. In Tennessee we say our r's. We let our tongues curl around the 'r' like a lemon drop before we let it go.

"Can I call someone for you?" he tried again when I didn't answer. I shook my head but I still didn't look at him. I kept my face forward, looking into the fog. I liked the white nothingness. It soothed me. I wanted to get closer to it. That's why I'd climbed the railing in the first place.

"Look, kid. I can't just leave you here." No 'r' again. I was fascinated by his accent, but I still wished he would give up and go away.

"I'm not a kid. So you *can* leave me here." I spoke for the first time, noticing how my 'r' rang out in defiance, just like my words.

I felt his eyes on my face. I turned and looked at him then. Really looked at him. He wore a knit cap pulled low on his forehead and around his ears the way I did. It was cold out. I'd stolen mine from my security detail, along with a huge hooded sweatshirt someone had left in my dressing room. His cap looked natural on him. He hadn't stolen his, I was sure. Shaggy blond hair peeked out beneath the cap, but his eyebrows were thick and almost as dark as the knit of his hat—black slashes above eyes of an undecipherable color. In the foggy darkness everything was just different shades of grey. His gaze was steady, and his mouth pursed slightly as if I'd surprised him. It seems we'd both been wrong. I wasn't a kid and he wasn't an older man. He was maybe a few years older than I was, if that.

"No, I guess you aren't," he said, his startled gaze flickering to my chest as if to verify that I was, indeed, female. I raised one eyebrow and lifted my chin, demanding that he lift his gaze in return. He did, almost immediately, and he spoke again, his voice measured, his tone mild.

"The odds are, if you fall, you'll die. Falling might feel good. But landing won't. Landing will feel like shit. And if you don't die, you'll wish you had, and you'll wish you'd never let go in the first place. And you'll cry out for help. But then it will be too late, because I'm not jumping in after you, Texas."

"I don't remember asking you to, Boston," I shot back wearily, not correcting him on my origins. Everybody with a drawl must be from Texas, apparently.

His eyes rested briefly on my boots and then slid up to mine, calculating. "You and I both know you aren't gonna do it. Cut the drama, climb down, and I'll take you wherever you wanna go."

It was the wrong thing to say. I felt the fury fill my empty gut and roar up my throat like flames in an elevator shaft. The tears started streaming down my cheeks, my body's natural, protective, response to the inferno raging in my chest. I was exhausted. Completely spent. Emotionally and physically done. I was tired of being told what to do, when to do it, how to do it, and who to do it with. I was tired of never making any decisions for myself. So then and there, I made a big one. His words cemented my resolve. And I saw the moment when he knew it. His mouth moved around a silent curse and his eyes widened.

I leaned into the fog and let go.

WHEN MY TWIN sister died, death became very real. It was something I thought about almost constantly. And because she was there, wherever dead people are, and because I loved her more than I loved anyone on Earth, part of me wanted to be there too. And so I started to consider my own death, to contemplate it, to wonder. I didn't just suddenly want to die. It's not something that happens suddenly. It starts as a thought that flickers in the darkest recesses of your brain for a second, like a birthday candle just before it's extinguished. But death is a trick candle. The kind that you rub out only to have it flame up again. And again. And each time it flickers back to life, it lingers a little longer and glows a little brighter. The light seems almost warm. Friendly. It doesn't feel like it's something that will burn you.

Eventually, the flickering thought becomes an option, and the option becomes detailed and precise, with a plan A and a plan B. And sometimes a C and D. And before you know it, you start to say goodbye in little ways. "Maybe this should be my last cup of coffee. The last time I tie these shoes, the last time I pet my cat. The last time I sing this song." And there is relief with each "last"—like checking chores off a long, burdensome list. Then the little candles in your head become burning bridges. People who want to die burn bridges right and left. They burn bridges, and then they jump off of them.

That night, I had kicked everyone out of my designated dressing room. I made them all leave. I smiled and spoke softly. I didn't scream or cry or have a diva moment. I never did. That was Gran's job. I just asked for a few moments by myself. It was the last night of the tour and everyone would want to celebrate. I'd sung at Madison Square Garden the night before and Gran was in heaven. Tonight we were at another "garden" arena—TD Gardens, they called it. I knew I should be thrilled. But I wasn't. I felt hollowed out like a big, empty watermelon. Daddy used to cut off the top and eat watermelon like ice cream, spoonful by spoonful, until it was just an empty gourd. Then he'd put the top back on so it looked brand new. More than once Mama had taken his name in vain when she discovered that the insides had been scraped clean.

They had all cleared out—my stylist, Jerry, my makeup artist, Shantel, and a few others, wives and girlfriends of the road crew who wanted to be there for the last night of the tour. The show was over, after all. Well, almost. I'd left the stage before the final song and my opening acts and the band were bringing it home in the medley we always performed together to close the show.

I'd said I was sick. But before leaving the stage, I'd performed just like I'd been trained to do. I'd sung the songs from my latest album, as well as favorites from the previous three. With four albums under my belt, not counting the rushed release of all the songs I'd sung on *Nashville Forever* a month after my big win, I was established in the business, a headliner, a Grammy winner, and my latest album, *Come Undone*, had gone platinum.

I had fulfilled my obligations. And no one could say I hadn't delivered. I had sung my heart out, belted out each note while prancing around on stage in the carefully chosen costume—artfully torn, skintight, blue jeans and a black silk shirt with high-heeled, red cowgirl boots—straddling the line between pop princess and country crooner to maximize my marketability.

The lights had been hot on stage, but my makeup was still in place, fake lashes and expertly applied shadows and liners made my dark brown eyes look deep and soulful, big puppy dog eyes framed by loose golden curls. Those long, blonde, Bonnie Rae Shelby curls that had become the style little girls everywhere tried to copy. I could have told them it was easy. Mine were store-bought. All the little girls could buy them too. Sure, now they were expensive, but they didn't start out that way.

When Minnie's hair had started falling out because of the chemo, we decided to shave our heads together, light brown hair falling to the floor in fluffy piles. We were twins. Identical twins. Mirror image twins. If Minnie was going to be bald, I had to be bald too. But Gran said I couldn't be bald on stage, so the day I auditioned for *Nashville Forever*, Gran took our bus money (and our food money) and bought me a wig with long, ash-blonde curls.

"Dolly Parton always wears wigs, Bonnie," Gran had said brightly, pulling the wig over my smooth head. "Look at you! Blonde hair suits you, Bonnie Rae. It makes you look like a little angel. That's good. That's what we want. Angel hair to go with your angel voice."

I'd had angel hair ever since. Except now I didn't wear a Dolly wig. I had extensions and professional dye jobs and a hairdresser that traveled with me everywhere I went. A hairdresser, a makeup artist, a stylist, and a team of bodyguards. I also had a publicist, an agent, and a lawyer on speed dial. And Gran. Gran was a little bit of everything. But mostly, she was my manager.

Gran hadn't wanted me to go up to my dressing room without her. Gran was smart. And tough. And sometimes a little mean and scary. And she smelled something off. She smelled the burning bridge. She just couldn't see the smoke.

"Give me a second, Gran. I'm twenty-one years old. I can be alone for thirty minutes without the world falling apart." My voice was placid, but inside I was flinching. I was such a liar. Her world was going to fall apart tonight. Such irony. She nodded once, and then turned away to attend to business.

Now, I was alone.

I looked at myself in the big mirror in front of me. There were mirrors everywhere. I ran my hand over my curls and blinked my eyes a few times. And then I pulled out the scissors I'd taken from Jerry's little bag of tricks. And I started to snip. Snip, snip, snip. And the angel hair started falling around my feet, just like it had six years before. A few strands landed on my shoulders and in my lap. A clump fell down the front of my shirt and I started to laugh, the hair peeking out of my cleavage like I was a man with boobs. I laughed harder as I cut. And then there was only a little hair left. It stood up in short tufts on my head and around my ears, jagged and uneven. It was even shorter than Damon's. Damon was the drummer for the Bonnie Rae Shelby *Come Undone* Tour. I thought he was cute but Gran kept him away because she heard he had Herpes. I was pretty sure it was because he had a penis. Gran did her best to keep all the guys away.

The laughter hiccupped into something closer to tears as I looked at what was left of my hair, knowing there was no turning back now, knowing Minnie wasn't here to go hairless with me. I squashed the regret and pulled off my fake eyelashes, wincing as the spidery legs resisted being plucked free. I scrubbed my makeup off with a handful of wet wipes and pulled a stocking cap down low over what remained of my angel curls. The knit cap smelled like Bear—it was his hat—and I felt pain again, pain that was harder to squash than the regret. I would miss Bear. He would miss me.

The red boots and jeans would have to stay. I didn't have anything else to wear or time to change. The oversized tour sweatshirt went on next, all of our 2013-2014 tour dates printed on the back in long rows. It made me tired just looking at them. I pulled the hood up over my stocking cap, shading my face like a gangster wannabe. I needed to hurry. I didn't clean up the hair. I left it strewn in a sloppy mess across the vanity and on the floor. I don't really know why I wanted Gran to see it. But I did.

I lurched for the door and skidded to a halt. How would I catch a cab or take a bus? I didn't have any money. I didn't have my purse or my credit cards. I never carried any of that stuff. I never needed to. When I needed something, Gran or someone made sure I got it. I panicked for a full ten seconds until my eyes fell on Gran's purse sitting on the vanity. I couldn't believe she'd left it.

Gran had been poor a lot longer than she'd been rich, and we poor folk liked to keep our money on hand. We stuffed it under our mattresses and in our bras and carved out holes in our walls for our treasures. Gran had the poor man's mentality, would have until the day she died, and she kept herself flush in cash at all times. I was guessing she had way more than what I'd need for a cab, but I was getting antsy, sure my time was up, so I grabbed it, not taking the time to look through it.

If I knew Gran, she had at least a hundred grand back in the safe on my tour bus. And she was welcome to it. I slung Gran's designer bag over my shoulder, put my head down and opened the dressing room door.

Then I walked away. No one was waiting outside the door, and as far as I know, no one looked at me twice. I was careful not to walk too fast.

When the lure of escape had started flickering in me several weeks ago, I had begun to make note of the exits wherever I performed. I would walk the perimeter, the concrete hallways, the vast underbellies and industrial labyrinths of the stadiums and arenas,

Bear on my heels, using the excuse that I needed to stretch my legs, to get some exercise. It had become a game I played. A game of "what if?" Wherever I went, I plotted a mad dash. Dreamed of it. Fantasized about it. And now I was here, walking away from an arena that symbolized super stardom. And I didn't look back.

AS SOON AS I let go of the metal truss, I was sorry I had. In that instant, I wondered if everyone felt that way at the end. No life flashing before your eyes, no silent movie reel. Just a brief, yet perfect awareness that it's over, and the finish line has been crossed. I tipped forward, a slow motion swan dive, with my feet still clinging to the metal rail. I felt the stranger beside me lunge for me. His hand fisted in the back of my stolen sweatshirt and yanked, changing my trajectory, and my feet lost purchase on the rail. My legs flew out from under me, and instead of falling forward, I was falling downward, and my left side connected with the metal railing we'd been standing on. His efforts must have knocked him off balance too, because I felt his weight glance off my shoulder. I landed in a painful sprawl, half on the stranger, half on the wet concrete that butted up to the guardrail, and I immediately tried to push myself up and away from his grasping arms, furious and fighting, robbed of my choice once again.

"Stop it!" he bit out, gasping for air as my elbow connected with his ribs, and I ground it in, trying to stand. "Are you crazy?"

"I'm not crazy!" I cried. "Who are you, anyway? Go away! I didn't ask for your help!"

My hat had come off in the tussle. I patted the ground for it, but I couldn't find it. I felt the loss of Bear's hat more than the near-death experience, and I wrapped my arms around my head, leaned back against the rail, and tucked my legs in against my chest, breathing hard, blinking back the tears. Maybe the tears weren't for the hat. Maybe it was relief or maybe it was fear, or maybe it was the weight of not knowing what came next. I hadn't thought beyond the bridge. I knew I couldn't climb the railing again, and I knew there would be no more falling into the fog. I was cured of the flickering lure. At least for now.

"I might cry too if my hair looked like that," the stranger said softly and crouched down at my side. And then he handed me my hat. I took it from his outstretched hand and pulled it fiercely over the ravaged clumps of hair.

"I'm Clyde." He left his hand outstretched, as if waiting for me to clasp it in greeting. I looked at it numbly. His hands were large, like the rest of him. But he wasn't big like Bear was. Bear was bulky, and bullish, and built like a blockade, which is what he was, essentially. Clyde was rangy, and long, and broad-shouldered, and his hands looked capable and strong, if that made any sense.

"Clyde," I repeated numbly. It wasn't a question. I was testing it out. The name didn't really fit him. He didn't look like a Clyde. Clyde was the name of the guy that ran the one-pump service station in Grassley, Tennessee, at the bottom of the hill where I had lived all my sixteen years, until Gran convinced my folks we could all be rich if they let her take me to Nashville. The Clyde of Grassley, Tennessee only had two teeth and he liked to strum his banjo that only had two strings. Two teeth, two strings. I hadn't made that connection before. Maybe two was old Clyde's favorite number.

"What's your name, crazy girl?" the new Clyde asked, his hand still extended, waiting for me to shake and make friends.

"Bonnie," I answered finally. And then I laughed like I really *was* crazy. My name was Bonnie and his name was Clyde. Bonnie and Clyde. Wasn't that just perfect? I shook his hand then, and he swallowed it up inside his, and in that second I felt both reckless and redeemed, like maybe I wasn't done yet, after all.

"Yeah. Right. You don't want to tell me, that's fine. I get it." Clyde shrugged. "I'll call you Bonnie if you want me to." Clyde obviously thought I was playing with him, but he seemed willing to play along. His voice was still mild, still that low-pitched rumble that made me think it took a lot to make him lose his cool and had me wondering if he could sing. He'd be a bass, hitting all the low notes and anchoring the chord.

"Are you running from something, Bonnie?"

"I guess I am," I answered. "Or maybe I'm just leaving something behind."

His eyes searched my face, and I bowed my head. I didn't know what kind of music Clyde listened to. Probably not the kind I sang. But my face had been plastered in enough high-profile places the last six years to make me extremely recognizable, whether you liked country/pop crossovers or not.

"Is there someone we can call?"

"I don't want to call anyone! I don't want to see anyone. I don't want to be your sidekick and rob banks, Clyde. I want to be alone now. I want you to go. Okay?" My voice sounded snarly but I didn't care. I needed him to leave. As soon as word got out that Bonnie Rae Shelby had "disappeared" he was going to figure out who I was. I just wanted to get far enough away that it wouldn't matter that he'd seen me.

He sighed and swore under his breath. Then he stood up and started walking away. Several cars whooshed by, each a blast coming out of nowhere, and I wondered suddenly if Clyde was on foot. Maybe that's how he'd seen me. I don't know how he could have otherwise. I looked around me, as if there were answers in the mist. Instead, I just got dizzy and more confused. I didn't even know where I was.

I stood up and hurried after Clyde. He was already lost in the fog, so I started to jog a little, stuffing my hands in the baggy pockets of the sloppy sweatshirt, listening for his footfalls, hoping he hadn't veered off. I shook myself. He couldn't veer off. There was only one direction he could go on the bridge without turning back toward me. I wasn't sure why I was chasing him, after having just successfully chased him off, but I suddenly didn't know what else to do.

The sound of my feet against the bridge changed subtly, and I realized I'd reached a place where it widened and construction cones separated the driving lanes from a pull-out area. There was a white work truck with "Boston Municipal" written on the side parked in the service zone. A beat-up, orange, older-model Chevy Blazer was pulled off behind it, hazard lights pulsing. Clyde sat on the thick bumper, knees wide, hands clasped between them, as if he'd been waiting for me to arrive.

"Is that yours?" I pointed at the Blazer.

"Yeah."

"Why did you park it here?"

"I couldn't very well stop back there in this fog. I would have caused a pile-up."

"Why did you stop at all?"

"I saw a kid, standing on the railing, getting ready to jump into the Mystic River."

"How?" My voice was slightly disbelieving, even accusing.

He looked at me blankly, obviously not understanding my question.

"How did you see me through the fog?"

He shrugged. "I guess I just looked at the right time. There you were." I stepped back in surprise and considered his answer, puzzled.

"So you pulled off up here, and walked back? For me?" I had gone from disbelieving to incredulous. "Why?"

He stood up and turned away, walking toward the driver's side door, ignoring my question. "Are you done jumping for tonight, Bonnie?"

"What if I said no?" I challenged and crossed my arms.

He stopped and turned slowly. "Look. Do you need a ride somewhere? A bus station? Home? The hospital? Wherever it is, I'll take you there. Okay?"

I didn't know what to do. I didn't know where to go. I turned in a circle and rubbed my arms, considering my options, plotting the next step, and I was at a loss. And I was tired, so incredibly tired. Maybe I could just tag along with Clyde until we passed a hotel. Then he could drop me off, and I could sleep for a few days or a few years, until my world righted itself and I had some clarity or some courage, both of which I seemed to be lacking at the moment.

A police car blazed past and then another, their lights making the foggy darkness feel like a smoke-filled nightclub, complete with a psychedelic disco ball. Clyde and I both flinched as the sirens wailed, and Clyde's eyes met mine. "You comin?"

I nodded and scurried to the passenger side. I had to wrench on the handle a little, but on the second attempt it came open. I slid up onto the tattered seat, pulling the door shut behind me, hugging it as Clyde inched away from the curb and merged into the trickle of traffic coming off the bridge. The inside of the Blazer was still warm, and the radio was set on a classical music station. I didn't like classical music much. It surprised me that Clyde did. He looked more like the Pearl Jam type, or maybe Nirvana. His knit cap and the week's worth of stubble on his jaw made him look a little like Kurt Cobain. He kept his eyes forward, but I guessed he knew I was scoping him out, as well as the inside of his ride. He was obviously going somewhere. He had a few boxes, a couple of army bags, a stack of blankets and a pillow, and a very ratty looking houseplant. Behind the second row of seats I could see what looked to be the neck of a guitar case. The urge to pull the case over the seats and into my arms was sudden and intense, as if cradling it would help me find my way, or at the very least, comfort me the way the instrument always had.

"You goin' somewhere?" I asked.

"Out west."

"Out west? What is this, a John Wayne movie? There's a lot that's west of Boston. How far out west?" I asked.

"Vegas," he said, and turned down the strings.

"Huh." Vegas. That was quite the drive. I wondered how long it would take. I really had no clue. It was all the way across the country. Major road trip.

"I'm headed that direction too," I lied enthusiastically. He looked over at me, his eyebrows disappearing under the thick edge of his cap.

"You're headed to Vegas?"

"Well, maybe not that far, you know, uh, just . . . west," I hedged. I didn't want him to think I wanted to tag along all the way to Vegas, although suddenly I thought I might. "Can I ride with you for a ways?"

"Look, kid—"

"Clyde?" I immediately interrupted. "I'm not a kid. I'm twenty-one years old. I'm not jailbait or an escapee from prison or a mental institution. I'm not a member of the Klan, or even a Bible salesman, although I do believe in Jesus and am not ashamed to admit it, though I will keep my love for him to myself if you've got issues with that. I have some money to contribute to gas and food and whatever else we need. I just need a lift out . . . west." I liked that he'd used "out west" first, because I was milking it for all it was worth now that I needed a destination.

Clyde actually smiled. It was just a quick twist of his lips, but I guessed that was saying something. He didn't seem like the smiley type.

"You don't have anything but the clothes on your back and that little purse, and your name isn't Bonnie, so you're obviously hiding or running, which means there's trouble on your ass," he objected. "And I sure as hell don't want trouble."

"I've got money. And I can pick up what I need along the way. I packed light." I shrugged my shoulder. "I didn't think I'd need a suitcase in heaven."

Clyde choked and looked at me in disbelief. I didn't blame him. I was joking, but I sounded crazy. I felt a little crazy. I continued talking.

"And, for your information, my name really is Bonnie. But you don't look much like a Clyde."

"Clyde's my last name," Clyde offered, somewhat hesitantly.

"I've been called Clyde for so long now, I use it automatically."

"So your friends call you Clyde?"

"Uh, yeah. My friends," Clyde agreed with an edge to his voice that made me believe there was something there he didn't want to discuss.

"Well, my friends and family call me Bonnie. So you can too. Even if it is kinda funny."

"Bonnie and Clyde," Clyde said under his breath.

"Yep. Let's just hope this little adventure has a better ending then theirs did."

Clyde didn't respond. I didn't know if he was going to let me ride along or not, but he hadn't said no. The little voice in my head that sounded like Gran told me I had officially lost my marbles. When I stood on that bridge and let go, my mind obviously hadn't been rescued with the rest of me. It must have tumbled down into the water below the bridge, leaving me a brainless zombie. So I leaned my forehead against the passenger side window, closed my eyes, and played dead.

2

Convergence

FINN CLYDE WASN'T a stupid man. In fact, he was brilliant. As a child he was fascinated by reoccurring themes in nature. Why do most flowers have five petals? Why are honeycombs shaped like hexagons? Why do numbers have corresponding colors? He was eight before he realized not everyone saw the colors.

Numbers also had weight. When he multiplied them, the numbers swirled in his head like a blizzard in a child's snow globe, the answers settling in his mind softly, just like the snowflakes, as if gravity were responsible for the solution. As he got older, the fascination with the patterns nature presented grew into a fascination for probability, using mathematical formulas to predict outcomes. And his predictions became eerily accurate. So much so that he could handily beat anyone at chess, poker, or even games that seemed governed by chance. There was no such thing as chance to Finn. Chance could be analyzed, sliced, diced, and pegged using a little brain power.

But even Finn Clyde couldn't predict that his brother, Fish, would get desperate, rob a convenience store with a stolen weapon, and drag Finn into the mess. Finn was brilliant, but he was also young. And he was loyal. And Finn had run toward his brother instead of driving away when Fish took a bullet in the stomach after demanding that the Vietnamese owner of the convenience store empty his cash drawer. Fisher Clyde died in the front seat of their mother's car in his brother's arms. And at barely eighteen, Finn Clyde's fortunes took a definite turn for the worse. Life had not been kind since then, and at twenty-four, six and a half years after that fatal night, Finn Clyde was still brilliant, but he wasn't nearly as young or loyal, and he wasn't running toward trouble anymore. And Bonnie was trouble.

She was asleep, her head resting against the window, her arms wrapped around her middle as if she was physically holding herself together. She was slim, almost too slim. She said she was twenty-one, but she could pass for younger. When he had seen her perched on the railing, arms braced, her slim form appearing through a sudden and almost suspiciously providential parting of the fog, he had thought she was a kid. A boy, maybe fourteen or fifteen. And he'd driven past. You didn't stop on Tobin Bridge. Hell, you didn't walk or bike on Tobin Bridge. He didn't know how the kid managed to be where he was. Where she was, Finn corrected himself.

He was heading northbound across the bridge into Chelsea. He had a stop to make—a goodbye—and then he was gone. The Blazer was packed with everything he owned in the world, and he was leaving Boston, leaving it all. New start, new people, new job. New life. But something about that figure in the fog, perched for flight, whispered to the old Finn Clyde, the Finn that didn't know better, the Finn that ran toward trouble. And before he knew it, he was pulled off in a maintenance lane, trotting back toward the jumper.

When she'd spoken he recognized his mistake. The kid was a woman. Her voice was a smoky drawl, a voice so completely at odds with her enormous sweatshirt and her tear-stained face that he'd almost fallen off the bridge himself. Then she'd looked at him, and Finn saw something he'd seen on a thousand faces in the last six and a half years. Beat-down, hopeless, finished, blank. It was a look he had battled in his own reflection. It was defeat.

Finn wasn't good with words. He didn't know how to talk her down. He'd been tempted to throw statistics at her—he'd started to—spouting something about odds. Then he'd seen her high-heeled red boots, and it had thrown him. Those boots weren't the boots of a runaway teenager or a penniless prostitute. Those boots looked expensive. They looked like they cost more than most people in his neighborhood in Southie made in a week. And he'd been immediately disgusted with her. He'd even taunted her a little, thinking that she was after attention or even a thrill, thinking in minutes her Harvard boyfriend was going to show up in his Beamer and beg her to come down.

Something in her eyes changed as the words left his mouth, and once again, Finn realized he had predicted wrong. He'd lunged for her as she let go, Fisher's death suddenly so fresh in his mind he could hear his brother's gurgling last breath. Fisher had died, but this girl would not.

She had thrashed angrily when she fell but she'd only cried when he'd handed her her hat. Her hair looked like someone had attacked her with a pair of pruning shears. If Finn needed more proof that this girl was in trouble—beyond the suicide attempt—the hair solidified it. So he'd eagerly left her when she'd demanded he go. But then he'd sat on the Blazer's rusted bumper, torn between his own survival and the survival of the weeping girl he'd walked away from. When she'd suddenly stepped out of the fog in front of him, he had felt a rush of relief, followed quickly by a flood of dread.

She had pulled herself together. She wasn't crying anymore, and her voice was steady, and after a minute of hesitation, she'd seemed determined even. She wanted a ride. With him. A complete stranger. Finn grimaced inwardly. Now, here they were.

Just two hours ago, he'd been heading across the bridge into Chelsea to say goodbye to his mother before he left town. Alone. Now he was on his way to Vegas with an unwanted passenger huddled against the door, sleeping like he'd shot her with a tranquilizer gun. He should pull over, wake her up, demand some answers, and insist that she let him drop her somewhere. But he just kept driving, like a man in a trance, each mile taking him farther from Boston and deeper into the mess he was sure he'd gotten himself into. And she slept on beside him.

I WOKE UP before I hit the water and swallowed the scream that was still trapped in the dream. I was cold, stiff, and I didn't know where I was. I jerked upright, and a thin, wool blanket fell from my shoulders. I took in the dusty dashboard and the broad windshield that revealed a rest area littered with tired stragglers, benches, and businesses, poorly lit in the pre-dawn darkness. And then my eyes found him—Clyde-who-didn't-look-like-a-Clyde—and I remembered.

He was slumped behind the wheel, his arms folded, his legs stretched out into the footwell where my own rested. It was colder than snot inside the car, and he'd fallen asleep with his hat on. I patted my own, making sure it was still there. We were twins in our snug caps, a pair of cat burglars staking out a hit. But that's where the similarity ended. His hat was slightly skewed, and I could see clumps of blond hair peeping below the edge of the cap at his neck. He had a strong, squared off jaw beneath the bristle of beard that looked more careless than cultivated. His nose was marred, or maybe improved, by a small bump on the otherwise smooth ridge. His lips were neither full nor thin but slightly parted in sleep, and I noted with surprise that all together, this catalogue of features combined to make an appealing face. He was handsome.

Gran would not approve. She was always more suspicious of the "pretty ones," as she put it. Gran got pregnant at fifteen with my dad, and I don't think she ever forgave Grandpa for that, though she was married to him for thirty years before he was killed in a mining accident the year Minnie and I turned ten. Gran moved back to Grassley, into our already crowded excuse for a house, and I started singing for my supper. Gran had big plans, even then.

I felt the bubbling anger that had become a gossipy, new friend wake up in my chest, viciously listing all of Gran's sins. I pushed the thought away before I got too caught up in her faults, my eyes finding Clyde's face again in the dark. I should call Gran and let her know I was okay. But I wasn't going to. I didn't care if she was worried. I didn't care if she was upset. I didn't care what she wanted. She'd gotten everything she wanted up to this point. She could deal.

I should have been afraid, sitting in the dark with a stranger named Clyde. No one knew where I was—hell, I didn't know where I was. For that matter, I didn't really know *who* I was, and for the first time in years, I didn't care very much. I felt a shifting and a settling inside me. My plan had gone all wrong, but maybe it was okay. I had let go and now found myself in a new dimension where there was just me, the sweatshirt on my back, and whatever money was in Gran's purse. I was in a different world, and in this place there was possibility and peace. And it felt liberating. I felt free.

Plus, Clyde had obviously put a blanket around me. And he hadn't groped or killed me while I slept. Two points for Clyde. Three, if you counted the episode on the bridge. I found myself smiling stupidly out into the darkness, the smile banishing the angry resident in my heart and the Jiminy Cricket on my shoulder, pestering me to make a call and turn myself in.

"You're scaring me a little," Clyde said suddenly, his voice thick with sleep.

I jumped a foot in the air and my hands gripped the dash like I was in the front seat on a roller coaster, heading downhill.

"I apparently just scared you too," Clyde muttered, lifting his feet back to his own side of the cab and pulling his hat back down over his forehead.

"Why am I scaring you?" I asked, and my voice cracked.

"You're sitting there smiling at nothing. It's creepy."

"It wasn't nothing. It was something." I shrugged. "How long was I asleep?"

"A while. By the time I got off in Chelsea, turned around, and came back across the bridge into Boston, you were dead to the world. It took me almost an hour to get out of Boston—there was some big event getting out at the TD Garden, I guess. Traffic was horrible. I drove for another couple of hours, and I pulled off here about an hour ago to close my eyes."

I tried not to wiggle in my seat. That traffic jam around the TD Garden was all my fault.

"Where's here?" I asked.

"We're just off the Mass Pike just about to cross into New York."

"So we're still in Massachusetts?"

"Yeah. But not for much farther." He was silent, staring forward. And somehow I knew what he wasn't saying. We were still in Massachusetts, so I could still turn back.

"I've never been outside of Massachusetts," he volunteered suddenly, surprising me. "This will be a first for me." He turned his head toward me slowly. "How 'bout you?" And he waited, holding my gaze.

"A first for me too. I mean, first time in Massachusetts."

"How long were you here?"

"What time is it?"

Clyde checked his watch, tipping the clock face this way and that to catch the paltry light from one of the street lamps rimming the rest area parking. Nobody wore watches anymore. But Clyde apparently did. "Four a.m."

"Well, then I guess I've been in Massachusetts about twenty-four hours." We had rolled into Boston early yesterday morning in our cavalcade—a bus for me and Gran and all the people necessary to make Bonnie Rae Shelby beautiful, a bus for the band and the sound crew, a bus for the back-up singers and dancers, and two semis filled with the sound equipment and all the staging. The Bonnie Rae Shelby *Come Undone* Tour was a huge undertaking. And I'd managed to come undone with just a sweatshirt, boots, and a pair of jeans. And Bear's hat. Don't forget that. I could have told my record label that we didn't need all that other stuff.

Clyde swore long and low, making the one syllable word into several. "What in the hell happened in the space of twenty-four hours to make you want to take a plunge into the Mystic River?"

"Maybe I wouldn't have jumped," I said after a long silence, not knowing what else to say without spilling my whole life story.

"You did jump. But that wasn't the question, Bonnie," Clyde said softly.

"That's the only answer I've got, Clyde."

"Then you and I are gonna have to part ways."

"Say that again."

"You and I are gonna have to part ways," Clyde repeated firmly, his gaze steely in the murky light.

"I like your accent. You don't say part. You say pat. Say it again."

"What the hell?" Clyde sighed, throwing his hands in the air.

"Now that, that didn't sound very cool," I said. "You say it just the way I say it. What the hell!" I yelled. "See? Exactly the same."

"I don't need this," Clyde muttered under his breath and ran his big hand down his face. He wouldn't look at me, and I knew I'd blown it. When would I learn to just shut up? I always tried to lighten things up and change the subject when things got uncomfortable or I was nervous. It was how I dealt. When Minnie got sick, I spent my days trying to make her laugh. Trying to make them all laugh. And when I couldn't make them laugh anymore, I let Gran talk me into "helping out" in a different way, making money. Which reminded me. I held up Gran's purse.

"I've got cash. I can pay you to take me to Vegas." I pulled a wad of bills out of Gran's wallet and waved it toward him, fanning his face, and his eyes widened.

"There's no way you're twenty-one," he said, pushing my hand away. "What are you, twelve?"

"I was born on March 1, 1992," I said, my voice rising with his. "There's an answer for you. What other answers do you need?"

"Nobody who's twenty-one years old would wave a stack of cash like that in front of a stranger's face. You are completely vulnerable, you realize that, don't you? I could take your money, push you out of my car, and drive away. And that isn't the worst thing I could do! What you just did, there? Not smart, kid. Not smart!" He was flabbergasted, angry even. I knew he was right. I'd never been smart. Gran said so. That's why I sang, because singers didn't have to be smart.

"You're right. I'm not smart. I'm as dumb as a fence post. And I need a ride." My voice wobbled pathetically and that seemed to work much better than trying to distract him or make him laugh.

Clyde groaned and rubbed his hand down his face once more. "You have money—plenty of it from the looks of it. Why don't you rent a car?"

"I don't have my driver's license with me or my credit cards."

"So take a bus!"

"Someone might recognize me," I answered immediately and then wished I hadn't.

"Oh, that makes me feel better!" he shot back. "Look, you gotta give me somethin' kid. Not money," he cut me off with a look as I lifted my cash as an offering. "Information! I am not taking you any farther if you can't convince me that it wouldn't be a huge mistake."

"I would really rather you didn't know who I am."

"Yeah. I got that when you told me your name was Bonnie."

"It is Bonnie."

"And your last name?"

"What's your first name?" I countered.

"This is my car. I ask the questions."

I bit my lip and turned away. I supposed I didn't have much choice. "Shelby," I said softly. "My last name is Shelby."

"Bonnie Shelby," Clyde repeated. "And how old are you, Bonnie Shelby?"

"Twenty-one!" I ground out. I was starting to reconsider my desire for a ride.

"Well, unfortunately for you, Bonnie Shelby, you can't prove that."

"Turn on the car."

"We're not going anywhere, kid."

"Just turn it on. I can prove it. You just need to promise me you aren't going to get all weird on me."

"I'm not the one who jumps off bridges, smiles like a lunatic, talks a hundred miles a minute, and wants to drive to Vegas with a total stranger." Clyde said, but he twisted the key, and the old Chevy roared to life. I flipped on the radio and spun the dial until I found a country music station. "Do you ever listen to country music?" I asked, hoping mightily that he didn't.

"No."

"I didn't think so." Hunter Hayes was singing about making a girl feel wanted, and I listened as the song ended. I'd met Hunter last year at the CMAs. He was cute and nice, and I thought maybe at the time he might be a good artist to open for me on the *Come Undone* tour. But Gran had other plans, so I never followed through on the idea.

Carrie Underwood immediately followed Hunter, and I sighed. It was too much to hope one of my songs would just conveniently be in the line-up when I needed one to be. I spun through the dial once more and then flipped it off.

"That's not gonna work. I need your guitar. It's got all its strings doesn't it?"

Clyde looked at me blankly. "Yeah. But it hasn't been played in ten years. And it wasn't played well before that. It's way out of tune."

I scrambled over the seat to the back, tugging the guitar behind me as I crawled back to the front. I could have climbed out the passenger door and walked to the back of the Blazer more easily, but I was afraid Clyde would drive away as soon as my feet hit the pavement. He was looking more wary by the second.

I pulled opened the case on the backseat and lifted the guitar free, hoisting it into the front seat and positioning myself around it so I could play. I plucked and tightened for a minute. It was so out of tune the strings moaned and whined as I coaxed them back into place.

"You can do that by ear?"

"I may not be smart, but Jesus gave me perfect pitch to compensate," I said matter-of-factly, and Clyde just raised his eyebrows. I didn't know if he was doubtful about my perfect pitch or the fact that Jesus was my benefactor.

"There you go, old girl," I crooned, as I strummed a series of chords, "not too bad for a girl that hasn't been touched in a while."

Clyde said a bad word under his breath.

I ignored him and picked my way through the intro of my most recent number one hit. Even if Clyde didn't know country music, he had probably heard this song. It had been on the soundtrack of last summer's big action blockbuster and had been my biggest crossover hit yet. It had been played so often even I was sick of it.

The movie was called *Machine* and so was the song. In the film, Earth had fallen to invaders—part machine, part human—from another planet, and one of these invaders falls in love with a human girl and has to choose which part of himself he's going to embrace. The song is bittersweet and filled with longing, a perfect counter-balance to the high-paced action sequences that built to a fiery crescendo as the machine sacrifices himself for the girl who thinks he's incapable of feeling, and she finds out too late that he was so much more than she had thought. America had eaten it up. I hoped Clyde would.

"Just a machine," I sang, "Too cold to run, expired and numb, call it love. You don't mind it, like I mind it, your hollow kindness. I should leave."

Clyde was watching me, his body still, his hands resting on the steering wheel. I couldn't tell what he was thinking so I kept singing, swinging into the bridge that launched the chorus.

"I'll cover your feet and kiss your hands. By the morning you'll forget who I am. Love is charity, but you're not an orphan, so I'll stay white noise that helps your sleeping. And if I'm useless, why do you use me, like a rusty machine, for your saving?"

"I've heard that song." Clyde didn't seem impressed.

"And do you know who sings it?"

Clyde shook his head.

"Bonnie Rae Shelby," I said.

"And you're telling me that's who you are?" I could tell he didn't believe me.

"That's who I am, although my family just calls me Bonnie."

"So what was Bonnie Rae Shelby doing on the Tobin Bridge last night?"

"I sang at the TD Garden last night. Last stop on my tour. I was finished." I rushed on, realizing that whatever I said wouldn't make much sense. "I took a cab. Told him to drive. I just needed some space, you know?"

"And the cab driver let you get out on the bridge?"

"He didn't have much choice when I opened the door and told him to stop. He slammed on the brakes pretty quick, and was glad to see me go, I think."

We sat in silence while Clyde seemed to mull it all over. The fingers of my left hand fingered the strings, finding chords and sliding up and down the frets. But I didn't play. I just let Clyde be until he sighed and sat back in his seat.

"That doesn't prove anything, Bonnie. I don't know anything about Bonnie Rae Shelby. You could still be seventeen for all I know."

I sighed. "You've got a phone, right? Look me up." I really wished he didn't have to. I just wanted to drive. Drive, drive, drive. And never look back. And odds were, as soon as Clyde figured out I was Bonnie Rae Shelby, he was going to see dollar signs just like everyone else did.

Clyde reached into his pocket and pulled out his phone. It was a flip phone. Ancient. "I'm not going to be able to do that with this, am I?"

"Uh. No. Where did you get that phone? A museum?"

"My mom insisted I have a phone on this trip. So she hooked me up."

"Does your mama hate you?"

Clyde shoved the phone back into his pocket, and his eyes met mine. I instantly felt bad. I was joking. I hated my big mouth. There was something about his expression that made me pause. He had sad eyes and a tired face. Too tired for a young man. I wondered if my eyes were as weary.

"How old are you?" I asked.

"Twenty-four," he answered.

I nodded, as if I agreed. Which was stupid. I would have nodded if he'd said twenty-three or twenty-five.

"Are you going to hurt me, Clyde?"

His eyebrows shot up, and he drew back, as if I'd surprised him.

"Are you going to cut me up in little pieces or make me do disgusting things?"

Shock widened Clyde's eyes, and then he laughed a little and ran that hand over his face. It must be what he did when he didn't know what else to do.

"No?" I persisted.

"You are a very strange girl, Bonnie," he muttered. "But no. I'm not going to hurt you, or cut you, or anything else."

"I didn't think so. Guys who do things like that don't play the hero and talk strangers down from bridges. Although you didn't really talk me down. You knocked me down. Thank you, by the way." My throat closed, and I pushed through the sudden, surprising emotion. "I'm not going to hurt you either, Clyde. I just need a ride. I can help with costs and keep you company and even spell you when you need a break."

It occurred to me suddenly that Gran's phone might be in her purse. I pulled it open again, shoving the cash out of the way and looking into the big zipper pocket where Gran kept Tic Tacs and lipstick. I found her phone laying at the bottom of the bag. It had been on vibrate, and there were thirty missed calls and twice that many new text messages. She'd obviously figured out I had taken her purse. I didn't look at any of them. Instead, I swiped across the screen and set to work googling my name. I found a couple of good shots, close-ups of my face, and handed the phone to Clyde.

"See?"

He took the phone and looked down at the images. Then he reached up and turned on the dome light, illuminating my face for his perusal. He looked from me to the screen for several long seconds and then reached out and pulled off my stocking cap.

"Why did you do that to your hair?"

"You don't like it?"

A ghost of a grin flitted across his face. "No."

I snatched the phone from his hand and clicked through a few links until I found a biography on Bonnie Rae Shelby. My date of birth was listed right at the top, March 1, 1992.

"And there's everything you need to know about me, including my age. Totally reliable information off the internet. There might even be stuff there I don't know."

Clyde took the phone again and read through the information I'd offered him. He read and read. And read. It was awkward, and I turned from him, strumming the guitar and hoping that there wasn't anything too far-fetched in the so-called biography—like romances that had never happened and bad acts I hadn't been fortunate enough to actually commit.

"Clyde?"

He looked up from the little screen in his hand.

"You got enough dirt now? 'Cause I need food. And a shower. And I'm thinking I don't like my hair much either."

3

Identity Equation

THEY DIDN'T FIND a shower, but they did find a pancake house. Bonnie dug into her stack like she was starving, but she seemed to fill up before she'd eaten even half of her food. She looked at what was left of the teetering golden pile with regret. Clyde watched her as he finished every last bite on his own plate and drank three glasses of milk. She insisted on picking up the tab, and he decided he would let her this once—if she truly was Bonnie Rae Shelby, she could afford it—but he didn't like letting her buy his food. It made him feel small in a way that his six feet two inch frame could never be. Small in a way that reminded him of the times he'd turned his head when he should have spoken up, or let someone get hurt because standing up would have made him a bigger target. He didn't like feeling small, so he made a silent promise to himself that he wouldn't let her pay for his meal again.

After breakfast they found a Walmart, and she skipped down the aisles throwing things into the basket until he warned her that the cargo space was limited. She looked at her purchases the way she had looked at the pancakes—regretfully—then put several things back. She still left the store with her arms full of sacks—jeans and T's, another stocking cap and a coat to match, underwear that he had studiously ignored, and all kinds of feminine things that made him truly grateful he was a man. She'd also purchased a couple of duffle bags to stuff it all in, and she'd made short work of organizing it, throwing her bags in the back seat with his. She seemed amazingly lighthearted and upbeat for a girl who had wanted to die less than twelve hours before. That worried him, more than the fact that she was apparently a pop-star on the run, more than the fact that she seemed to completely trust him.

"Just one more stop," she insisted, and looked at him as if she were sure he was going to refuse her. He sighed.

"There's a Quik Clips right there." She pointed toward a strip mall across from the Walmart. "I need to fix this hair. I can't wear a beanie forever."

It was nine o'clock in the morning. They had driven another two hours before they'd burned three hours on food and shopping, and Clyde had driven all night. He was growing irritable, and really wanted to get a few more miles down the road before he found a cheap hotel and crashed for a solid eight. But a quick nap would sure take the edge off.

"Fine. You take care of the hair. I'll sleep for an hour while you do."

Clyde pulled in front of the Quik Clips and turned off the engine. The parking lot was empty. Good. Then she wouldn't be long.

"You won't drive away while I'm inside, will you?" Bonnie asked, her hand on the door handle.

"I won't leave."

"You swear?"

"I swear."

Bonnie worried her lip with her teeth, her eyes boring into his, trying to determine whether she could take him at his word.

"Can I have the keys?" Her voice was so soft Clyde wasn't sure he had heard her right.

He almost laughed. The girl was no pushover. He pulled the keys from the ignition and laid them in her palm. "Here. Now go. I'll be here when you're done. You paid for this tank of gas, so you paid for your ride. I won't leave."

She flashed him a grateful smile, dropped the keys into her purse, and was out of the Blazer without another word. Clyde lowered his seat all the way back, folded his arms across his chest, and was asleep almost immediately.

Clyde was awakened an hour later by the excited voices of a small group of women who had gathered on the sidewalk in front of the Quik Clips.

"Brittany said she was here!"

"Why would someone like her be getting her hair cut here, of all places?"

"I don't know, but Brittany is sure it's her!"

Four or five females were pressed up against the windows, trying to get a clearer view of what they obviously couldn't see through the large doors of the establishment. Then a white van with Channel Four emblazoned across the side and a satellite attached to the roof pulled into a parking spot beside his Blazer.

"Holy shit," Clyde breathed, as the realization hit. This was all about her. Bonnie Rae. She had drawn a crowd. At ten o'clock in the morning, barely an hour since she'd set foot inside the little salon, she'd drawn a crowd and the gig was up.

Clyde opened his door and, slouching down, stretched his long arm under the Blazer, feeling for the key box he kept for emergencies. He found it immediately and had the Blazer started and was backing away from the cheap hair joint without anyone in the growing crowd giving him a second glance. For a moment he thought about driving away. He didn't want any part of that mess. But Bonnie's bags were in the back seat, and she'd paid for the gas. And he'd told her he wouldn't leave her.

Clyde pounded on his steering wheel, frustrated by his damn conscience. So what? She could replace the Walmart clothing easily enough. It wasn't like she needed him. Not really. She was trouble. And Finn Clyde had had enough trouble in the last seven years to last him a lifetime. But he'd said he wouldn't leave.

Clyde cursed again, but he swung around to the back of the strip mall, parking at the entrance to the alley that ran behind the line of businesses. There were no crowds or cameras back here yet, but there would be. People weren't stupid, and if he drove down the alley, he might get boxed in by a television van or two. Plus, by parking his Blazer there, nobody else could drive down the alley either. He jumped out of the Chevy and started running, counting doors as he went, making an easy calculation as to which door was the back entrance for the hair joint. The door was locked, but he pounded on it, calling her name.

"Bonnie!"

The door swung open almost immediately, as if someone had been waiting for him to knock. A heavy-set girl with hair like a skunk and a phone stuck to her ear eyed him warily and then stuck her head out around the door to view the alley beyond him.

"Are you from Channel Five?" she asked with a doubtful raise of her painted on eyebrows. "Where's your camera? They told me they would interview me on television!"

Clyde pushed past her and ran into the establishment, kicking a mop bucket out of the way as he burst through another door into a room lined with sinks and low, backless chairs on one side, and mirrored hair stations on the other. Bonnie sat at one of the stations, facing the mirror, apparently the only patron in the place. Her head boasted a new, shiny cap of dark hair, and her eyes widened as she caught his reflection in the mirror. A girl wielding a blow dryer was chattering above the din, making Clyde wonder if either of them were even aware of the crowd outside the salon. From where they stood, the front windows weren't visible.

"Clyde?" Bonnie's mouth moved around his name as he strode forward, yanking the black apron from around her neck and pulling her from the chair.

"I think someone called a few friends and told them a certain singer was getting a haircut," he clipped, by way of explanation.

Without a word, Bonnie snagged her purse, pulled out some bills, and tossed them toward the wide-eyed, stuttering, stylist who still held the bellowing blow dryer in her right hand.

"It wasn't me," the girl squeaked, trying to gather the bills as they fluttered to the ground, but blowing them in all directions instead.

"Let's go out the back." Clyde grabbed Bonnie's hand as they ran into the back room toward the skunk who was now positioned in front of the exit door with her arms and legs spread wide, barring their escape.

"You can't go out this way!" she cried as they tried to push past her out the exit. "You're trespassing," she yelled desperately, and clung to Clyde's arm as he barreled through the door. He shook her off while shoving Bonnie in front of him, pushing her out into the alley. The woman grabbed at him again, and he flung his arm wide to evade her. He heard a thwack as the back of his hand glanced off the side of her face. He spun in horror and she stumbled back, wobbling, her hand pressed to her cheek.

"You hit me!" she shrieked.

"Clyde! Come on!" Bonnie pulled at his hand. "Clyde!"

The woman leaned down to pick up her phone, obviously not injured enough to miss an opportunity for a quick picture or another phone call, and Clyde turned and ran behind Bonnie down the alley toward the Blazer. The Channel Five van the woman had been anxiously awaiting rounded the corner just as Bonnie and Clyde threw themselves into the front seat. Bonnie hit the locks and buried her face in her lap as Clyde gunned the Blazer forward, taking an immediate hard right and flying down the street.

"What the hell was that?" Clyde hissed, unable to believe that there were actual news stations that cared if a country singer was getting her hair done. Did Bonnie put up with this every time she set foot out of doors?

"Just drive, Clyde. Go!" Bonnie's voice was muffled against her lap, and he did as she asked, squealing around corners and taking side streets until he was a little carsick and more than a little lost. Bonnie eventually raised her head from her knees, but her eyes were wide and scared, and her hands shook when she ran her fingers through her newly-styled hair. She looked as lost as he felt, and he wanted to tell her he wouldn't let anything happen to her. But he stayed silent, winding his way around the city until he found his way back to the freeway.

"I'm so sorry, Clyde. I should have known better," she said suddenly. "I thought I was bein' so smart. I locked the door of the salon when I walked in, just in case. It was one of those little twisty locks. The girls didn't see me do it. I figured I would leave a huge tip to compensate for the fact that nobody was gonna be gettin' in for a haircut while I was there. And I didn't think they would recognize me. I can't believe they recognized me! It was probably this damn tour sweatshirt. I shoulda changed."

"If you hadn't locked that front door, they would have been crawling all over you. Luckily, the other girl was out back, awaiting the news van that had promised her air time. Is it always like this, everywhere you go?"

Bonnie shook her head. "No. Not like that. I don't know what that was all about. I get swarmed when I show up at a place where people are expecting me, or in very public places, but mostly by fans, not by cameras, unless it's an event or a high profile hang out."

Bonnie sat up straight, flipped down the visor above her head, and peered at her reflection in the little mirror. She quickly looked away, snapping the visor back into position. Her hair was boy short and chocolate brown, a neat little pixie cut framing her large, dark eyes. She didn't look much like the girl he'd watched dance across the stage on the YouTube video, golden curls bouncing, one hand in the air, one hand clutching a microphone.

"I don't think that news van got any pictures. I think we got away just in time. They probably didn't even realize I was inside your vehicle." Her voice sounded hopeful, and she looked at him for the first time since they'd tumbled into the Blazer. He met her gaze, and the hope he saw there turned to trepidation as he asked softly, "What happened last night, Bonnie?"

∞

"DO YOU WANT to drop me somewhere, Clyde? I will understand if you do," I said, suddenly resigned to the impossibility of the whole situation. I felt around in Gran's purse for her phone, noting once more that the missed calls and incoming texts had risen to an alarming number. "I'll call Bear and tell him where I am. He'll come and get me, and you can just be on your way."

"Who's Bear?"

"Officially? My bodyguard. Unofficially? My friend."

"So why didn't you just take off with Bear last night?"

"He wouldn't have let me go. Last night I was sad and tired and I wanted to die, remember? Today? Today I'm pissed and fed up and thinking maybe I want someone else to die." I liked this phase much better. "Bear will come and get me if I call. But he won't run with me. He'll try to talk me out of it, try to cheer me up the way he always does, and he'll tell me I just need time—"

"Time for what?" Clyde pushed again, and I stepped away from the question. Again.

"Time heals all wounds, right? Isn't that the saying? An old woman in Grassley we called Appalachian Annie used to say, 'Time may heal all wounds, but it ain't no plastic surgeon.'"

"What wounds, Bonnie?"

"You want to hear the poor pop star complain, Clyde?"

"Yeah. I do."

"I'll show you my wounds if you show me yours, Clyde. Starting with your first name. I admit, Clyde's growing on me, but I'd really like to know the rest of it so I can send you flowers and a thank you card for not leaving me at the Quik Clips with Skunk Woman even though you apparently had two sets of keys and coulda left me any time." I pulled his keys from Gran's purse and tossed them toward him. He swiped them out of the air with barely a glance and tossed them in the ashtray that served as a catch-all for wrappers, pennies, and the random bottle cap.

"Finn. My name is Finn."

"As in Huck Finn?"

"As in Infinity."

"Infinity? Your mama named you Infinity Clyde?" I was stunned. His mama definitely hated him. It was almost as bad as my own name.

"No. It was my dad's idea. Mom named my brother, so Dad got to name me, and for once Mom gave in. But they both just call me Finn."

"Why Infinity?"

"I was born on August eighth. Eight eight. My dad is a mathematician. He thought those eights were a sign. An eight looks like the symbol for infinity, so . . ."

"Whew! And I thought our names were bad! My oldest brother is Cash after Johnny Cash, next is my brother Hank after Hank Williams, and my sister was Minnie after the one and only Minnie Pearl."

"And Bonnie Rae. Where did that come from?"

"I was named after both my grandmothers." I heard the bitterness in my voice and shook my head, mentally shaking her off. I didn't want to think about Gran. "Bonita and Raena. My birth certificate and my driver's license say Bonita Rae Shelby. Luckily, no one has ever called me Bonita."

"All right. I gave you Finn. Now you give me something," Finn demanded.

"Well, Huckleberry." I grinned at him cheekily, enjoying the fact that his name represented so many possibilities for teasing, which is probably why he went by Clyde. "I am a Pisces, and I enjoy long walks on the beach, sunsets, and romantic dinners." Clyde sighed and shook his head, clearly not enjoying my sarcasm.

"You said your sister *was* Minnie. Isn't she Minnie anymore?"

I lost the cheeky grin. It was too much work to keep it in place. "She will always be Minnie, but she died last October." I shrugged as if time had already stitched up that particular wound without leaving me uglier for it, the way Appalachian Annie said it would.

"I see." Clyde didn't say he was sorry the way most people did. He just stared at the road, and I noticed for the first time that we were back on the freeway, the trees shooting up on either side, reducing our visibility of the world to the space between us, the road behind us, and the never-ending ribbon of black beyond us.

"Are you still taking me with you?" I asked in surprise.

"Is that what you want?"

I looked at him again, wondering if there was something in his words I was missing, some warning signal that I should see, a detectable, cautionary bleeping urging me to get out while I still could.

"Finn?" I liked the way his name sounded. It fit him in a very non-fitting way. Finn was a whimsical name, a name that would be right at home with Peter Pan and the Lost Boys. Finn Clyde was big, scruffy-jawed, and a little intimidating. Definitely not whimsical. But it worked all the same.

"Yeah?" he answered.

"I don't really want to die."

Clyde's eyes slid from the road to search my face before they slid back again.

"I just don't want to live very bad," I said. "But maybe that will change if I can just get away for a while, figure out who I am and what I want. So yeah, I want you to take me with you."

Finn nodded, just a quick jerk of his head, and that was my only response for several minutes.

"Your sister . . . was she older or younger?" Finn asked.

"Younger. By one hour."

Finn's eyes snapped to mine in shock.

"What? We were twins," I explained, his reaction confusing me.

"Identical twins?" His voice sounded funny.

"Yes. Mirror-image twins. Ever heard of that?"

Finn nodded, but the expression on his face was so inscrutable that I thought maybe he needed more explanation.

"If we stood looking at each other, it was like looking in a mirror. Everything was reversed on our faces. I have this mole on my right cheek?" I touched it, drawing his eyes to my face. "Minnie had the same mole, in the same place on her left. I was right-handed, Minnie was left-handed. Even the natural part in our hair is exactly the mirror image of each other. We didn't ever think much of it until we got into high school and took biology. There was actually a unit on twins. We didn't realize there was a name for what we were."

"Mirror-image twins," Finn said quietly.

"Yeah." I nodded. "In identical twins the egg actually splits, but in mirror-image twins, it splits later than usual. Quite a bit later. The original right half of the egg becomes one twin and the left half becomes another." I remembered the text book definition perfectly. I was a half. Minnie and I together made a whole. How could I possibly forget something like that?

"How did she die?"

I looked out the window and laid it out. "Minnie died of leukemia. She was diagnosed when we were fifteen. She got well for a while. Remission. But she got sick again two years ago, and everybody kind of played it down so that I wouldn't get distracted, so that I would keep singing and touring and sending money home. That was my job. Send money home."

"You weren't there when she died?" Finn's voice was hushed, reverent even.

"No," I answered woodenly, my attention on the landscape, letting the trees rushing past whisk away the emotion that was brewing beneath the words. "They didn't tell me until after her funeral, a week later. I was on tour, see. And Gran didn't want me to cancel the dates. We're talking big money, sold out shows, powerful interests. Obviously, much more important than Minnie's funeral or my feelings on the matter."

The anger came whooshing back, and I opened my mouth to take in more air to release the heat in my chest, but everyone knows that you have to suffocate a fire. The rush of air down my throat only fed the flames. I sat, gasping, my face turned away, and then I held my hand over my mouth in a belated attempt to dampen the blaze. I wondered if Finn could see the smoke curling between my fingers and out my ears. I was so hot with fury that I reached out and unrolled the window, fiercely turning the old handle, letting the icy wind fill the interior of the Blazer and nip at my face and kiss my cheeks. Clyde didn't complain about the cold or try to speak over the bellowing wind, and I closed my eyes and wished it would whisk me away. But I leaned my face too far out, and without warning, my hat, Bear's hat, was snatched off my head. I watched it tumbling down the freeway, lost to me, just like Minnie.

Suddenly I wanted to throw everything out the window. I wanted to start grabbing things and hurling them out, as if tossing things out the window would purge me. It was the same feeling I'd had when I started attacking my hair in the dressing room.

But I couldn't do that. I couldn't throw my newly acquired things out the window. I couldn't throw Finn's things out the window, either. I had to get a grip. I grabbed the handle and starting winding, watching the space narrow, listening to the wind wane and finally cease altogether as the pane reached its destination. I sneaked a look in Finn's direction. He was looking straight ahead, just waiting. I shrugged.

"According to Gran, she didn't tell me because Minnie was gone, and me crying at her funeral wasn't gonna bring her back." I didn't cry now either.

"Gran said we all knew it was coming, and that we had all said our goodbyes a hundred times. But I hadn't said goodbye. Not even once." I was proud of how calm I sounded. Clyde just continued to drive, not commenting, but I could feel the intensity of his attention, and it spurred me on.

"When they told me, I threw a fit worthy of a pop princess. I broke things, and I screamed and cried, and I told my Gran I hated her and I would never forgive her. And I won't either. And then I packed my bags and headed home to Grassley. Which was fine with Gran. She had waited to tell me until I had a week-long break for Thanksgiving. It was the first time I'd been home in eight months. But when I got there, nobody was home but my mama. Daddy had moved out, Cash was in jail, and Hank just got out of rehab for the umpteenth time—he'd moved into Gran's house in Nashville. And Minnie was in the ground.

"I spent a week with my mama, and she seemed like she was handling it all pretty well. She told me my dad got an apartment in Nashville not far from Gran's and is pursuing his dreams. Isn't that special? I think I'm paying for that, too. I have been making money for my family since I was ten years old. And I don't have a relationship with any of them anymore. I never had much with my brothers in the first place. Cash was okay, but Hank has always scared me a little. Hank on drugs is even scarier. Gran's the only one who can stand him. It's because they're two mean peas in a pod. Minnie, and my parents, I suppose, were my reasons for keeping on." I shrugged like it wasn't that important.

"When Thanksgiving was over, I was an obedient little Bonnie Rae, and I went back out on the road. I didn't go back home for Christmas. I just kept working, and last night, I finished my tour."

"So your parents have split up?"

"Yeah." I leaned my head against the window. "I found out a couple of days ago that Mama's got a boyfriend, and he's moved in with her. We can all just go our own way now, I suppose. It's just . . . everything I thought I was working for was just a lie. You know? Money makes things easier. It can even transform your life, but it doesn't transform people. And all my money couldn't save Minnie, and it sure as hell didn't fix my family."

"Is that why you wanted to jump off that bridge?"

"Maybe. I don't know. I kind of lost it last night. Gran had a surprise for me during one of my songs. That set me off, I guess."

"What was it?'

"Gran had someone make a film, a series of shots of Minnie, pictures of us together. Pictures of her last days. And they ran it on the screen behind me as I sang 'Stolen.'"

I heard Clyde curse under his breath, just a whisper of sound, but his sympathy chipped at my composure. "I couldn't sing."

What an understatement. I couldn't sing because I could only stare at that huge screen. In that moment, I had nothing left that was mine. Gran had stolen everything. Every part of me. Just like the song said. And then she'd sold it all. And I had allowed it.

"What did you do?" Clyde asked.

"I walked off the stage. Bear and Gran were waiting backstage, just like always. I told them I was sick. That I couldn't go on. The concert was almost over anyway. My exit only made the moment more meaningful, Gran said. Everyone would understand, she said."

The heat was building again, and I started to pant. I paused and leaned back against the seat, collecting myself. I ran my hands through my hair, over and over, the short silkiness evidence of what came next. I continued more calmly.

"Bear walked me back to my dressing room, and then he went back down to take care of some other security issues. Gran went out on the stage and made my apologies, apparently. I don't really know. I chopped off my hair, pulled on this sweatshirt, took Gran's purse, and I left. And here I am."

"You took your Grandma's purse?"

I laughed—a loud gasp that popped my ears and burst the bubble of anger that I'd been floating in. After all that, Mr. Finn Clyde was worried about Gran's purse?

"Yep. I sure did. Mine was still on the tour bus." I pulled the purse from where it sat between my feet and started pulling items from it. Gran's phone, handfuls of bills, her wallet with her shiny credit cards.

"I was a minor when I got started in the business, and Gran has always controlled the money side of things. Her name is on every one of my accounts, and I've never taken her off." I was pretty certain she paid the balances on these cards from accounts with my name on them. So I didn't feel too bad that I'd used one of them at Walmart and then again to fill up Clyde's gas tank in Albany.

"I should probably give her purse back to her, huh?" I rolled down the window and threw the designer bag out onto the freeway. I kept the wallet and the cash, though. And the Tic Tacs. Orange Tic Tacs are tasty.

"I should probably let her know I'm okay too. But I can't actually call her since I have her phone, now can I?" I laughed as if that was the funniest thing in the world. The phone vibrated in my hand like it was laughing with me, and I almost dropped it. Instead, I decided it was probably time to face the music.

"Hel-lo?" I said in my best sing song voice.

"Bonnie Rae?"

"It's Gran!" I said to Clyde, as if I were thrilled to hear from her.

"Bonnie Rae? Who are you with? Where are you?"

"Why, Gran, I'm with Clyde! Haven't you ever heard of Bonnie and Clyde?"

"Bonnie Rae? Tell me where you are!"

"You know what, Gran? The tour is over. I am an adult, and I am officially on vacation. You need to leave me alone for a while. And Gran? You're fired." And then I returned her phone the same way I'd returned her purse.

4
Indirect Proof

"POSSIBLE SIGHTINGS TODAY of country singing sensation, Bonnie Rae Shelby, who reportedly left the stage without finishing her concert at the TD Garden Arena in Boston, Massachusetts last night and disappeared into thin air. Police were called in several hours later after her manager and security team were unable to locate her. In a statement made early this morning, police reported there were items stolen from her dressing room, prompting them to get involved, although it is still too early to file a missing person's report on the twenty-one year old singer."

∞

FINN CALLED IT a day about five o'clock that afternoon. He was drooping at the wheel and promised we would get an early start the next morning. We pulled into a simple, roadside motel, one with a six or an eight on it . . . I didn't pay much attention to the name. I was too busy worrying that he was going to sleep for a few hours and cut loose of me. I was ready for a shower and clean sheets myself, but not if it meant being alone somewhere between Boston and Cleveland without a friend in the world. I told him as much, and he sighed like he was getting a little tired of my insecurity.

"We'll get adjoining rooms, okay? We'll leave the door between them open for as long as you want," he said.

"Done." I jumped out immediately, grabbed my two duffle bags, and headed inside. The desk clerk looked like she'd had even less sleep than Clyde and I, the bags between her eyes dusky and plump, and she hardly looked at me as I made the request for two adjoining rooms and plunked down Gran's card. I didn't want to use the cash if I didn't have to. Having it made me feel less vulnerable. Maybe it was my hillbilly blood, wanting to stick it somewhere safe, or maybe it was just the tangibility of the bills, but I wasn't parting with it.

I signed the receipt with a granny flourish, our names were almost the same, after all, and had the keys to the two rooms in my hand before Clyde even made it inside. He looked like he wanted to argue about the fact that I'd paid for both rooms, but then he sighed and took his key from my hand. He shot a glance at the desk clerk and was visibly relieved when she seemed oblivious to us, already tuned back into the TV in the lobby. A pair of skaters twirled across the screen, and I realized she was watching the Olympics. I'd forgotten they were even going on. We left the desk clerk to cheer for the red, white, and blue, and made our way to the second floor.

True to his word, Clyde opened his door between our rooms, and the little bilious knot in my stomach eased immediately.

I didn't want to turn on the TV because it would drown out the sound of Clyde moving about in his own room, a sound that was comforting to me. I realized part of my problem was that I wasn't especially good at being alone. I rarely was, and rarely had been since I'd been crowned America's sweetheart and had hit the road running . . . or singing. Before that, I'd lived in a double-wide trailer with six other people, and there had been no such thing as solitude. I wondered if it was an acquired taste. I thought maybe I could learn to like it, and I definitely wanted more of it. But not now.

FINN ORDERED PIZZA, keeping his promise to himself that he wouldn't let Bonnie buy his dinner, though she'd paid for his room, which had cost a whole lot more. He heard the shower in her room start up and relaxed a little, knowing he was as alone as he was going to get for the near future.

She was the most peculiar girl he'd ever met. Sad, sassy, temperamental, introspective, funny . . . and all of that in the space of ten minutes. She was troubled. That much was obvious. But she wasn't scared of him, surprisingly. He wasn't sure what to do with that information, and he felt a flash of guilt that she might be afraid if she knew his story as well as he knew hers, which was fairly well considering he'd done a lot of listening throughout the long day. After she'd told him about Minnie she seemed spent. So he'd asked her to sing to him, thinking she would roll her eyes and refuse him, or give him some line about being on "vacation." Instead, she'd been happy to oblige, and he'd marveled at her lack of artifice, considering she was who she was. She'd plopped one red boot up on the dash and regaled him with one ridiculous song after another.

She sang a song called "Little Brown Jug," which was apparently about moonshine, and one called "Goober Peas," which was about, well, goober peas, whatever the hell they were. Another song, "Black-eyed Daisy," wasn't too bad. Bonnie said her dad changed it up, singing Black-eyed Bonnie, because her eyes were so dark. Something about Cherokee blood back in her mother's line, and she and Minnie got what was left of it. There was a song called "Nelly Gray" that seemed to make her sad, and she'd stopped singing it abruptly, half-way through a verse about a girl being taken away in chains. He was sorry she stopped. He'd liked the story in that one.

Bonnie said the songs were the ones she grew up singing, the songs of Appalachia that her dad had taught her and that had been passed down through the generations. She could apparently play several instruments, some of which he'd never heard of, like one she called a mouth bow, which was basically a stick, rounded like a bow, with a guitar string strung from one end to the other. Bonnie said folks hadn't always used a guitar string. They used to use a stick and a cat gut.

"A cat gut? You mean like an intestine?"

"Yep."

Clyde was pretty sure she was lying. Fairly sure. Not really sure at all.

"You don't like these old-timey songs, huh, Clyde?" she had asked. Funny . . . he had told her his first name but she'd kept calling him Clyde.

"This isn't what you sing at concerts, is it? People don't still listen to these songs, do they?" he'd asked, incredulous.

"Sure they do. But, no. I sing new country. Cross-over country. Some of it sounds like pop music—in fact it's so close the only difference is a few steel guitars and a fiddle. And me. I add my own whine and twang to give it that down home feel." She had winked at him then, and Clyde found himself smiling with her like he was an idiotic fan. "I get lonesome for these old songs, though."

Finn didn't especially like the old songs, and he was pretty certain she enjoyed the fact that he didn't. Bonnie Shelby was a tease. But he liked hearing her sing. And Bonnie could sing, no doubt about it. It was as effortless and sweet as cold water sliding down his throat on a hot day. And she seemed to love doing it. She was a performer, a storyteller, a commanding presence even in the front seat of his old Blazer. He could see why she'd been so successful. He could see how America had fallen in love with her.

He remembered her now. He'd seen her on TV many years ago. *Nashville Forever* had been one of the only shows they had been allowed to watch when they earned a little recreation time. They all complained because it was country music, not exactly the popular preference among the guys.

She'd been a wisp of a girl—all hair and eyes. She'd grown up since then. He remembered thinking, watching her sing, how young she was. But she had seemed absolutely fearless. And when she'd smiled, everyone in the audience had smiled with her. She'd even won over some of the hard asses who complained about her song selection but found themselves rooting for her anyway. Finn had only seen the show a couple of times. But he remembered her. He hadn't realized she'd won. It seems she'd not only won, but she'd gone on to be a big star, apparently. A big star who wanted to kill herself.

Finn grabbed a quick shower and was just pulling on a clean T-shirt and a pair of jeans when the pizza arrived. He shot his head through the open adjoining doors to tell Bonnie and could still hear the shower running. It sounded like she was singing in there too. He stopped, wanting to hear her again, and realized she wasn't singing this time. She was crying. He backed out of her room like he'd inadvertently seen her naked, and realized he would be less embarrassed if he had. Naked, he could deal with. Naked he would even enjoy. Tremendously. But tears? No.

She stayed in her room for another hour. He heard the shower cease, heard her pad through her space, riffling through bags, flipping through the channels, and then turning the television off again. Finally, she popped her head into his room and asked if she could "have a slice?"

Finn inclined his head and searched her face for signs of tears. There were none. He smiled with relief, and she returned the smile, the flash of dimpled cheeks and white teeth framed in pink lips made his heart lurch in his chest. He immediately stopped smiling. She was too pretty. Especially now that her hair didn't look like she'd survived the apocalypse. She was too pretty, he was a lonely man, and the combination scared him, for her sake and for his.

"You look different without the shag." She was talking to him now, perched on the edge of his bed, enjoying her pizza. Clyde pulled his attention from her pretty face and settled his eyes back on the fascinating sport of curling on the screen in front of him.

"Shag?" he asked. Wasn't shag another term for sex? God help him.

"You know, the scruff," Bonnie reached out and touched his clean-shaven cheek with the knuckles of her left hand, and the Olympics didn't stand a chance. "You look younger. And I'm jealous. You have more hair than I do." Finn saw the slight quiver of her bottom lip and then watched her take a huge bite of pizza as if to make it stop.

Finn ran his hands through his damp, shoulder-length hair and shrugged. "It's coming off when I get to Vegas. It just felt good to let it grow." Dangerous territory here. He stopped talking.

"You haven't always worn it long?"

"Nah. It's been short my whole life, up until the last couple of years, or so." He fidgeted, pretending he was interested in a commercial for car insurance, but mostly he was hoping she would change the subject.

"I look like a boy, don't I?" Bonnie burst out suddenly, the quivering of her lower lip back in full force. She set her pizza down abruptly and grabbed a napkin, wiping her hands and face with agitated motions.

"What?" Finn asked, stupefied.

"I was getting in the shower . . . and I caught my reflection from the corner of my eye, and I screamed! I screamed 'cause I look like my brother Hank! I look like Hank, and I always thought he was the homely one in the family."

"What the . . .? Is that why you were crying? Because you think you look like Hank?" Finn tried not laugh. He did. He tried. But he was not successful.

"It's not funny, Clyde! I didn't want angel curls anymore, but I didn't think about the consequences of short, brown hair on this square, Shelby face. But now I know." Bonnie hung her head and her shoulders shook as she dissolved into noisy sobs. She seemed almost as alarmed by her tears as he was, and she shot from the bed and into her room without another word

He didn't go after her. He wasn't her mother, her twin sister, or the guy she was sleeping with. He was just . . . Clyde. And he didn't have a clue what to say. He could say she didn't look like a boy. Because she didn't. At all. Her hair was short and that was where the similarity ended. But he didn't think he could support his argument without pointing out her more womanly attributes, which was a very bad idea. So he stayed on his side of the door and worried. He had no wisdom where women were concerned, especially a woman he hardly knew, who had literally fallen into his lap, and who he now felt strangely, infuriatingly, responsible for.

He scrubbed his hand down his jaw, immediately missing the feel of whiskers against his palm. The friction against his fingers eased the friction in his head, and he wondered what he'd been thinking when he'd shaved it off. Stupid. He knew what he'd been thinking. He'd been thinking that he should show Bonnie more of Finn and less of Clyde. He'd been thinking maybe he could shed some of the old skin and become a little more suitable for someone like her.

She didn't come back through his door, though he left it open, just like he'd said he would. He ended up turning off the television and staring up at the ceiling in the dark, the way he'd done a million times in his young life. He wished he had some colored chalk. He wanted to write on all that empty white space. His fingers clenched and stretched, imagining how it would feel to scribble an equation across the expanse, something he could stare at and puzzle over until the numbers blurred and sleep lifted him up and away, where he could merge with the universe, a place rife with endless formulas and figures transcribed across the heavens.

But he was in a motel room, and writing on walls was frowned upon. When he had lived at home, he and Fish had shared a room. Fish's two walls were covered with posters and pictures, and his parents had finally given in—his dad even encouraged it—and let Finn cover his two walls with numbers. When they were full he would paint over one wall and start over. His next apartment was going to have walls covered in chalkboards.

But the numbers were forced to remain in his head, crowded, irritable, and hot . . . or maybe that was just Finn. He sat up in frustration and threw off his covers. He had turned off his heater when he'd turned off his TV, but Bonnie had hers cranking in the next room, and the heat billowed through their adjoining door. He pulled his shirt off, wadded it up, and threw it toward his duffle bag. He lasted all of five seconds before he stalked over and retrieved it, knowing he needed to put it back on.

"Finn?"

Finn jolted, bumping his head against the wall as he shot up from a crouch. The sudden light from Bonnie's room sent a fat streak of light shooting across his floor, pinning him against the wall like an inmate caught trying to scale the prison fence. Bonnie was outlined in the opening. He immediately turned back around, facing the wall.

"Finn?"

"Yeah." He felt like an imbecile, his back bare, his eyes to the wall, unable to move.

"I'm sorry. For crying like that . . . over something so stupid. I'm embarrassed."

"Don't be. Hank sounds hideous. I would cry too." He wished she would go.

She giggled. She sounded like a sad, little girl, and he winced at his predicament. The giggle died when he remained motionless.

"Finn . . . are you okay?"

"Yeah. Fine. Just . . . uh. Yeah."

"Oh. Okay. Goodnight." Seconds later the light was gone, and Finn heard Bonnie's bed creak and the headboard jostle the slightest bit. He stayed where he was and lifted his hand to his chest, and the twisted black cross etched into his skin. Maybe she hadn't seen it. But she'd seen the ink on his back. No doubt about that.

He had only been eighteen. And he had been terrified. Terror makes a man do things he would not otherwise do. Finn pressed his hand over his heart once more, covering the ugly tattoo. Then he crossed the room to his bed and willed himself to sleep, his hand curled against his chest.

He remembered the feel of the needle in his skin, the weight and the smell of Grayson sitting across his shoulders and head, suffocating him, his arms stretched out to the sides, his legs similarly pinned, a man on each limb, Maurice straddling his back. He had eventually lain motionless, allowing the indignity of being marked and branded against his will, the pain of resisting—the blows, the stabbing needle skittering across his skin—greater than the humiliation of holding still. And when they were done, the blood had welled and seeped from the messy outline of three playing cards on the center of his back. One card had a big diamond on its face, a symbol that Finn was a cheat. One card was decorated with a spade, a symbol that he was a thief—and both were stamped on his skin for everyone to see. But it was the third card, the one with a heart on it that made Finn's blood run cold. The heart was a symbol to the population that he welcomed romantic attention. And that was the one thing he didn't think he would survive. Not that.

It had all started with a card game. He'd thought if he ingratiated himself with Cavaro he would be safe. So he'd taken a chance.

"Don't go all in," he had said.

The play stopped, and eyes were leveled at him in outrage.

"What did you say?" The response was laced with equal parts anger and curiosity.

"He's got to be holding the ace of clubs. You'll lose."

The table erupted, and Finn was brought down, the long point of a sharpened bolt nicking the skin beneath his right eye, drawing a line of blood before a sudden command demanded his release. The bolt disappeared, and Finn was pulled upward by a hand in his collar and a hand in his hair. His hair was released as he straightened, his height making it difficult to keep a good grip.

"Let me see your cards," Cavaro demanded, looking across the table at the only man left in the game.

Without argument, the man laid his cards down, revealing them.

"How did you know he had the ace?" Cavaro asked, not looking at Clyde. "You weren't anywhere near his cards."

"I know all the cards that have been played. Three aces have been played, and I can see your cards. You don't have it, he must."

"You know all the cards that have been played," Cavaro had repeated, not questioning, but mocking.

"Yes. And the order that they were played."

The laughter had risen around the table and from the men lining the walls, watching the play.

"Prove it." With a look, one of Cavaro's men had sat at the table and pulled the pile of cards toward him.

"Turn around, kid."

Clyde had turned his back on the table. Behind him, he could hear the rustling of cards and knew they wouldn't be in the order they had been played. But maybe they would be close enough, and all he could do was tell them the order they had been lain down. Whether they believed him or not was beyond his control.

He'd proceeded to lay it out, from the first card played to the players who laid down what, replaying it all in clear monotone, interrupting when someone disagreed, correcting them and moving on quickly until he described the cards that Cavaro's opponent was left holding.

The silence in the room had felt like razors against his skin and it had been all he could do not to move, to run from the slicing stares and the sharp doubt cutting away at his courage. But he hadn't turned. He hadn't run. He'd waited, nervous sweat pooling in his hands hanging loosely at his sides.

"How did you do that?" Cavaro had asked. The mockery was gone.

"I'm good with numbers."

∞

THERE WAS A big, black swastika on Clyde's chest. I lay awake in the hard, double bed, gripping the covers, my mind churning, my thoughts racing. The door between our rooms stood wide, like the gates to hell, and I wanted to run and fling it closed and bolt it for good measure. But I didn't dare. I'd surprised him, it was clear. But I'd seen the mark before he'd turned away. What kind of man put a swastika on his chest?

Not a good man. Not a man I should be riding with, across the country, going on a trip that had no destination or purpose. I had grabbed on to Finn Clyde like he was a lifeline, but I was suddenly realizing his raft might have a big leak. Served me right. It wasn't like he'd invited me to jump in, to attach myself to him. I'd done that all on my own.

It was strange. I had trusted him immediately. I had liked him immediately. The music industry had made me suspicious of everyone. But Clyde hadn't known who I was. And he'd put himself out there for me, simply because . . . because, as he said, he'd seen a kid about to jump off a bridge. Still, there had been something about him that had felt right to me, something that made me feel anchored and safe. Gran always said I didn't have much sense. Gran was obviously right.

I lay perfectly still for a long time, my ears straining in the dark until I thought I was going to lose my mind . . .or what was left of it. He was shirtless, and the bare skin had drawn my eyes, but instead of seeing the well-muscled contours of his arms and chest, the ripples of abdominals, or the width of his shoulders, my gaze had narrowed in on the tattoo. He'd turned, allowing me to hide my reaction, to play it cool, to doubt my eyes and pretend I hadn't seen a thing. His back was decorated in various black, poorly executed tattoos, as well. Playing cards and numbers, from what I could tell before I dropped my eyes and turned away.

Finally, when I'd figured I had given Clyde plenty of time to fall asleep, I eased out of bed, inch by inch, and crept toward the door on my side of the adjoining rooms.

What if it squealed or moaned and gave me away? I held my breath and carefully swung the door closed. It was silent on its hinges, and I almost whimpered in gratitude. Then I turned the lock. It cracked loudly as the bolt shot home and my heart echoed the thunderous report. If Finn was still awake he would have heard it. And he wouldn't have misinterpreted what it meant, especially after I'd made such a big deal about leaving the doors between us open.

In the morning, I would get up early and check out. Then I would check into a different room, safe from the stranger on the other side of the door, and I would call Bear and wait in the motel until he could come and get me. Adventure over.

5

Diametrically Opposed

REPORTS OF A Bonnie Rae Shelby sighting at a Quik Clips hair salon have been confirmed. Brittney Gunnerson, an employee at the business, said Bonnie Rae Shelby got a cut and color and left in a hurry out the back entrance with a tall, white male, approximately 6'1 or 6'2, in his mid-twenties, wearing a black, knit cap and a worn, jean jacket. The employee said Miss Shelby addressed the stranger as Clyde, although there are no further clues as to his identity. Gunnerson is considering pressing assault charges against the unknown man, claiming he pushed her and struck her across the face when she asked him and the singer to leave through the front entrance. Bonnie and Clyde? Folks, you can't make this stuff up.

∞

SHE WAS GONE. Fine by him. He'd known as soon as he'd heard the lock being engaged last night that he'd scared her off. Good. It was better that way. He'd knocked on her door this morning just to make sure. He'd called her name and even waited around until the maid had entered her room to clean it, just to make sure she wasn't still in there, fast asleep, or worse. With Bonnie, he didn't know. She hadn't seemed suicidal. But she had been less than forty-eight hours before. But the maid bustled in and out, and obviously there was no sleeping guest or dead body in room 241.

He had lost over an hour waiting for the confirmation. He grabbed up his bags, angry at himself and at her, and left his own room, taking the stairs instead of the elevator, and headed for the parking lot. Snow had fallen overnight, and a sloppy, wet mess met him as he shot through the exit and out into the parking lot, hoisting his bags over his shoulder. His eyes shot to the gunmetal grey sky, trying to gauge what was coming. Winter weather wasn't fun to drive in, but winter weather was February's best girl, and unless he wanted to wait until April to head to Vegas, he was stuck with her.

Finn's eyes swung back down and settled on his rusted Blazer. Speaking of getting stuck with a girl, the parking lot had cleared out while he'd waited upstairs. The clientele of the Motel 6 were travelers, and no one hung around for the in-room movies or the accommodations. Only two cars remained in the entire lot, and sitting next to the Blazer, perched on a plastic bag spread over the curb, ostensibly to keep her butt from getting wet, was his own little pain in the ass. She wore the puffy, pink coat and the stocking cap she'd purchased from Walmart the day before. The hood was pulled up over her cap, and her hands were pressed between her knees. Her nose was as red as her boots, and she looked miserable. She'd seen him before he'd seen her, and her eyes were locked on his face. She didn't smile, didn't greet him, didn't try to explain herself. She just watched him walk toward her.

He bit back a curse and strode to the driver's side. Unlocking the door, he tossed his bags in the back, climbed in, and slammed the door. He turned the key and backed out resolutely, trying to ignore that she had risen, her hands on her bags, and that her hood had slipped from her head. She didn't move forward, didn't call out to him to wait. She just stood there, watching him go. He shifted into drive and made it a hundred feet before he let his eyes find her figure in the rearview mirror.

"Unbelievable," Finn ground out, and slammed the wheel with the palm of his hand. He slowed to a stop. "UNBELIEVABLE!" He reprimanded himself even as he engaged the brake, pushed the door open, and lurched out of the idling vehicle. Bonnie still stood with her two duffle bags in her hands, but now her lips were slightly parted, clearly stunned that he'd stopped.

And she wasn't the only one. Finn felt like he was split right down the middle. The rational part of his brain, the side that ensured his survival and his sanity, was outraged, demanding that he keep driving, while the side of his brain that was connected to his heart and his nether regions was breathing a sigh of relief that he hadn't let her get away.

She didn't move, as if she were sure that the moment she did he would change his mind, climb back inside the Blazer, and drive away. So he walked back to her, battling with himself every step of the way. He walked until they were practically toe to toe, her dark eyes wide and lifted to his, his hands shoved into his pockets so he wouldn't strangle her. But his pockets felt like manacles around his wrists, and he yanked them free, fisting them in the front of Bonnie's puffy, pink coat and raising her up on her tip toes and into him until they weren't toe to toe any longer but nose to nose. His emotions were a big, tangled ball of anger, longing, and injustice all wrapped up in impatient outrage, and Finn couldn't separate one feeling from another. So he did the only thing he could do. He kissed her.

It wasn't a soft kiss or a sweet kiss. It was a "you-scared-me-and-messed-with-me-and-I'm-mad-and-relieved-and-frustrated-as-hell" kind of kiss. It was teeth and lips and nipping and bruising, and Finn couldn't make himself stop, even when Bonnie's teeth tugged at his lower lip, and her hands pulled at his hair. Especially then. And when she wrapped her arms around his neck and stepped up onto his toes so that she could press herself flush against him, he decided revenge really was sweet, and enjoyed the feel of her face against his, the wet heat of her mouth making him forget he was standing in the middle of a Motel 6 parking lot with his car rumbling behind him, the driver side door still hanging wide open. The rational part of his brain was stunned into peaceful silence . . . for all of ten seconds.

"I don't know what I'm doing, Bonnie Rae," he gasped, pulling away abruptly. He took a deep breath and pushed her gently back, releasing his toes from beneath her boots and his clenched hands from her coat. The thin nylon stayed wadded and crinkled in two big circles above her breasts. Her hands fell from his shoulders to her heaving chest to smooth the wrinkles, and he looked away to give them both a moment.

He was still pissed but he held it in check, keeping his voice low and firm when he continued speaking. "I don't know what I'm doing, and I don't know what the hell you're doing either. But don't get back in my ride if you're going to play games. Don't do it. Hide and seek is only fun if you're ten, and everybody knows the rules. Just call your posse, turn yourself back over to your keepers, and leave me the hell alone."

Bonnie nodded once, her eyes big, her lips bruised. "I got a little worried that you might be a bad man."

"Well, it's about damn time," he said on a sigh.

"What does that even mean, Clyde?" she asked.

"More games, Bonnie?"

"No." She shook her head emphatically.

"So say what you need to say."

"What's with the swastika?"

Finn felt his heart sink. Even though he had known what she was going to say, he had still hoped it was something else. He wasn't ready to have this conversation with snow starting to fall around their heads and his toes growing numb from the slush that had seeped into his old boots.

"It's a very long story. And I'll tell it. But not right now. I will promise you it wasn't about hate. It was never about hate. Does that make sense? I was a scared kid. That's all. And it seemed like the only solution."

Bonnie released her pent up breath, nodded slowly as if she understood, and then picked up her bags. "I can live with that. But I can't live with wet clothes, and these bags are both wet on the bottom. For that matter, I'm a little wet on the bottom!" she called over her shoulder as she hurried to the Blazer. "Let's go, Huckleberry."

Finn rolled his eyes and immediately obeyed, but he couldn't completely smother his grin. And just like that, Fisher strolled through his mind—blond, smirking, and way smarter than anyone gave him credit for being. He used to call Finn *Huckleberry* sometimes too. And Finn had hated it.

∞

"YOU GONNA MAKE your move, Huckleberry?" Fish was suddenly by his side, and he hadn't missed the back and forth looks going on between Finn and the lovely Jennifer.

Jennifer was pretty. And she kept staring at him. Finn studied her, wondering if he would still like her when they were done making out. He found he usually didn't, which made him hesitant to approach her.

"Nah." Finn sighed.

"Why not?" Fish was obviously perplexed.

"I'll be bored as soon as I do. Plus, she's more your type than mine."

"Oh yeah?" Fish pursed his lips, as if considering whether this might be true. He shook his head as if he, too, was going to pass.

"What is your type, Finn? So far, I really don't think you have one."

"I don't know. Tall, thin, smart. Quiet. Good with numbers." Finn shrugged.

"You're describing a ruler. Not a girl."

"I'm describing myself," Finn conceded with a laugh.

"Oh, and wouldn't that be fun. Dating yourself. What happened to Libby? She was hot, she was into you, and she's a damn good

kisser."

Yeah. She was hot, Finn thought to himself. And she was a very good kisser. She'd taught Finn a few things. Things he'd like to try . . . with another girl. Plus, he didn't like being with girls Fish had already sampled. If you thought about transference, which he did, it was disgusting. But Libby had been talented, he had to agree with Fisher there.

"I liked the kissing. But that was all. Quit trying to set me up. I'll choose my own girlfriends." He shot his brother a warning look. As usual, Fish was not deterred.

"Not a good idea, Bro. None of us know what's good for us. We think we know what our type is, but we have no clue. That's why I burn through as many girls as I can. See, I'm tryin' to find what's good for me—'cause I just don't know. And neither do you. You think you know because you're a genius."

"If I'm the genius, why are you the know-it-all in the family?"

"You think you're the only one who studies? I study. But I study girls. I study music. I study life." Fish took a swig of whatever was in the cup. It was probably beer, but it must be his first or second round because he was still his slick self, smiling and waving and working the crowd all the while giving his brother his unsolicited opinion.

"It's my own theory. I may not think like you and Dad, but this is solid math, man. The girl you think is the perfect girl for you is never *the perfect girl for you*. One of these days, a girl is going to come along, and you won't even see her comin.' And she'll rock your world." Fisher said this like it was a done deal.

"Oh yeah?" Finn already wanted to leave. But he wouldn't. He would stick around until Fish was ready to go. And who knew when that would be.

"Yeah! And I guarantee she won't be your type. And you're going to strategize, and think, and make lists. And it's not gonna add up."

"That's not your own theory, Fish. It's chemistry. Opposites at-

tract."

"Yeah. But it's more than that. You can have opposites that don't attract. It has to be just the right kind of opposite. And you won't know what you've got . . ."

"Til it's gone?" Finn finished the tired cliché, not really listening, his eyes straying back to Jennifer, reconsidering.

"Til it's gone, baby. And then you're gonna wonder what the hell hit you, and I'm gonna laugh my ass off and say, 'who's the genius now?'"

∞

"GRAN CLOSED HER credit card. My credit card, I should say. I tried to get another room back there at the motel, and the clerk told me it was declined. It kind of scared me. She knows I have it." I shrugged. "Guess it's her way of telling me she's still in charge."

"They can track credit card usage . . . you know that, don't you? If you want to disappear, using your gran's card was never a good idea in the first place."

"I don't want to disappear. I just want to be left alone. Just for a while," I said.

"Have you tried to talk to her?"

"Not since Minnie died. No. I've been too angry . . . and tired. And sad. I haven't been able to muster the energy to make her hear. And making Gran hear anything other than what she wants to hear has always been close to impossible."

"So you were just going to get another motel room and wait for the cavalry to arrive? Screw you, Clyde?"

"Yep. Screw you, Mr. White Supremacist with a scary-ass tattoo on his chest."

Clyde laughed. "No games. That's good. Say it like it is."

I laughed with him, but his laugh gave me that same drop and slide feeling in my stomach I had felt when he'd smiled at me in the motel room last night, before I'd seen his tattoo and bolted.

"Do you have a girlfriend, Clyde?" The words popped out before I had a chance to register that they were even on my tongue, but I didn't regret them.

"No."

"Why?"

"Because I'm moving to Vegas."

"So you had a girlfriend, but broke up with her because you're leaving town?"

"No."

"No, you didn't have a girlfriend, or no, you didn't break up with her because you're leaving town?"

Clyde just lowered his eyebrows and shot me an irritated look. I shrugged.

"You're probably smart to end it now—long distance relationships never work. There was a boy I liked back in Grassley, but after I won *Nashville Forever*, I didn't ever go back to school. In fact, I didn't even go home for almost a year. Minnie was the only one from home I kept up with. I talked to her almost every night. When I finally made it back to Grassley, the boyfriend, Matt, was dating another girl. I can't really blame him. A year when you're that age feels like ten dog years. It's forever."

Clyde just grunted, not participating in the conversation at all. Time to shake things up.

"When I was nineteen, I asked my bodyguard, Bear, if he would have sex with me."

Finn swore and swung on me, his eyes darting between me and the road. "You don't have a filter, do you? You just say whatever the hell comes into your head!"

"You just told me no games. You just told me to say it like it is. That's what I'm doing."

"There's a big difference between saying it like it is and telling all there is to tell!"

"You're probably right." I nodded. "I've always been . . . blunt, but something happened to me when I let go on the bridge," I explained softly. "My give-a-damn broke. I don't care anymore. I just don't. I'm not afraid. I'm not feeling suicidal, but I don't give a rat's ass. Does that make any sense?"

Finn nodded. "Yeah. It does. I've been there myself. But I just fixed my give-a-damn, unfortunately. So you need to have a little respect and show a little restraint. Deal?"

"Okay." I sighed. "Tell it like it is, but only in doses Clyde can handle. Got it."

"Thank you," he said sarcastically.

I resolved to freeze him out and didn't say another word, staring out the window, composing song lyrics in my head so I wouldn't go crazy.

Finn sighed again. "Why do you call him Bear?" he asked, all but admitting he had been thinking about what I'd said for the last twenty minutes.

"He says he got the nickname because he's big, black, and cranky. His mama even calls him Bear. He's a forty-five-year-old, divorced father of two. He's actually a grandpa. But I love him, and I thought if I could have my first time be with someone I loved, someone I trusted, then I would be safe while getting it over with."

"He didn't take you up on it, I hope."

"No. He didn't. He said that was the most disgusting thing he'd ever heard, and he was going to wash my mouth out with soap, tell my Gran, and let her do her worst. And she would have too. He said I was like a daughter to him. A scrawny, white daughter to boot. His words, not mine. He said I shouldn't feel bad, but he didn't find me attractive. At all."

"Nice." Finn was smiling a little now.

"Yeah. Really boosted my ego. So, I was hurt and more confused than ever, and I managed to hook up with a rising star who'd had one decent hit and was looking for more air time and a little one-on-one time with someone who could boost his celebrity status. Enter Bonnie Rae Desperate. And it was awful. And humiliating. And I realized something then. I'd been lied to. I'd been singing, and dreaming, and writing songs about something that was a big, fat lie. So I convinced myself that surely it must get better, otherwise, why would everyone do it? So I endured it a few more times. It didn't get any better."

Finn was tense again, listening, probably wondering where I was going with this confession. He fiddled with the radio when I didn't continue and then flipped it off with finality. I was waiting him out again. He was going to have to ask for the juicy tidbits after his lecture on saying it like it is versus telling it all.

"And the point to that very personal story was?" he prodded finally.

"When you kissed me, Clyde? I felt more in that one, pissed-off kiss than I felt in those three or four attempts at making love. And I realized it wasn't a lie, after all. That was the best kiss I've ever had. By far. So tell me what I have to do to earn another one, because embarrassingly enough, I always seem to be the girl begging for affection, and even with a broken give-a-damn, I don't know how much more humiliation I can take."

"That kiss didn't mean a damn thing, Bonnie Rae. I kissed you so I wouldn't kill you. That's all. There won't be another one, because the next time I want to kill you, I'll just drive away without you."

I would have been hurt, but Finn Clyde was blushing and that just made me like him more. For someone so big, bad, long-haired, and tattooed, he was remarkably uptight. I put my boots up on his dashboard and started to laugh. I liked this new feeling. When you stopped caring, things got very interesting and a whole helluva lot easier. Finn flipped the radio back on, and I sang along loudly, feeling lighter than I'd felt in a very long time.

6

Horizontal Reflection

THE SNOW THAT had started falling that morning continued in fits and starts as we crossed into Ohio and beyond. We moved slowly through patches of rough into patches that seemed untouched by the storm. Not knowing what was coming was part of the adventure, and neither of us were particularly worried at that moment about the world outside of the vehicle. It definitely wasn't blizzard conditions yet, and the old Blazer hummed along, windshield wipers flying. But as day descended into night, the snow that was on the ground was caught up in high winds, and it was almost impossible to tell what was coming down, what was going up, and which way was what in the dizzying swirl.

"Let's get off at the next exit. I think we should stop for the night. It's getting bad," Finn said.

I tried to make out what services were available on the large green road sign, but it was covered in a fine layer of snow and what little was visible was obscured by the flakes sticking to the passenger side window.

"Where are we?" I asked.

"We're somewhere between Cleveland and Columbus. I can't tell you much more than that." Clyde slowed to a crawl, not wanting to miss the exit. We inched along that way for several miles and had almost decided we'd missed it when I spotted the exit marker.

"There's an exit!"

Even at the crawling speed, the fat, black tires on the Blazer were no match for freezing sleet and snow and roads that had not been cleared, and the Blazer fishtailed as we descended the off-ramp. I squeezed my eyes shut and crossed my fingers, a habit from childhood that I still fell back on when a situation required luck or divine intervention.

"Try clicking your heels together in those boots, too," Clyde teased, but his eyes were clinging to the barely visible road in front of him, and both of his hands were on the wheel as the tires finally found purchase, and the slide down the off-ramp was halted.

In those few, nervous moments, when our attention was on the ice and the snow, maybe we missed a sign or a landmark, or maybe we should have gone left off the exit instead of right, but regardless, as we inched along the road, heading with hope and little else, we definitely missed a vital piece of information that would have saved us from what came next.

The blinding white was relentless, and we may as well have been in outer Siberia for all the luck we were having finding signs of life. There weren't even any other cars traversing the road in either direction.

"I'm going to turn around. There's nothing here." Finn eased the Chevy around and headed back in the direction we had come, retracing the path we'd just created.

"We'll just get back on the freeway and drive until we hit the next town. We can't be too far from Columbus." Clyde said. But as we neared the point where the on-ramp should be, the visibility was so poor we ended up missing it and turning around for a re-attempt. I even rolled down my window and stuck my head out, getting a face full of frosty flakes, as I searched for the freeway entrance.

"Is that it?" I peered doubtfully at the looming underpass, and Finn tried to take the right onto the on-ramp a half second too late.

The Blazer swung in a complete circle, moving sideways as it spun, sending us hurtling in the opposite direction, snow flying into the cab through my still-open window. Without warning, we were off the road, back tires wedged into a snow bank, front tires spinning uselessly against the ice and the steadily falling snow. Clyde jumped out and tried to push us free, rocking the vehicle as I matched his motion on the gas pedal.

But we were stuck.

The back wheels, all the way up to the bumper, were buried, the snow several feet deep where we'd come to a stop. We couldn't get the traction we needed to get back on the road. I climbed into the passenger seat as Clyde tumbled back into the Blazer, his boots soaked, his pants wet to above his knees, and his hands red and raw. He pulled out his old cell phone and, with frozen fingers, called his insurance company to send out some roadside assistance. An automated voice told Clyde it was "very sorry, but could he please hold?" Clyde held on for fifteen minutes until his phone started bleeping pathetically and died in his palm, at which point I started apologizing for acting like a spoiled baby and throwing Gran's phone out the window when we really could have used it.

"I've got a charger. We'll just sit tight, I'll get warm, and I'll try again in a few minutes."

The problem was, when he tried again and finally got through to a real, live operator, he couldn't tell them where we were. He did the best he could, giving them the last sign he'd seen off I-71, but I didn't think it would help much, especially in the whiteout conditions. The operator promised to get a tow truck sent out in our general direction, promising that they would find us, which, comforting as the words were to hear, was a lie.

We waited for two hours, heat blazing in the marooned Chevy before I had to vacate the warmth of the cab for an embarrassing bathroom break behind the bumper, where my bare butt got an icy bath, and I accidentally peed on my red boots. I made sure to bury the yellow snow, mortified at the thought of Finn seeing where I'd marked my territory. Clyde took his turn next, and then we were both back in the Blazer with nothing to do, nowhere to go, and no hope for rescue, at least until the snow stopped falling or morning came, when we could walk a ways and get a better idea of our location so help could be sent.

Clyde worried about the amount of gas we had left, just in case we had to make it through the night before someone found us.

"It's midnight. I figure it will get light about six or seven, right? We can't just run the Blazer all night." He paused as if he didn't quite know what to say next. He ran his hand down his face, and I suddenly felt like laughing from sheer helplessness. I bit my lip hard, the inappropriate giggle perched at the back of my throat just waiting to jump out. I really was crazy.

"I have a sleeping bag and two pillows, plus those three old blankets. It's going to get cold when we turn off the Blazer." Finn stopped again, as if he were uncomfortable, and the giggle escaped through my clenched lips.

"Are you laughing?"

"No."

"You are. Here I am feeling like a dirty old man because I'm about to suggest that we make a bed and cuddle up to keep warm, and you are laughing."

"You were going to suggest we . . . cuddle?" My shock immediately cured the giggling problem.

Finn ran both hands over his face, scrubbing at it like he wanted to erase what he'd just said.

"Okay," I said in a tiny voice. He looked at me in surprise, and I couldn't help it. I smiled. A big, wide, you-are-my-sunshine smile.

"You do realize we're in trouble here, right?" Finn shook his head like he doubted my sense, but a smile teetered around the corners of his mouth. "This isn't a slumber party with your girlfriends and trips to the fridge for snacks."

"Hey, Clyde?"

"Yeah, Bonnie?"

"You will have officially slept with Bonnie Rae Shelby after tonight. You aren't going to ask me to sign an autograph, are you? Maybe sign your hiney in permanent marker so you can take a picture and sell it to *US Weekly*?"

"Got a little ego, there, huh?"

I dove over the seat into the back, laughing. "Dibs on the pillow with a pillow case!"

Within ten minutes, we had rearranged Finn's boxes and our gear between the front seat and cargo area so we could lay the middle seat flat, making it approximately the size of a double bed, an extremely handy feature of the 1972 Chevy Blazer. At least, I thought so. Clyde said it wasn't a "handy feature," it was a broken seat, but I thought it was awesome.

We laid the sleeping bag down, topped it with the two pillows, and then shucked our wet shoes, pulled on several pairs of socks each, donned our coats and beanies, and then Finn turned off the Blazer. He didn't want to open the door and let in the cold, so he crawled over the seat too. Six foot two didn't fold down very small, but he made it, and then lay down next to me, pulling the layered blankets up and around us.

There was a little adjusting and wiggling until we each found a position we could live with—or sleep with—which ended up being my back to Finn's chest, a pillow clutched in my arms, and my head on Finn's left bicep. We lay there quietly, trying to find comfort in an awkward situation. My mind raced but Finn seemed content to let the silence win, and his breath above my head was slow and steady, his weight against my back pleasantly heavy but distracting in a way that made sleep difficult, and the detail that had been demanding introspection all day took center stage.

Clyde had kissed me. Just when I'd thought he was gone, he'd come back. And instead of yelling or pointing his finger in my face, like I'd expected him to do, he'd kissed me. I felt the frustration in that kiss. But I felt something else too. His mouth had been several degrees hotter than mine, and the heat was delicious. He had tasted like toothpaste and buttered toast—a combination that shouldn't have worked but did, like he'd eaten breakfast, brushed his teeth, and then blown my mind, all in the space of ten minutes. I hadn't been lying when I'd teased Finn earlier. It was the best kiss I'd ever received.

It had been rough and abrasive, invasive even. No practiced technique, no smooth manipulation. Lips, teeth, heat . . . and hurt. His hurt, not mine, and I felt remorse for causing it and surprise that I even had the power to do so. He'd said he'd kissed me so he wouldn't kill me. And maybe that was true, but it hadn't felt like that.

The desk clerk at the motel had been falsely sweet and apologetic when Gran's card was rejected, and she had oh-so-regretfully told me that she would need a card for incidentals if she was going to rent me another room. She'd also hovered when I asked to use the phone, and I knew then, even if I could convince the woman to take cash, I wouldn't be staying another night at that motel.

That's when I'd sat beside the orange Blazer and waited for Finn, knowing I was going to have to explain myself, knowing I was going to have to trust him. And yet, when he finally showed up, I didn't do either of those things. I couldn't find my voice, the voice that never failed me. And even though I stood, bags in my hands, and watched him leave, I didn't try to stop him. I was still undecided. And in that moment, all I could do was watch him go.

But then he'd stopped. He'd gotten out of his truck. He'd walked back to me. And he'd kissed me. If he'd done anything else—yelled, cajoled, tried to explain or intimidate, I wouldn't have gotten in the car with him, not again.

But he'd kissed me. And I woke up. The Bonnie that sassed and sparkled and didn't let Gran push her around, the Bonnie that laughed hard and fought harder, the Bonnie that had made the world love her against impossible odds, that Bonnie, that ME, woke up.

Some people might laugh or roll their eyes and accuse me of tired clichés. But there it was—hot food in an empty stomach, water on a parched throat, that first glimpse of home just around the bend, or that first bite of something you thought you'd never have the courage to try, only to realize it was the best thing you'd ever tasted. That was what Finn's kiss was like. And in that moment, I realized I was starving and had been for a long time. I was starving. Hungry for companionship, affection, connection. And strangest of all, hungry for Finn Clyde.

Maybe it was because I was raised in Appalachia, raised in faith and poverty and little else, but I believed in things like fate and destiny. I believed in angels, and I believed in God's ability to direct our paths, to guide us and move us in unseen ways, and I believed in miracles. Suddenly, Finn Clyde felt like a miracle, and I felt sure that Minnie had sent him to me.

"What do you believe in, Finn?" I whispered, giving voice to my thoughts, the darkness and quiet necessary ingredients for a discussion so important. I thought for a minute he wasn't going to answer, that he'd fallen asleep beside me and there would be no sustenance for my suddenly ravenous appetite. But then he spoke, his voice drowsy and slow, and I tipped my face toward him to soak up the safety of his voice in the dark.

"I believe in numbers. The ones you can see and the ones you can't. The real and the imaginary, the rational and the irrational, and every point on lines that go on forever. Numbers have never let me down. They don't waffle. They don't lie. They don't pretend to be what they're not. They're timeless."

"You're smart then . . . aren't you, Finn?" I heard the awe in my own voice. It wasn't a question. I had never been school smart, and marveled at those who were. "I thought you were. I was never any good with numbers. Math has always been like a murky pond, and me, a hillbilly stabbing at the fish with a pokey stick, trying to get lucky."

"That doesn't make any sense, Bonnie." Finn laughed softly.

"That's my point, Clyde."

"You're your own kind of smart." I loved the way he said the word "smart."

"Smat," I mimicked softly, and he pinched my side in response but continued his argument.

"Music doesn't make any sense to me. I couldn't pull a pitch out of the air the way you do no matter how hard I studied, no matter how many theorems I proved. Some are born with an ear. I was born with a calculator."

"Does it come that easy for you? Like music does for me?" I marveled at the idea. "I've never had to work at it . . . or maybe it's just that it never felt like work to me. The music was just always there, easy for me to hear, easy for me to re-create. I can't imagine math being like that."

"When we were little my dad would ask me and my brother to tell him about numbers. He would say, 'Tell me about the number one.' Fisher wasn't interested, but I was. I would tell my dad everything I knew from my limited perspective. I would point to myself and say 'one.' I would point to Fish and say 'one.' And he would say, 'Ah, but Finn, together you are two, aren't you?' And I would say, 'No. One Finn. One Fish.' As if we were the same—two halves of a whole.

"As I got older my dad would demand more. And I would recite everything he'd taught me, everything I'd learned. 'Tell me about number four, Finn,' he'd say. And I'd respond with something like 'the first composite number, the second square, and the first square of a prime.' Not difficult stuff, but more difficult than the 'one Finn, one Fish' stuff of my three-year-old answers."

"That's not difficult stuff?" I asked, and I could see my breath puff out from my lips as the temperature in the Blazer continued to fall.

"No. By the time I was in my mid-teens, my answers included things like Fermat's last theorem, or Euler's assertion, or Goldbach's conjecture."

"Holy crap! You won't feel bad if I don't ask you to explain what any of that means, will you?"

"No." Finn laughed, creating a heavy white plume above my head that dissipated immediately. "Math is lonely in that way. Isolating. It's the reason my parents split. My mom always felt excluded. She said my dad would go off into his own little world. Then he started taking me with him, and it was the final straw.

"My dad got offered a position at a college in another state, and my mom said she wasn't leaving. They gave me and my brother a choice about where we wanted to go. But I was almost seventeen—I'd spent my whole life in Boston. I had friends and I played ball, and deep down, I didn't want to leave Fisher or my mother, even though I blamed her for the fact that my dad was leaving us. I should have gone, though. Looking back, I should have gone. Because in the end, I left my mother anyway." Finn stopped short and changed the subject. "You asked me what I believe in. What do you believe in?" I sensed his discomfort, talking about his family, and decided to let him pass the stick this once.

"I believe in music. I guess music is for me what numbers are for you. There's power in music. There's healing in it. God is there in it too, if you let him be. Growing up, in Grassley, everybody was so poor, Jesus was the only thing we had left . . . so I believe in him too. And God and music, once they are truly yours, are the two things people can't take away from you."

"I haven't figured God out yet."

"What's there to figure? God is all the good stuff. God equals love."

"Hmm. You just wrote an equation."

"I did, didn't I?" I felt kind of proud of that, like I'd said something smart . . . or "smat." I smiled in the dark.

"So why is everyone so poor in Grassley?" Finn asked.

"Lots of reasons. It's a tradition, I guess. A tradition of hopelessness. Drug addiction and alcoholism are high almost everywhere in Appalachia because people are hopeless, and when you're hopeless you look for ways to feel something else . . . anything else. Drugs are good for that. So parents let their kids down because they are slaves to the pills. Politicians sell pills for votes, keeping them that way. The government gives us stuff but then when someone gets a job, they take it away, so everyone becomes afraid of work, not because they're lazy, but because the job doesn't cover what the handouts do, even if the handouts make you feel like trash and keep you poor. Being poor becomes the easiest thing to be . . . and the hardest too, because nobody really knows how to do something different."

"You did something different."

"Yeah. Look at me! Ain't I somethin'?" I laughed softly, mocking myself. "I'm not poor, but I haven't beat hopeless yet." I tried to laugh again, but the truth wasn't especially funny. My laugh didn't sound very convincing. Time to talk about something else.

"How's this for an equation: Bonnie plus Finn equals one big Popsicle," I said and shivered for affect.

"Yeah. It's damn cold." Finn rose up onto one arm, the arm beneath my head, dislodging me and the blankets and making me squeal and burrow down even farther as he looked out the window. "It's stopped snowing. Someone will come along eventually. And if they don't, we'll find a mile marker in the morning and make another call."

"Come back down here, heat supply," I commanded. "I'm going to close my eyes and you are going to tell me about math so I can fall asleep. Tell me some theorems. Is that what you called them? Tell me how Einstein knew e equals mc squared. And start with once upon a time . . . okay?"

"You're a little bossy, you know that?"

"I know. I have to be. It's to make up for not being born with a calculator. Now share your wisdom, Infinity."

"Once upon a time—"

I giggled and Finn immediately shushed me, continuing on with his "story." I closed my eyes, more content and less hopeless than I'd been in months.

"Once upon a time, there was a man named Galileo."

"Galileo Figaro!" I sang, interrupting the story immediately. "Name that song."

"'Bohemian Rhapsody' by Queen." Clyde sighed with pretended long-suffering.

"Excellent. I just had to make sure you and I could be friends. Continue." I nestled down again and prepared to be bored to sleep.

"Galileo isn't usually considered one of the greatest mathematicians of all time. He was a physicist, a scientist, but it was people like Galileo that made me believe that math was magic." Finn's voice was a rumble in my ear, his breath tickling the hair against my forehead, and I closed my eyes as he began to expound on something he called Galileo's Paradox—how there are just as many even numbers as even numbers and odd numbers combined, which should defy reason, Finn said, but which made perfect sense if you compared them in terms of infinite sets. My eyes started to feel heavy immediately, too tired to try to follow the concept for long. Who woulda thunk it? Big, blond, and beautiful also had a brain.

7

Twin Primes

RUMORS CONTINUE TO swirl about the reported disappearance of country superstar, Bonnie Rae Shelby. Police are now involved after several sightings of the star with an unknown male have been reported. One sighting resulted in an assault against a salon worker, another sighting led to an altercation outside a Motel 6 just east of Buffalo, New York, where Shelby attempted to use a credit card that had been reported as stolen and was later seen arguing outside the establishment with the same, still unidentified, man. The desk clerk at the motel was concerned for Shelby's safety after the man grabbed Miss Shelby, at which point the desk clerk called the police. The clerk, in an interview with police, said she had talked to the singer before the altercation and claimed Miss Shelby seemed frightened and under duress. The singer asked to make a phone call when her credit card was declined but was unable to reach whomever she was trying to call. Shelby's family has issued a statement that they are very concerned for Bonnie Rae and will cooperate with police to ensure her safe return.

∞

IT WASN'T SUNLIGHT that woke him. It was brighter than that. The world around the Blazer was so white he wouldn't have been surprised if a chorus of angels had surrounded the partially buried vehicle and pointed him toward the pearly gates. But heaven couldn't possibly be this cold. And the girl in his arms was no angel, though she looked pretty damn sweet with her short brown hair sticking up at her crown and her bow-shaped lips parted on a soft snore. Her hat had come off in the night, and her face was buried where his armpit met his chest.

Finn looked down into her face and waited for the dread and disbelief he'd been feeling, in varying degrees, since becoming shackled with Bonnie Rae Shelby. Instead, he remembered the way she'd looked after he'd kissed her, her lips all pink and swollen. He thought about her diving over the seat to claim the pillow with the case, the way she'd returned her gran's phone by chucking it out the window, how she'd sung "Bohemian Rhapsody" and fallen asleep to his mathematical mumblings, all in the middle of a crisis. It made him curious as to how she would behave when she wasn't overcome with grief, when her world wasn't coming down around her ears, when she wasn't stranded in a snowstorm with someone she'd only known three days—two and a half, actually.

He grinned and laid his head back down.

"You're scaring me. Grinning like that, at nothing," Bonnie mumbled.

"It wasn't nothing. It was something."

"Ha ha. Are we going to die in this Blazer?"

"No. But I can't feel my left arm, and that place where you drooled on my chest has frozen solid, freezing my nipple in the process."

Bonnie started to laugh and rolled away from him, sitting up and throwing blankets this way and that, looking for her hat. Finding it, she pulled it over her bedhead, yanked her boots on her feet and threw herself back over the front seat, like she'd done it a thousand times.

"Ladies first, and it's not dark anymore, so no peeking out the windows. I'm going to test you on the color of my panties, and you better not know that they're red with black skulls." Bonnie pushed the passenger door open, snow falling from the roof onto the seat as she climbed out.

An immediate image of Bonnie in red panties decorated in black skulls filled Finn's mind and he half laughed, half groaned.

"Skulls are not sexy," he said out loud. "Skulls are not sexy." He pulled on his boots, taking the time to lace them tightly, his eyes on his hands, keeping his focus from wandering outside. "Skulls *are* sexy, dammit, and my boots are still wet."

He ran his hands through the strands of his hair and pulled it off his face with an elastic band he'd shoved into his pocket the day before. He folded up the blankets and the sleeping bag, righted the seat, and moved their gear from the front seat. Then he pulled on his beanie and climbed out of the Blazer after Bonnie.

An hour later, after a bit of recon, Clyde had a much better idea of where they were, along with the number of the exit they'd taken the night before. But another call for roadside assistance was unnecessary. As he made his way back to Bonnie and the Blazer, his feet frozen solid in his wet boots, a pick-up truck pulled alongside him, and an old man wearing a Cleveland Browns hat with furry ear flaps stuck his head out the window.

"That your vehicle stuck up there in the snow?"

"Yes, sir."

"I've got chains. I can pull you out. Jump in."

Finn was only a hundred yards from the Blazer, but he didn't argue. When they pulled up, Bonnie climbed out of the Blazer, her face wreathed in a relieved smile.

The old boy in the funny hat knew what he was doing, and within minutes, with Clyde pushing, Bonnie steering, and the pick-up pulling, the Blazer was freed from the snowbank. Bonnie left the Blazer running, letting it warm as she and Clyde walked to thank the owner of the pick-up for his help.

"You folks lucked out," he said, unhooking the chains and stowing them in the back of his truck. "You're in the middle of Cuyahoga National Park. I usually wouldn't have been out this way, but my sister and her husband own a farm just west of here, outside of Richfield. Her husband got sick last year and died, right out of the blue. I go check on her now and then."

"I thought we were on I-71 last night, but from what I can tell we're now on I-80," Clyde said.

"Well no wonder nobody found you if you told 'em you were on 71! I-80 intersects 71 a ways back. You must have headed down the turnpike in that blizzard and not even realized it."

"It was pretty bad." Finn extended his hand to the man, thanking him. Bonnie extended her hand as well, but the old man was in a talkative mood and kept his window down as he climbed into his truck.

"It was terrible! There were a lot of stranded motorists out last night. Kept the snow plows and the highway patrol busy, that's for sure. I have one of those police scanners, and it was lit up all night with people needin' help. There was even a report of an ex-con who they think mighta run-off with that little singer comin' through here. You heard about that? When the call went out to the highway patrol you shoulda heard the buzz on that scanner!"

Bonnie stiffened beside him, and Finn felt the bottom drop out of his stomach. Run off? What the hell was going on? His assistance call would most likely have been transmitted to the local highway patrol. That made sense. But the rest of it didn't.

"Cute little gal, that singer. Little blonde gal. I like some of her songs. Shelby's her name. We got a Shelby, Ohio, too. Did you know that? I've got a cousin in Shelby." The old boy started singing something about a big blue moon and big green mountains and a great big broken heart, apparently one of Bonnie's songs that he was fond of.

"Well, my feet are cold, and my hands are too, so thanks again!" Ever the performer, Bonnie reached through the window and patted the old man's shoulder. Finn just stood there, the ache in his feet suddenly the least of his worries.

"Just get back on 80 here, heading east. You're going to intersect I-271 right away. Head south on 271, and it will take you right back down to I-71. You'll be in Columbus in two hours." And with that, and a little wave, the clueless old man rolled up his window and rumbled down the road.

Clyde and Bonnie watched him go, their hands pressed into their pockets, their eyes trained on the *Dodge 4X4* stenciled across his tailgate. They watched until he was out of sight. Then Bonnie turned on him.

"You're an ex-con?" she asked flatly.

"Yeah. I am," he said swinging around, arms folded against the cold. "And apparently, I *ran off* with a cute, helpless, little country singer, and everybody's looking for me!" Finn kicked the tire of the Blazer with his soggy boot, wincing as his frozen toes connected with the hard surface.

"Son of a bitch!" He yanked the driver's side door open and climbed in, slamming the door behind him. He glared at Bonnie through the broad windshield, challenging her, knowing he wouldn't leave her, knowing she knew it too.

She walked slowly to the passenger side and climbed in. The Blazer was warmed up now, blasting heat in their faces and urging them to resume their journey. But they sat, unmoving, and not surprisingly, Bonnie was the first to speak.

"You said you would tell me about that tattoo. That swastika. You never did. You didn't tell me because you would have had to tell me you'd been in prison."

It wasn't a question. She'd put two and two together pretty quickly. Who says she wasn't good at math?

When Finn didn't reply to her opening statement, Bonnie tried again.

"The old guy said they were looking for an ex-con. Not an escaped convict. So I'm assuming you did your time. Did you violate your parole? By leaving the state, I mean."

"No. I didn't. And I don't owe you an explanation, Bonnie." And he didn't. He didn't owe her anything. At this point he figured she owed him. Big time.

"What did you do?" she asked, undeterred.

"I killed a famous country singer."

Bonnie didn't laugh. He didn't blame her. It wasn't very funny.

"How long were you there? In prison, I mean."

Finn gripped the wheel and tried to rein in the helplessness that filled his chest and made the palms of his hands sweat. He didn't want to talk about this.

But Bonnie did.

"Come on, Clyde. Tell me. You've heard my sad tale. Let's hear yours."

"Five years. I've been out for a year and a half," he said, relenting, the response short and sharp, a verbal whip that left Bonnie temporarily stunned. But she was silent for all of five seconds.

"And you're twenty-four?"

"Turned twenty-four in August. Eight, eight, remember? Heil Hitler."

"What's that supposed to mean?" Bonnie hissed, offended, just like he'd intended. He was angry. He wanted her to be angry too.

"You didn't notice? I have a swastika on my left pec, and a double eight on the right. H is the eighth letter in the alphabet—Heil Hitler, HH, 88. The Aryan Brotherhood has all kinds of cute little symbols like that. It just so happens to correspond with my birthday. Nice, huh? Convenient too."

"What did you do?" She went back to her previous question. Maybe the Hitler stuff was too much.

"My brother robbed a convenience store. To this day, I don't know what he was thinking. I was in the car. I didn't know he had a gun, and I didn't know he was going to rob the store. Unfortunately for Fisher, the owner had a gun too. And he knew how to use it. Fisher got blasted. He ran out of the store, but not before he pulled the trigger too. I don't know how he managed to get a shot off, because he had a huge hole in his stomach. But I heard the shots, and I saw him fall. I grabbed him, got him into the car. Took him to the hospital. He died on the way. And I went to prison." Finn kept his voice clipped, his answers short, making it seem like it was no big deal, just water under the bridge.

"Your brother?" Bonnie sounded as stunned as he had been when she told him about her sister.

"My twin brother," he answered, not looking at her. But after a few seconds of silence he had to look. She was staring straight forward, but tears streamed down her face, and her hand covered her mouth like she was trying to hold something in. He turned off the key, climbed back out of the Blazer, and shut the door behind him. He had to. He had to get away from her. Just for a minute. He knew he should have told her about Fish when she told him about Minnie. But he'd been too stunned. The similarities had felt wrong, strange, and even false somehow, and telling her then would have felt like he was trying to one-up her story after she'd bared all.

Fish had always done that. From the time they could talk, Finn would share something, and Fish would immediately have to top him. Finn would finish his dinner, and Fish would ask for seconds he was too full to eat. Finn would get a solid double in baseball, and Fish would kill himself trying to hit a home run. He kept track of all their stats, their grades, their girlfriends. Finn would tell him something, and Fisher would always come back with, "Oh, yeah? Well . . ." And Finn had hated it. He'd hated how competitive Fish was. How animated, how bossy. He'd hated how Fish could always wear him down. He hated how he always gave in to whatever Fish wanted. But most of all, he hated how much he loved him, and he hated how much he missed him.

Finn heard Bonnie behind him. The snow crunched beneath her boots, and her breathing was ragged. He noticed suddenly how ragged his own was.

"Why didn't you tell me?"

"I told you I had a brother named Fisher."

"But a twin? Finn, I . . ." her voice trailed off. She seemed as lost for words as he had been. Then she slid her arms around his waist and pressed her face into his back. She never failed to surprise him. He thought she would grow colder with the revelation—that she would feel betrayed that he hadn't shared all there was to share. Instead, she held onto him. For a long time, she just held on. And they stood there in the road, surrounded by white and nothing else.

"He died?" Her voice was a stunned whisper, more a statement than a question, though her voice rose a little on the end like she couldn't believe it.

"Yeah. He did." Finn hadn't wept for Fish in a very long time, but his mouth trembled as he verified that truth. Fish had died. And that had been far worse than what had come next.

"Why did they send you to prison?" Bonnie asked, the question muffled, her face pressed into his jacket, but he heard her.

"Armed robbery. Seven year maximum sentence for a first time offender."

"But you didn't shoot anybody or take anything, right? You didn't even have a gun."

"I took the gun out of Fish's hand. I threw it in the backseat on the floor. My prints were on it. I was there with him. I helped him get away," Finn said humorlessly. He'd helped him get away. And Fish had gone far, far, away. "It wasn't hard to assume I was in on it. We were both high. And Fish shot the owner of the store. The guy almost died."

Finn could almost feel Bonnie's dismay, her wonder, gauging his remorse, the truthfulness of his tale, but she stayed silent.

"They offered me a deal. It was three days after my eighteenth birthday, and I had no priors. Five years and no attempted murder charge if I would plead guilty to possession and armed robbery. I would have been out in less time, but I didn't adjust very well."

"So you got a tattoo of a swastika . . ." Bonnie moved to stand in front of him. She was biting on her lip, worrying it between her teeth like it held the answer to her dilemma. "I still don't understand that. Was that something Fisher was involved in too?"

"No!" Finn shook his head vigorously, not wanting Bonnie to lay that on his brother's head. "I got that tattoo a month after I arrived at Norfolk. I'd tried to impress some people by showing them what I could do with numbers, with cards. It didn't go over very well. I got beat up, they marked up my back, and I was sure if I didn't find a gang, I was going to die just like my brother, and die soon. So I joined up with the only gang who would have me."

Bonnie's eyes were wide like she was putting it all together.

"Funny," Finn said, though it really wasn't funny at all. "What feels necessary on the Inside makes you a freak on the Outside."

"The inside?" Bonnie asked.

"Inmates call prison the inside."

"And the outside is . . ."

"Life. Freedom. Everything beyond the walls. I thought the tattoo was necessary. I thought it was survival. In the end, though, the tattoo didn't save me. I was saved by numbers. I was attacked, yeah, but I'd made my point, and eventually I had people coming to me, powerful people, and I didn't need the tattoo after all."

There was a long silence between them, Bonnie staring wordlessly at him, Finn staring back, wondering if she could really understand. Finn touched his chest and her eyes followed his fingers.

"The tattoo is a reminder that choices made out of desperation are almost always bad choices." Finn paused, hoping Bonnie was thinking about her choice to climb the bridge. She'd been desperate too, and it had been a bad choice. "I don't take off my shirt at the beach or in the weight room or when I go for a run or play ball with my friends. And I would never have shown you. It's there, over my heart, making me look like something I'm not. Pretty hard to get past, I know. But it's over my heart—not *in* my heart. And hopefully that makes a difference."

Bonnie nodded and reached over and placed her left hand over his right one, peeling it off his chest so she could hold it. Finn was so surprised that he let her. It hung between them, and she wrapped both of her smaller hands around it, cradling it.

"I'm sorry about Fisher," she said sincerely.

Finn snorted in disbelief and pulled his hand away. She grabbed it back and swung on him fiercely, bringing their conjoined hands to her chest, his arm resting between her breasts, her right hand clinging to his forearm.

"I'm sorry that happened to you, Finn." She repeated the words with a vehemence that had him snapping back at her.

"Don't do that, Bonnie! Don't be one of those girls who thinks I'm something to save! You can't save me. I can't save you. I sure as hell didn't save Fish, and you couldn't save Minnie, could you?"

Bonnie's brow was furrowed, resistance written all over her face.

"Could you?" He was being a son-of-a-bitch. But it was the truth, a truth he didn't think Bonnie had come to terms with.

"No." Her lips trembled, and she shook her head. "No. I couldn't. I didn't."

Finn swore, an ugly word for all the ugly feelings in his chest, and he tried to pull his hand free. Instead he just pulled her with it.

"But you did save me, Finn." Her face was tipped up to his, his arm pinned between their chests.

"No, Bonnie. I interrupted you. If you wanna die, you're gonna die. You know it, and I know it. I just hope you change your mind, because you're better than that. Fish and Minnie are gone. Maybe we failed them. Hell, I don't know. But we don't help them by jumping off bridges."

"I am?" she asked, still clinging to his hand.

"What?"

"I'm better than that?"

"Yes!" Finn sputtered. "You are!"

She smiled at him then, just a wry twist of her lips and a softening through her eyes. But her tone was wry as she said, "You're gonna have to make up your mind whether or not you hate me,

Clyde."

"I don't hate you, Bonnie." How could he hate her with her lips inches from his and her chocolate eyes so full of compassion? "I just don't know what the hell to do with you. And now, I've got the police looking for me, thinking I've kidnapped you."

"You don't hate me, but you don't like me very much." Bonnie ignored the part about the police looking for him. She was still holding his hand and Finn felt ridiculous and irritated and more than a little turned on with his hand clasped between her breasts. He tugged again but she held fast.

"I do like you, Bonnie." Damn it all. He did, too. "But you've got to call your gran, your friend Bear, and everyone else who needs to know where the hell you are, and clear this up. Do you understand? Remember what I said about games? This isn't one. This is my life, my freedom, and I don't want to go back to prison."

Bonnie sighed but didn't respond. She just held tight to his hand for a minute longer and then released it. Together they walked back to the Blazer, climbed in, and without further fanfare, headed down the road.

Finn was tired, and he felt filthy, the result of sleeping in the car all night, wearing the same clothes for two days solid, and brushing his teeth with snow and his middle finger—his way of saying eff-you Mother Nature. They needed to find a hotel and recoup. And Bonnie was going to make those calls if he had to hold her down and dial for her.

8
Continuous Compounding

THE MAN WHO has been seen with singer Bonnie Rae Shelby has now been identified as Infinity James Clyde, a twenty-four-year-old ex-con from the Boston area. Clyde served five years for armed robbery and was released from Norfolk Penitentiary in Massachusetts in 2012. A vehicle registered to Clyde, an orange, 1972 Chevy Blazer, seen leaving the scenes of both recent sightings of the young superstar contributed to his identification. Bonnie Rae Shelby's family is convinced that Miss Shelby had never met Infinity James Clyde before and had no relationship with him prior to her disappearance, leading police to believe that Miss Shelby either met or was bodily detained by Clyde in Boston, the last time her family or friends saw her. Infinity James Clyde resides in South Boston and left the area the night Bonnie Rae Shelby performed at the TD Garden.

Infinity James Clyde is a white male, approximately six-two, two-hundred-ten pounds, and twenty-four years old. He has dark blond hair and blue eyes and is currently wanted for questioning by the police. If you have any information for police, you can call the number at the bottom of the screen.

∞

WITHIN MINUTES THEY were on 271 which, just like the old man said, eventually spit them out back on 71, heading toward Columbus, but they'd burned through most of their gas keeping warm the night before, and before too long Finn pulled off the freeway in a town called Ashland to refuel. Bonnie hadn't said a word since they'd hit the road again. She was full of contradictions. Most of the time she couldn't shut up, and then there were moments like this, stretches of time when she just turned it off and went somewhere else. They had both sat in contemplative silence, looking anywhere but at each other. She'd stared sightlessly straight ahead, and he had stared at the road while his gut had churned, and his mind had raced, the peace from that morning destroyed.

He pulled into the gas station feeling like he wore a target on his chest, worried that any moment someone would step forward and point, yelling for the police who would swarm in and haul him off. But the world seemed oblivious to him, the way it usually was, and cars and trucks caked in dirty ice and snow rolled in and out of the gas station, refueling and recharging without taking note of the old, orange Blazer or its occupants. The knot in his gut eased slightly.

Bonnie slid a pair of sunglasses on and stepped out of the passenger side, not looking right or left, and headed inside. He washed his salt and sleet covered windows before he noticed that Bonnie had put $70 down on the pump. He supposed that was her way of telling him they were going to be together for a few more miles. He just shook his head and commenced refueling.

He was usually good at figuring things out, good at unraveling complicated equations and ferreting out solutions to problems most people wouldn't even attempt. Here he was, surrounded by a complex, puzzling, and elusive problem, and he wasn't talking about math. Bonnie was a woman, and the functions and formulas that ruled one had no obvious bearing on the other. Bonnie should be running from him as far and fast as she could, and for the life of him, he couldn't figure her out.

Finished fueling, Finn headed into the convenience store to take advantage of the bathroom break and secure some coffee for the road.

Bonnie nodded at him as he came through the doors and held two large Styrofoam cups aloft, indicating she was one step ahead of him. He couldn't complain that she wasn't conscientious. He nodded back and headed toward the bathrooms, but not before he noticed that Bonnie's attention was fixated on a child who sat in one of the tables in the corner, an uneaten breakfast sandwich in front of her. The child had the smooth, hairless appearance of someone undergoing chemotherapy. A sock monkey hat covered her head, but her non-existent eyelashes and brows gave her away. A woman sat beside the little girl, bouncing a baby on her knee and talking into a cellphone. The woman was obviously agitated, and the bouncing baby was not mollified by the motion.

When Finn came out of the restroom five minutes later, Bonnie had approached the woman and was now sitting at the small table next to the little girl who was smiling at her shyly. Finn bit down on a curse and shook his head in wonder. Wasn't keeping a low profile kind of important?

He strode toward the table, and Bonnie welcomed him with a smile and patted the chair next to her.

"Finn, this is Shayna and her two daughters. Riley and Katy." She looked at the little girl when she said Katy, so Finn assumed Riley was the drooly baby now happily chomping on a paper cup. Finn didn't want to sit, but his height and the fact that the females were all sitting, staring up at him, forced his hand.

"Shayna's car broke down, Finn."

"We've been in Cleveland since Friday at the children's hospital, and we're on our way home," the woman named Shayna rushed to explain. "The transmission's been slipping, but I've always been able to coax it into cooperating. But I pulled in here to get gas, and I couldn't shift it back into drive again. I'm blocking a pump. The owner isn't too happy with me, I don't think. But I can't move it. The wheels are all locked up because it's stuck in park."

"Finn's really smart. I know he can help you," Bonnie said, nodding her head and smiling at Finn. Finn almost growled, but Shayna looked so relieved, he set down his coffee and stood.

"Let me take a look. Show me which car."

"I'll stay with Riley and Katy, Shayna." Bonnie held her arms out for the squirming Riley, and Katy seemed completely fine with the suggestion. Her eyes were glued to Bonnie's face as if she couldn't believe what she was seeing. Finn truly hoped she wasn't a Bonnie Rae Shelby fan, but given his luck as of late, that was probably expecting too much.

"Are you sure?" Shayna was doubtful, looking between Finn and Bonnie as if she weren't sure she could trust them, but not knowing what other options she had.

"We'll stand right there at the windows so you can see us and so they can see you, all right?" Bonnie said kindly, and they all trailed after Clyde as he made a beeline for the entrance. The front of the store looked out onto the busy pumps, and Bonnie waved them away as she dug some quarters out of her purse, and she and Katy began feeding the sticker machine to the right of the front doors.

Shayna led him to a green Ford Fiesta that had seen better days and stood, her attention shifting back and forth between him and her children, who watched from inside the store. She looked exhausted, and Finn felt instant remorse for his ill feelings. He climbed inside and turned the key, hoping that the woman was wrong. The gear shift wouldn't budge. He turned the key off and then just to the right, turning on the radio and the interior lights, but not starting the engine. Then he pumped the gas a few times and turned the wheel. Then he tried the key once more. No luck.

He remembered something he'd read once, just a snippet from some popular mechanics article. Funny—he could even remember the page number. His mind was like that, always associating a number with a piece of information. He called Shayna over and had her follow his instructions, turning the key to the alternator position and pumping the gas pedal while he bounced lightly on the back of the car.

"See if you can pop it into neutral," he said, and felt the moment the car shifted out of park.

"You did it!" Shayna squealed.

"Now you steer as I push. Let's get you out of the way before we try anything else."

Bonnie and the kids came trundling out of the gas station, following them to the far side of the parking lot, sure that he'd fixed the problem. But in spite of the small success, the car still wouldn't shift into drive, and Clyde didn't dare shift it back into park for fear he wouldn't be able to get it out again. He tried everything he could think of and then looked at the young mother in defeat. Her jaw was clenched, and she was blinking hard, and he could tell she was about to cry.

"How far is home?" he asked.

"We live in Portsmouth."

"Where's Portsmouth?

"It's directly south of here, about a three hour drive. My in-laws live in North Carolina so they can't help, but I can call my parents. They both work, though, and can't leave until after six." It was now noon.

"Husband?"

"My husband's in Afghanistan."

Well, shit.

"Finn?" Bonnie only had to say his name, and he knew what she wanted. She waited, her eyes on his.

"We'll take you home." Clyde said before he could think too hard about it. "It's not that far out of our way." Just three hours.

"I can't leave the car. I have to get it back to Portsmouth, and I can't pay to have it towed all that way." Shayna was trying to hold it together, but the loss of the car was apparently the last straw.

"Finn?"

Clyde had no idea why that one word was so effective coming out of Bonnie's lips, but he found himself suggesting something so horrendous he had to question if Bonnie used her voice to carry out mind control. Maybe that's why she was a super star.

"We'll pull it behind the Blazer. I've got a hitch, and I can get my hands on some chains. It'll be slow going, but we'll get you home."

Bonnie beamed at him. Yep. Mind control.

Finn went to secure some chains and Bonnie bustled around rearranging bags and boxes to clear out the middle seat. Shayna took what she needed from her car, and the women went back inside for a final bathroom break.

Within a half hour, the green Ford Fiesta was rolling along behind the old Blazer, traveling at a blistering speed of forty-five miles an hour. It was going to be a long, long drive. Finn almost wished the cops would pull him over and haul him off.

∞

I PULLED OUT Finn's guitar about a half hour into the trip. I'd placed it in the front to make room for our passengers, and I'd sung a few songs just to keep them entertained. I was pretty sure little Katy knew exactly who I was. Finn was pretty sure of it too, and he kept shooting me looks, and I kept giving him smiles. He needed to relax. He hadn't done anything wrong, and nobody was going to be sending him to jail. He clearly wasn't used to having people talking about him, having news stories about him, having to live with the whole world thinking they were entitled to your business just because you sold records. I wasn't worried about the police, and I definitely wasn't worried about Katy Harris and her mama and baby sister calling the tabloids the minute we reached Portsmouth.

"Your name is Bonnie and you sound just like Bonnie Rae

Shelby," Katy said, her voice hushed and her eyes wide. "You look like her too, but with different hair."

"That's because I *am* Bonnie Rae Shelby," I said. Finn looked at me and rolled his eyes. I stuck out my tongue and Katy laughed.

"How come you cut off your hair?" Katy obviously had no trouble believing I was who I said I was.

"I needed a change," I lied. She didn't need to know about the meltdown I'd had over my resemblance to Hank. "Just think, your hair will be as long as mine soon, and then you'll be able to say you have Bonnie Rae hair, right?"

"Yeah! Except my hair is blonde . . . when I have hair, that is."

"Well, then. I might just have to go blonde again so that we can be twins. Will you send me pictures so I can get the color just right?"

Katy's mama, Shayna, was staring at me with her mouth hanging wide open. She blinked a few times and then closed her mouth without saying a word.

"Will you sing another song?" Katy asked.

"Sure. What's your favorite one?"

"I love all of them. You choose."

"Well, Finn likes a song called "Goober Peas"—I think baby Riley would like it too." Finn just shook his head, and I tried not to laugh. He was such a grouch. I launched into an exuberant version of "Goober Peas" which the baby did indeed enjoy, kicking her chubby legs in her car seat, but which had Finn wincing.

"There's a song my daddy used to sing called "Down in the Valley." It's kind of a sad one, but Riley looks a little sleepy. Maybe I can sing her to sleep, whaddaya think?" Shayna looked like she was ready to keel over too, and maybe if the baby slept, she would get a much-needed nap.

"Okay." Katy smiled, nodding.

"Down in the valley, valley so low
Hang your head over, hear the wind blow
Hear the wind blow, love, hear the wind blow

Hang your head over, hear the wind blow"

*"Roses love sunshine, violets love dew
Angels in heaven know I love you
Know I love you, love, know I love you
Angels in heaven know I love you."*

I had to stop suddenly, the words getting to me. Katy had pulled off her sock monkey cap and laid her head down on her mother's lap. Her thin neck looked scarcely big enough to hold up her bare head, and her mama stroked the smooth skin as I sang. There was a time Minnie had looked just like Katy, bald head and all, and the sight of Katy's little hairless head was almost more than I could bear.

Finn glanced at me, his gaze sharp, not missing much, I was sure, and I played a few measures on the guitar, trying to control the emotion that had caught me off guard. It was the line about angels in heaven, I supposed. I winked at Finn, pretending I was just fine, and sang a different verse that wouldn't make me think of Minnie.

*"Write me a letter, send it by mail
Send it in care of the Birmingham jail
Birmingham jail, love, Birmingham jail
Send it in care of the Birmingham jail."*

"Nice, Bonnie Rae," he said under his breath. I winked again and blew him a little kiss to let him know I was just teasing him. I could have changed the words to Norfolk Penitentiary, but it had too many syllables and didn't rhyme with mail.

"He's in jail?" Katy asked.

I stopped playing in surprise. "Who?"

"The guy in the song," Katy answered. "He's in jail, and she's an angel in heaven?"

"No. I mean, yeah. He's in jail, but she's not an angel . . . she's just a girl he loves, and he wishes she would love him back," I said.

"And write him letters?" Katy asked.

"Yep. Write him letters while he's in the penitentiary," I answered cheerfully.

Finn sighed the sigh of a man with little patience left. I did my best not to laugh.

"There's another verse too, Katy. You'll like this one. It's about a castle.

Build me a castle, forty feet high
So I can see her as she rides by
As she rides by, dear, as she rides by
So I can see her as she rides by."

"It's Rapunzel!" Katy whispered and tried to sit up from her mother's lap.

Shayna's eyes were getting heavy, and the little girl slid out from under her mother's arm and scooted up until she was leaning between the front seats, completely tuned in to the song that was about another apparent favorite. I didn't point out that the man was the one in the castle and the girl was riding by.

"It's kind of like you, Bonnie. You cut off your long hair too. Just like Rapunzel."

"That's right, Katy. That's because a mean old witch locked me up at Tower Records, and I had to wait for my boyfriend to get out of jail and come rescue me."

"What the fu—heck are you talking about?" Finn asked, amending his curse at the last minute for the sake of the little girl who was hanging on every word.

A little snort escaped out of my nose at the incredulous look on his face, and Katy giggled.

"Bonnie Rae," Finn choked out, finally laughing, "can we please change the subject?"

"Well. Singing is what I do best. Why don't you entertain for a minute, Clyde?"

"What are you good at, Clyde?" Katy asked sweetly.

"Finn's good at math," I answered for him when he stayed silent.

"Oh, yeah? What's twenty times twenty" Katy challenged.

"Four hundred," Finn answered. "But that one wasn't very hard. I bet you knew that one too."

"Ask him one you don't know. Something really hard," I instructed.

"What's six hundred and ninety . . . five," Katy scrunched up her nose trying to make the number as complicated as she could. "Times four hundred and . . . fifty-two?"

Finn hardly stopped to think. "Three hundred fourteen thousand, one hundred forty."

Katy and I both stared. I'm sure my face resembled Shayna's stunned expression of not too long ago. I should have known.

Katy was immediately digging in her mother's purse, rifling through wadded-up receipts and hair bands until she pulled out a dinky, red calculator that looked as if it had come out of a kid's meal. She asked Finn several more problems, checking his answers on the little device. One time she crowed that he was wrong, only to realize she'd entered the numbers incorrectly.

She kept at it for at least a half hour, and Finn answered correctly, and quickly, every time. Katy was blown away. I was blown away. She continued grilling him until Finn shot me a sideways glance and mouthed, "Help."

"What's infinity plus one?" I interrupted Katy, asking Finn my own question.

"It's still infinity," Finn said, sighing.

"Wrong. It's two."

"Oh yeah? How do you figure?"

I pointed at Finn and said, "Infinity." Then I pointed at myself and said, "Plus one. That's two, genius."

"I really wish I hadn't told you my name."

"Ha. Gotcha! You think you're so good at math, but I just stumped you."

Katy clapped, and I distracted her further by saying, "Here Katy. I have a cooler trick than Finn's. I can show you how to write *poop* on a calculator . . . now that's awesome." I pulled the calculator from her little hands and proceeded to teach her some potty humor every kid should know.

Finn grabbed it from my hand and punched in some numbers and passed it back. When I turned it upside down it read "hILLBIL-LI." Well, I definitely was that.

9

Countably Infinite

THE RIDE THAT should have taken three and a half hours took almost six. We rolled into Portsmouth after the sun had already gone down. Shayna lived in West Portsmouth, across the Scioto River, and she said you could still see what was left of the old Ohio-Erie Canal, but it was pretty overgrown, and in the dark it was impossible to see. I was too tired to care much about seeing any sights anyway. The baby had slept most of the way, which probably meant a sleepless night for her mother, but it had made the drive more bearable. Katy and Shayna had dozed off and on too, but I stayed awake with Finn, watching the Ohio landscape drift by, pondering the twists and turns of fate and fame, wondering how it all shook out.

We'd stopped once for a bathroom break and food, which I insisted on buying. Shayna let me. I could see there were things she wanted to say, but for whatever reason held back. With Shayna directing us the last few miles, we finally found ourselves in front of the Harris home at a little after six o'clock that night. I helped carry kids and luggage into the tidy rambler while Finn unchained the Fiesta from behind the Blazer. I referred to it as the "party in the back." Get it? Fiesta? Yeah. Nobody else thought it was very funny either.

Katy was asleep by that time, and though she was too old to be carried to her bed, and it was still early in the evening, I scooped her up, cradling her slight figure in my arms, knowing that my tenderness for her was partially due to her illness. Minnie's illness. I'd even slipped and called her Minnie once on the long drive. She'd looked at me blankly, and I'd stuttered and corrected myself immediately, but Finn had shot me a look. He didn't miss much, but I really wished he'd missed that.

Shayna pointed me toward Katy's room, and I swung through the opening, laid her on her bed, and untied her sneakers before I pulled a blanket up around her shoulders. I straightened, took a couple of steps back, and noticed the posters on the wall were mostly of me. Weird. And kind of cool. I found a black, felt-tip marker among a handful of colors protruding from a tin pencil can on a dresser littered with crayons and paints and drawings. I went around the room and autographed all of the posters.

"Bonnie Rae?"

I turned, and Katy was looking at me sleepily, trying to keep her eyes open. "I don't want you to leave."

"I don't want you to leave." Minnie had said the very same thing the night before I'd left for Nashville the first time. I had clung to her and she had squeezed me back.

"Then I won't," I'd said simply. "I'll stay here. There's always next year."

She'd sighed and let me go, pushing away from me in our double bed. "No. I'm just feeling a little sad. You need to go, Bonnie. You're going to win. I can feel it. Then you'll make a million dollars, and we'll travel all over the world together."

I was feeling sad too. Scared. I'd never spent a single night away from Minnie. Not in all our fifteen years. "Can't you come with me?" I'd asked. I knew the answer. We'd been over it.

"You know there's only enough money for you and Gran to go." And she'd been too sick to go. She'd been too sick for me to leave

her too.

"Can't you stay?" Katy's voice. Not Minnie's. Katy was trying to sit up, and I crouched down beside her bed.

"Where would I sleep?" I tried to smile. "I can't fit in your bed. And what about Finn? I don't think Riley wants to give up her crib."

Katy snickered at the thought of Finn in Riley's crib.

"You and Finn must be as tired as we are," Shayna said from the doorway, and Katy and I looked up at her.

"Look, Mommy. Bonnie Rae signed all my posters." Katy pointed at the walls.

"Uh, yeah." Shayna had that same dazed look she'd gotten when I told Katy who I was. "What . . . I mean . . . how, I mean, I know it's not my business. But, what are you . . . doing?"

"I figured I should make them valuable in case you wanted to hawk them." I felt a little stupid, suggesting my signature was something special, but Katy seemed pleased.

"No! I don't mean the posters. What are you and Finn doing tonight? You should stay here. The couch in the family room folds out into a bed."

"Yeah! Yeah! You and I can sleep in the family room and have a sleepover!" Katy's eyes were huge, and she no longer looked the slightest bit drowsy. She was up and out of bed immediately.

"Slow down, Katy. You know you get lightheaded," Shayna said.

I thought I heard Finn come in the front door. He was probably standing there, just inside the entry feeling awkward and not daring to venture any further.

"And I don't think Finn, Bonnie, and you can all fit in the foldout bed. A little crowded, sis, don't you think?" Shayna was trying to discourage the group sleepover, and Katy wasn't hearing any of it.

"I have to pee! Don't leave, Bonnie, okay?"

I stood and headed for the door, wanting to reassure Finn. Wanting to make sure he didn't leave without me.

"I saw something about you and Finn on Entertainment Buzz or one of those shows at the hospital," Shayna blurted out as I moved to walk past her. "I was just flipping through channels. I stopped when I saw they were talking about you, thinking that Katy would want to watch, but she'd fallen asleep. They said you'd been taken, or something. They tried to sound serious, but mostly they all just sounded really excited. I felt really sad for you, and I was glad Katy was asleep. It would have upset her to think you were missing."

"Leave it to E-Buzz to get it all wrong," I said and forced a laugh. "Finn didn't take me, obviously. I think you can see that I'm fine. And he's a good guy."

"So you're . . . okay?"

"Tell me this, Shayna. Do I seem like I'm in trouble? Does Finn seem like the kind of guy who steals pop stars for ransom?"

"No," she said with a smirk. "Actually, if I had to guess, I would say you'd kidnapped him."

"Shayna, you're a smart woman," I said, patting her shoulder. And she laughed.

"Why did you help us?" Her laughter faded, and her eyes were suddenly bright, like she wanted to cry.

"Because you needed help." I shrugged. "And my sister had leukemia too." Damn it all. I felt emotion rise in my eyes too.

"Finn?" Katy ran out of the bathroom and shot past us in the hallway, in search of Finn, and I followed her gratefully, not wanting to continue the sensitive conversation with her mother.

"Finn?" Katy shouted again, and ran to the front door. Finn sat on the front stoop. I'd guessed wrong. He hadn't even come inside, though Shayna had left the door propped wide open, welcoming him.

"Finn! Bonnie and I are sleeping on the fold-out bed. We're having a sleepover. You're sleeping in my bed."

And that was that. We were staying. You didn't say no to a kid like Katy. Finn just closed his eyes briefly and avoided my gaze, but he seemed resigned to the fact that it made as much sense as anything else, and when Shayna thanked him profusely and produced a pair of army boots that were almost new, claiming they were too big for her husband, he accepted them with quiet dignity. I too had noticed his boots were worn out and his feet kept getting wet, and I had made my own plans to replace them when I could. Maybe it was better this way. Finn didn't seem to like it when I paid for him.

Shayna started dinner—spaghetti—and Finn left for a while, claiming he needed to get some exercise. I resisted the urge to tag along as much as I longed to stretch my legs and match my stride to his. I was pathetic and needy, and we both knew it, and I didn't like that I felt that way where he was concerned. Plus, I really thought Finn might explode if I asked to go with him. He threw on a pair of basketball shorts, a T-shirt, and some worn running shoes and was out the door, his hair pulled off his face, his expression stony.

He was gone for an hour, but when he finally came through the door, dripping with sweat, he looked a little less explosive than he had before. Still, even sweaty and ornery, he was impressive to look at. Shayna tried not to stare as she informed him of the clean towels in the bathroom and invited him to help himself to the shower. It had been a while since there had been a man in the house, obviously, and Shayna looked at me apologetically, as if she were having lascivious thoughts and felt guilty about them. She bit her lip and turned away, and I felt bad for her once again. Shayna Harris was juggling a lot of crap. And shit is incredibly difficult to juggle. No matter how hard you try, it still falls apart and slips through your fingers, and even when you're managing to keep it aloft, it still stinks.

After dinner, with Finn's permission, I lightly sanded his old guitar, and Katy and I drew little flowers all over it, intertwining the blossoms with curling long green vines. We painted the blossoms in different shades of pink, using some of the little tole paints on Katy's dresser. When we were done, Katy and I both signed our names on the back, and Shayna applied a clear overcoat to seal our efforts. I could tell she was one of those crafty ladies that was good at making tin cans and weeds look pretty.

Finn told Katy she could keep it, that it would be a collector's item someday. I don't think Katy knew what he meant, but I hoped Shayna did, and told her if she needed the money she shouldn't be afraid to sell it. I would send Katy a new one to replace it. I also left three thousand dollars in her cookie jar. I was frustrated that I couldn't leave more because I had so much more. I just couldn't *access* more at the moment, and I needed to make sure I still had some cash to get myself and Finn to Vegas.

I didn't know why I needed to get to Vegas so badly. There was nothing there for me. But I was focused on it like it was the ribbon strung across a finish line, as if the journey itself held the answers to my questions. And I believed if I could just have until Vegas—just a few days is all—I would figure out how to live again.

∞

COULD YOU FALL in love with a voice? Finn shut his eyes and listened from the little room, lying in the little bed, covered in a little pink spread, surrounded by life-size pictures of Bonnie Rae Shelby wearing skimpy outfits and long, blonde curls, making love to a microphone. Katy was requesting one song after another, and Bonnie Rae was giving the sweet ten-year-old a private concert . . . in her pajamas. Talk about Make-A-Wish.

You would think he would stare at those pictures while he listened to her sing. But Finn didn't stare at the images. He didn't need to. The real thing was a room away. So he had turned off the lights, climbed into bed, and now lay with his eyes closed, just listening.

He heard giggles—childish and adult—and he wondered how Bonnie was still going strong at ten o'clock at night. He was exhausted, and she hadn't had any more sleep than he had in the last twenty-four hours. And she still hadn't showered or had a minute to herself. He wondered if this time with Katy was good for her, healing maybe. It was the only reason he hadn't insisted they leave. He'd wanted to get on the road. He'd needed to press his foot to the gas and leave Portsmouth behind, to get back on track.

What had happened to his road trip, the road trip he'd been so eager to make that he hadn't even waited until morning to leave home as originally planned? He hadn't been able to sleep that last night in Boston, the night he'd found Bonnie on the bridge. He'd gone to bed and lain there for an hour and then thought, "Why wait?" So he'd folded up his bedding—the only thing left in his basement apartment—and pulled on his clothes. Then he'd headed out. His mom worked the swing shift at the hospital, so she would be getting home about midnight too. He planned to catch her right as she got home, say goodbye, and be on his way. That was the plan. That was Saturday. And that plan, and every other one since then, had been shot to hell.

Now it was Tuesday. Only three nights later. And he was in a strange house, in a child's bed, in southern Ohio.

He almost laughed then, so damn bewildered and incredulous that laughing was all he really could do. He rubbed his face, too tired to give in to the urge to howl, and just sighed instead, noting wearily that Bonnie Rae had closed her concert and was saying goodnight to Katy, promising she'd be back after she showered, telling the little girl to try to go to sleep.

Bonnie Rae had called Katy Minnie. It had happened only once, but he'd seen the stricken look on Bonnie's face before she'd corrected herself and patted Katy's cheek. It was the same look she'd worn when she'd been watching them in the convenience store, before she'd befriended them.

The bathroom was right next to Katy's bedroom. He saw the light pool in the hallway as Bonnie entered, and then watched it narrow to a long thin line as she closed the door, and the light seeped out beneath. The shower came on next, the sound soothing the way rushing water always was. Someone had told him in prison that God's voice sounded like rushing water. That's why babies love to be shushed. That's why the sound lulls people to sleep. He wondered how anyone would know what God's voice sounded like. Especially someone convicted of homicide.

He felt himself drifting off when he heard Bonnie crying. He was pretty sure that this time it had nothing to do with short hair and a resemblance to her homely brother, Hank. She cried like she'd been holding it in all day. Maybe she had. Maybe spending time with Katy had been a very bad idea. He sat up immediately, wondering if they should go, if he needed to get her out of here.

Then he swore, loud and foul, pulled at his hair, and lay back down. It wasn't his job to save her! He couldn't save her! Hadn't he told her, just today, not to try and save him? It was all bullshit. And it was her fault they were here in the first place! He pulled the pillow over his head so he couldn't hear her. There. That was better. God's voice didn't sound like rushing water, it sounded like silence.

Finn commanded himself to sleep, keeping the pillow smashed into his face. But the light curled around the edges of the pillow when Bonnie left the bathroom, and the hallway went black when she flipped it off. He moved the pillow off his face and bunched it under his head, telling himself he still wasn't listening. And he wasn't listening, he was straining. With every muscle, he was straining to hear.

"Finn? Are you awake?" He could hear her feeling along the walls, trying to make her way to the bed where he lay. When she reached it, she sat gingerly on the end.

"Yeah," he admitted quietly. She sat for a minute, not saying anything, and he didn't demand a reason for her presence.

"Do you still miss Fisher?" she finally whispered.

He could say no. Maybe she needed to be reassured that the pain would go away eventually.

"Yeah," he said. So much for reassurance. "I still talk to him sometimes. Fish and I were identical too. Sometimes when I look in the mirror, I imagine it's him. I talk to my reflection. Stupid. But yeah."

"I can't stand looking at myself for that reason. All I see is her."

"You should look. Let yourself look. If it makes you feel better, let yourself pretend."

He heard her sniffle in the dark.

"It's better than seeing Hank. Right?" he was trying to make her laugh, but he didn't know if it worked. It was too dark and she was too still.

"Do you ever feel like you've forgotten something, only to realize it's not something, it's someone . . . it's Fisher? I feel like that all the time. Like I've overlooked something important—and I'll check to make sure I haven't left my phone, or my keys, or my purse. Then I realize it's Minnie. I've lost Minnie."

"My mom used to say Fish and I were two sides of the same coin. Fish said he was heads, and I was the ass. Not tails, the ass. But if that's true, I guess he won't ever be lost—as long as I exist, so does he. You can't lose the other side of a coin, right?"

"Were you alike?"

"We looked alike, but that was all. He was right handed, I'm left. He was random, I'm sequential. He was loud, I've always been a little shy."

"Sounds like me and Minnie," Bonnie said. "Only I'm like Fisher and she was more like you." Finn smirked in the dark. Yeah. He'd figured that one out all by himself.

"Finn? I'm a twin. You're a twin. But our twins are gone. So what does that make us? Are we halves?"

Finn waited, not sure how to respond. Bonnie sighed when he didn't speak. His eyes had adjusted to the dark, and he stared at her shadowy form, perched beside his feet on the little bed. Then she curled up like a kitten, laying her head on his legs like she had no intention of leaving.

"When Fish was alive, I tried to keep the numbers in my head from spilling out into everything we did together. Sometimes he would get jealous. It made him feel left out that Dad and I loved mathematics, and he was clueless. He was very, very competitive. And I'm not." Finn shrugged in the darkness, trying to shrug off the weight of the memories.

"I just wanted him to be happy. I wanted my family to stay together. And from the time I was just a little kid, there was the Finn who loved numbers, the Finn who happily read about Euclid and Cantor and Kant. And then there was the Finn who everybody called Clyde, the Finn who played ball and hung out with Fish and a bunch guys from the neighborhood. Guys who were always up to no good, smoking pot, drinking too much, and chasing girls that I didn't particularly want to catch. I did it for Fish. Always for Fish. I never told him no. In that way, I've always been split in two."

"I never felt that way. Minnie never acted like she minded the attention I got. I hope she didn't. I hope she wasn't just good at hiding it. It's possible. She hid other things from me." Bonnie sounded sad and bitter, and Finn guessed there was a part of her that was angry with Minnie, the way he'd been angry with Fish for a long time. Maybe it was sick and wrong to be pissed off, but the heart doesn't understand logic. Never had. Never would. Evidence of that truth was curled around his feet at the end of the bed.

"She didn't tell me how bad off she was, how sick she was," Bonnie continued. "Every time we talked she would tell me she was feeling better. She didn't warn me. She knew I would have come home right away. I never told Minnie no either. I would have done anything for her."

"Maybe that's why she didn't call you, Bonnie."

He felt her shaking her head against his legs, rejecting his suggestion. "But she left me without a word, Finn!"

"Fish left without a word, too, Bonnie. One minute he was looking up at me as I tried to stop the blood pumping out of his gut. And the next minute, he was gone. Without a word."

"What word would you have wanted, Finn?" Bonnie asked, and he could tell she was trying not to cry. "If you got one word, what would you have wanted him to say?"

It was Finn's turn to shake his head. "I don't know, Bonnie. No matter how many words we get, there's always going to be the last one, and one word is never enough."

"I would have told her I loved her," Bonnie whispered. "And I would have told her to save me a mansion next to hers."

"A mansion?" Finn asked gently.

"There's a song we always sang in church. "My Father's House has Many Mansions." Ever heard it?"

"No."

"My Father's house has many mansions, if it were not so, I would have told you," she sang the line softly.

"Maybe God lives in the Grand Hotel," Finn murmured, wanting to sit up and beg her to sing the rest. Instead, he folded his arms beneath his head and pretended that her voice didn't make him feel things he didn't want to feel and make him consider things he refused to consider.

"What's the Grand Hotel?" she asked.

"It's a little paradox about infinity—Hilbert's paradox of the Grand Hotel."

"What's a paradox?"

"Something that contradicts our intuition or our common sense. Something that seems to defy logic. My dad loved them. Most of them are very mathematical."

"So tell me about the Grand Hotel. Tell me the paradox." The tears had faded from her voice, and Finn eagerly proceeded, wanting to keep them at bay.

"Imagine there's a hotel with a countably infinite number of rooms."

"Countably infinite?"

"Yeah. Meaning I could count the rooms, one by one, even if the counting never ends."

"Okay," she said drawing the word out, like she wasn't sure she understood, but wanted him to keep talking.

"And all those rooms are filled," Finn added.

"So infinite rooms, and all are full."

"Uh-huh. Pretend someone comes along and wants to stay at the Grand Hotel. There's an infinite number of rooms, so that should be possible, right?"

"Yeah, but you said all the rooms are occupied," she countered, already confused.

"They are. But if you have the person in room one move to room two, and the person in room two move to room three, and the person in room three move to room four, and so on, then you just cleared out some space. You have an empty room—room one."

"That makes no sense."

"Sure it does, you can't find the end of infinity. There *is* no end. So if you can't tack space onto the end of infinity, you have to create space at the beginning."

"But you said all the rooms are filled."

"Yes. And they will still be filled," Finn said, as if this were completely reasonable.

"So if ten people come along and want to stay at the Infinity Hotel . . ." her voice trailed off, waiting for him to fill in the rest.

"Then you have the person in room one move to room eleven, and the person in room two move to room twelve, and the person in room three move to room thirteen, and so on, clearing out ten rooms."

She laughed quietly. "That makes no sense whatsoever. Eventually someone's not going to have a room."

"There are infinite rooms."

"Yeah, yeah, yeah. And infinite people," she muttered, as if her mind were a little blown.

"That's why it's called a paradox. In a lot of ways, infinity makes no sense. It's impossible to get your mind around that type of vastness," Finn said thoughtfully. "But no one argues with infinity. We just accept that it's beyond visualization."

"I don't know about that . . . I frequently argue with Infinity." Bonnie rubbed her face against his leg as if she liked the feel of him beside her.

"Ha ha," Finn said dryly, wondering if he should pull away. He probably should. But he didn't.

"Do you think heaven is filled with countably infinite rooms filled with countably infinite people?" she asked.

Maybe Bonnie wondered if Minnie was in her own heavenly room. Maybe Fisher was there too, in a room near Minnie's. Maybe they had found each other the way Finn and Bonnie had, Finn mused to himself. And then he swallowed a groan at his romantic thoughts. He was getting delusional. And it was all Bonnie's fault.

"I don't know, Bonnie Rae," he said.

"People in Appalachia have been singing that song since the dawn of time. They're hoping there are infinite rooms and that the rooms are all mansions."

"That's kind of sad." The cynic in Finn didn't like the thought of people singing about mansions that didn't exist. It felt like buying lottery tickets to him—a huge waste of emotion and energy.

"Yeah. I guess so. But it's hopeful too. And sometimes hope is the difference between life and death."

Finn had no answer for that.

"Hey!" she said suddenly, her voice rising with her epiphany. "I know how we can make some room at the Infinity Hotel without making everyone move. I've officially solved the paradox. Call it Bonnie Rae's Solution."

"Oh yeah?"

"Yeah. We'll all double up. Problem solved. You wanna double up, Infinity Clyde?" Finn was sure if he could see her face she would be waggling her eyebrows. She liked to tease. And she was damn good at it.

Yeah. He wanted to double up. Instead he decided to poke back a little. "The problem is, when people double up, they start to multiply."

She giggled, and Finn found himself smiling in the dark.

"And then we're right back at square one," he whispered.

Bonnie snuggled further into his legs, throwing her arm across his knees. It was several minutes before she spoke again.

"How did we end up together? Don't you think it's . . .

strange?" she mumbled into the blanket. "I mean . . . what are the odds?"

He had asked himself the same thing over and over. But he wasn't ready to admit that, so he pulled out his mental math book and dusted it off, speaking softly, but impersonally.

"Mathematically speaking, they're pretty low. But not as low as you might think." Finn's mind settled into the comfort of percentages and the odds of certain coincidences with relief, not wanting to linger on thoughts of fate or destiny. He offered Bonnie a few examples of how oddities weren't really oddities at all when you examined the numbers. It was all true. And it was all bullshit.

Bonnie's head had grown heavy on his legs and she hadn't offered up so much as a "hmm" for several minutes. Finn sat up and looked down at her. He'd done it again. Two nights in a row. He talked about numbers and she was instantly asleep. Asleep. In his tiny bed—in Katy's tiny bed. He sighed and looped his hands under her armpits, pulling her up beside him. It was narrow, but doable. He threw the pink comforter over them and closed his eyes, willing himself to ignore the press of her body against his, willing the numbers in his head to take him away, the way they'd done for Bonnie.

10

Negative Direction

THEY LEFT JUST after seven the next morning, before Shayna and her girls were even up. Bonnie thought it would be easier that way, and had shaken Finn awake with a light hand against his shoulder. He'd scared her, shooting up from the bed, the slam and slide of prison doors ringing in his ears, carried over from a dream that visited almost every night.

Finn couldn't have felt much worse if he had actually woken up to find himself still behind bars. He'd spent the night snuggled up to Bonnie in a glorified Barbie bed, a bed as hard and small as a pink, plastic shoebox, and his back hurt and his hips ached and he had a headache that only sex or black coffee would ease. Since sex wasn't an option, he got himself ready in a hurry and was out in the Blazer within minutes of rising, hoping for black coffee and unfortunately, still thinking about sex.

Bonnie climbed in beside him and they were off. Off—just long enough to go through a McDonald's drive thru for coffee, long enough to get half of it in his belly, long enough to be driving along at maximum speed on highway 51, headed toward Cincinnati, when they heard the awful thumping sound that only means one thing. Steering became almost impossible.

The rest of Finn's coffee landed in his lap as he gripped the wheel and maneuvered the galloping Blazer to the side of the road. He spent an hour changing the tire, thankful that he had a spare, even though the spare was really just a donut, and he would have to stop and buy a new one as soon as possible. The only way to Cincinnati from Portsmouth was on an old highway that wound in and out of little towns, making the going slow and the services limited. The spare got them as far as a town called Winchester, and at that point, Finn was wishing he had a Winchester to put himself out of his misery. Bonnie had been very quiet throughout the long morning, and surprisingly, the silence hadn't been welcome.

She hadn't complained or groaned when they'd blown the tire, and she'd stayed beside him while he'd changed it, though he'd barked at her to get back inside the Blazer. She'd ignored him and huddled in a squat as the traffic flew by them, handing him this tool and holding that one, not saying a word. He preferred the Bonnie that told lame jokes about his name and poked and teased him, nonstop. This Bonnie made him think of the girl perched on the bridge, surrounded by mist.

They were in Winchester for two hours, awaiting service. The tire cost $200, and he and Bonnie fought about who should pay for it, resulting in a few stares and unwanted attention, reminding him again about the fact that the police were looking for them. Looking for her. Because they believed he had "taken" her. But maybe the people in the service station just stared because his crotch was stained with coffee, and his hands were smeared with grease. Nobody approached them, though, and in the end, Finn let Bonnie pay cash for the tire so he wouldn't have to show his ID or hand over his credit card with his very memorable name engraved along the bottom.

When they were on the road again, he reminded her that when they reached Cincinnati, she had to call her gran. The longer they let things lie, the worse it would get for both of them. Especially him. She just nodded, but didn't commit to anything, and Finn resisted the urge to scream. Her moody silence was killing him. And scaring him. He reached for the radio and flipped it on, needing something, anything to occupy his thoughts.

"The tattoo on your hand. The five dots. What does it mean?" Bonnie asked, her eyes drawn to his hand by his sudden motion. He flipped off the radio once again.

"If you connect the four outer dots, they make a square. See?" he held out his hand so she could see what he meant.

She nodded, her eyes on the dots. "Yeah?"

"That represents a cage."

"And the dot inside?" Bonnie asked.

"The man in the cage," he answered stiffly. "You'll see a lot of guys who've served time with this tattoo. But I actually wanted to get this one." Finn smiled humorlessly and felt the slice of nausea in his stomach that always accompanied thoughts of his other tattoos.

"Why did you want this one?" She reached out and touched the small grouping of dots on the back of his right hand between his forefinger and his thumb. The touch made him want to grab her hand and hold on, but he pulled away and gripped the wheel instead.

"There are five dots. Five is the only odd, untouchable number . . . as far as we know," he said, trying to ignore his reaction to her brief caress.

"Odd and untouchable?" she asked, not understanding.

"You know what odd numbers are. Five is odd, but it's also untouchable—meaning it's not the sum of any of the proper divisors of any positive integer."

Bonnie stared at him blankly. "I could ask what an integer is, but I'm not sure that would help me understand what you just said."

"Integers are the natural numbers—one, two, three, four, etc., as well as the negative of the natural numbers. Negative one, negative two, negative three, negative four, and so on. Zero is an integer too. Integers aren't fractions or decimals or square roots," he explained easily.

She nodded as if she understood. "Odd and untouchable. Is that what you are then, Finn?" He could tell she was trying to tease him, but he didn't feel like laughing.

"In prison I wanted to be untouchable. I've always been odd." His eyes shot to hers and then returned to the road. "But, yeah. I wanted to be different than the rest of the prison population, and I wanted to be left alone. Interestingly enough, eighty-eight is also an untouchable number." He rubbed the double eights on his chest through his shirt.

"What was it like, the day you got out?" she asked suddenly.

"Of prison?" Finn found he didn't mind the personal questions as much as he'd minded her silence.

"Yeah." Bonnie said nodding. Her dark eyes were probing, and her usually smiling mouth curved down at the edges.

"Terrifying."

"Why?"

"It was almost as scary as the day I went in."

Bonnie looked stunned and waited for him to continue.

"When you go in, everybody is counting the days 'til they can get

out . . . if getting out is even an option. The strange thing is, the longer you're in, the less you want to get out. It starts feeling safe. It starts feeling like the only option.

"One guy, five years older than me, had been in since he was seventeen too. Ten year sentence. He got out a few months before I did." Finn looked over at Bonnie, making sure she got what he was about to say next. "But he was back before I was released. And he was relieved. Being out here, in the real world, living? It scared him shitless. He didn't know how to be on his own. He didn't have any skills. The world had left him behind, and he crawled back in his hole the only way he knew how—he hurt somebody, stole their wallet. Problem solved. And you know what? I felt sorry for the bastard. I understood his thought process. I didn't like it, but I understood it."

"I guess that makes sense." Bonnie was nodding. "Being out here, in the real world, living? It is pretty scary. It makes me wonder what I'm running away from."

It was Finn's turn to wait. He didn't get the similarities between the two at all. Super stardom and prison? Um, no. But she'd used his words exactly.

"But then I think about going back. And I get so sick I just want to find a . . . a . . ."

"A bridge?" Finn finished for her.

"Yeah," Bonnie whispered, and Finn felt apprehension quiver in his gut. He studiously ignored it and resumed his own story.

"I promised myself I would be different. I promised myself I would not go back. But I won't lie and say there weren't times it would have been easier. It's been almost two years since I got out. I can't find a full time job. I can't really blame people. I was in prison for five years. Easier to hire the guy who doesn't have prison tats and a rap sheet.

"I lived in the basement of the house I grew up in because my mom had rented out the upstairs. She remarried while I was in Norfolk and moved to a nice house in Chelsea with her new husband. She said I could come live with her, but it would have caused problems in the relationship, and I didn't want that. Plus, living with my mom wasn't my idea of independence. So, I've lived in the basement and used a hot plate and a mini fridge for the last two years, sleeping on a mattress in the corner, lucky to have my own bathroom, lucky not to pay rent."

"Doesn't sound so bad," Bonnie said, and she sounded wistful. The wistful tone made him angry. She had no idea what she was talking about.

"You say that because you have money to burn and a life most people dream about. I have worked every odd job I could. My mom lined some things up for me. Painting, fixing this, fixing that. I'm not half bad at fixing things. It's a whole lot easier to fix things than it is to fix myself. But it wasn't working, Bonnie. So when Cavaro, a guy I met in prison, called me and told me he had something for me in Vegas, I decided it was better than what I had going. His brother owns several casinos. I don't know if there are mob ties. He told me my job will be to watch the tables. To watch the dealers. Follow the numbers. Nothing illegal, nothing shady." Finn stopped talking and shook his head. He didn't really know if it would involve anything shady or not, if he were being honest.

"So the numbers are saving you again, huh?" Bonnie said softly, and he remembered his confessions of the morning before.

"Yeah. Sometimes I think numbers are all I've got . . . but they go on forever, so it could be worse."

"They go on for Infinity." Bonnie replied wryly, waggling her eyebrows.

"Yeah. Just for me."

They let the conversation die, and Bonnie resumed her pensive position, feet on the dash, knees hugged into her chest, thoughts inward. So her sudden outburst as they pulled into Cincinnati caught him by surprise.

"I remember Cincinnati. I was here about a month ago. See? Up there! Time to change the billboard, folks." Bonnie said in a sing-song voice.

Just to the right, on a giant sign, Bonnie, blonde hair swirling, red lips parted, eyes beseeching, looked down onto the afternoon traffic flowing into Cincinnati, Ohio, reminding them all, belatedly, that she had been at the US Bank Arena on January 25th and making every man sorry he'd missed it.

Finn forgot to breathe, and if it hadn't been for Bonnie's shrill warning, he would have rear-ended the car in front of them.

"Fun venue," was all she said. Finn swore and kept driving.

∞

WE DIDN'T NEED to stop in Cincinnati. We could have kept going. It was only one o'clock when we settled on a motel. But Finn was still wearing his coffee-stained pants, and he was grubby from changing the tire. It had been an incredibly long twenty-four hours for both of us, and some regrouping was in order, so I didn't argue. Plus, he was determined that I make that call.

I didn't have a credit card, not counting Gran's stolen, useless ones, and Finn was worried about using his, considering there was a bit of a man-hunt on. Finn said no decent establishment would want to rent us a room without a card, and if we insisted on paying cash it was going to draw attention.

So we opted for a less than decent establishment. One room, two beds, one night—$100 plus a $50 deposit in case we broke something that wasn't nailed to the wall or to the floor, which left the mirror and each other, which could happen, I supposed. I was pretty sure Finn had fantasized about breaking me in half a few times since we'd thrown in together . . . or I'd thrown myself on him. At least he'd put us in the same room. If I was going to be sleeping in the shabbiest, scariest motel in Ohio, I wasn't going to do it alone.

We walked into the room, threw our bags down, and Finn handed me his phone. I looked at it, the small black device laying on his long palm. But I didn't take it.

"I'm not calling Gran," I said quietly, sinking down on the bed.

"Bonnie!" Finn's voice rose in warning.

"I'll call Bear!" I said, offering up the solution I'd spent all morning stewing over. "I'll tell him where I am and what I'm doing. I'll tell him to call Gran off because you can bet she's the one who's got everyone stirred up. The Golden Goose has flown south . . . or west. Where we heading? What big city is next?"

"Indianapolis. But it's less than two hundred miles away. We'll be there in three hours, tops. I wasn't going to stop in Indianapolis. I was going to go straight through to St. Louis, which is another four hours or so. Long day, but doable, if the weather holds."

"What's in St. Louis?" I asked, trying to distract him, trying to stall.

"My dad."

That surprised me. Finn was going to stop and see his dad. The only things he'd mentioned about his dad were related to math—the childhood promptings, the fact that his parents divorced when he was seventeen.

"He's head of the math department at Washington University."

"I see. Well, maybe I could go to St. Louis too." I had a sudden inspiration and hurried to share it. "I could call Bear, and he could overnight my things—my driver's license and my credit cards—to your dad's address. Then I won't . . . need you . . . anymore. You can go your way and I'll go mine. That's an idea!" An idea that sounded very reasonable to me.

Finn sighed and sat down on the little table positioned in front of the large window that looked out onto a parking lot adorned with two very large dumpsters. He shook his head and leaned forward, holding my gaze.

"You have to call her, Bonnie. If you don't, I'm calling the police. And you're going to sit beside me and tell them every damn thing that's gone down. Your choice."

"That's not much of a choice, Clyde." I meant to sound flip, but the words stuck in my throat. I lay back on the bed and looked at the ceiling. The texture looked like oatmeal laid on thick and painted in white sparkle. I had the urge to jump up and down on the bed so I could reach it, so I could grab giant handfuls of the texture and fling it around the room. I wondered if our $50 deposit would cover it.

"I can't talk to her, Finn," I whispered. "I can't do it yet."

Clyde sighed and swore, but I didn't look at him. I kept my eyes on the crusty ceiling, willing him to let me be, just for now.

"Here's what I'm going to do, Bonnie Rae. I'm going to take a shower. And when I get out, I'm calling the police. That's what I'm going to do. I'll let you decide what you want to do." He shoved up from the table, grabbed his duffle, and went into the closet-sized bathroom and shut the door. The shower started up a few minutes later.

Funny. Clyde said he would let me decide what I wanted to do.

So I decided.

But it wasn't at all what I wanted.

I shot up from the bed and grabbed the keys to the Blazer. Clyde had left them next to the TV—dropped them like everybody does when they walk into a motel room. His wallet was beside the keys, along with his phone, like he'd emptied out his pockets when he'd set down his bags.

I took his phone too. Then I counted out $2000 and laid it out next to his wallet, so he couldn't miss it. I'd given him half of the money I had left. The motel had provided three sheets of stationary and a pen with the motel chain on it, as if people still sat and wrote long letters to their loved ones back home. Still, I was glad it was there, because I had a letter to write, and very little time to do it.

Meet me in St. Louis, Louis, Meet me at the fair. The words to the old song tripped through my brain. My high school had done the musical, *Meet Me in St. Louis*, the fall of my sophomore year. I'd tried out for the part played by Judy Garland and had every song memorized a week after auditions. I'd gotten the part but never ended up being in the play. Jackie Jacobson had ended up taking my place. The *Nashville Forever* audition had been the same day as opening night, so I'd had to back out. I put down my pen and left the room, closing the door quietly behind me.

Ten minutes later, the phone rang. I was back on the interstate, reading road signs as I listened to Blake Shelton do his thing, hoping that Indianapolis was easy to find. I flipped down the radio and greeted my friend, Clyde.

"Bonnie Rae, turn around and get your ass back here with my Blazer."

"I'm driving to St. Louis, Finn. I left you some money. You can rent a car and meet me there. Or . . . you can call the cops if you want to, but I think it might be a little hard to explain everything when I'm not there to back you up. They might think you have me tied up somewhere."

The anger coming through the phone was palpable, and I winced and rushed ahead when he didn't speak.

"I'm calling Bear. I'll tell him to straighten things out with the police. Okay? I'm going to have him overnight me the things I need, just like I told you. But he needs an address to send them to, Clyde. Can you tell me where your dad lives? I'll meet you there, with the Blazer. I'll hand it over, get my things and be on my way. Deal?" My voice squeaked at the end, undermining my tough girl play.

Finn hung up on me.

I kept on driving, both hands on the wheel, holding on to the Blazer like it was my only friend in the world—a stolen best friend. It was only two o'clock in the afternoon but I felt like I'd been up for days, the pressures of the last 36 hours creating a time warp where time felt stretched and surreal, like I'd lived it all before and would live it again, over and over until I got it right. Whatever "right" was. "Right" felt like a very relative word at this point. Since the moment

I'd walked off the stage in Boston, I couldn't think of one single thing I could have done differently. Finn Clyde was certainly wishing he'd let me fall into the Mystic River at this point. But me? I didn't feel like I'd had much choice in the matter.

I didn't die on the bridge. Finn Clyde saved me, and then he kissed me. And I had to keep moving, because the minute I stopped, the momentum that kiss had given me, and the life that kiss had breathed into me, would be snuffed out like everything else. What Finn couldn't understand was if I called Gran and turned my life back over to her, I might as well just find another bridge.

The phone vibrated against my thighs where it sat nestled between them, and I grabbed for it, flipping it open on a breathless hello.

"Write this down," Finn snapped, not returning my greeting.

"Can't you just text it to me?"

"I'm on a motel phone, Bonnie," he roared.

"Oh. Yeah. Okay." I scrambled for the purse I'd purchased at Walmart, but the only thing I could find was the red lipstick I'd kept from Gran's bag—no pen or paper.

"Bonnie?"

"Uh, okay. Go!"

Finn clipped out the address, and I wrote it on the window with the lipstick as he did. Not bad. I could read it, and I wouldn't lose it.

"Call Bear." Click. Finn was not happy.

I called Bear, and I managed to make it to Indianapolis. Finn was right. It only took about three hours. But by the time I got there I was so tired I found a Wendy's, used their restroom, and bought a salad and a couple of bottles of water. I ate in the car, afraid someone would recognize me, even in my pink coat and beanie. It had happened before. When I finished, I locked the doors and crawled in the back seat, falling asleep parked in the far corner of the Wendy's parking lot.

I awoke to chilly darkness tempered by street lights and the comforting sounds of nightlife. The blankets around my shoulders smelled a little like Finn, and I wondered how far he was behind me, and what he would say to me when I saw him again. I thought about that kiss, and felt slightly devastated that there wouldn't be another one. Not now. No more Finn kisses. No more Finn smiles. No more Finn.

I crawled into the front seat and started the Blazer, cranking up the heat and drinking the second bottle of water.

It took me several seconds to realize that Finn's phone was buzzing again, and I snatched it up gratefully, feeling incredibly alone now that darkness had fallen and I was, well, alone.

"Finn?"

"I have been calling you for three hours. Where are you?" Finn still wasn't happy.

"I'm in Indianapolis. I had to rest my eyes for a minute. That minute lasted a few hours." I still sounded tired, even to my own ears, and I muffled a yawn. "Are you still at the bugs-r-us motel?"

"No. I'm on the road. Finally. I rented a car, and I got one of those little throw-away phones, the reloadable kind, from Walmart. My mother's probably calling my phone. Don't answer it. I'll leave a message on her home phone and tell her I'm okay, and that I didn't kidnap anyone," Finn snapped.

"I called Bear. He doesn't like me very much right now either. It must be something in the water. I told him you had only given me a ride, that I was just fine, and that I just needed some time off. He's sending my things, and he said he'd talk to Gran."

"And the police?"

"And the police."

Silence.

"St. Louis, Bonnie."

And then he was gone. Again.

The phone rang again almost immediately, but the number wasn't the same as the one Finn had just called me from, so I didn't answer it, aware that it would be for him, well aware that I didn't want to explain his absence. It was probably his mama, just like he'd warned, and I had a feeling that just like Bear and Finn, she wouldn't be too happy with me.

I held the phone for a long time, wondering if Finn would call back or if I dared call him, wondering if he would listen if I tried to explain why I was so crazy, if I tried to explain what life had been like for me for the past six years. We weren't so different, Finn and I. Cages come in lots of different colors and shapes. Some are gilded, while others have a slamming door. But golden handcuffs are still handcuffs.

I studied the maps, waiting for him to call, but when he didn't, I gassed up the Chevy and headed for St. Louis, a straight shot westbound on I-70 from point A to point B. I wouldn't have to look at the map again for this leg of the trip. So I drove and let the miles take me far away.

Harmonic Progression

I DIDN'T THINK I could find the address in the dark, but Finn's instructions were detailed and precise, even smudged in red lipstick on my window. St. Louis looked peaceful and picturesque in the quiet moonlight. There was snow on the ground, but just a dusting, a bit of glitter in the shadows. The streets were lined with trees, and as I neared my destination, I realized I wasn't far from the university. I thought about Clyde senior—Clyde said his name was Jason—and whether or not he knew a runaway celebrity was about to crash his pad. It was midnight, and morning was a long ways away. Dread filled my stomach, and I decided to drive around for a while, or find a place to park and sleep until morning came, a place that wouldn't invite curiosity or cops.

A pretty park edged in trees not far from the campus seemed like a logical place, and I hugged the curb and turned the key with sudden relief. I needed to breathe. I grabbed the keys, shrugged into my coat and was out of the Blazer and stretching my legs within seconds. The park looked old—like it had been built when ladies strolled while holding a man's arm. Curving benches with wrought iron edging, stately fountains, and winding cobbled pathways meandered through the park. I followed them for several minutes until I came upon a little fence, complete with fleur-de-lis edging and a swinging iron gate that enclosed a towering swing set, a see-saw, and a metal slide easily as old as the park, and just as well preserved. I laughed and thought of Minnie. When we were little she loved to fly on the swings, and I was happy just to push. For all my bluster, I didn't do well with swings. Heights didn't bother me, but swinging made my stomach flip and tumble in unpleasant ways.

The playground called to me. It echoed with silent laughter and ghostly twins chasing each other through the trees and down the slide. It made me ache for moments lost and the little girls Minnie and I had been together. Those little girls were both gone. And I missed them so much that I held my breath, gripping the wrought iron bars of the decorative fence, waiting for the wave of painful longing to abate. When the sorrow ebbed enough for me to breathe again, I moved to the gate, hoping it wasn't locked, hoping I wouldn't have to risk impalement trying to scale the spiky fence. I smiled when the latch lifted easily. Feeling a bit like Goldilocks entering unknown territory, I pushed through the gate and let myself in.

∞

FINN WAS ONLY blocks from his dad's house when he passed a little park and saw a familiar orange Blazer snuggled up to the curb, not another vehicle in sight. He slammed on his brakes and slid in front of his old Chevy, relieved that Bonnie was actually in St. Louis, mystified that she had stopped at a park in an unknown city after midnight, and still pissed about what she'd pulled in Cincinnati.

He could see that Bonnie wasn't in the Blazer as he approached, but he peered into the back windows to make sure she hadn't crawled into the backseat and fallen asleep again. He couldn't make out anything but a few of his boxes, Bonnie's duffle bags, and a lumpy blanket, but as he pulled back and turned away, he noticed the dark streaks on the driver's side window. In the half-light of the tall street lamps, the streaks looked like blood. Finn grabbed at the door handle, suddenly afraid of what he'd find slumped across the front seat, but the door was locked.

His stomach filled with ice and his hands shook as he framed them around his face to see inside the dark interior. He couldn't make out a shape or a form, but the light made strange patterns against the seat and camouflaged the floor in shades of black.

"Bonnie?" he yelled, and looked under and around the Blazer. There was no trail of blood outside the vehicle, no macabre footprints walking away. He wished he could open the damn door! He tried to see in again from another angle, looking this time through the passenger window, and felt a measure of relief when he confirmed that Bonnie wasn't unconscious in the front seat.

"Bonnie?"

He set out through the park at a brisk pace, his eyes scanning benches and quiet corners until after about five minutes, the path curved around and he saw, among the trees, a small play area. He rushed toward it, knowing intuitively that she was there. A girl like Bonnie would be drawn to the playground. Sure enough, standing tall on the top of a steep, metal slide was Bonnie Rae Shelby, feet planted on the platform, hands in her pockets, face to the sky. Was it the bridge all over again? It felt like a loop of the first time he saw her, and the relief he felt at finding her was immediately overpowered by the same dread he'd felt when he'd seen the blood on the car window.

The gate was hanging open, evidence that she'd passed through it. He slipped through it too, grateful that he wouldn't have to make a sound. He wanted to call out to her, to tell her to come down, or to at least *sit* down, but he was afraid he would startle her and cause her to fall. So he froze, her name on his lips, his heart at his feet. She didn't seem upset. She didn't seem to be crying. He moved a few steps closer, but her face was angled away, the curve of her cheekbone the only thing visible from the angle he approached. There were no dark streaks on the pale pink of her coat, so no obvious bleeding. She seemed entranced by the view from the top of the slide and completely at ease with the height.

I'm just a poor wayfarin' stranger
Travelin' through this world of woe
There's no sickness, toil or danger
In that bright land to which I go

Her voice rang out like bells across the park, and Finn took a step back, the sound as shocking as it was sweet.

I'm goin' there to see my Father
And all my loved ones who have gone on.
Just a poor wayfarin' stranger
Travelin' through this world of woe.

He didn't recognize the song. He'd never been to church, and the only song his mother had ever sung was the theme song to *Cheers*. And she'd sung it badly. This was something different, so different as to be incomparable. And Bonnie, singing for no one but the stars and the hovering trees, sang the words like a broken hallelujah, a heartsick hosanna, and the song echoed in his chest as if he hummed along with her.

I know dark clouds will gather 'round me
I know my way is hard and steep
But wide fields arise before me
Where God's redeemed, their vigil's keep.

I'm goin' there to see my brother.
He said he'd meet me when I come
Just a poor wayfarin' stranger
Travelin' through this world of woe.

The last note hung in the air for a full five seconds and Finn realized he was holding his breath. He told himself that was the reason for the tightness in his chest and the moisture at the corner of his eyes. He wanted her to sing again. But she had clearly finished the only number she was going to perform. She dropped her chin to her chest and sank to the little metal platform, her legs stretched out in front of her, positioned for a turn down the slide.

Relatively safe from being startled into a fall, her arms wrapped around the bars at the top of the slide, Bonnie didn't even turn as Finn approached, and she seemed oblivious that anyone might have heard her concert in the park. He circled the slide and stood at the bottom, looking up at her.

She blinked and then gasped a little, as if she thought for a moment he wasn't real. Then she smiled. It was a smile that said she was thrilled to see him and overjoyed by his presence. She'd smiled like that when he'd promised her he would wait for her outside of the Quik Clips. She had smiled at him like that when he'd told her they were going to have to spend the night in the Blazer in the middle of a blizzard. She'd smiled that way when he told Shayna and her girls he would get them home. Now she smiled at him, sitting there on top of the slide as if it made perfect sense for her to be there, like she hadn't just stolen his vehicle and led him on a chase across two states. She smiled at him, her whole face infused with light, and he forgave her. Instantly. No longer furious. No longer scared. No longer ready to strangle her, tie her up, and call the police. All of that was gone—evaporated like snowflakes on his tongue.

It was one a.m. on a Thursday, the end of February, in a cold, deserted park in St. Louis, and there was no place he would rather be.

"Hi," she said.

"Hi." Dammit. Now he was smiling too. And shaking his head in surrender. "What in the hell am I going to do with you?"

"You could move so I can go down this slide." She winked. He didn't move. So she let go. He knew she would. She flew toward him, whooping all the way down, and at the last second he stepped back so he didn't take two red cowboy boots to the shins. She barreled into him anyway, all momentum, wrapping her legs around him, and he grabbed her, falling back as he did. Thick, rubber playground bark broke their fall, for the most part, but Finn still found himself flat on his back with Bonnie sprawled across his chest.

"I told you to move." She laughed, her face above his, her knit cap clinging to her head. He reached up and pulled it all the way off, and she immediately ran one hand over her hair self-consciously, smoothing down the strands that floated with static. He followed her hand with his, a caress that had nothing to do with her hair and everything to do with needing to touch her.

∞

HE DIDN'T PULL me to him, didn't wrap his hand around my body to urge me closer. My mouth hovered above his, waiting. I didn't dare move. Not because I didn't want to, but because I was worried that Finn would suddenly jolt wide awake, wipe the cobwebs from his head, shake me off, and leave me in the park.

I wouldn't blame him if he did. He should hate me. Yet he was looking at me like everything was going to be okay. He was looking at me like he wanted to kiss me again. And I wanted him to kiss me more than I'd ever wanted anything in my life. His mouth was so close I could taste his breath on my tongue, and I wanted to lick my lips to savor the sensation.

Then his lips weren't close, they were there. And here. Above. Inside. Around. My eyelids fluttered, and my belly plunged, and the heaviness in my limbs made me want to sink into the kiss like an anchor in the sand, digging in, yet strangely weightless. Then both of his hands were in my hair, securing my mouth where he wanted it, holding me still as he tasted my lips and asked me to let him in. And I welcomed him with a sigh that slid into the cold night and drifted away just like my song. It was a new verse, a duet of lips and the merging of mouths. It was rising crescendos and crashing cymbals, and it was unlike any song I'd ever sung. And even as he withdrew, the kiss echoed around me, inviting me to repeat the music of his mouth against mine.

Clyde's hands were still framing my face, but he had knifed up from his back as he kissed me, sitting with me straddling his lap, my knees on either side of his thighs. And I wanted to stay there, connected, and press my body against him, but he rolled me off and stood, brushing the playground debris from his jeans. I wished I could crawl up his legs and pull him back to the ground, but he pulled me to my feet instead.

He searched my face for several long moments, as if composing a tongue lashing of a different sort than he'd just given me, but then he sighed and turned, pulling me along after him.

"Tomorrow," he said.

We walked hand in hand through the gate and back through the park, winding our way toward the entrance. I followed slightly behind, the sidewalk not quite wide enough for us to walk side by side, so when he stopped short, I ran right into his back and then had to lean around him to see what had caused him to halt.

"The Blazer's gone."

"What?" I stepped around him and followed his gaze to the place I'd left the Blazer forty-five minutes earlier. Finn was right. The Blazer was gone. A small, dark-colored car was the only car parked along the curb.

Finn started to jog, to run toward the place the Blazer had been, and I clomped after him, the boots of my heels sounding like applause against the pavement.

"It's a tow-away zone!" he yelled, pointing at a sign about a hundred feet beyond where I'd parked his Blazer.

"But . . . why didn't they tow that car?" I protested, unable to believe I'd screwed up once again.

"I'm sure they will if we don't move it!"

"This is your car?" I asked.

"This is my rental car, Bonnie. How do you think I got here?"

Oh, no. I turned in a circle, as if the Blazer had moved itself somehow, as if maybe we'd gotten turned around inside the park and come out on the wrong side. But we hadn't. Finn's rental car was there, and he'd obviously parked it beside the Blazer and come looking for me. I had parked in a tow-away zone, and Finn's Chevy was gone. I sat down on the curb and rested my head on my knees. My money and my things were in the Blazer. But I could deal with that. I couldn't deal with his displeasure. Not now. Not when he'd just forgiven me.

A few minutes later, Finn sat down beside me, a solid presence on my right, stretching his long legs into the street. I held my breath, waiting for him to tell me he never wanted to see me again. And then he laughed. It was quiet at first, just a chuckle, a soft murmur that made me lift my head from my knees. Then he started to shake with it, laughing so hard that he fell back against the grass that butted up to the curb. I turned toward him, stunned, not quite ready to laugh with him.

"Finn?"

"Unbelievable," was all he could say, his hands covering his eyes as if he needed a break from reality. "Unbelievable."

∞

WITH FINN'S DISPOSABLE phone we called the number for the towing company printed on the sign—the sign that was so small and far enough away from where I had parked to engender some serious righteous indignation on my part. The Blazer was indeed in the impound yard, and it would cost $250 for us to get it out. Added to that, we couldn't get it out immediately, because it was after hours, and the tow truck driver on duty had been called out on an accident and didn't know when he would return. He said we could come in the next morning during office hours, which would run us another $100 in storage fees, by the way. Finn said college campuses were notorious magnets for towing, especially during the late night, early morning hours when confrontation was less likely. He said we were lucky they hadn't had time to get both vehicles. I didn't dare tell Finn how truly unlucky we were because my/Gran's wallet was still in the Blazer, along with all my money and his phone.

Unable to do much more at one-thirty in the morning, Finn drove us to his father's house. His dad wasn't home, and wouldn't be until sometime later the following day, which made me wish I'd just come straight there like Finn had told me to do. If I had, the Blazer wouldn't be in the impound yard. But if I had, I wouldn't have been kissed in the park. Once again, I found myself unable to regret the decisions I'd made. The events of our journey seemed unavoidable and pre-destined, almost as if Finn and I were being pulled against our wills toward an inevitable conclusion.

Finn's father's house was a narrow two-story that sat on a cul-de-sac at the end of a busy street littered with cars and similarly small houses. Finn said the neighborhood was filled with students, and most of the houses were split up into rentable rooms. It was a two bedroom, two bath bachelor's pad with the kitchen, family room, and a half bath on the main level and the master suite and a small bedroom up the stairs. The spare bedroom featured a desk, a plaid sofa too small to sleep on, and a few boxes that Finn's dad apparently couldn't part with but hadn't cared enough about to unpack in the seven years he'd lived in the little house. The rest of the house was equally sparse, the tell-tale signs of a man who works too much and has little life outside his profession.

Finn pointed me toward the master bedroom, and I stumbled into the small adjoining bath, pleasantly surprised by the tidy space. I stripped and entered the shower, letting the water run over me, streaming over my hair until the tears streamed from my eyes in sheer, exhausted gratitude. I lathered with Irish Spring because it was available and soaped my hair with Mr. Clyde's anti-dandruff shampoo. I used the razor that was there as well, and promised myself I would replace it the next day. I hit the jackpot when I discovered an unopened toothbrush in the vanity and wrote another mental IOU for that.

When I finished, I pulled on a T-shirt Clyde had given me from his own things, and reluctantly pulled my red panties with the black skulls back on again. I was back where I'd started from, with only the clothes on my back—the clothes that were now in a heap on the bathroom floor. Actually, I was worse off than when I'd started. I didn't have a single, solitary dime in my pocket. Amazingly enough, though, the idea didn't scare me one bit. Finn was with me. And right now, he was the only thing I really wanted anyway.

I stumbled into the little bedroom off the bath and crawled into the double bed. Finn was already there. He'd been quicker than me, using the bathroom on the ground floor, and he pulled me close and wrapped me up without comment. I could have easily been convinced to do a whole lot more than sleep, but sleep was all we did there in his father's room, in his father's bed, saving our words for later, letting the things that needed to be said slide over the side of the mattress and onto the floor, like extra pillows, waiting for the morning when we would be forced to pick them up again.

12

Extraneous Solution

NEW DEVELOPMENTS IN the possible kidnapping case of country singer Bonnie Rae Shelby. Sources close to the family say there has been a ransom demand for her safe return. The FBI has been consulted on the case, and authorities have not confirmed an amount or even that there was a demand made, but again, sources close to the family have confirmed that a ransom demand has been made.

∞

THEY SLEPT LIKE the dead, and when Finn woke and stared blearily at the bedside clock it said 10:30. He hadn't slept so late or so deeply since he was a teenager. Maybe it was the feel of the girl in his arms, the smell of soft skin and clean hair tickling his nose. He buried his face deeper into the fragrant strands and tried to go back to sleep, not yet wanting to be conscious, because consciousness brought heightened awareness, and he was already far too aware of the slim thigh thrown over his and the arms wrapped around his torso. Bonnie tucked her head when she slept, burrowing in, and he could feel her breath tickling his naked chest. He hadn't donned a shirt the night before because he'd only had one clean shirt left, and

Bonnie was wearing it. She'd seen the tattoos. It wasn't like he had anything left to hide.

He had thought that once Bonnie got her ID and credit cards, the two of them could go their separate ways. But it was too late for that now. Too much had happened, and even if Finn wanted to let her go, which he didn't, they were inextricably tied, and he was as afraid for her as he was for himself. She obviously wasn't afraid, so he had to be. The girl was trouble, but she was also *in* trouble, and Finn knew he couldn't walk away. Maybe it was Bonnie's penchant for disaster. She'd apparently used up every bit of luck she was ever going to get in this life on the lottery of superstardom, because she was an accident waiting to happen. Everywhere they turned, everything she touched seemed to go south in a hurry. And yet he was here, beside her, trying to figure out what to do, what was best for her, and whether or not she'd be the death of him . . . or worse, be the reason he lost his freedom again.

But consciousness reawakened the nagging worry that last night's fiasco was a bigger deal than just an impounded vehicle and hefty fees. If the police were actually looking for him, then he wouldn't be getting his Blazer back. Every tow company called in license plate and VIN numbers when they towed a vehicle. He knew that much. The cops could be crawling all over his Blazer at that very moment for all he knew. And Bonnie's bags were inside. The noose kept tightening around his neck. It wouldn't take much for them to discover his dad lived in the area. And then they would come calling.

The thought had him untangling his limbs from Bonnie's and sliding from the bed. He pulled on his jeans and headed down the stairs, eager for coffee and needing reassurance that a SWAT team wasn't, at that very second, assembling outside the house. He yanked the front door open and found himself face to face with a giant with a raised fist. Apparently, the man had been about to knock. That, or Finn was about to get popped between the eyes.

The man was huge, not fat so much as wide. His skin glistened it was so black, the whites of his eyes the only color in his face, and Finn only saw the whites of his eyes when the man shoved the black Ray-Bans up on his forehead and glared with a cold, flat, venom that made Finn quickly readjust his opinion of the neighborhood his dad was living in. This guy wasn't a door-to-door salesman, and he wasn't a cop. He didn't know what he was—but he was scary. The huge, sharply-dressed black man looked a little too old to be a student and too slick to be in a gang, although the big diamonds in his ears did shout drug dealer, in Finn's opinion.

"Are you Finn Clyde?" the voice was higher-pitched than Finn would have expected, coming from the chest cavity of the bear-sized man on his father's front porch. As soon as the comparison with the bear crossed his mind, Finn knew who the man was.

"Are you Bear?"

"I am. And you better move your white trash ass aside and get Bonnie in front of me real fast or you will find out why my mama named me Bear. It ain't 'cause I'm cuddly."

Finn figured he deserved the white trash assessment, standing there with his bare chest marked with offensive tattoos and his blond hair loose around his shoulders, so he let the comment slide and stepped aside.

"Come in."

Finn stepped back, and Bear stepped forward into the small living room, filling the space with malevolence, his eyes taking in everything at once.

"Bonnie's upstairs. She was asleep the last time I checked. If you'll excuse me for a second, I'll pull on a shirt and tell her you're here. Bear's eyes widened at the mention of Bonnie still being asleep at almost eleven o'clock in the morning, as if that detail was too intimate for Finn to be privy to, but he folded his arms across his massive chest and spread his legs in a stance that said "hurry" as he watched Finn climb the stairs.

Finn raided his dad's closet for a T-shirt. His dad was a tall, thin man who spent his time in dress shirts, sweaters, and the occasional golf shirt, so finding a T-shirt was harder than you would think. Finn found a pale blue T-shirt at the back of the closet that had a corny slogan only a math teacher would find funny. It had a beer can and the limit definition of the derivative on the front of it. On the back it said *Never Drink and Derive*. It was stretchy enough to fit, unlike the dress shirts and the polos, but snug enough to make Finn feel like he'd borrowed his brainy little brother's T-shirt. He ran a brush through his hair and pulled it back in a smooth tail, hoping that made him look a little less trailer park and a little more Steven Segal. He would need all the help he could get with the grizzly downstairs. Somehow, he didn't think Steven Segal was much of a mathlete, however. The ponytail was completely undermined by his stupid T-shirt.

Bonnie was awake, but just barely. Her eyelids were at half-mast and her hair, wet when she went to bed, looked as if she'd spent a wild night doing all the things he wished they'd done.

"Bonnie Rae, you've got a visitor downstairs. And if you don't show your face right away, he's going to kill me. And it won't be a quick death. It will be a mauling. Do you understand?"

"Huh?"

"Bear's here, and he's loaded for . . . well, bear."

"Bear's here?" she shot straight up in bed, immediately awake, and made for the door, bare legs flying, oversized T-shirt slipping off her slim shoulders.

"Bonnie!" She halted and turned in question. "If you want me to live, pull on some pants and do something with your hair. Please."

A sheepish grin lifted the corners of her mouth, and she ran for the bathroom where her discarded jeans still lay in a heap. Within minutes, she was out again, teeth brushed and hair slicked down a la Hank Shelby. She was still wearing Finn's T-shirt, but she'd thankfully added her jeans for modesty's sake. Finn followed her downstairs and was just reaching the bottom step when Bonnie launched herself into Bear's arms.

To the big man's credit, he didn't immediately throw her over his shoulder and leave. Instead, he held the slim girl to his chest, her feet dangling a foot off the floor, his arms wrapped around her. He had lowered his glasses back over his eyes, but his big, lower lip trembled suspiciously as they both took a minute to communicate their devotion.

"Baby Rae. What in the hell is going on, baby girl?"

Baby Rae. Finn tried not to smile. It seemed he wasn't the only one with a nickname. He turned to leave the room to give them a little privacy, but Bonnie called after him.

"Clyde. Wait. Don't go. I want you to meet Bear."

"We met," Bear said, and he didn't sound pleased.

Bonnie turned on him fiercely. "Bear. Don't use that tone with Finn. He hasn't done anything but help me. And believe me, I haven't made it easy for him."

Bear set "Baby Rae" on the ground and stared into her face. She glared back, her chin jutting forward and her expression stony.

"I'm going to make some coffee," Finn grunted, not comfortable being the topic of a thorny confrontation.

"Sit!" Bear barked, and Finn stiffened, turning back toward him.

"Bonnie loves you," Finn said, keeping his voice mild. "And you obviously love her. That's all that counts in my book. But if you think that gives you the right to come in here and tell me what to do, you're going to have a fight on your hands. I was in prison for five years, and I don't fight pretty." He turned and walked into the kitchen, and the silence behind him convinced him that his comments had momentarily stunned the pair. But not for long.

Bear stalked after him, and Bonnie was right on Bear's heels.

"Who the hell do you think you are?" Bear was practically breathing down his back.

"I'm nobody," Finn said, opening cupboards until he found his father's coffee can. Same brand as he used to drink.

"You got that right, man. And what makes you think I'm going to let Bonnie Rae spend another minute with a piece of shit like you?"

"Bear!" Bonnie stepped between the two men, sensing both were about to explode. But Finn held himself in check. He didn't blame the guy. He couldn't blame him. He knew exactly how it must look, and he knew how he felt. And Bonnie's feelings were written all over her face. She liked him. He didn't know why, but she did. And if Finn could see it, Bear could too.

"He's an ex-con with a swastika on his chest and prison tats all over his back, Rae! What are you thinking?"

"I'm thinking you need to sit down, Bear. You need to back off. Now." Bonnie pointed at one of the kitchen chairs, and Bear growled but did as she commanded. He was a well-trained Bear, apparently. Bonnie remained standing close enough to Finn to touch him, and her proximity reassured him more than anything she could have said. Her nearness said she didn't think he was nobody.

"You're in trouble Bonnie. Your gran is going crazy, and after seeing this guy, I don't blame her!" Bear started in again.

"You talked to her, right? You talked to the police. You told them I was okay. You told her I was fine. Right?" Bonnie asked.

"I didn't talk to the police. I needed to see for myself that you were okay. I did tell your gran that you called me and told me you were fine, but she didn't buy it. Hell, Rae. I don't buy it! She's shouting from the rooftops, giving interviews to TMZ, hounding the police."

"Is she worried about me, or worried about my reputation?"

"Both!"

"Why? Why doesn't she just back off for a little while?"

"She's afraid everything she's worked for—"

"Oh, that's right. Gran's done all the work," Bonnie interrupted, and Finn touched her hand briefly, comforting her, before he continued his preparations.

"She's afraid you've gone off the deep end, Rae," Bear said, his tone softening to couch his words.

"And what do you think, Bear?"

Bear studied Bonnie Rae, his eyes lingering on her cropped

hair—glaring evidence of all that had gone wrong—and on the way she hovered near Clyde.

"I think you've been standing on the edge for a long time, Baby Rae. You haven't been yourself. I'm not the only one who's noticed it either. Some of the crew think it's drugs, but nobody's ever seen you taking pills or shooting up. Everyone knows the troubles your brother Hank has had, so they're wondering if it's a family habit. You've been off, way off, for months now."

"It isn't drugs, Bear. It isn't anything like that. And you know it, Bear."

"I know it isn't Baby Rae." He sighed heavily. "You're grieving, and your spirit's broken. But I'm thinking you're going about fixing it the wrong way." The black eyes rested firmly on Clyde once more.

"I just need some space . . . and some time, Bear," Bonnie Rae whispered, pleading.

"You aren't gonna get much more, Rae. This thing is ramping up every minute that you're gone. I'm surprised someone didn't follow me here. I'm even more surprised you don't have reporters camped outside. If your gran can make it look like you are innocent as the day is long, just a sweet little girl at the mercy of a big bad thug, then that's what she's going to do. This is country music, baby. This is big business. You've got an image to protect."

"But what about Finn?" Bonnie protested.

Bear looked at Finn who stood leaning against the sink. Bear's jaw tightened, and his eyes grew hard.

"Mr. Clyde can take care of himself, Baby Rae."

"But this is all my fault. I won't let Gran do this!"

Bear kept his eyes on Finn as he addressed him.

"I'm sorry, man. But you're going down. Rae's gran is going to take you down."

Bonnie gasped, and Bear turned to her. "And Rae? You're coming back to Nashville with me."

"No, Bear. I'm not. I'm not going with you. I'm going with Finn to get his Blazer, and I'm going to make things right. You tell Gran that if she ever wants to see me again, she will make this all go away for Finn. She better start singing a different tune, or I won't sing again. I won't, Bear. I love you, but I won't be bullied one more day. I don't owe you, or Gran, or anyone else one damn thing."

"Bonnie." Finn spoke up for the first time, and Bonnie turned to him, tears threatening, apology written all over her face.

"We can't get my Blazer. They would have called in the plates when they towed it. Maybe the police didn't pick up on it, but I'm guessing it has been flagged by now. If the cops are really looking for me, the moment we go get it, I'll either be arrested or they'll keep it impounded until I've been cleared."

"But . . . but . . ." Bonnie collapsed into her chair, and Bear and Finn considered each other for several long minutes. Then Bear turned to Bonnie and pointed a thick finger at her.

"You should be at the Kodak Theater on Sunday, in that audience, ready to accept that award if you win, Rae." He looked at Finn and explained. "Bonnie's song "Machine" got nominated for best original song in a motion picture." He looked back at Bonnie like he couldn't believe he was having to remind her. "You remember that, right, Bonnie Rae? You wrote a song that could win you an Oscar? That's a big damn deal."

"I remember, Bear." Bonnie shrugged and looked at Finn as if she were a little embarrassed.

The coffeemaker finished, and Finn busied himself with cups and creamer, setting mugs in front of Bear and Bonnie and keeping one for himself. Bonnie wrapped her hands around it but didn't make any move to sweeten or lighten the black brew.

Bear wasn't finished. "You show up there, on the red carpet, smiling in front of the cameras like nothing has changed, holding hands with Clyde here like he's your boyfriend and not a convict who dragged you off. You'll undermine everything your gran's tellin' everybody, and you'll do it on national TV, without having to say a word to the police or anyone else. If you win, you go up there and be your charming, loveable self, thanking everybody and their dog—or should I say 'Bear.' You do that, and all this just might go away."

"Finn?" Bonnie asked. "You ever been to the Oscars?"

She knew he hadn't been. But that's not what she was asking, and he understood the question, loud and clear. Bonnie wanted him with her. And in spite of everything, he wanted that too. He was all in, and he'd known it last night when he heard her sing, standing at the top of the slide, telling the night sky that she was a traveler going through the world alone.

"I'll get Bonnie to California by Sunday," he said to Bear, and Bonnie's face lit up with that same old smile that kicked his ass and made him beg for more. "It's Thursday now. We'll show up at the Oscars, put the rumors to rest, and after that, Bonnie can decide what happens next without any of us telling her what she will or won't do."

Bear was watching Bonnie as she beamed at Finn over her coffee mug. He shook his head a little, as if denying what his eyes were telling him.

"You need wheels?" Bear asked abruptly.

"I've got a rental car out there," Finn said doubtfully. "But I'm supposed to turn it in today. If I'm in trouble, I don't want to be flashing my driver's license and using my credit card again to rent something else. We won't make it very far."

"Nah. That won't do. I drove in from Nashville this morning. It's only four hours from here. You take my car, and I'll drive your rental back to Nashville. You call the rental company, tell them you'll turn it in there. They don't ID you when you bring the car back. They just want money. I'll give it to them."

"They might charge us an arm and leg for changing the check-in location," Finn said.

"You can pay me back when this is over. I will expect a raise, Baby Rae." He turned his attention to her for a brief second and then was back to glaring at Finn. "I'll get my car when I come to LA for the awards." Bear looked at Bonnie. "Don't let Bonnie drive."

"Bear!" Bonnie said, offended. Judging by Bonnie's penchant for trouble, it wouldn't surprise Finn if she were a terror behind the wheel. Finn considered himself fairly warned.

"There's your purse, Rae." Bear indicated the buttery yellow, leather bag he'd placed on the table upon entering the kitchen. "I got you a new phone. Your gran took yours since you lifted hers. Don't ask me how I got my hands on this bag. The phone's on my account, and it's for my own peace of mind."

Bonnie rose and kissed the top of his shiny, bald head. "Thank you, Bear. And the raise? Consider it done."

With a quick smile for Finn, she bounded up the stairs, and Finn could hear her in the upstairs room, gathering their things. Good. They needed to leave while they still could.

"I've been a bodyguard for twenty-five years, and I've been Bonnie's head of security and fix-it man for the last five," Bear said seriously, and Finn's attention moved from the bedroom to the kitchen table where the glowering black man demanded it. "I've played babysitter to a lot of celebrities in my life. Made a good living at it too. Some of them are nice people. Some of them aren't. But most of them are screwed up in some way or another. Just comes with the territory. Too much of everything. And everybody knows too much of anything makes you sick. Sick in the belly, sick in the head, sick in the soul. Too many of 'em got too much yet they don't ever feel full, it seems like. They think they should be happy but they aren't, so they do stupid shit to make the emptiness go away.

"But Bonnie Rae isn't like that. Some of it's due to her gran being a hard-ass. Bonnie might not admit it, but that woman loves her. Unfortunately, Gran saved Bonnie from being bitten by the celebrity bug, but she's fallen victim to it herself. She's let it become the most important thing.

"Rae's always been steady, though. Sweet. Full of life, and never full of herself. But when her sister died the fire went out. She just lost it. I thought she was done when she went home. I thought we'd be canceling the rest of the tour and taking some time off. But that didn't happen. It shoulda happened. I shoulda stepped in as her friend. But I didn't. So that's why I'm here, and that's why I'm stepping in now. I don't know what's going on with you two. She says you found her on a bridge in Boston. She told me if it wasn't for you she might not be here. So I'm gonna walk away now. And I'm gonna trust you. But if you hurt that girl in any way, I will kill you." The flat black of Bear's eyes didn't flicker or shift. He wasn't making idle threats.

"I'm ready!" Bonnie spilled into the kitchen, hopping on one foot as she pulled a red boot on her other foot. Finn's bags hung off her shoulders, and one arm was stuck in her fluffy pink coat.

"Keys!" Bear demanded, standing from the table, abandoning what was left of his highly doctored coffee. Finn dug the keys from his pocket—he'd hidden them the night before so Bonnie couldn't steal them and drive off again—and he'd put them in his pocket as soon as he'd pulled his pants on that morning. Bear tossed his own set toward him, and Finn caught them deftly before doing the same.

"My car is the black Charger parked down the street, and I'm guessing yours is the tin can in the driveway. Lucky me. I suggest you two get the hell out of town. You keep moving and you should be fine. Once you get to LA, lay low at the Bordeaux—those people have dealt with stars and scandals for decades, and they are discreet. You've stayed there before so you know the drill. Nobody will even know you're there. I'll take care of the details, and I'll see you both in LA. Call me, Baby Rae."

13
phase shift

CLYDE AND I did as Bear suggested and left soon after he did, locking the front door behind us. Bear had parked the Charger almost a full block down the street, in front of a dumpy house with several other vehicles pulled up on the grass. College kids. I couldn't help but feel like someone, a cop or a reporter, was going to jump out at us at any moment, but very few people were on the street, and those who were didn't give us a second glance.

Finn wouldn't get to see his dad, after all. I felt bad about that, and told him as much as we slid into the Charger, the luxury of Bear's car feeling almost exotic after days spent in the rumbling old Blazer.

"I'll ask him to get the Blazer when this is all cleared up. Then he can drive to Vegas and spend a few days with me there. I think he'd be willing. He's been trying to get me to come to St. Louis since I was released, hoping that I would go to school." Finn shrugged and let his father's suggestion hang in the air.

"Why don't you? Go to school, I mean. You're so smart. Then you could do math all day long, right?"

"Nobody wants to sit and do math problems all day, Bonnie. It isn't like that. I love numbers and patterns, and I see them everywhere, but I don't need to sit in school to do that. Plus, I don't want my father to have to explain me to his colleagues. People in his circles don't have kids who spent their college years in jail."

"I'm guessing people in his circles don't have kids who can multiply large numbers in their heads, and who can remember every card that's been played in a poker game either."

Finn grunted, like he didn't have an answer for that and started Bear's car.

I reached over and turned it back off. He looked at me in surprise, and I took a deep breath.

"I'll do whatever you want to do."

Finn raised his eyebrows, waiting for me to explain myself.

"I've been selfish. I can make this go away. We'll just go to the police. I'll make a statement. Then we'll get the Blazer. And it'll all be over."

"I just told Bear I would get you to Los Angeles," Finn said, his face blank.

"I can get myself to Los Angeles."

"With what? You don't have any money."

"I have cards."

"I'm guessing every last one of those cards has been suspended. Your gran strikes me as the thorough type."

"So take me to a bank. I have my ID now, I have my account numbers. I'll get what I need."

"I'll take you to a bank."

I nodded, a lump rising in my throat. "Okay."

"But we'll do what we planned. We'll call the shots. We go to LA—you let the world see that Bonnie Rae Shelby is just fine—and then you decide what comes next. Not your gran. Not me. You."

I nodded again, the lump now lodged behind my eyes, making them water. I blinked hard and pulled my sunglasses out of my purse.

"Why?" I whispered, as I pushed them up my nose. "Why are you doing this for me?"

"I don't know." Finn answered. And I could see from his frank expression that he didn't. He was telling me the truth. "I don't know. I don't want any part of this circus. I don't want cameras in my face. I don't want people talking about me. I don't want to see my face on a magazine. I don't want any of it."

"So . . . why?" The tears leaked out from under my glasses.

"I don't want any of that . . . but I do want you."

When a man says something like that to a woman, he's supposed to lean forward and kiss her. Hard. Then he's supposed to make love to her. Harder.

But Finn didn't. Of course not. He looked like he wanted to take the words back as soon as he'd said them, and he scrubbed his hands over his face, Finn-style, letting me know he was agitated and extremely uncomfortable. He reached over and yanked my glasses off my nose. I guess he needed to see what I was thinking. He swallowed when he saw my tears, his Adams apple working in his strong throat, and then he looked away from me, tossing my glasses on the dashboard, like he was tossing away his good sense.

"You drive me crazy! You irritate the hell out of me. You make me want to pull my hair out, and every damn thing has gone wrong since the moment we met."

I nodded, agreeing with him, and dug for something to wipe my nose. I found a napkin in Bear's middle console and mopped at my face. I thought Finn was done, that he'd said what he was going to say, but then he spoke again.

"But I still *want* you." Finn sounded stunned by the admission, and emphasized the word *want* like he couldn't believe it himself.

"You want to have sex with me?" I squeaked, wanting that too, but hoping there was more.

"Yes!" Finn didn't sound especially happy about it. "Yes! But if that were all, I wouldn't feel like this. I wouldn't be doing this. But I want *you*." This time he emphasized the word you, and I felt myself relax a little, and I smiled through the tears that hadn't stopped falling through his tirade.

"Good." I laughed. "I want *you* too. So we're even. Infinity plus one does equal two, see? Me and you."

His hand shot out and wrapped around my neck, pulling me to him, taking my mouth with equal parts impatience and reluctance, like he could no longer help himself, but was trying to talk himself out of it right up until his lips touched mine. My hands curled in the front of his T-shirt as his tongue curled in my mouth. And we didn't come up for air for a very long time, oblivious of anything beyond the black windows of the tricked-out ride, completely unaware of the two television vans that had pulled up in front of Jason Clyde's home at the end of the cul-de-sac.

∞

I SENT A text to Bear as soon as we were back on the road, telling him we were on our way, and got an immediate reply.

I've got you registered at the Hotel Bordeaux under my mama's name, just like we always do. Call before you arrive and they will bring you in through the back per our usual – no check-in required. Bill covered. Mr. Clyde can act as your security until I roll in on Sunday. Your tickets for Sunday will be with the concierge. The hotel will have a limo available for the big show. You got wardrobe covered? You won't have a team there. Just you and me, Rae. That's what happens when you go AWOL.

I responded:

I don't have any hair left, I think I can handle my makeup, and I'll buy a dress in Vegas. It's just the Oscars. No big. :P I Love you, Bear.

And his final text:

Love you too, Baby Rae. Be wise. I'll see you Sunday.

∞

THE BANK WAS small, but it was still a bank. Normally, this wouldn't bug me. The bank back in Grassley had been a little, brown brick building that had bats in the rafters and smelled like mold—a fitting statement for the state of Grassley's financial situation. I hadn't spent much time in any bank, truth be told. I had opened a little checking account and received my own debit card when Minnie and I got our first job at fourteen. It was a job at the Grassley Grill. We shared it, splitting shifts when there was only enough work for one of us. We started out scrubbing toilets and cleaning fryers and then worked our way up to cashier, making $6.75 an hour. I think minimum wage has risen since then, but half of every paycheck went into my bank account, and I watched my money like a hawk. Gran and I had emptied that account and Minnie's account when we went to Nashville. It had taken all of our savings and hers, which wasn't much, to buy our bus tickets there, and if I hadn't made it all the way through the competition and won, we wouldn't have had any money to get home because Gran spent it all on that damn wig.

But I knew how it worked, even though it'd been years since I'd managed my money. As long as I had ID and my account numbers, I should be able to withdraw whatever I wanted at my bank, no matter what branch I went into, anywhere in America. I was nervous, though. I was going to walk right up there and tell them I was Bonnie Rae Shelby, hand them my ID that didn't look much like me anymore, and ask for ten grand. I would have asked for more than ten, but I wanted cash, and I didn't want there to be a problem getting it.

Ten thousand would get me and Finn to Los Angeles, with plenty to spare. I was going to have to buy an Oscar-worthy dress, and Finn was going to need a tux. Plus, I was going to have to wire some money to Finn's father to get the Blazer from the impound yard. And after a few days, the charges would be steep. Ten thousand shouldn't be a problem—there was fifty times that in this one account. This was my cash account, and Gran's too, I supposed, since her name was on the account as well. I had money in mutual funds and trusts and stocks and bonds, money in property and land, and, like Gran, money stuffed in my sock drawer at home. But in the last five years, I'd hardly dealt with my finances at all. I had people for that. Now I wished I had been more hands-on.

The bank smelled like new carpets and leather, with just a hint of Windex thrown in to convince bank patrons that the facility was squeaky clean and therefore, safe and secure. The girl behind the marble counter smiled at me from her little open partition and asked me how she could help me. She was as clean and tidy as the shiny floors, and a gold plaque at her workstation identified her as Cassie. I felt a little grubby in Finn's over-sized T-shirt and my tight jeans that needed a wash, but I still flashed her a giant Bonnie Rae Shelby grin on full wattage and pulled out my driver's license.

"I need to withdraw some money from my savings account."

"All right. Do you need a withdrawal slip?"

"No ma'am. I have one."

I handed her the withdrawal slip I had already filled out, along with my driver's license and watched as her eyes grew big. She glanced at me furtively and looked away, two bright red dots appearing high on her smooth cheeks. She either recognized me, or I was in trouble, or both.

She started click clacking away on her computer, her fingers flying over the keys. Then she opened a cash drawer and set five bundles on the counter, each bundle encircled with a band that said "two thousand." She slid all five bundles into an envelope and pushed a button on a funny little machine to print out my check-sized receipt. Thank you, Cassie. Thank you, Lord.

"Cassie?" Another woman who had been manning the drive-up window behind Cassie, approached the young teller and pointed out something on Cassie's computer screen. Then they both looked at me. The older woman pulled her aside just to the left of the partition, and I heard her explain something in dulcet tones. Cassie stepped back to her position and tried to smile. The spots on her cheeks were now the size of tomatoes. She looked mortified.

"Um. I'm sorry Miss . . . um Shelby. I'm new . . . and I haven't seen something like this before. Um, there's an alert on this account. There's been some fraudulent activity reported, and no money can be released from the account without the presence of both parties listed on the account." She said all of this like she was repeating exactly what her superior had just told her.

"But this is my account." I tapped my driver's license. "And I am here in person—standing here in front of you . . . not fraudulent. You have verification that I am who I say I am. And that's my money." I tried to keep my voice level, my smile in place, but my heart was in my throat, and I felt the burn of shame creeping up my neck in a scarlet line. I had felt this way often growing up in Grassley, using food stamps at the grocery store or having Mama's debit card declined at the gas station. Shame was like a loud, embarrassing cousin who constantly tagged along and always made sure everyone knew who he was related to. But everyone had cousins in Grassley, so at least then I wasn't alone.

But I was alone now, staring at the slightly uncomfortable face of a girl who knew who I was . . . who Bonnie Rae Shelby was. Her supervisor stood behind her, prepared to jump in if she needed to.

"So I can't get any money from my account even though there's half a million dollars in there."

"Actually, ma'am," the supervisor spoke up. "There's only about ten thousand dollars in the account. A large sum was removed two days ago."

I choked as if I'd been sucker punched. Gran was the only one who could walk into a bank and pull five hundred grand from my account. "But you just said no money could be removed from the account without both parties present," I gasped.

"The money must have been withdrawn before the alert was

placed on the account," the older woman answered neatly. The expression on her face indicated she believed I was the reason there was a fraud alert on the account. And I guess I was. But it was my money.

I stood staring at them for the space of two deep breaths. They stared back. I didn't stop to think about the consequences of what I did next. I was too angry. I reached forward and snatched up the neat little pile of cash still sitting in front of the fresh-faced teller. Sorry, Cassie. You snooze you lose. The receipt was tucked inside the envelope as well.

"Consider the account closed then, ladies," I called out over my shoulder as I walked swiftly toward the door.

"Ma'am! You can't do that!" the supervisor called out behind me.

"I just did. And I have a receipt."

"We'll call the police!"

"I'm sure you will. Tell them I said hi."

I pushed out of the little building, the money still clenched in my hand. There was no security guard to stop me, no alarms clanging as I reached for the door of Bear's black Charger.

"Drive," I said, as I slid inside.

14

Odd Number

ST LOUIS WAS BARELY in their rearview mirror before they were pulling off in a little town called Pacific to gas up. Finn was jittery, and Bonnie seemed rattled too, because when he wasn't looking in the rearview mirror, he caught her throwing furtive looks behind them too. She was trying to be sneaky about it, but she wasn't great at keeping her feelings hidden. She'd been upset when she came out of the bank in St. Louis, though she hadn't said much about it. She'd muttered something about a "reckoning," but when he'd questioned her, she just shook her head and said, "I'm damn tired of my life. And I'm tired of the people in it, present company excluded. I've made a lot of people wealthy, and you better believe there will be a reckoning."

She sounded cute when she said reckoning. Reckonin' was how she said it, like she was on the set of a Clint Eastwood western. But Finn didn't laugh. Bonnie Rae had been used and emotionally abused on her road to fame and fortune, and he was going to help her get her reckoning, even if it meant putting his own ass on the line. Even if it meant showing up at an event like the Oscars in all his bad boy glory, just so Bonnie Rae could stick it to her gran.

While he'd filled the tank and picked up two sandwiches at the gas station, Bonnie ran across the street to a little clothing store for a few things. Finn had groaned inwardly, thinking he would be waiting forever, but Bonnie was back in roughly the same amount of time it took him to fulfill his assignments. She had a clean shirt for each of them, plus underwear and socks for both of them as well—which she cheerfully informed him she was wearing, along with a white V-necked T-shirt that looked a whole lot better than the one she'd borrowed from him, although he'd kind of liked the idea of her wearing his shirt.

He wondered what she'd done with the skull panties, but didn't ask. He marveled how easy she was to please, how such little things like clean panties and a new shirt could make her smile, and thought again about the reckoning. Interesting that he was thinking about meting out justice as he slowed and came to a stop at the red light just before the freeway entrance.

A panhandler stood on the median entreating drivers for mercy and cash. Bonnie watched him as Finn waited for the light to turn—Finn always felt bad not giving people who begged for help the dignity of eye contact, but eye contact was a signal that the window was coming down, and money was going to exchange hands. Sure enough, Bonnie reached for her purse, and Finn shot her a look that said "no." She sat back regretfully. Good girl. Maybe she was learning.

The panhandler's hair was a wild mess—Finn had never seen a bigger fro, not even at Norfolk, where hair like that was a symbol of rebellion. The man's beard was greying and equally matted, and he had crazy eyes, wide and bulging, reminding Finn a little of Samuel L. Jackson in *Pulp Fiction*. He wore socks—no shoes, just socks—and a huge, pea green army duster. From what Finn could see, the man wore all his clothes layered beneath, making him impossibly bulky and probably extremely ripe, even in the cold sunshine. He turned his cardboard sign toward them just as the light turned green, and Finn looked away as the cars in front of them started to inch forward.

"Stop! Finn! Pull over! Pull over!" Bonnie cried, her hand on the door handle as she turned in her seat, staring at something beyond her shoulder.

"Stop!" she screeched again, so instead of turning and following the line of cars in front of them onto the ramp, he went straight ahead and flipped on his hazard lights as he veered across traffic onto the narrow shoulder of the road. Maybe he was so responsive because Bonnie was pounding on his arm and shrieking for him to stop.

Bonnie was out of the car before the Charger had even come to a full stop, and it was Finn's turn to cry out, warning her to hold on, but she didn't listen. She ran down the side of the road until she was standing across from the panhandler who still stood on the median, watching the cars fly past him in both directions. Bonnie was separated from him by a lane of traffic, but she waved her arms, trying to get his attention. Finn waited until there was a break in the traffic, and then slid out of the car, not wanting to open his door and risk having it removed by an oncoming truck. Luckily, it was a small town, and the traffic wasn't heavy, but his inability to follow Bonnie had given her plenty of time to reach the panhandler, who she now stood talking to on the median, as seemingly comfortable with the grizzled man as she was behind the microphone. As Finn watched, she looped her hand through the man's arm and led him across the road toward Bear's car and Finn, who could only watch the two of them approach in horror.

"Finn! William's heading in the same direction we are! I thought we could give him a ride."

Holy. Shit. Bonnie Rae Shelby was a lunatic. He was in love with a lunatic! The thought brought Finn up short. In love? He didn't love her! He just . . . wanted her. Like he'd told her this morning. He just wanted her. That was all. He wanted a lunatic.

"I'm needed in Joplin." The panhandler's voice was strident and powerful, but he smiled at Finn as he and Bonnie neared the vehicle, his beard parting like the waters of the Red Sea, revealing that he didn't have all of his teeth. "My friends call me George Orrin Dillinger the III, but as I told the lady, you can call me William." He drew out each syllable like he was delivering a sermon.

The fact that the panhandler's friends called him by his full name yet he and Bonnie could call him another name entirely made absolutely no sense, but Finn just nodded numbly and watched as Bonnie popped the trunk, threw their few belongings inside, and made a spot for William, aka George Orrin Dillinger the III, aka the crazy man who would be sitting behind him for the next three hours until they reached Joplin, the next stop on Finn's plotted route.

William climbed into the car, and just before he shut the door, Bonnie asked him if she could borrow his cardboard sign, just for a second. He acquiesced, obviously, because Bonnie Rae grabbed it as William pulled the door closed, and then she held it over the roof of the car, showing Finn, who still stood next to the driver's side door. Bonnie's eyes were almost as wide and crazy as George Orrin Dillinger's. She pointed at the words on the sign fiercely, not speaking.

I Believe in Bonnie and Clyde the sign read. Finn read it again, and then again, not sure what to make of it. Then he looked at Bonnie and shrugged.

"So?"

"So?" she hissed. "It's a sign!"

"Yeah. It is. A cardboard sign."

"Finn! It has our names on it!"

"Names which happen to be the same names as a very well-known pair. He could have written 'I believe in Sonny and Cher' or 'Beavis and Butthead' or 'peanut butter and jelly.'"

Bonnie looked a little crestfallen. He'd taken the magic out of the moment. He was good at that.

"And now we have a smelly guy named William with the initials, G.O.D. in our backseat. And I'm not happy about it, Bonnie Rae."

"His initials are G.O.D!" Bonnie's eyes were seriously going to pop out of her skull. The magic was back. Finn moaned and then started laughing, once again not even sure how any of this could possibly be real. He even pinched himself, just to make sure he'd actually woken up this morning to a pop star in his arms, a Bear on his front steps, and now, God in his backseat.

He just shook his head and got in the Charger before a passing car took a chunk out of his ass, and Bonnie followed his lead, the cardboard sign still clutched to her chest.

The interior of the car already reeked. Bonnie made polite noises about it being a beautiful day and rolled down the windows a bit. Finn immediately lost his appetite.

"You hungry, William?" he asked.

"Yes sir. I am." William nodded, his powerful voice a little too loud for the interior of the car.

"Here!" Bonnie Rae handed William her sandwich as they headed southwest toward Joplin.

"What does this sign mean, William?" Bonnie reached back and set it on the seat beside him, though he barely looked at it.

William was devouring the sandwich like he hadn't eaten in a week. Finn handed his sandwich back too, along with a bottle of water. William tried to answer Bonnie between bites, lettuce and pieces of tomato and onion falling into his beard, caught like flies in a spider web, but William didn't stop to free them.

"I had a dream," he said, sounding just like Martin Luther King. "I had a dream about Bonnie and Clyde. I always be dreamin'—I dream of lots of things," William said, chewing.

William was too theatrical to be taken seriously, but Bonnie shot Finn a look, as if to say, "See?"

"Well, my name is Bonnie," Bonnie said triumphantly.

"And what's his name?" William didn't seem surprised by Bonnie's revelation.

"I'm Finn." The devil in Finn wasn't about to tell William his last name.

"Ahh. Mr. Infinity," William boomed.

"Mr. Infinity!" Bonnie hooted with laughter. "Mr. Infinity

makes you sound like you should be covered in oil, wearing a speedo, and flexing your muscles on a stage, Finn."

"You wish." Finn smirked.

"Yes. I do," Bonnie said deadpan. She was being silly, but it was still hot, and Finn really wished stinky William wasn't in the backseat so he could kiss her.

"Mr. Infinity, the Almighty, King of Kings, Lord of Lords, the Everlasting Father, the Prince of Peace. Mr. X himself. The unknown quantity!" William was done eating the first sandwich and he delivered the names like he was announcing professional boxing.

"Are you ready to ruuuuuummmmble?" Finn said under his breath.

Bonnie giggled.

"I don't think I've heard God referred to as Mr. Infinity or Mr. X, or even the unknown quantity, for that matter," Bonnie said as William started in on his second sandwich.

"X and the unknown quantity are mathematical terms," Finn offered, enjoying himself, amazingly enough. The next three hours would not be boring. William's beard was so full of veggies he could make a salad later on, unless of course, the sonic boom of his voice shook everything loose.

"Do you like mathematics, Mr. Infinity?" William asked. Finn met William's gaze in the rearview mirror, but he didn't answer. It had just occurred to him that he hadn't told William his name was Infinity, but Finn.

"Tell me this, does mathematics exist because it's a reflection of our world, or does the world exist because of mathematics?" William said, making Bonnie's eyebrows shoot up and causing Finn's heart to stall. It was obviously not a question he expected them to answer, because he finished the sandwiches, and with a small burp, sat back heavily against the seat.

"I was hungry and you fed me, thirsty and you gave me drink. And now I will rest a little while," William declared in much more normal tones, and within seconds he was snoring in the backseat, one of his filthy, stocking-clad feet propped on the armrest between Bonnie and Finn.

"Aren't you glad I offered him a ride?" Bonnie said, trying to keep a straight face. When Finn didn't respond she poked him.

"That question that he asked—does mathematics exist because it's a reflection of our world, or does the world exist because of mathematics—did you hear that?" he asked, distracted.

"Yes. I heard it." Bonnie snickered. "How could I not? It blew the top layer of skin clean off my face. I won't have to exfoliate any time soon."

"My dad always used to ask us that." Finn felt strange, unnerved even. "I guess other people may have asked the same question. But it was weird hearing William just shout it out like that."

"Well, his initials are G.O.D." Bonnie said softly, smiling. Finn could tell she was trying to ease the sudden tension he was feeling.

And then a memory surfaced. His dad had posed a paradox for the second time in as many days, and Fish had altered the question, inserting their names. He'd said, "Does Finn exist because he's a reflection of me, or do I exist because I'm a reflection of Finn?"

His father had looked at Fish as if he had no idea what Fish was talking about, and Fish had burst out laughing, enjoying the feeling of stumping his father for once. That night they'd gotten drunk, though, and the question had been posed again, this time with a slightly different paradox.

"Fisher! Wait! You're going to fall."

Finn felt the fog in his own brain, in the way his lips struggled to form the words. He was drunk. He hated being drunk. Fish was drunk too. Which was why walking along the roofline was a bad idea. But Finn followed him, just like he always did, climbing the ladder that wouldn't hold still, placing his feet on rungs that wavered before his eyes.

Fish just laughed. "I'm not gonna fall. What was that thing Dad told us about the arrow in flight? The paradox? Or was it the pair o' dicks? The arrow isn't really moving, remember? It's motionless. If we fall, we aren't really falling." Fish laughed uproariously at himself, and Finn laughed too.

Pair of dicks. That's what they were. They shared the same face, the same room, the same friends, but at least they didn't have to share the same dick. That was good. Fish was a little too free with his. He had terrible taste in women.

The paradox Fish was talking about was another one of the Greek philosopher Zeno's—Dad loved Zeno. Zeno said in order for an object to move, it has to change position. But in any given instant, the arrow isn't moving to where it is, because it's already there, and it's not moving to where it's not because no time has passed for it to get there. So in essence, if time is made up of instants, and if in any given instant the arrow is not moving, then motion is impossible.

The tangle the paradox created in Finn's head became a tangle in his feet, and about halfway up the ladder he slipped, proving motion is indeed possible and extremely painful as he hit the ground.

He laid there, stunned, the wind knocked from his chest, his eyes on the sky. It was unclear and the air felt wet and heavy as he struggled to pull oxygen into his deflated lungs. You couldn't see stars in Southie. He wondered if you could see the stars in St. Louis, where his father was moving. The thought made him angry, the anger clearing the muddle from his head better than the fall from the ladder.

"Since when have you ever listened to anything Dad says, Fish? And you **are** going to fall," Finn shouted, and struggled back up the ladder, wondering if he was already too late. He hadn't heard anything.

Fish was sitting on one of the little gables above the two windows that overlooked the front yard. Finn made his way gingerly to the other, straddling it like he was taking a turn on the mechanical bull at O'Shaughnessy's, and the roofline swam and bucked a little, making the comparison even more apt. The alcohol in his belly sloshed and rose in his throat, and Finn realized that the bull was going to throw him if he didn't hold on. He lay against the shifting shingles and gripped the edge of the dormer weakly. But instead of getting tossed he did some tossing of his own, throwing up the contents of his stomach, watching as it waterfalled over the side of the roof and down onto the front walk. He was pretty sure he hadn't made the eight second whistle.

"You throwing up already, Infinity?" Fish laughed. "For someone who soaks up so much shit, it's amazing you can't soak up a few shots."

"Yeah, yeah," Finn mumbled wishing he could take a shot at his brother, but knowing he probably should just hold still. Very still. "Why are we up here, Fish? You wanna die?"

"Nah. I wanna live. I wanna live!" Fish shouted into the fog, and laughed, raising his arms and throwing back his head, his balance seemingly unimpaired by the alcohol. Finn shut his eyes, wondering how in the hell he was going to get back down.

"You're trying to kill me," he groaned.

"Nobody said you had to follow me up, little brother." Two hours separating their births officially made Finn the little brother.

"Of course I have to follow you. We're a pair, remember?" Finn sighed, willing the world to settle so he could climb down.

"Are we really? Let me tell you the paradox of the pair o' dicks, my young friend. If a dick can do what it does, completely independent of the other dick, what's the point of being a pair?"

Fish impersonated their father so perfectly, his tone of voice so thoughtful and serious that Finn couldn't help but laugh, and he decided to play along.

"If you lose one, you have a spare." Finn offered a solution to the ridiculous riddle.

"Ah, but that's the paradox." Fish stroked his chin just like their father did, as if he had a little goatee. "We're a pair, but we're nothing alike. So are we really a pair? And if you lost me, would you truly be my spare?" Fish shook his head in a very professorial manner, tsking like Finn wasn't trying—something else their father did *sometimes.*

Then he answered his own question, but he abandoned the impersonation. "You are Infinity, and I am Infinity's opposite."

"Infinitesimal," Finn said. "Infinitesimal is the twin of infinity."

"Oh, that's rich!" Fish replied. "Infinity means immeasurably large, and infinitesimal is immeasurably small—I know that much math."

"Exactly," Finn smiled, going in for the kill. "I mean, we are talking about our dicks, right?"

Finn smiled at the memory, the humor banishing the discomfort he'd felt at William's uncanny question. Fish had laughed so hard he'd almost fallen off the roof, and they had ended up helping each other down the ladder in what could have been a disaster instead of a sweet memory. It was just one of many close calls leading up to the ultimate disaster six months later.

Finn looked at Bonnie and pondered Fish's question—did Finn exist because he was a reflection of Fish? Or had Fish existed because he was a reflection of Finn? Maybe neither. Maybe both. One egg, two people. Maybe in the beginning they were one, but that day had long since passed. He didn't dare pose the question to Bonnie. He wondered if she still thought she existed as a reflection of her sister.

William snorted in his sleep and another large, smelly foot found its way onto the console between them.

"He's a little crazy, isn't he?" Finn sighed, turning his attention to the problem at hand.

Bonnie shrugged. "I don't know. What has he really said that's so crazy? People like to throw words like crazy and emotionally unstable around when people are just . . . different. It's a way to shut people up. It's a way to control. Nothing scarier than someone who is bat shit. Nothing more intimidating than someone who is 'mentally ill.'" Bonnie lifted her hands and made quotations in the air. "Slap that label on someone and it's over, whether it's true or not. Their freedoms and their credibility are gone forever—little notations on driver's licenses, little files that follow them through life, closed doors, suspicious looks, ready medication. I say let William preach. He's not hurting anyone."

He'd touched a nerve. Bonnie was a little too vehement and ready in her argument, like she'd had it in her own mind a hundred times. He wondered again about her relationship with her grandmother, about the road that had ended on a bridge a little less than a week before. Bonnie wasn't mentally ill. Bear had said it right. Her spirit had been broken. Maybe not entirely—she still had more light and personality in her little finger than Finn had in his whole, big body. But she had sustained some pretty serious fractures.

And it was time for a reckonin'.

∞

WILLIAM LEFT US in Joplin with a fervent sermon about taking care of each other and watching for angels in disguise.

"If you have done it unto one of the least of these, my brethren, ye have done it unto me!" he quoted boisterously before he thanked us for feeding and clothing him . . . well, clothing his feet, anyway. Finn had given him his old boots. Luckily, neither the old boots nor the new ones had been in the Blazer when I'd ditched Finn in Cincinnati and then ended up losing our ride and everything in it.

Before William left he handed me the cardboard sign that had reeled me in and won him a ride to Joplin.

"Here you go, Miss Bonnie. You keep this."

I believe in Bonnie and Clyde.

On the back side he'd written a new message.

I believe in Bonnie for Infinity.

"Don't you mean Bonnie *and* Infinity?" I laughed.

"Yeah. That too." He smiled and waved as he walked away, hoisting his backpack onto his shoulders, his eyes on his new (old) boots, like a kid in new sneakers who can't quit looking at his feet. And I felt like I had missed something important.

15

Common Denominator

OUR HOTLINE HAS received multiple sightings of Bonnie Rae Shelby in the company of ex-convict, Infinity James Clyde, ranging as far north as Buffalo and as far south as Louisiana. We even have what appears to be an armed robbery of a liquor store outside of Chicago carried out by none other than the wanted felon, Infinity Clyde, with Bonnie Rae Shelby herself behind the wheel of a dark colored Bronco, waiting at the curb. Other witnesses claim there was no woman in the driver's seat, but that there was a woman in the backseat, who appeared to be restrained in some way. Witnesses say she even called out to pedestrians. So far these sightings are unconfirmed and police aren't commenting on leads. Raena Shelby, Bonnie Rae Shelby's grandmother and longtime manager, gave a brief interview to Buzz TV about her granddaughter last evening. She claims Bonnie Rae was taken against her will and openly pled with Mr. Clyde at one point, to release the superstar.

∞

THE CONVENIENCE STORE in Joplin, Missouri where we dropped William was kitschy and fun, a little of this and a little of that, and I found myself lingering over a display of books, wondering what Finn liked to read when his head wasn't filled with numbers. I'd never been much of a reader. The words in my head always came with a tune, and I wondered if books would hold my interest longer if they were written in rhyme, so I could sing them.

My hands ran over the titles of the books, cookbooks that boasted "a taste of Missouri," romance novels from "local authors," and even a copy of *Huckleberry Finn*, the cover a picture of a boy and a black man who looked a little like William without all the hair, gliding down the Mississippi. I had to have it and snickered at the thought of Finn's face when I asked him to sign it. I started to turn away in anticipation of that face, when something caught my eye.

On the top shelf of the display, propped so the cover could be seen, was a flimsy, dusty book that looked like someone had produced it on a home printer. It was the title that caught my eye, and I pulled the booklet from the shelf, my eyes on the picture of a couple dressed in 1930s clothing, smiling at the camera, the girl perched on the left arm of the guy, clutching him as he clutched her, his left arm holding her aloft, almost in a childlike pose, which showed his strength and her affection.

He held a white hat in his right hand, which partially obscured the license plate of the car behind them. Above the picture were the words *Bonnie & Clyde*. Below the picture, the words *Their Story*. It was simple and unsophisticated. It wouldn't take me more than an hour to read it from cover to cover, twice. But I was spellbound by that picture, by the couple that shared our names. I snatched up all the copies on the shelf, a thin stack of them, as if it were our story and the pages held our secrets.

The cashier seemed surprised that I needed six copies of the glorified pamphlet, but was "glad to see them go," as they'd been sitting on that same shelf for as long as she'd worked there, which would be ten years in May.

"It's supposed to be pretty accurate, though. The gal that put that book together was a relation or distant cousin of Clyde Barrow's, I guess. She was real protective of those two—kind of obsessed with them, actually. She said theirs was a love story first and foremost, and people got distracted by the violence. She's gone now, but I didn't have the heart to throw them away."

The friendly cashier bagged my purchases, which included some lunch to replace the sandwiches William had eaten, as well as a couple of homemade suckers and a stack of pralines because I had a sweet tooth and wasn't in the mood to deny it any longer. Gran had made me ultra-self-conscious about everything I ate because "being thin was part of the job description."

"You know, you should drive by Bonnie and Clyde's hideout while you're here, since you're buyin' the book and all. It's on your way outta town. It's just off Highway 43." She indicated the street we were on. "Head south and take a right on 34th street. There's a big liquor store on the corner, you can't miss it. The house is between Joplin and Oakridge Drive, on your right." She took one of the books out of my bag and turned a few pages, finding what she was looking for. She tapped a picture and showed it to me.

"Here it is. It looks just the same. They stayed here in Joplin back in 1933, according to this here," she quoted. "You can't go inside anymore, but you can see it from the road." I thanked her again and strolled out to the car with my finds and climbed in beside Finn. His eyes were focused on a police car parked at another pump, his brow furrowed.

"Finn?" I asked, not liking the look on his face.

"That cop has just been sitting in his car since he pulled up. No big deal, but he keeps looking over here, and a second ago he picked up his radio and started talking into it, still looking at me the whole time."

I shrugged. Finn was nervous around the police, understandably. But we hadn't done anything and I was eager to see Bonnie and Clyde's hidey hole.

"Let's go. Maybe he just thinks you're hot."

"Most likely he thinks this car's hot—as in stolen."

"But it isn't . . . so we don't have anything to worry about." But I thought about the scene at the bank and didn't argue with him.

Finn pulled away from the pump and eased out into the intersection, heading south down Main Street. He kept his eyes on the rear-view mirror, as if expecting to be followed by the police car still parked at the pump. I was too busy looking around me, making sure we didn't miss 34th street. I'd been part of a group of country singers that had raised money to help rebuild Joplin after the tornado hit in 2011. Sections of Joplin had been completely leveled by the twister. In fact, it had headed straight down 32nd street, but the town was already thriving again, building going on in every direction. The old gas station hadn't been new, however, and I marveled at the sheer randomness of a storm that would take out one business and leave another, take one life and spare another. It was the randomness that made it fair, I supposed.

"Turn right!" I yelped, realizing I should have given Finn a better heads up. He turned without hesitation, and our back wheels squealed a little. The car behind us honked, but I laughed, and Finn lost the worried look he'd had since spotting the police car.

"What are we doing?" he asked.

"We're sightseeing." I peered down the street, doubtfully. It felt like spring in Joplin. Late winter could be like that in the south. The sun was shining, the trees looked like they were thinking about sporting some green, and 34th street looked sleepy and content, hardly the place where a shoot-out with a pair of bank robbers cost two policemen their lives eighty years earlier.

"Between Joplin and Oakridge on the right," I said, repeating the directions the woman at the gas station had given me. "There!" I pointed at a boxy, light-colored stone home facing the street. A pair of large windows sat above two garage doors, just like in the picture. It was neat and well-kept, pretty even, with a side yard. But there was no sign indicating it was a historical landmark. There was a chain link fence around the yard, and the houses around it looked lived in—a tetherball pole with a faded ball stood in the yard of the house next door. It was just a demure house on an old street in a quiet neighborhood. I looked down at the book again to make sure we were in the right place.

"What are we looking at?" Clyde asked, parking in front of the two garage doors and staring up at the big windows above us.

"*The infamous bank robbers lived over this garage for less than two weeks before the April 13, 1933 shootout with the authorities, who had been tipped off about the apartment hideout. Two officers died, and Bonnie and Clyde escaped,*" I read out loud from the pamphlet.

"Here? This is their hideout?" Finn marveled and looked around once more at the surrounding homes. A boy of about nine or ten pedaled by on his bike, eyeing us curiously.

I lifted up the little paper book and showed him the cover. "I bought this at the gas station. The lady there thought I might want to see their love nest."

Clyde took the book from my hands and opened it to the first page.

"*You've read the story of Jesse James,
Of how he lived and died
If you're still in the need
Of something to read,
Here's the story of Bonnie and Clyde,*" he read.

Apparently, Bonnie was a poet. She'd written two poems, stories really, and I could imagine them set to some bluegrass music, a little harmonica between the stanzas, maybe a fast fiddle in the getaway scenes. One poem was called "Suicide Sal," about a woman who had loved a man who betrayed her, landing her in jail, and the other, "The Story of Bonnie and Clyde." I started to read as Finn drove, leaving the inauspicious hideaway and merging up onto I-44, Joplin at our backs, but Bonnie and Clyde still very much with us as we headed toward Oklahoma.

I read for almost an hour, the account very detailed and elaborate, and obviously written by someone who cared for Clyde Barrow and Bonnie Parker. I thought it was funny that Clyde's middle name was really Chestnut—not Champion like some accounts claim—and resolved to add that to my list of nicknames for Finn. He only volunteered comment once, when I read about Clyde's time in prison.

"Clyde was sent to Eastham Prison farm in April 1930. While in prison, Barrow beat to death another inmate who had repeatedly assaulted him sexually. This was Clyde Barrow's first killing. A fellow inmate said he 'watched Clyde change from a schoolboy to a rattlesnake.'

"Paroled in February of 1932, Barrow emerged from Eastham a hardened and bitter criminal. His sister Marie said, 'Something awful sure must have happened to him in prison, because he wasn't the same person when he got out.'"

Finn reached over, grabbed the book, and tossed it out the window. I watched it tumble behind the car before turning to Finn in astonishment.

"I wanted to see what happened next!"

"We don't need to read that, do we Bonnie?"

"But . . ." I protested. I had several more copies. It wasn't like I couldn't pull another one out. "It's fascinating."

"I don't find it especially fascinating," he said, his eyes straight ahead.

"Oh." I felt sick, and we sat in silence as I tried to figure out what to say. He glanced over at me eventually. I guess I was too quiet.

"You look like you're going to cry, Bonnie Rae."

"Did that happen to you, Finn?" I asked, sorrier than I'd ever been in my whole life. Finn cursed and shook his head, like he couldn't believe I'd just come right out and asked him. But I didn't know how else to do it. And because I cared about him, I had to know.

"No. It didn't. But it happens. All the time. And it was the thing

I was the most afraid of. The thing I was most desperate to avoid. So I feel for him even though I don't like him very much."

"Who, Clyde?"

"Yeah. Clyde. It makes a lot more sense why he lived his life the way he did after that."

I pulled another copy of the book out of my grocery sack. Finn just shook his head, but he didn't protest.

"Clyde had another inmate chop off two of his toes in an effort to get released from hard labor. Instead, he got paroled."

"Holy shit."

"He was desperate." I couldn't imagine that kind of desperation. Or maybe I could. I don't know. Cutting my hair was one thing, cutting my toes off was another thing altogether.

"And what did I tell you about desperate? Desperate people make bad choices."

I had nothing to say in response, and Finn didn't interrupt as I continued on with the story, though he listened intently with his arms crossed over the wheel, his eyes on the road and occasionally on me until I read the final page.

"Bonnie's mother refused to have Bonnie buried with the man that led her daughter into a life of crime. So although they died together, and Bonnie predicted they would be buried side by side, they were buried apart, in two different cemeteries in West Dallas." Then I read the last sentence, a stanza from Bonnie's poem.

To few it'll be grief –
To the law a relief
But it's death for Bonnie and Clyde.

"They robbed banks and killed nine police officers," I said, looking out over the wide open space, serene in the noonday sun, so unlike the dense, tree-lined freeways we'd started our journey with.

"Yep," Finn said.

"They weren't good people," I added, but even I heard the reluctance in my voice.

"No."

"So why the fascination? Why are movies made about them, museums built for them? Why did this little old lady—I read the author's name off the bottom of the booklet—love them so much?"

Finn's gaze was sober and probing, like he was waiting for me to come to a bigger conclusion. His eyes were a bright, sky blue, completely opposite from my own, and when he leveled them at me my mind tripped and my thoughts went spilling out in all directions. I forgot my own question for a minute. But then Finn looked away from me, out his window, but his jaw was tight.

"You tell me, Bonnie. Why the fascination?"

I studied Finn's profile, the line of his jaw and the firm set of his lips. A few strands had worked their way free of his smooth tail and brushed his lean cheeks. I wanted to brush them back so that I could touch him. It was strange how I always wanted to touch him. And he tried so hard to be untouchable.

"Because they loved each other."

The answer came out of nowhere. Or maybe it came from instinct or from that place in the human heart that knows the truth before we tell our heads what to think, but I felt the truth in the words even as I spoke them.

"They loved each other. And love is . . . fascinating." I almost whispered the words, they felt so intimate. I was confessing my own feelings under the flimsy guise of discussing two long-dead outlaw lovers. And I was pretty sure he knew it.

"There's that word again. Fascinating. You find them fascinating. But they were criminals." Finn's bright eyes were probing again, looking for something from me.

"But that's not all they were." Again, the truth resonated like a gong in my heart. "People aren't one dimensional. They were criminals. But that's not all they were," I repeated.

"I'm an ex-con."

"But that's not all you are."

"Oh yeah?" Finn asked, his eyes heavy and troubled. "But how long will I be fascinating to you, Bonnie?"

I wanted to laugh. And then it made me mad. Was he serious? "People who don't even know me claim to love me, Finn, and people who *should* love me are more interested in claiming me. Maybe I should be asking you that question."

"I'm a felon. You're a superstar. Enough said."

"But that's not *all* I am!" I said, angrily pulling my hand free from his.

"So you and I, what are we? What else? Tell me," he reached out and grasped my chin with the hand that wasn't on the wheel, making me look at him as he looked between me and the lonely road, demanding an answer.

I gasped at his vehemence and bit down on all the things I wanted to say, but the words rose within me anyway, flashing like neon in my head.

"We're Bonnie and Clyde! Wanted and unwanted. Caged and cornered. We're lost and we're alone. We're a big, tangled mess. We're a shot in the dark. We're two people who have nowhere else, no one else, and yet, suddenly that feels like enough for me! I'm sorry if it's not enough for you."

I was angry, spitting the words out at him, so it caught me by surprise when I started to cry. I pulled my face from Finn's grip, pushing at his arm, and I put my head down in my lap, not wanting him to see my nose swell and my eyes run, fearing I would look more like Hank than ever.

He didn't say anything. But after a minute, he reached out and stroked my hair, tentatively at first. His big hand, gentle and heavy on my head, made the tears come harder, but lessened the agony of release.

"It's more than enough for me, Bonnie Rae," he said, and I was reminded of the way his voice had sounded the first time I'd heard him speak, the night I stood perched on a bridge and thought about becoming my own version of Suicide Sal.

"Tell me about numbers, Clyde," I whispered, the tears still dripping off my cheeks and soaking my knees through my jeans. I wanted to listen to his voice. I wanted him to unravel the mysterious. "I want to hear you talk about numbers."

"Which number?"

"One." I responded immediately, because that is how he made me feel. Whole.

"One is the number of unity. One is the number that the ancient Greeks equated with God. It's the number all others spring from . . . so I guess that makes sense." Finn continued on, his head in the clouds, far beyond where I could follow, but his hand was in my hair, and that was enough for me. More than enough. As his hand stroked and soothed, there was a silent roaring in my ears, a roaring so loud that I wondered how he didn't hear it too. Maybe it was our own song, the song we created together. The ballad of Bonnie and Clyde. The words to Bonnie's poem suddenly echoed through the roaring.

"The road was so dimly lighted.
There were no highway signs to guide.
But they made up their minds,
If all roads were blind,
They wouldn't give up 'til they died."

In that moment, I understood with a clarity that was frightening, exactly what Bonnie Parker—outlaw, lover, girl on the run—had meant. There was a point, a place in time, where all roads but one are blind. And there is only one way you can go, one direction. For me, for Bonnie Rae Shelby, Finn Clyde was that road, and I wouldn't give him up. Not 'til I died.

16

Hero's Formula

OUR SOURCES ARE telling us that just this morning in St Louis, police recovered the orange, 1972, Blazer owned by Infinity James Clyde, as well as items that were reported stolen inside the vehicle, including a large amount of cash, several credit cards, and identification belonging to the manager of singing sensation Bonnie Rae Shelby, furthering suspicions that Miss Shelby was taken against her will.

Reports of a message written on the window of the vehicle, an address, led police to a residence near Washington University, but the residence was empty when police arrived. Apparently, the home is owned by Jason Clyde, father of Infinity Clyde, who police have since confirmed has been out of town and is not a person of interest.

Then, just hours ago, we started getting reports of Bonnie Rae Shelby attempting to withdraw a large sum of cash from a small local bank. Bank personnel said Miss Shelby seemed upset and frightened and ran from the bank when she was refused access, causing sources to speculate that she had been sent into the bank under duress, possibly to pay her own ransom. Police aren't commenting on this latest development, and we don't have all the details, nor can we completely confirm this report, but our sources say that Miss Shelby may now be under some suspicion as well, as some of her recent actions have invited legal scrutiny.

This story just keeps getting stranger by the minute . . .

∞

YOU COULD DRIVE across America and not see much, I decided. The cars were all the same, one road looked like another, and most of the roads were tree-lined, making it impossible to see the land and space beyond. As we made our way farther west, the trees became sparser and the landscape opened up and flattened out, but so many highways bypassed the towns, the people, and the flavor of a place, that the only thing that really provided any color and texture was Finn himself. He had a game he played called finding primes. It wasn't a game I could play with him. He replaced the letters on license plates with its alphabetical number, for instance, A was replaced with 1, Z with 26, and so on. A license plate that read KUY 456 would be 112125 456 or 112,125,456, and Finn would then proceed to tell me what the factors of the number were. He told me he won when he found a prime, a number that was only divisible by itself and one. He hadn't found a prime yet.

Since I couldn't participate, I would make up little ditties for the different states on the license plates. Clyde would be ripping out factors while I sang about Texas, Vermont, and North Dakota, tapping a rhythm on the dash board, wishing I had Finn's guitar, and creating songs that distracted him from his never-ending supply of numbers.

I had a good song for West Virginia and had been searching for a license plate from that state all day long when I spotted one attached to a maroon van at the side of the road, obviously experiencing car trouble. A grey-haired man was gamely looking under the hood while a child stood near him, watching the cars pass them by.

"Bonnie. No." Finn was shaking his head. I hadn't even said anything, but he'd seen them too, and he spoke before I could. "We aren't stopping. Not this time."

"But Clyde . . . they need help. And they're a long way from home, too! They're from West Virginia, for heck sake."

Finn passed them, and I felt a little sick, swooshing by, just like that. Swooshing by with every other car.

"Please, Finn? Can't we just stop and make sure he's got help coming?"

Finn just shook his head and sighed. But he signaled and slowed, pulling over to the side of the road. Then he reversed the Charger and backed up for about a hundred yards, eating up the space between us and the old, maroon van. The man turned toward us, pulling his head from beneath the hood. He was an older man, probably the child's grandfather, and he looked relieved that someone had stopped. He reached for the child's hand as Finn climbed out. Finn told me to stay put, it would only be a minute. But he should have known he was wasting his breath.

The smell of burnt rubber was heavy around the vehicle, and I immediately held my hand to my nose.

"Hey. You need to borrow a phone?" I noticed Finn didn't offer a ride. But I kept quiet. I'd pushed my luck with Finn way beyond breaking.

"No. I've got one. My engine light isn't on, but I'm getting that burnt rubber smell, have been for the last hour. I've only got about an hour to go, so not too much farther, but it's got me nervous."

"You noticed any oil leaks on your driveway?"

"This isn't my vehicle. It's my daughter's. She and her husband are going through a divorce. She's moving in with us. Long story." He waved his words away, obviously not wanting to go into detail.

"Is it driving okay?"

"Yeah. Doesn't seem to be overheating."

"You've probably got a small oil leak. The motor oil might be leaking onto the exhaust and burning, giving you that smell. It could also be your catalytic converter overheating, but if that were the case, your engine light would be on. Did you check the oil?

The old man nodded. "I checked the oil first. It was maybe a tad low, but still in the normal range. We should be fine to get home. I've got a mechanic friend who can take a look at it when we get there."

"We'll stay behind you until you turn off just to make sure you don't have any more problems." Finn offered, almost pleasant now that he realized we weren't going to be taking on passengers or trying to pull the van behind Bear's Charger. The image made me laugh a little as Finn and the old man turned toward the engine to take a final look. The little boy looked at me in confusion. Apparently, he wasn't enjoying himself and my laughter seemed odd. He was probably eight or nine and had chubby cheeks and bright red hair. I leaned down and introduced myself, offering my hand for a shake.

"Hi. I'm Bonnie."

He stuck his hand in mine awkwardly. "I'm Ben."

"Hi Ben. I like that name. I reached in my pocket and pulled out some of the money I'd stashed there. Most of it was in my purse, but I was through leaving it all in one place. I had some bills stuck in my boots and some in my bra and some in my pockets too. You can take the girl out of Grassley . . .

I peeled off five one-hundred-dollar bills and folded the money up in Ben's small hand.

"You give that to your grandpa when you get home, okay? Not before, because he might try to give it back. He can use it to help you and your mom."

The little boy's eyes were wide, and with his full cheeks he resembled a squirrel caught in the headlights. "Okay," he squeaked as he stuffed the money deep into the front pocket of his jeans. I held my finger to my lips and stood.

The boy's grandfather lowered the hood and called to Ben, thanking us as he waved us away, and we were back on the road, following the maroon van, within a few minutes.

"I hate that smell." It lingered on our clothes.

"Burnt rubber?" Finn could still smell it too, obviously.

"Yeah. It reminds me of burning tires. In Grassley, people would burn tires to melt the rubber away from the rims so they could sell the scrap metal. One time, when Minnie and I were about fourteen, we actually pulled a guy away from his pile of burning tires. He'd been burning and drinking, which is never a great combination. He passed out too close to his pile. Minnie and I happened along and Minnie was convinced it was a test."

"Do you think it's Jesus?" Minnie asked.

"That guy?" I couldn't imagine it was.

"Not Jesus, exactly, but someone Jesus put in our path. Maybe he's an angel."

"He sure doesn't look like an angel," I said doubtfully.

"If he looked like an angel then it wouldn't be a test. Remember what Pastor Joseph said? That story about the couple waitin' for their special guest and the special guest never coming? Instead, it was all the people who needed something?"

"The couple asked the special guest why he never came, and he said he did. He was the beggar, and the old woman, and the hungry child . . . that one?" I looked at the man lying far too close to the pile of burning tires like it was just an outdoor barbeque built for roasting weenies instead of a roiling, greasy, smelly tar pit.

"Yeah. He might be an angel in disguise. He might be testin' us!" Minnie said.

"So what should we do?" The smell of tires was so thick I could hardly breathe.

"He's passed out, Bonnie. We should pull him away from the fire."

We pulled on the neck of his coat and ended up pulling it right over his head and pulling him right out of it. He didn't have a shirt on underneath.

"Ew!" I said, trying not to look at his jiggling white flesh, but failing miserably. "This one ain't Jesus, Minnie. He ain't an angel either. I guarantee it."

"Come on, Bonnie. Grab his other arm." I did as she instructed, and together we heaved and tugged, and managed to pull him closer to the house with the sagging porch and the plastic covered windows. The yard was littered with cans and broken bottles, and I worried about what his back would look like if we kept pulling him that way. We were probably doing more harm than good.

Unfortunately, he wasn't wearing a belt or suspenders, either, and by the time we reached the front of his house, breathing hard and sweating, our muscles protesting our lifesaving efforts, his pants had been dragged down around his knees, his underwear too. When I saw what we'd done I released his arm and pointed.

"Look, Minnie!" I laughed. "We depantsed him."

Minnie looked down, screamed, dropped the arm she'd been tugging on, and backed away hurriedly, like she'd seen a snake. Which, I suppose she had. I was a little more curious and didn't back up nearly as far. Plus, I wasn't afraid of snakes.

But it was pretty horrifying. We had two brothers and because of it, had a fairly good idea what boys looked like naked, but this was a full-grown man, not related, and definitely not attractive.

"I don't think Jesus would approve of our efforts, Minnie," I said with mock solemnity. "I think he frowns on young girls lookin' at naked men."

"Throw his coat over him," Minnie hissed.

I did as I was told, tossing the coat I was still holding toward the mostly naked, unconscious man. It wasn't a very good toss. It landed over his face. His nether regions were still completely uncovered, just blowing in the wind.

"If he throws up he's gonna die laying on his back with that coat over his face, Bonnie!"

We'd seen Hank and Cash drink enough that they threw up. Daddy had even thrown up in his sleep before, and if Mama hadn't been there he'd have choked in his own vomit. Mama never drank more than a beer a day, and she said it was for her health—"to flush out her kidneys."

"Well, feel free to move it, Minnie." I gestured toward the man's covered head. I didn't know why I had to do everything. Minnie shook her head frantically.

"Fine." I sighed. I hunched down and inched toward him, leading with my leg and keeping my upper body shifted to the side. Then I yanked the coat from off the man's face and dropped it over his lower body.

His eyes were wide open.

He stared up at me unblinking, and I screamed and fell back on my butt.

"What the hell?" he slurred. Then he reached out and grabbed my ankle.

I pulled away, kicking my foot, and Minnie was there, helping me up. Our feet got a little tangled, and we tripped and fell and were up and running again immediately.

"Hey! Come back! Why you leavin'?" The man yelled behind us. "Did I miss all the fun stuff? I don't remember nothin!'"

"Definitely not Jesus," I puffed, and we ended up giggling all the way home.

"We smelled like burnt tires, and I kept seeing his sad manhood in my head when I closed my eyes," I told Finn, laughing. "But Minnie was back at her do-goodin' the next day, and the next. She was convinced that behind everyone in need was an opportunity to make the world a better place. It was like she knew she had only a little while to leave her mark, and that's the way she decided to leave it. It wasn't a bad way to be. But I still hate the smell of burning tires."

"There can't be much money in burning tires." Finn sounded skeptical.

"It's something. We never did it, but lots of folks did. Daddy made money traveling around singing, and Gran went with him. When we were old enough, Minnie and I did too. We sang up and down the Appalachians at county fairs and churches and family reunions. Daddy took cash or trades, and never claimed any of it on his taxes so he could keep his welfare check. With the government money and the money we made under the table, we did better than most families in Grassley and better than all the other families in the holler."

"What's a holler?"

"A valley, you know. A hillbilly neighborhood. A hollow." This time I said it like the rest of America said it, with "o" on the end instead of "er."

"You realize when you say things like 'holler' you sound like you're from the early 1930s talking about the Great Depression," Finn said mildly.

"You mean I sound like Bonnie Parker? I guess I can relate to her a little, after all." I could relate to her a lot. "Appalachia hasn't changed much since then, from what I can tell. Up and down the Appalachians—Iowa, Kentucky, Tennessee, West Virginia, North Carolina—there are hundreds of towns just like Grassley. And most of America doesn't even know we exist. They just fly over us, and from the clouds, everything looks pretty."

Finn reached over and rested his hand on my leg, trying to soothe me, I supposed. And I stared for a minute at that big, strong hand resting on my thigh, wishing for a moment that I was small enough to crawl beneath his palm and pretend places like Grassley didn't exist. But they did. And try as I might, they always would.

"Minnie's doctor said the poverty of the mountain people, people in Appalachia, rivals the poverty she saw in places in India when she spent time there on humanitarian missions. Nobody talks about Appalachia . . . so nobody really knows. I built my parents a nice little four bedroom house and they have nice things, but I still dream about Grassley, and I wake up with the smell of burning tires in my nose. To me, that's what despair smells like. Burning tires."

"So is that the reason you have to put yourself out there for everybody you see? Stranded moms, homeless preachers, people on the side of the road?"

I shrugged. "That's what Minnie did. I thought about her when William was preaching to us about angels in disguise and clothing the naked and feeding the hungry. I told you about that song we always sang. The one about the mansions? I believe in mansions in heaven, but it'd be nice if people stopped hoping and started doing."

"Doing what?" he asked.

"Doing something more than just dreaming of mansions in the sky. Minnie and I started a foundation called Many Mansions. I was the money and Minnie was the manager. We wanted to help kids make a detailed plan to accomplish their dreams, and then help them carry out their plan. We wanted to make 'many mansions,' and not just in the sky."

I felt tired just talking about the foundation. It was Minnie's baby. Maybe I should change the name from Many Mansions to Minnie's Mansions. The idea actually cheered me.

"You said Minnie was trying to improve the world before she left it. Is that what you're trying to do? Improve the world before you leave it?" Finn's eyes were intent on my face, his voice flat.

I guess I deserved questions like that, considering how Finn and I met. I didn't know why I was compelled to do the things I did. I just got an impulse, and I went with it. Usually it served me well. Sometimes, not so much.

"I think I'm just trying to find what's real. Dreamin' of mansions isn't a bad thing. But there's got to be more to life than just enduring or dreaming. And too often, it feels like hope is the only thing most people have. Rich, poor, sick, healthy—we're all just drowning in dreams and hoping someone else will make them come true."

17

Instantaneous Velocity

"ENTERTAINMENT BUZZ HAS been following the ongoing drama surrounding singer Bonnie Rae Shelby which began with her abrupt departure from the stage last Saturday night. Just a recap, Bonnie Rae's inner circle called police in the early hours of Sunday, February 23, after they were unable to locate the star. Cash, credit cards, and personal items were also reported missing from the vicinity, heightening concerns that someone was involved in the disappearance of Miss Shelby, and that she might not have left the premises of her own free will.

Later sightings paired Miss Shelby with this man, an ex-convict named Infinity James Clyde. Clyde was incarcerated for armed robbery six years ago, and recently resided in the Boston area. He was last seen the night Bonnie Rae Shelby disappeared from the TD Garden in Boston. Police have contacted his mother, Greta Cleary, who still lives in the area, and have said she is cooperating with police. Police contacts say Ms. Cleary claimed her son had a job offer in Las Vegas, but close friends of Infinity Clyde's mother say she did not see him before he left and was hurt and surprised by his sudden departure.

Miss Shelby's manager, Ms. Raena Shelby, claims her grand-

daughter, Bonnie Rae Shelby, did not know Infinity James Clyde before that night, making these sightings very troublesome.

We have since had reports of assault, theft, an impounded vehicle owned by the ex-con containing Miss Shelby's clothing and items stolen from her dressing room at the TD Garden the night of February 22, as well as a bizarre confrontation at a small bank just outside of St. Louis—"

I flipped the television off immediately. I didn't want to listen to the rest. We were in a miniscule Oklahoma town in a roadside lodge that was actually a series of little individual red cabins not too far off the freeway, and we'd made the mistake of turning on the TV the moment we were settled in the room. The newscaster was cut off mid-sentence, and our stunned silence immediately filled the void. But her words hung in the air as if she stood there between us, waiting for us to defend ourselves. And the words weren't the worst part.

They'd shown stock footage of me singing, signing autographs, and waving at fans. But they showed mug shots of Finn. The pictures of him in an orange jumpsuit facing both forward and in profile, with numbers stamped across the bottom, made him seem dangerous, like he was an escaped, armed convict on the loose. His hair was short in the pictures, and he was younger, but it was undeniably him.

"This is gossip. It's just gossip, Finn," I whispered. "There's no meat in it. Shows like that take bits and pieces of what they think they know, and they try and stitch it together so it seems like they've got a real story."

Finn nodded woodenly, but his face was drawn and his lips were pressed into a tight line.

"Do you know how often I've seen stories like this? Not just about me, but about friends and acquaintances in the industry. Sometimes, there isn't a shred of truth to be found in any of it. And eventually? The story just disappears. No apologies, no recants. They just move on to someone else."

But Finn still didn't respond. And I felt a sudden rush of anger, so swift and so alarming that I almost gasped at the intensity. I placed a hand on the wall to steady myself.

"You haven't done anything wrong, Finn!" I made myself whisper so that I wouldn't shout. "I haven't done anything wrong! I just wanted to be left alone for a little while. You helped me. We haven't hurt anybody. We haven't *done* anything!"

Finn looked up at me, and the expression on his face was so discouraged I wanted to slap him. I wanted to wipe the sorrow from his eyes, to slap the sadness away. I wanted to make him angry like I was. Anger was so much better than grief. Instead, I fisted my hands in my hair and repeated myself, the words coming out much louder than they had before.

"We haven't *done* anything!" I wanted to run from the room, and shout those same words to anyone who would listen, but as suddenly as my anger had appeared, it morphed into fear. I'd so enjoyed my brief hiatus from caring, but my interlude with ambivalence was apparently over. All at once, I'd never been so afraid in my whole life. Not when I stood on a stage for the first time in front of thousands of people, not when Minnie got sick, not when her cancer came back. Not after I fell forward into the fog on a bridge in Boston. Not ever.

There was no way we were going to survive this. And I wasn't talking about life and death survival. I wasn't talking about incarceration. I wasn't worried about the police. We really *hadn't* done anything wrong. But *we* weren't going to survive. Us. Finn and me. Bonnie and Clyde. The two of us. I wasn't going to be able to keep him. He wouldn't want to stay.

I ran into the bathroom and slammed the door, shedding my clothing in a frenzy, as if removing them would ease the panic that was coursing in my veins. My chest felt tight, incredibly so—so tight that I couldn't breathe, and I wondered if I was having a heart attack the pressure was so intense. I flipped on the shower and stepped under the spray before I checked the temperature. The blast of icy water shocked me, distracting me from the vice around my heart for several welcome seconds, but as the water warmed, the fear came back, and I moaned at the simultaneous pressure and pain.

I thought I heard the door open and close. Not the door to the bathroom. I would have welcomed Finn, even in the state I was in. But it was the door that led outside. Finn had gone.

∞

HE RAN AS fast as he could for the first fifteen minutes or so, up and down the streets of the little town, the little blip on the map that he couldn't even remember the name of. All he knew was they were hugging the northern border of Oklahoma, more than five hundred miles from St. Louis, Missouri, where they'd started their day. And Bonnie was back at the motel, crying in the shower where she didn't think anyone could hear her. He'd wanted to step beneath the spray with her, damn the world, damn them all, and just be with her. That's what he'd wanted to do. But instead, he had pulled on his shorts and running shoes and fled out into the cold, quiet streets trying to purge the fear that warred with his desire for the girl who cried for him and confounded him, and made everything so much more complicated than it had to be. And none of it was really her fault. He understood that. But fault or no fault, the situation still existed.

He loped past what appeared to be an elementary school, resting beneath the soft glow of street lights, and he circled the campus until he found a playground and, using the monkey bars, hoisted himself up, over and over again, one pull-up after another, until his back, shoulders and arms were as weary as his legs. The sight of the tall slide made him smile, in spite of himself, and he wished Bonnie were there so she could climb it and sing to him, sing the worry away like she had the night before. Had it only been twenty-four hours ago? Finn became dizzy at the thought. The number of life-changing, plan-altering experiences wedged and crammed into the last few days was mind-boggling.

He resumed his run back toward the direction of the motel, his legs weary, his thoughts heavy, and failed to notice until it was too late, the police cruiser that had idled up next to him. Shit.

"Kinda late for a run, isn't it?"

"That depends," Finn said mildly, keeping his pace, and hopefully his tone, steady and unconcerned. "I like it best when it's quiet. Helps me unwind so I can sleep."

"Hmm," the officer said, non-committal. "You from around here?"

"No sir. Just staying at the motel off the freeway up there." Finn pointed in the general direction of the group of cabins that called themselves something quaint but looked like a row of fish shacks.

"What's your name?"

Now why in the hell did this guy need to know his name? He was obviously jogging, not bothering anyone. Finn wanted to punch something, but he decided lies would get him nowhere. Lies only made people look guilty when they were uncovered. If this was it, so be it. He would almost welcome it, and Bonnie's words rung in his ears. *"We haven't done anything wrong!"*

"Finn. Finn Clyde." He jogged over to the officer's open window and extended his hand, the friendly neighborhood felon. His forthcoming answer seemed to satisfy the officer, who shook his hand briefly but didn't act as if he recognized the name at all.

"Well, Finn. It's kinda cold out and you aren't very warmly dressed, and our streets are more like country roads. Not very well-lit and full of pot holes."

"I'm warm enough. And it's not too much farther." Finn tried not to let his relief show. The officer hadn't typed his name into a computer or called it into dispatch, as far as he could see. A call came in, and Finn stepped away with a quick wave of his hand. The officer answered the call with his badge number, and then tossed some parting words toward Finn before his attention was pulled elsewhere.

"All right, then. Welcome to Freedom. Have a good night." The cruiser pulled away and slid down the road. Finn almost stopped running he was so dumbfounded. Then he started to laugh as he remembered. Freedom was the name of the town.

∞

THE ROOM WAS dark when he stepped inside. He let the door swing shut behind him and turned the lock. The drapes were pulled wide, providing enough light to find his way to his bags. He didn't know why he was digging. His only relatively clean shirt was the one Bonnie had bought him earlier in the day—and it was in the car. He'd had plenty of clothes in the Blazer. Little good that did him. He walked back into the bathroom and pulled off the sweat soaked T-shirt. At least he could get clean beneath the shirt.

When he stepped out fifteen minutes later, Bonnie was sitting in the dark, perched on the end of one of the beds, wearing a little white top and very little else, judging from the bare length of her legs folded beneath her. He had hoped she was asleep. He stopped a few feet from her, rubbing the towel across his head, hand drying his hair before he tossed it toward a chair. He wore his shorts but hadn't pulled his sweaty shirt back on after his shower. Seeing Bonnie made him wish he had. He felt naked with this girl, defenseless, exposed, and it had very little to do with his bare chest or lack of clothing.

"I thought maybe you left," she said softly.

"And left you here?"

"I did it to you."

"And left me a note and two thousand dollars. I was pissed, but I didn't feel abandoned. I knew why you ran. I didn't like it. But I understood." They were both almost whispering, and Finn wasn't sure why.

She nodded, but stood slowly, her eyes on the ground. Finn kept his eyes on her down-turned face so he wouldn't see what she'd paired with the white undershirt.

"Will you hold me, Finn?" Bonnie asked, her voice so faint he wasn't entirely sure that was what she'd said. Because he wasn't sure, his response was cautious, questioning even.

"It won't end there, Bonnie—"

"It'll begin. And that's what I want," she interrupted, and he welcomed her honesty, reveled in it, even as he made himself reject her.

"It's what I want too. But it's not what's going to happen."

"Why?" she whispered, and the sadness in her sigh softened his response even further.

"Because I will hold you, and I'll want more. And I'll take it, Bonnie. I won't be able to stop. And then it will be over, and you and I will have crossed a line we can't uncross."

"I want to cross it."

"Really? 'Cause I'm not sure you know what that means. You and I go down this road, there won't be any going back for me and the things they're saying out there? About me being a loser? And a criminal? And a piece of shit, taking advantage of you, hanging onto you because you're somebody and I'm nobody? All that stuff will be true."

"No it won't! But why do we care what people think?"

"Because it *will* be true! Don't you see? Right now . . . right now I'm your . . . your friend." Her eyes shot to his in disbelief, and he almost flushed thinking about the way he wanted her, the way he'd kissed her. Several times now. Friends didn't kiss like that. He ignored the qualm. That was all before he saw the news report. It changed things, and he had to make her understand.

"I've done right by you, Bonnie. I have. I've taken care of you. And I've watched out for you. And I can feel good about that. I haven't taken anything from you that I didn't earn or that wasn't fair. But I haven't earned this, Bonnie. I haven't earned you. And if I take you, all that stuff people are saying will be true."

Bonnie stepped toward him, raised herself up on her toes, and pressed her lips against his, halting his words with her mouth. Finn needed her to cooperate if he was going to be able to stay away from her. But when had she ever done a damn thing he'd asked her to? Her kiss was so sweet, so honest, and so Bonnie Rae. And then she sighed against his lips as if she was exactly where she wanted to be, in spite of everything he'd said.

And Finn couldn't help himself.

His convictions were immediately reduced to eggshells. Call it weakness. Call it lack of conviction. Call it love. But he just couldn't help himself. His hands were on her hips, in her hair, sliding down her arms, around her waist, and then back up to cup her face, trying to be everywhere at once and not knowing where to start. Their breathing grew ragged, and together they sank to the bed, Bonnie pulling his body back onto hers as he willed himself to slow down.

"I don't know what the hell is happening between us," he whispered, hovering above her mouth, his voice tickling her lips. "I feel like I'm free falling, and any minute I'm going to touch down, and this is all going to be over, or worse, just a dream." His voice was so low that he wasn't sure if he was talking to her or talking to himself, but either way, he needed her to hear him. He kissed her again, anxiously, but then pressed his forehead into hers, pulling away as if their mouths were magnetized and it required conscious effort to suspend the kiss, needing to speak but unwilling to entirely disengage.

"I have a bad feeling about this, Bonnie. Not you and me exactly. But this, the media frenzy, the fact that everyone seems to know who I am. This is going to end badly. I can feel it, the way I felt it the night Fish robbed that store. He lost his life, but I lost mine too, just in a different way. I don't want you to lose your life because of me, Bonnie. Mine's not worth a whole hell of a lot, but it's all I've got, and you . . . you can do anything, go anywhere, be anything. This isn't going to end well, Bonnie."

She shook her head adamantly, her forehead rocking from side to side against his, her eyes squeezed shut, her bottom lip between her teeth.

"Please. Please don't say that. I believe in Bonnie and Clyde! Why does it have to end at all?"

There were tears in her voice, but she didn't let them fall, and she raised her hands to his face and pushed him away just enough to find his eyes. She held his gaze until she seemed satisfied that there would be no more talk of endings. Then her lips found his again, briefly, before she let her hands slide from his face and down his neck until they rested against his pounding heart. Then she rose up and kissed his chest. Sweetly, softly, entreating him without words.

Finn braced himself above her and watched her hands and her lips, as they soothed and smoothed, bestowing small caresses and velvet kisses against his throat and arms, against the marks that brought him shame. And in her reverence of his skin, he felt that shame wither and curl, like paper on a flame, and float upward, disintegrating into nothing more substantial than ash, and with her breath, she blew it all away. *I believe in Bonnie and Clyde.*

Finn's eyes stung and his throat grew tight as she drew him close and cradled his face in the slope of her neck, as if she knew he had let something go. The words Finn had pressed upon her with such urgency slipped away from his head like the silky camisole she wore that allowed his hands to slide from her waist to her breasts without resistance. He lifted his hand and pulled one little strap from her shoulders so he could press his lips to her skin, unimpeded. And then his hands framed her face, and he felt the whisper of her sigh as she pressed her lips into his palm.

He wanted to close his fingers over that kiss, to grip it tightly, to crush it into his skin so it couldn't fly away. But the swell of her lips and the curve of her jaw demanded a gentler touch, a touch he felt incapable of delivering when the intensity of his response pounded in his veins. So he slid his hands into her hair, curling his fingers desperately into the short strands, and pulled her mouth back to his. And this time, instead of words, he used his kiss to impart his trepidation into soft lips that he feared would one day wish him gone.

Flashing red and blue lights filled the room through the uncovered window, circling the walls, one color chasing the next, and Finn and Bonnie froze, their breath and lips halting, even as their bodies demanded they continue. Finn shot up and off the bed, and Bonnie followed, reaching for her jeans and pulling them on without a word, shoving her feet into her boots without bothering with socks. Finn stood to one side of the window, watching the slow-moving cruiser glide past the short row of cabins. Finn was yanking off his shorts and pulling on his jeans as he watched, and he saw Bonnie pause, taking in the expanse of long, smooth, uninterrupted skin before he clipped out her name in warning.

"Bonnie. We've gotta go. Nobody knows what we're driving but they're looking for something. I ran into a cop tonight on my run. That looks like the same guy." The cruiser had slowed to a stop by the cabin that served as the front office and the officer that had pulled alongside Finn earlier stepped out of the vehicle, looking this way and that like he was, indeed, looking for someone or something.

Bonnie didn't take the time to pull on a shirt. Instead, she pulled her pink coat over the camisole she'd been wearing beneath her shirt and stuffed their T-shirts into his duffle bag. She grabbed her purse and swept up their toothbrushes and they were out the door within forty-five seconds of being rudely interrupted from the only thing either of them really wanted to do.

They'd parked Bear's car right outside the door. But they were only thirty yards from the lobby entrance. And there were only three other cabins that appeared to be occupied. Freedom apparently wasn't popular on Thursdays. Finn disengaged the locks and winced at the chirp and the flash of light that innocently welcomed them. Without looking toward the office to see if they'd been spotted, he and Bonnie slid into the car and said goodbye to Freedom with their eyes on the rear view mirror.

"What name did you give them when you registered us?" Bonnie asked. She was turned around in her seat, watching to see if they were going to be pursued. So far so good.

"Parker Barrow."

Bonnie laughed and groaned. "And you thought that was a good idea?"

"No. I just thought it was funny. And at this point, funny is about all we've got," Finn said with a rueful smile.

"We really aren't anything like Bonnie Parker and Clyde Barrow."

"I've decided that the media doesn't care, Bonnie Rae. They want us to be . . . and so that's the story they'll tell."

18

parallel Lines

WE DROVE FOR an hour in the dark, half scared, half euphoric, not really knowing where we were going, but driving because that was the only thing we could do. Every second had taken on a relevancy that I didn't want to miss. I was in love, I was in lust, I was afraid, I was fearless—contradictions that made perfect sense and no sense at all. Maybe it was the adrenaline of running from circumstances that seemed determined to hunt us down, but it was more likely the unfinished lovemaking back at the motel, and I was struggling not to beg Clyde to pull over and let me have my way with him in the back seat.

The tension simmered between us, a buzzing undercurrent that felt as intoxicating as a pounding bass line and a killer beat, and a song started to form in my mind, more a feeling than real words, but when I started to hum, Finn just looked at me, a smile on his lips and his eyebrows raised, and I almost moaned right out loud, closing my eyes against the desire that had to wait, just a little longer. I felt simultaneously weightless and endless, floating there beside him, as if he held me on a string.

Weightless and endless. Timeless and restless. Hopelessly breathless. The words seeped into my head, my yearning composing a chorus without conscious thought. I knew what the chords would be, and took note of the arrangement in my head, creating verses and a bridge to go with it. I wished I had Finn's guitar. I hummed as I went, composing feverishly.

"Don't just hum. Sing," Finn urged.

I didn't want to sing the words out loud. I didn't want to scare him. Finn wasn't as far along in his feelings as I was. I was there. All in. Love. But he wasn't. And me, singing songs about needing Infinity probably wasn't going to make him get there any faster.

"What's your favorite song?" I asked instead. "If I know it, I'll sing it."

"What's that song you sang, standing on the slide?"

"Wayfaring Stranger?" I asked, surprised.

"Yeah. That's my favorite song." Finn nodded once, definitively.

"You know that song?"

"No. I'd never heard it before," he said frankly, his eyes cutting to my face and then back to the road.

"And now it's your favorite?"

"Now it's my favorite."

His sweetness moved me, and my desire for him swelled again, stronger, and I trembled, wishing I were brave enough to say what I wanted to say.

"Sing it. Please?" he asked.

And so I did. I sang until the interior of Bear's car reverberated with my voice, and my heart was shredded from the feelings clawing to get out.

∞

WE WERE BOTH too tired to drive for long—even with me singing to keep us both awake. Finn told me to sleep, but I didn't want to drift off when I knew he was struggling to keep his eyes open. We agreed to stop at the next big town and pulled off in a place called Guymon. A large, white, water tower gleamed softly in the dark, the name of the town written boldly in black, telling wandering strangers like Finn and me exactly where we were.

There was a Walmart that was well lit and apparently open all night. We were both in desperate need of clothing and supplies, but we needed sleep even worse, and sleeping in a dark parking lot liberally spotted with cars seemed safer than checking into another motel at the moment. We would shop in the morning.

We parked at the far edge, tucking ourselves into a corner close to an exit, far enough away from the other cars to afford us some privacy, but close enough to make us look like just another patron who didn't want his ride scratched or dented by a wayward shopping cart. The windows were dark, and we laid our seats back as far as they would go and tried to rest for even a couple of hours. The closest I could get to Finn was his hand in mine, and I thought wistfully of the Blazer sitting in an impound yard in St. Louis. I marveled once again that Finn was even talking to me, not to mention holding my hand in his and gently stroking the skin above my wrist as he lay beside me in the dark.

I listened to him breathe, soothed by his fingers and the steadiness of his presence. And right before I let sleep pull me under, I whispered the words I needed to say.

"I love you, Finn." And maybe it was my tired mind or my wistful heart. Maybe it was just a dream, but I thought I heard him whisper back, "I love you too, Bonnie."

∞

WE'D LEFT THE blizzards behind, but it was still February, and Oklahoma wasn't warm. We were fortunate to have our coats and for the relatively mild overnight temperatures, but we still woke up shivering several times. Finn would restart the car and get it warm before shutting it off and giving us another hour of sleep before the cold woke us up again. All in all, it wasn't a great night's rest, and when the sun rose and started to warm the inside of the car, we both welcomed the heat and slept more deeply than we had all night. It was mid-morning before we sidled into the Walmart, slipping into the bathroom with the appropriate stick figure on the door, and made use of the facilities. Finn still had some of his things, and I had reinforcements in my purse. I made use of them after washing my face and hands with cheap soap, brushing my teeth with gusto, and sticking my head under the tap to tame the little turkey tail in the back before applying moisturizer, mascara, and lip gloss, which was all I had in my bag.

It was a Friday morning, and Walmart was populated only by the occasional mom with very young children and the random senior citizen, which made my bathroom makeover less conspicuous. Only one woman came in while I stood in front of the mirror, and she went straight to the toilets. I made sure that when she came out I was no longer standing in front of the mirror but was huddled with my palms stretched out beneath a loud hand dryer, my face completely averted. No one expects to see a celebrity in their local Walmart bathroom. Most of us don't really look at each other anyway. Our eyes glance off without really registering what we're seeing. It's human nature. It's polite society. Ignore each other unless someone is grotesquely fat or immodestly dressed or disfigured in some way—and then we pretend not to see, but we see everything. I was none of those things, and so far human nature was working in my favor.

I found Finn waiting on a bench outside the bathroom, hair slicked back into his customary tail, his face a little shiny from scrubbing, and the stubble he'd been sporting shaved away.

"You shaved?"

"There wasn't anyone in there, but I soaped up and went into the stall and shaved by feel. Got a little soap on my shirt, but I feel a helluva lot better." He looked good too. I smiled at him as I told him so.

We stuffed his brush and shaving kit into my purse so we weren't quite as conspicuous and made our way around the store, grabbing up what we needed. Finn threw a Bonnie Rae *Come Undone* CD into the basket, as well as my four other albums, claiming it would save me from having to sing all the way to LA. I pulled the tag off a pair of non-prescription glasses and set them on my nose, further changing my appearance, and put a matching pair in the cart so I could pay for them at the register without taking them off.

I might be the only girl ever to go to the Academy Awards made up in cosmetics purchased at Walmart, but I hit the makeup aisle, selecting a variety of the most expensive products in several shades, along with everything I would need to apply them. I threw in some hair product that wasn't going to make my little boy hairstyle look any different than it did at that very moment, but at least I wouldn't have to stick my head under the faucet.

I saw Finn's eyes rest on the magazines at the checkout stand, my face plastered across several with screaming headlines and little insets of Finn's mug shots. He looked away immediately, and I reached for him, sick all over again. He squeezed my hand, and I felt like crying in gratitude, but sent him out ahead of me, not wanting the clerk to get an eyeful of us together, so close to the tabloids.

Several hundred dollars later, I was heading to the front entrance when over the intercom a voice that sounded a little like Reba McIntire informed Walmart customers that the owner of a black Dodge Charger with the Tennessee license plate BEARTRP needed to please return to their vehicle.

My heart sank to my knees along with my hopes. Bear trap. That was Bear's license plate. Finn had already left the store. Were the police outside waiting for us? And if so, why would they have a Walmart manager tell us to return to the car. Wouldn't they just wait until we returned? All of these questions shot through my mind instantaneously, and I decided the only option was to exit the store and hope to hell Finn wasn't handcuffed in the back of a police car.

He wasn't. He was waiting by the entrance, his eyes trained on the far corner where the Charger was parked. There wasn't a police car in sight, but there was an older model Suburban idling nearby, and a man surveying Bear's car with a phone to his ear.

"What's happening?" I asked.

"I think that guy ran into Bear's car," Finn said.

"And instead of driving away, he did the honest thing and is waiting for us to come out to exchange insurance information," I finished.

"Yeah." Finn sounded grim. "Let's go. We're not in trouble yet."

As we approached, the man on the phone turned toward us and seemed as relieved as he was apologetic. He was a middle-aged, heavy-set man in a tie and slacks that were a tad too short, making him look slightly pathetic and unkempt. If the paper doll family decal on the back window of his Suburban was any indication, he had ten zillion kids and several pets, and his clothes were probably way down on the list of priorities. His Suburban only had a few scratches that may have been there before his collision, but that was obviously not making him feel any better.

"Oh, hey! Are you the owners? Man, I am so sorry. My Burban sits high, and I couldn't see your car in my rear view. I was in a hurry, and I pulled out too far, too fast, and just nailed the back of your car."

Bear was going to kill us. The whole panel above the bumper was caved in, one taillight was broken, and the trunk had sprung open from the impact.

"I already called the cops because I wasn't sure if you were in the store or if you'd parked here for a car pool or something and weren't coming back for a while. There are quite a few people who do that here in Guymon—'course you're from Tennessee. Guess I should have thought of that. Man, I am so sorry!"

Finn pushed the damaged trunk all the way open and unloaded the basket swiftly, his eyes darting between the adjacent street and the entrances into the Walmart parking lot. He hadn't said anything to the honest Abe who was wringing his hands and talking non-stop. Then Finn slammed the trunk several times, trying to get it to catch, even though it didn't quite line up with the latch anymore, causing the agitated driver of the Suburban to pause mid-sentence and frown at Finn in confusion. I slid a folded hundred dollar bill into the man's wrinkled breast pocket, gave it a pat, stepped by him, and climbed into the passenger seat. Finn slammed the trunk once more and luckily it held. He slid in beside me a second later.

"H-hey! Hey! Don't you want my insurance information? You can't just leave! I messed up your car!" he cried.

We backed out, gliding by the dumbfounded man who had pulled the bill I'd given him from his pocket and stood staring down at it, holding an end in each hand. A police cruiser turned onto the street that led to the enormous Walmart parking lot, passing us without a glance just as our light turned green, and we merged into the traffic headed toward the freeway nearby.

"Doesn't drive any different," I said optimistically.

"You're the one who's telling Bear," Finn said.

∞

"I CAN'T GET a hold of him. I texted and left a message. I think I'm going to be buying Bear a new car when it's all said and done. Do you think we need to find some new wheels?" I chewed my lip, and Finn reached over and pulled it from my teeth with his middle finger, making me forget, momentarily, about conspicuous license plates and missing bumpers.

"Where? I'm sure the guy in the Suburban gave the license plate to the police. But he was the one at fault, and judging from what we saw, he'll take full blame. The police might run the plates, but that will just lead them to Bear. Which is why we need to give him a heads up. He'll handle it." Finn was playing the role of the optimist now, apparently. It made me breathe a little easier.

"So what next?"

"Vegas."

"How far?"

"I don't know exactly. We'll be dropping into the northern edge of Texas, and we'll make New Mexico tonight, but I've got to get some gas. We'll get some things from the trunk and make a plan and figure out how far we've got to go."

Finn used my new phone for a quick Mapquest check, and reported that we still had fourteen hours to go and another four after that to get to LA. We fueled up at a truck stop, using the bathrooms to change into clean clothes. We didn't eat inside or even go in and out at the same time, trying to lower the odds of being recognized together. We were both nervous and were eager to be away from people, now that the story seemed to have garnered national attention. I'd been on the covers of magazines before, but Finn hadn't, and I didn't want him seeing them at every turn. Even as crazy as I knew press coverage could be, I didn't understand what was happening. Why was my life of such interest? And what could have possibly prompted any magazines to run a story on me and Clyde? And that brought the fear back. How could I be so afraid of losing someone who I'd just found? In less than a week, he had become the only thing that mattered.

We drove for four hours, the day clear and sunny, the temperatures climbing into the low 60s, signaling February was almost behind us, and that we had officially arrived in the desert. Finn listened to all of my albums, remarking on this and that, and he seemed intent on every word, like he couldn't get enough. He skipped through the songs with heavy instrumentation, perky melodies, and flying fiddles. He seemed drawn to the ballads, the stripped down vocals, and the songs that told a story. It was a little strange for me, listening to myself sing for hours on end, but his intense focus on my voice was almost erotic, and I leaned my seat back and watched him quietly, letting my thoughts wander.

I'd been with Minnie this time last year. I'd gone home for our birthday. Minnie was going through chemo again, and had lost all her hair for the second time. I'd felt guilty that I hadn't shaved my head with her, like I'd done before, and she'd told me I was ridiculous.

"You're not required to be my twin in every way, Bonnie. Looking alike is a pain in the butt. Plus, you look a whole lot better than I do right now, so the fact that I look like you, but not nearly as good as you, is a little painful for me.

"It is?" I don't know why that hurt my feelings. But it did. Minnie must have seen the hurt in my face, because she grabbed my hand and smiled.

"I've always loved that we looked alike. I thought it was fun. And I thought you were beautiful—which comforted me. Because if you were beautiful, I must be too," Minnie soothed.

"I would tell you that you are indeed very beautiful, but that seems a little self-serving." I lay back on the bed beside her, still holding her hand. We lay quietly for a minute.

"Why are we spending our birthday in Grassley?" I whined abruptly. "I have loads of money, and we're twenty-one. We should go to Atlantic City!"

"Nah. Let's go to Vegas. I've always wanted to go to Vegas."

"You have?" I immediately started to plot how I could get us there as soon as possible.

"Yeah, I have." Minnie nodded thoughtfully. "I want to dance in one of those shows where the girls wear feathers on their heads—"

"And nothing on their chests?" I interrupted, sitting up so I could grin down into her face.

"I think it would be very freeing!" Minnie protested. "Just dancing and kicking my legs—"

"And shaking your ta tas," I interrupted again and jumped up on the bed, kicking and shimmying and bouncing her around.

"Everyone looks exactly alike under all that makeup and all that bling. Nobody would know which boobs were mine." She giggled, flailing helplessly as I jumped as high as I could.

"I would! Your boobs look just like mine!" I shrieked, laughing.

"Ha! Not anymore." Minnie lifted up her shirt and looked down at her shrunken chest, and I stopped jumping, my legs suddenly weak, my laughter gone. I fell down beside her on the bed, horrified and grief-stricken and unable to hide my reaction. I looked at her. At all of her. And I saw what I'd been refusing to see. She was right. Her breasts looked nothing like mine. Her body looked nothing like mine. Even her face, impossibly angular with her weight loss, looked different from mine. And I wanted to cover my eyes and break every mirror so I could keep the image of us the way we were fresh in my mind. She was being ripped from me, piece by piece.

"Minnie. Oh, Minnie May." I put my arms around her, and I couldn't stop the tears. *"I'll take you to Vegas, baby. I'll take you when your ta tas grow back, and you and I will dance topless with feathers and high heels, and Gran will be so scandalized."*

Minnie didn't cry with me—she just let me hold her, and she laid her head on my shoulder as I rubbed her back.

"She'll be scandalized. But if we're any good, she'll be the first to call the press. Anonymously of course," Minnie whispered, and I laughed wetly, the truth simultaneously hilarious and tragic. Minnie let me hold her for a few minutes longer, and then she pulled away and met my eyes seriously. Hopefully.

"It's not as bad as it looks, Bonnie Rae. I actually feel pretty good. You'll see. I'm getting better. The next time you come to Grassley, I'll have the biggest boobs you've ever seen. You've got Dolly hair, but I'll have Dolly boobs. And I forbid you to get them too. No twinner boobs! I want everyone to be looking at me and only me when we go to Vegas."

I would be in Vegas tomorrow. And Minnie wouldn't be with me. I wouldn't be dancing topless with a feathered headdress alongside my sister. I would be dancing sister-less, like a feather in the wind, a spinning top, the world around me like a colorful stream of nothing.

I closed my eyes, suddenly impossibly dizzy. And Finn reached out and touched my face.

"Where did you go, Bonnie Rae?" he said softly.

"What do you mean?" I liked the way his fingers felt on my skin and leaned into his palm. The dizziness abated instantly.

"Sometimes you're right there, right on the surface, full of life and so crazy and beautiful that it makes me ache."

His deep voice was melancholy, and I hated that I had caused it.

"Then there are times, days like today," he continued softly, "when you're buried deep, and your beautiful face is just a house where you live. But the lights aren't on, and the windows and doors are locked down tight. I know you're in there, but I'm not with you. Maybe Minnie's with you. But I don't think so. You're alone. And I wish you would let me in."

I climbed over the space between our seats and slid into his lap, laying my head on his shoulder, wrapping my arms around him as tightly as I could, breathing him in. I lifted the blinds on my metaphorical house, the one he described so well, and I gave him a glimpse inside. He continued driving, left arm wrapped around me, right arm on the wheel, and he settled his lips on my forehead.

"Our birthday is tomorrow," I said, placing my mouth by his ear so I didn't have to speak up. "Sometimes I miss her so much, that dark corners and locked doors are all I can manage."

"Ah, Bonnie. I'm sorry," he whispered.

"Are birthdays hard for you too?" I asked.

"Fisher and I were born two hours apart. Fish was born first, on August 7th, at around eleven pm. I was born on August 8th, a little after one am. So we each have our own birthday. But, yeah. Birthdays suck." Finn was silent for several heartbeats. "So when you're sad like this . . . and quiet, it's because of Minnie?"

"Today is hard because I'm thinking about tomorrow. And I'm

thinking about what I've lost. But I had days like this even before Minnie died. Days I just checked out. Gran says it's just the blues. Everybody gets the blues. Maybe that's all they are. But they feel more like grays than blues, and more black than gray sometimes. It's always worse after I've been working too hard, singing night after night, pouring myself out all over the stage so people can lap me up. I love it, the singing, the performing, the people, the music, but sometimes I forget to save something . . . the something that is essentially me, and my light goes out. Sometimes it takes a while to get it burning again."

"I see." Finn's hand stroked up and down my back, soothing me. His fingers traced the line of my jaw and dipped into the whorl of my ear and down across my lips. I turned and pressed my lips into his neck in response and felt an easing in my chest and a corresponding tightening low in my belly.

"But you have a key, Finn, and I give you permission to come on in," I said. "Even if it's dark, and you don't know what you'll find, you come on in, okay?" I felt an ache in my throat that grew as I spoke. "I want you in here with me, even if it isn't pretty, even if I don't invite you."

Finn's arm tightened around me, and he nuzzled my cheek with his, pulling me so close I could barely breathe, and I pressed my face into him and closed my eyes, and willed him to join me there behind my lids. Within minutes he pulled off an exit that led to somewhere else, pulling into a gas station that had long since closed its doors. A sign that lied about snacks and cold beer hung loosely on a pole, seesawing back and forth in the brisk February wind, the ancient advertising almost illegible, the sun having stolen its color, leaving it faded and on the brink of extinction. I wondered if the bright lights would eventually do the same to me.

With the heat billowing out around us and inside us, the lights of the dash our only stars, Finn let his hands slide over me, breathing life into me, letting his colors flow through me, his mouth call out to me. And I met him at the door.

19

Curve sketching

MALCOLM "BEAR" JOHNSON, long time body guard to singer Bonnie Rae Shelby, was the apparent victim of a carjacking at a gas station between St. Louis, Missouri and Nashville, Tennessee some time yesterday. Sources tell us he was unconscious when paramedics and police arrived at the scene and his wallet and phone were taken, as well as his vehicle, making identification difficult, but police have confirmed that it was indeed Malcolm Johnson, that he was shot at close range, and that he is in critical condition at an area hospital. There is no word on whether there are any witnesses or possible leads to finding the perpetrators of this vicious attack, and the police are not commenting further at this time.

Bonnie Rae Shelby was believed to be in the company of ex-convict Infinity James Clyde in the St Louis area around the same time, leading to rampant speculation about a possible meeting between the star and her bodyguard, Bear Johnson, which may have turned violent. At this juncture, police still aren't willing to say definitively whether Miss Shelby is being held against her will. But the similarities between the attack on Mr. Johnson and another crime committed by Infinity James Clyde are hard to ignore. Infinity Clyde served time for the 2006 armed robbery of a Boston convenience *store. One person died and another was seriously wounded.*

∞

THE BLANKET BENEATH them was actually an unzipped sleeping bag, purchased earlier that morning. Another sat nearby, still tightly bound, waiting for use. It wasn't cold, but the sun was setting, and it would be soon. Finn considered pulling it over Bonnie, where she lay nestled beside him, her head burrowed like she was hiding from something, the way she always slept, but he waited, not wanting to make them look like vagrants.

They were about sixty-five miles outside Albuquerque, New Mexico in a little town that claimed it was the nicest place on Earth, which didn't say much for the planet.

They had found a city park and backed Bear's car into a spot, the trunk hugging the curb, hiding the plates as best they could. Finn didn't think they were being chased through the southwest, but in the same breath wouldn't have been surprised if an entire brigade of Texas Rangers were bearing down on them. It had been that kind of journey. They spread a blanket in a far corner of the park beneath a few scrubby pine trees, far from the playground and the empty ball field and hungrily consumed a Walmart picnic.

Bonnie had curled up after their meal, sleepy and satisfied, and he'd stroked her hair, needing to touch her, even if it was only that, a hand in her hair. Her breathing had eventually slowed, until he realized she'd given in to the exhaustion that had pursued her since he he'd seen it flicker across her face a lifetime ago, when he'd found her braced on the metal railing of an enormous bridge. A lifetime ago. A week ago.

A father with two small children, a girl and a boy, had crossed the park a half an hour before, not too far from where they lay, and was now pushing his kids on the swings in the opposite corner of the park. He'd noticed them, no doubt about it, but he didn't keep looking their way and seemed intent on his children.

Two boys—brothers, he would guess from the way they fought—were throwing a baseball to each other nearby. One boy, obviously the superior athlete, threw the ball up and tossed out suggestions with each pitch. The younger boy seemed distracted, and his attention kept wandering as if he found other things more fascinating.

"Catch it, Finn. Man! Pay attention." Fish's voice rang in his head, echoing the boys as they argued nearby.

"Watch out!" Fish hollered as Finn stared at the ball curving toward him, not lifting his mitt at all. At the last minute he raised his glove and the ball smacked his palm with a satisfying thwack, as if he'd been faking Fish out all along.

"Where are you?" Fish grumbled.

"I was thinking about parabolas," Finn answered, his mind still pondering the curve the ball made, as Fish threw it high in the air, thinking about how it climbed slowly only to fall in ever increasing speed as it found its way back to Earth.

"Ah, man! You and Dad. It's bad enough that he's always thinking about that stuff. Why do you have to too?"

"I can't help if, Fish." Finn said honestly. "They're everywhere." He threw the ball to his brother as high as he could, and Fish positioned himself beneath it, perfectly judging where it would fall.

Curved lines. They *were* everywhere. Finn stretched out on the sleeping bag, resting his head on his hand, caught between the memory of his brother and the woman who lay beside him, the curve of her rounded hip drawing his eyes the way the ball, curving into the sky, had caught his attention and caused the wheels in his mind to spin, taking him away from his brother and the game at hand. Fish had asked the same question Finn had asked Bonnie earlier. *Where are you?*

Is that how Fish had felt when Finn went inside his head? Where are you? Why can't I come with you?

Finn touched Bonnie's cheek, another slope, a sweet curve, a quadratic equation that he could easily solve.

"A curve is just the conjunction of many straight, infinitesimally short, lines," Finn whispered, as if the mathematical definition of something so lovely would lessen its allure. It didn't.

Everything about Bonnie called to him. He wanted to peel off her clothes and answer that call, pressing his skin against hers from thigh to chest, sinking into her, consuming her so there was no more room, no more space, no more distance.

He knew they were moving too fast, yet he worried they would never get there. He didn't mean sexually—although the fear that that would be denied them too was very present. The almost desperate need to have her was something he had never experienced, but sex was as fleeting and infinitesimal as his longing was infinite and never ending, and he didn't just want a million infinitesimal lines stitched together to create a curve that they would both simply slide down. He wanted something beyond the rise and fall of physical satiation, he wanted a moment that stretched out long and straight, where it was just Bonnie and Clyde, where fate released them from the rollercoaster they were on. And that moment seemed unattainable.

He felt like Achilles constantly pursuing the plodding tortoise, unable to close one gap without a new gap springing up between them. The distances were growing smaller and smaller, but so was time, and Finn feared they would run out before he could solve the paradox.

In spite of his morose thoughts, the reminder of the paradox made him smile again, and his eyes found the boys once more, now racing to the playground, the older brother easily out in front.

Instead of stories at night, Jason Clyde would tell his boys paradoxes—the Greek philosopher Zeno had written many of them, all seemingly simple yet filled with mind twisting questions. They were stories, but not. Fish had come to hate them and wrote his own endings, the philosophical musings and mathematical conundrums irritants to a boy who craved action, motion, and uncomplicated solutions.

Fish had listened attentively to the paradox of Achilles, declared it ridiculous, and promptly challenged Finn to a race, giving him a head start just like the tortoise, eventually overtaking him, just as he always did. Fish was faster, just like Achilles.

"See?" Fish had said to Finn and his father. "Stupid. Achilles would have passed that dumb turtle before the turtle could even create another gap between them."

"It's not about speed, Fish," his father had explained. "It's supposed to challenge the way we think about the world versus the way the world actually is. Zeno argued that change and motion weren't real."

Finn had puzzled out the paradox all night long and had written his own solution and proudly presented it to his dad the next day, complete with ideas about convergent and divergent theory. His dad had been so proud, but Fish had just sighed gustily and challenged Finn to another race.

The paradox reveals a mismatch between the way we think about the world and the way the world really is, his father had said.

Finn had no illusions anymore about the way the world really was. It had shown itself too many times—and it always worked against you. They were running, the gap was closing, but he feared the paradox of Bonnie and Clyde might be insolvable.

∞

I AWOKE TO darkness and the feel of Finn beside me, his body large and warm, the air on my cheeks cool and crisp. We were still in the park. I could see stars through the pine needles above us—tiny, sharp pieces of broken glass. I stared at them for a while, and the song, "Nelly Gray," tiptoed into my head—the line about the moon climbing the mountain, and the stars shining too. Minnie and I would sing it to each other, changing the name from Nelly Gray to Bonnie Rae or Minnie Mae, depending on who was singing it.

Oh, my poor, Minnie Mae, they have taken you away
And I'll never see my darling, anymore
I'm sitting by the river and a weeping all the day
For you've gone
From the old Kentucky shore.

Now my canoe is under water, and my banjo is unstrung
And I'm tired of living, anymore
My eyes shall be cast downward, and my songs will be unsung
While I stay on the old Kentucky shore.

I hadn't stayed on the old Kentucky shore. I was somewhere in New Mexico, and I had no idea what time it was. I had been so tired, but now I was wide awake, and not nearly as tired of living as I'd been just days before. I rolled carefully from beneath the sleeping bag Finn had obviously pulled over us. He needed all the sleep he could get, but I had to visit the little girl's room. Or the little girl's concrete out house, which was what the bathrooms at the park were, but they had running water and a toilet, which was all I really needed at the moment.

Using my phone for a flashlight, I did my business, washed my face and hands, and brushed my teeth. I ran my fingers through my hair, fixing the damn turkey tail that was the first to spring to attention any time I rested my head. I'd set my phone on the sink, and the white light shining up from below me made me look ghoulish.

The little display informed me that it was 11:00 pm. I had been asleep for at least six hours. I felt recharged and did my best to make myself look that way. I'd filled my purse with my new cosmetics, and I wanted to be beautiful for Finn, but it was almost impossible to see by the light of my phone. When I was done, I peered at myself, holding the phone close to the mirror, hoping I hadn't made a mess of my face. The upside was that if Finn still liked me after all this, and I still liked him, then we had something. No candlelight dinners and best behavior, no pressed shirts, salon visits, and perfumed hugs. This was us. Real and unplugged.

I found I preferred real. Like I told Finn, I'd been searching for it. There had been so little of it in my life in the last seven years, so little that was genuine and foundational, that I wanted to cling to it, even if it wasn't pretty. The problem with life is that sometimes it's hard to know what's real. I figured it was the reason some people weigh six hundred pounds. Because in that moment, while the food is in front of you, while it is being lifted to your mouth, and then swallowed, that moment when it hits your stomach, that moment is bliss. And it's real. Sure you feel too full, but being too full is also real.

I turned away from the mirror, slid my belongings back into my purse, and left the restroom, picking my way across the grassy expanse that separated me from Finn. He was crouched down, rolling up the sleeping bags. He saw me coming and paused, looking up at me.

"I woke up and you were gone. I thought maybe you'd been dragged off by the brothers playing catch. I fell asleep to them arguing. It reminded me of me and Fish."

"Brothers? At eleven o'clock at night?"

"Nah. Hours ago. You ready to roll? We've got to drive if we want to make it to Vegas tomorrow."

I peered down at him, trying to make out his expression in the darkness. I brushed his hair back from his face. He'd taken off the elastic band, and it hung loosely around his shoulders. The strands I touched were damp, and I could smell soap and toothpaste. He must have woken up not long after I did.

"Where are we?" I was talking about our distance from Las Vegas, but I looked up at the stars as I asked him. The stars were brilliant, the night so still and cool that each glittering speck competed for my attention, and I wished I could turn the world upside down and fall into them, snatching them up as I floated by. Curse gravity for keeping me earthbound.

The song I'd been composing since the day before danced through my head, and I added the missing line that I'd been searching for. *No matter how I try I'm bound by gravity.* That was it. I could hear the melody and feel how my fingers would move across the strings as I sang the words.

"We're in the center of the universe." Finn had risen and now stood with his face lifted skyward as well.

"New Mexico is the center of the universe?" That seemed like a much better slogan than Nicest Little Place on Earth. They needed to change their sign.

"If you travel in any direction from this point, you'll never run out of space." He didn't look at me as he spoke, but I'd stopped looking at the stars so I could look at him. "You could be anywhere on Earth, and technically you'd still be the center of the universe. We're surrounded by infinite space."

"All that space makes me feel like floating away. And never coming back." I didn't mean to sound forlorn, but I suppose I did. It just looked peaceful, and I liked the idea of being surrounded by infinity.

I told him that too, wrapping my arms around him, surrounding him as best I could, but I could tell he was still thinking about me floating away. I always managed to say the wrong thing. He was silent as we loaded our things and left the park.

We flew through the dark as if we owned it—the late hour clearing the roads, the mild weather clearing the skies. And it felt like we were indeed at the center of the universe, the fulcrum, Finn had called it. He'd turned up the music until it made the dashboard shake, listening to me tell him how I was coming "undone," the title track to my most recent release.

*I've lost a shoe,
A few buttons are gone
The dress I'm wearing
Has come undone*

*It's come undone
But nobody stares
They don't seem to notice
My shoulders are bare*

But I'm coming undone.

Finn flipped the music off abruptly, as if he'd suddenly decided he couldn't stand the song. Then he looked at me, the dim light from the dash highlighting the angular planes of his face.

"Did you write that song?" he asked.

"I write all my songs. They didn't trust me on the first full-sized album, the one that came after my *Nashville Forever* release. Management picked most of the songs and only let me write a couple. The two I wrote out-sold and out-performed their songs in a very big way. My producer decided to let me write a few more on the next album. Same thing happened. On the fourth and fifth albums, I either wrote or co-wrote every song."

Finn nodded, but I could tell he wasn't thinking about all my number one hits. "Didn't anybody wonder about you . . . after they heard that song? Bear, your gran, anyone?"

"It's a sad song. Heartbreak sells. They all loved it. But most people can relate with heartbreak. What was it Bonnie Parker said in her poem?" I had a head for lyrics, and poetry wasn't much different. I pulled the lines up easily and spoke them without thought.

*"From heart-break some people have suffered
from weariness some people have died.
But take it all in all;*

our troubles are small,
'til we get like Bonnie and Clyde."

"Til we get like Bonnie and Clyde?" Finn asked. He sounded funny, like the line bothered him.

I looked at him, not sure what he was getting at, waiting for him to tell me. He seemed to be thinking about something and was quiet for several minutes.

"Are we there yet, Bonnie Rae? Are we like Bonnie and Clyde? Desperate? Hunted? Driving on a dark road that just leads to more trouble?"

"I hope so," I answered instantly, half-teasing.

Finn stared at me, shaking his head. "What in the hell does that mean?"

"They were together. Through it all, they were together." I wasn't teasing now.

He looked away immediately, staring out at the road and the lights of Albuquerque twinkling in the distance. His eyes, when he looked back at me, seemed impossibly bright. Brighter than the city lights, and I couldn't look away.

I shrugged my shoulders, not understanding the intensity of his expression.

"They were doomed from the start," he said flatly.

"Not doomed. Immortalized," I said automatically, surprising myself.

"I'm not interested in that kind of immortality, Bonnie Rae. I'd rather grow old and unknown than die young by your side and have the world write books and make movies about my sad, short life. I don't want to be Bonnie and Clyde!"

I gasped, rejection slapping me in the face and stealing my breath. It was my turn to stare ahead, eyes wet, trying to control my emotions. "Don't worry, Infinity. Didn't you tell me infinity plus one is still infinity? Without me, you'll still be you," I said finally.

Finn swore and pounded on the horn, an angry blast no one

heard.

"I don't want to be without you, Bonnie! Don't you get that? I am in love with you! I've known you for one week. And I'm in love with you! Crazy, drive-off-a-cliff-if-you-asked-me-to, in love with you. But I don't want to drive off a cliff! I want to live. I want to live with you! Do you want that? Or do you still think about jumping off bridges and going down in a hail of bullets?"

Finn slammed his hand against the horn again, over and over, cursing as he did. And I realized there were tears on my cheeks. His face was a study in contradictions, fury and despair battling it out across his features. I hadn't been able to move, to even speak. I was too stunned.

"Finn?" I whispered, reaching out my hand. He pushed me away, like he couldn't bear to be touched. He rolled down the windows, filling the interior of the car with roaring cold, effectively drowning out any attempts at conversation, but I screamed into the wind anyway. I screamed that I loved him too, but the wind whisked the words away. I never took my eyes from his face, watching him as he gritted his teeth and drove, never looking my way, shaking off my every attempt to reach him.

I stopped screaming and fell into silence with him, wondering what had happened, knowing something had, knowing another bridge had been crossed and not sure we were still on the same side.

20
Critical Point

FINN PULLED OFF at the first exit, an exit surrounded by businesses closed and dark and locked up tight. The gas station was well lit, boasting twenty-four hour service and the lowest prices in town. Bonnie had stopped trying to touch him and had turned in the passenger seat, averting her face. He knew she was crying, and he swiped at his own face, making sure his own humiliating emotion wasn't visible.

That damn song. Bonnie singing about coming undone, falling apart. And here he was, coming apart too. She seemed so blasé about death, so hell bent on floating away, and he'd lost control. He told himself it was anger, frustration. He told himself it was an anomaly. He never got emotional. Never. Not since Fish died. Not when he'd been sent to prison. Not when he'd been beaten up and marked in his cell, not ever.

Fish was the emotional one. The loose cannon. Not Finn. He was the opposite of Fish. He had been the counter balance to his wild brother. He told himself he needed to be that for Bonnie, too. He needed to be the voice of reason, the ballast. But instead, he found himself completely out of control, passionate, impulsive, and emotional.

He shoved the door open and stepped out, unsure of whether he should risk recognition by paying cash inside or use his card and mark their path if someone was really looking for them. Bonnie seemed to think the frenzy was more media driven than legally instigated, but they didn't really know anything for sure. That thought had him trudging inside, keeping his head down as he shot a fifty-dollar bill at the clerk, grunting out the pump number and immediately turning away. The clerk repeated the request cheerily, and Finn pushed back out of the doors hating that he had to hide his face and look over his shoulder.

He didn't want to get back in the car. He was hungry and agitated and he and Bonnie needed a distraction. But everything in the vicinity looked dark, though he could hear a pulsing bass line coming from somewhere, and he turned his face toward the sound as he finished filling the tank.

A car pulled up on the other side of the pump, and Finn eyed the occupants of the black Escalade from the corner of his eye. Definitely not cops or the kind of people who wanted anything to do with cops.

"Is there a bar around here?" he found himself asking, as he met the eyes of the driver of the Escalade over the top of the pump.

The driver raised his eyebrows in surprise and gave Finn a quick once over, as if making sure he was club material, worthy of the information. Finn must have passed because he answered without much hesitation.

"Yeah, man. There is. Hear that?" He stopped, listening, and Finn assumed he was referring to the throbbing bass he'd noticed. The man pointed in the direction of the music.

"That's Verani's. It's a club. They stay open until three a.m. Down the block on your left. It's completely dark on the outside, except for the big, red V. Parking lot in back, basement entrance. No cover charge, good food, and anything else you might want." His eyes flickered away when he said this, and Finn knew he wasn't talking about beer.

Finn nodded, hanging up the nozzle. He wasn't interested in "anything else." But music, darkness, and food sounded just about right. And he needed to hold Bonnie, now that the rage had passed. He'd told her he loved her. Now he needed to show her. Maybe they could dance in the shadows, maybe pretend they were a normal couple and not outlaws or runaways for an hour or two. They had time.

"Thanks," he nodded to the Escalade driver, who nodded back.

Bonnie had flipped down the visor, which lit up accommodatingly. She was smoothing a makeup brush over her face as he slid back into the Charger. She didn't comment as he pulled back onto the road, her gaze on her reflection, reapplying the shadow around her dark eyes, but she looked at him, her brow creased, when he pulled into the parking lot behind the black, windowless building with the slashing red V and turned off the car.

"I don't want to be Bonnie and Clyde. I want to be Bonnie and Finn. Just for a little while. Okay?" It was all the apology she was going to get—he was still angry. And he was still very, very afraid. Afraid of loving her, afraid of losing her, and mostly, afraid of losing himself in the process. But he did love her. And that emotion was stronger than all the others.

She nodded, her eyes wide. "Is this a club?"

"Yeah, it is. Hopefully it's dark and smoky and full of criminals who never listen to country music or watch entertainment TV. People who would never make a concerned citizen's call to the cops or the news channels, even if they happened to see a famous singer eating at a table next to theirs." He stopped, wondering if he was being an idiot. He decided he was, and he didn't care. "I'm guessing you love to dance. I don't. But I'm thinking I might like to dance with you."

The smile—the big, beaming one that had started it all, stretched across Bonnie's pretty face. She turned and added a couple strokes to her eye makeup, deepening the effect. She slicked color on her lips and ran her fingers over her hair. She even dug some earrings from a little, plastic, Walmart sack she'd tucked into a pocket of her purse. The dangling loops made her look dressed up, and when she pulled off her heavy sweatshirt and tucked the black tank top beneath into her snug jeans, he grabbed her brush and ran it through his hair, deciding maybe he'd better spruce up too. He gathered his hair into a tail and unzipped his leather coat so he didn't feel so buttoned up, but he grabbed Bonnie's from the back seat, a whim he would be grateful for later, though he didn't know it then.

They descended the stairs into Verani's, and no one stood by the door to greet them or to turn them away, so they slipped inside, the murky light welcoming, the music deafening. Finn snaked his arm around Bonnie, looking around for a place to sit. A long bar stood to his immediate left, and they sidled up beside it, waiting for the bartender to look their way.

He was a young guy with gauges in his ears and a hair do that was severely short on the sides and swooped back, Elvis-style, on the top. He was non-stop motion, filling and fixing, sliding and squeezing, his hands sure beneath the never-ending orders. But when he looked at Finn his eyes skittered away as if he was amped on something and couldn't hold still long enough to maintain eye contact. Someone called him Jagger, and when Finn asked him if they were still serving food, Jagger called out to one of the girls all in black, weaving in and out of the crowd.

She led them to an alcove that had a lousy view of the stage and the dance floor, which was probably why it was still unoccupied at after one in the morning. The waitress plopped two slim menus on the table and promised she'd be back. She wasn't very friendly or chatty, which was fine with Finn.

There wasn't a large selection, but he and Bonnie had been eating pretty simply since they left Boston—the last meal where they had actually sat at a table was the spaghetti in Shayna's little kitchen in Ohio.

It didn't take them long to decide, and the waitress came back with their water and took their orders. Finn wanted a beer in the worst way, but he didn't want to be carded, so he and Bonnie both abstained. As they ate, Bonnie kept looking toward the stage and the little sliver of dance floor that she could see better than he could.

Her nose was wrinkled, and she had a perplexed look on her face.

"Maybe it's because I'm a hillbilly, but I hate this music. It's like being in a maze, or in one of those little hamster wheels, where you just keep spinning and spinning, and you never get anywhere." She had to shout at him in order for him to hear her, and he ended up moving to sit by her side instead of across from her, so that they could speak into each other's ears.

Finn wouldn't have minded it so much had he not been listening to Bonnie sing for the last week. Bonnie's songs were anything but a hamster wheel. She told stories and revealed secrets, and made him believe she sang just for him. He had a feeling that's how everyone felt when they listened to her songs. That's why she was Bonnie Rae Shelby.

He told her this, his mouth pressed to her ear, and she smiled up at him when he finished and then leaned toward him to respond.

"But Finn—I was singing to you. I just hadn't found you yet. Don't you see? From now on, every song will be yours."

Her words were too sweet. Corny even. But she said them with such conviction, her hand against his opposite cheek, holding his face as she spoke into his ear, that he was moved by her words anyway. In spite of himself. He'd heard her yell into the wind, telling him she loved him too, but he'd been too upset with her to let himself believe anything she'd said in the heat of the moment. He didn't know if Bonnie really loved him. He knew she liked him. He knew she was infatuated with him. He knew she was sad and lonely and lost. And because she was all those things, she needed him. For now.

He kissed her forehead and finished his meal in silence, feeling her eyes linger on his face, knowing he was confusing her, but not knowing how to explain himself without prompting more professions of love and devotion that he wouldn't be able to believe. When the band took a ten-minute break, Finn eased himself from their booth to search out the men's room and a chance to clear his head. Bonnie said she didn't need to go, and that she would wait for him there.

He should have known he couldn't leave her alone. Not even for five minutes. When he returned to their booth, she wasn't there. He spun around, his eyes searching through the poorly lit space, wondering if she'd changed her mind about the bathroom, when he saw her.

She was on the stage. She stood beneath the lights on the little platform that had been vacated by the jumping trio and their drummer, so totally opposite of Bonnie Rae in every way, only a few minutes before. All four of them were sitting at a table nearby, clearly cool with her entertaining their audience while they took a breather. One even raised his glass, as if to say, "Have at it."

"Shit! Bonnie Rae!" he hissed, trying not to draw attention to himself as he eased toward the stage, anxious and furious and stunned that she would pull such a stunt. She had slung the fat one's electric guitar over her slim shoulders and was fingering the strings like she was as comfortable on the stage as she had been in his Blazer, her feet on the dash, her eyes on his face. She plugged it back into the amp nearby and leaned forward.

"Hey." Her mouth kissed the mic as she breathed her greeting, and the crowd instantly quieted. Vocal magic. He'd witnessed it before.

"Y'all don't care if I sing you a little somethin', do ya?"

Her arms were slim and golden, toned and taut, her cap of dark hair sleek and shining under the flickering strobe that obscured her features and shadowed her face in half-light. He didn't think anyone would realize they were about to be serenaded by an international superstar. Nobody would guess how many miles she'd come, or that she hadn't prepared to sing or be seen. But she was up there doing both, just for the pleasure of doing her thing. Her snug jeans, cowgirl boots, and tight blank tank looked very natural on stage, and Finn fought the urge to swing her into his arms and run into the night, keeping her safe, keeping her hidden, keeping her close.

"It's just somethin' I've been thinking about," she said, as if she were talking to her best friend. The electric guitar was a little at odds with her down home style, but she kept it simple as she began to play, her fingers plucking effortlessly at unfamiliar strings, picking out a tune Finn instantly recognized as the one she'd been humming last night. The one he'd asked her to sing. Seems she was granting his request. And then her eyes found his.

I cannot describe
Or explain the speed of light
Or what makes thunder roll across the sky
And I could never theorize about the universe's size
Or explain why some men live and some men die

Her voice filled the space so effortlessly that Finn felt a shot of fear, certain she'd be rushed by fans who recognized her signature sound, that she'd be swept off the stage in a deluge of frenetic humanity. But everyone was listening, a few couples dancing, and Bonnie Rae kept singing, pondering out loud the things she didn't know.

I can't even guess
I would never profess
To know why you are here with me
And I cannot comprehend
How numbers have no end,
The things you understand, I can't conceive

Infinity + One
Is still infinity.
And no matter how I try
I'm bound by gravity.
But the things I thought I knew
Changed the minute I met you.
It seems I'm weightless

and I'm endless after all.

Finn felt heat and heartache rise in his throat as Bonnie threw back her head, singing a song that could only be for him. And the audience moaned with her as she climbed an entirely different kind of bridge.

Weightless and endless.
Timeless and restless.
So light that I'll never fall.
Weightless and endless.
Hopelessly breathless.
I guess I knew nothing at all.

Infinity + One
Is still infinity.
And no matter how I try
I'm bound by gravity.
But the things I thought I knew
Changed the minute I met you.
It seems I'm weightless
and I'm endless after all.

She hadn't panted and strutted, she hadn't moved her body in sultry ways. She hadn't serenaded the crowd with suggestive lyrics, but she'd bared her soul and Finn's soul too, and he didn't think he would have felt more naked or exposed if he'd participated in a strip-tease.

I'm weightless and I'm endless after all. That was it. He felt weightless. Her eyes were on his as she stepped back from the mic and shrugged the strap back over her head. The bouncing band seemed momentarily stunned as she set down the borrowed guitar, fully aware that their audience had completely abandoned them for a slip of a girl with a pixie hair-cut and red cowboy boots. The crowd took a collective breath and released it in shouts and applause and stomping.

Finn had been moving toward her as she sang, walking toward her because he couldn't walk away, and now he closed the gap, sidestepping dancers and drinking observers and swept her up bodily as she moved to step off the stage. She gasped a little as her feet left the ground, but then his mouth found hers, hot with need, but laced with anger at her foolishness. It was the second time he'd kissed her in frustration. But regardless of the reason, it didn't take Bonnie long to catch up, and she kissed him back, unaffected by the crush of people around them.

And then Finn heard the whispers. He heard the name Bonnie Rae Shelby ricochet around the room in hissed wonder, as if people guessed but weren't sure. She didn't look the same. But her voice was distinctive, and once you saw through someone's disguise, it was completely useless. The moment question became belief, there would be a stampede. He pulled his lips from hers and barreled toward the back entrance he'd noticed upon arriving. Bonnie had taken her purse to the stage with her, and it now hung across her body. But their coats were back at their table, and they hadn't paid for their meal. Shit! He set Bonnie down and pushed her toward the side entrance, across from the bar.

"Stand by the exit. Don't go out! Wait for me! I'm going to grab our coats and leave some money on the table." He strode toward the alcove that housed the booth where they'd tried to hide before Bonnie gave in to the lure of the microphone. Digging out his wallet, he tossed more than enough money to cover their dinner among the plates and napkins that had yet to be cleared. He grabbed their coats and was heading back toward the exit, pushing around people that were still watching, still wondering, although the band had begun to sing again, desperately trying to recapture their audience after Bonnie's performance. The pounding drums were sufficient distraction for most of the patrons, and Finn had never been more grateful for obnoxiously loud music in his life. His eyes were on Bonnie, on the ten steps it would take to reach her and exit the building, when the lights flickered, the sound system lost power, and the band was upstaged once more.

Cops flooded into the room from every entrance, SWAT team style, all in black, shields and weapons raised, DEA written across every chest. Finn lunged for Bonnie and narrowly missed the advancing stream of police shouting for everyone to get down. He obeyed immediately, pulling Bonnie with him, but he didn't stay put. He crawled toward the bar just to his right, finding himself nose to nose with the wide-eyed bartender, the college kid who he suspected had a cocaine habit and a side business that paid for it.

"Is there a way out that nobody knows about? A window, a cellar, the roof, anything?" he shouted into the bartender's face, the din around them making it impossible to do anything but yell.

"They're DEA! I'm in so much shit, man!" Jagger started to babble.

"So let's get out of here!" Finn coaxed, willing the bartender to pull a disappearing act out of his hat for all of them. Jagger nodded, gulping, and eased himself deeper behind the bar and Finn followed him on his hands and knees, pushing Bonnie in front of him, his hand on her rear end, urging her along. The bartender opened what appeared to be a large cabinet built into the wall behind the bar, about three feet by two feet, and Finn worried for a second that the wiry bartender was going to crawl inside and pull the doors closed behind him, a hiding spot for one.

"It's the recycling—there's a delivery dock on the other side of this wall and a dumpster where we keep the empty glass bottles until they are picked up. This shoot feeds the dumpster. Careful. There's lots of broken glass."

Jagger shimmied into the opening, feet first, and disappeared almost immediately. Bonnie didn't need prodding and copied his exit. The opening was a little narrow for someone Finn's size, but he turned his shoulders, squeezing himself through, and dropped into a half-full bin of glass bottles, most of them still in one piece. The dumpster was shoved into the right angle between the back wall and the wall with the recycling shoot. There was only one way to go, and the young bartender was already loping down the narrow loading dock toward the sliding metal door.

Finn called out to him, warning him. He knew what would be on the other side of the door. The police weren't stupid. They would have the exit covered, and if he went out, they would come in. Jagger halted and ran back as Finn swung out of the dumpster behind Bonnie and looked around for another way out that wouldn't be as obvious and destined for failure.

A door opened across from them, and an old man with a janitor's uniform and a haggard face stepped out onto the blacktop, pulling a cigarette from his breast pocket, the pocket with a laminated employee badge with a picture, an employee number, and a barcode clipped to it for all to verify. Apparently Verani's wasn't the only business that used the loading dock. The janitor patted his pocket for a light and Bonnie ran toward him, Finn and the bartender on her heels, digging in her purse as she did.

She held a hundred dollar bill out to the man as she approached him.

"We need to get out of here. Can you take us through there?" She nodded toward the door he'd just exited.

The man looked at her as if he didn't understand English and lit his cigarette, puffing as he ignored the money in her outstretched hand and stared at her face sullenly. Bonnie looked at Finn and shrugged helplessly.

Finn took it from her and held it in front of the eyes of the man who didn't seem inclined to help, or even acknowledge them. The movement drew the man's attention from Bonnie's face to Finn's hand. The man's eyes clung to the five dots on Finn's skin between his thumb and his pointer finger.

"You do time?" he grunted, and his eyes swung up to meet Finn's.

"Yeah. You?" Finn said, not batting an eye.

"Yeah." Another grunt in the affirmative. "Long time ago."

"Verani's is crawling with cops," Finn said. "And I don't especially want to serve any more."

The man stubbed out his cigarette on the concrete wall and nodded once.

"You two runnin' 'cause you're guilty?" he asked, looking from Bonnie to Finn.

"No. We're running because we're not. What's going down in there has nothing to do with us."

He nodded again, like that made sense to him.

"I'll let you two go through. Not him." He used a jut of his chin to indicate the jittery bartender.

"Wh–what?" The bartender bounced nervously.

"You're dealin'. I've seen you out here. Selling snort. To kids. You go out that way. Take your chances." He used his chin once again to point toward the entrance to the loading dock. "I'm not helpin' you."

The bartender looked to Finn for support, but Finn shook his head, not giving it.

Jagger shrieked out a string of obscenities as he realized he was on his own. "I'm telling everyone I saw her! I'm telling! I'll tell them Bonnie Rae Shelby came here tonight looking for a hit," he said, pointing at Bonnie, threatening to tattle like he was nine years old and had been snubbed on the playground.

Finn turned on him with a curse and a well-placed swing to his wagging jaw, and the bartender crumpled into a heap. Out cold. For the second time in five minutes, Finn's time in prison had come in handy.

"If he does, you can bet I'll be telling what I know too," the janitor said, swiping his employee badge in the card reader by the heavy door, disengaging the locks. He held the door wide for Bonnie and Finn, and seemed almost pleased as he tossed a final look at the unconscious dealer laying on the concrete.

"Karma's a bitch, but I sure like her tonight," was all he said, and the door swung shut behind them.

It was an office building, cubicles and phone systems packed into the large room that the janitor led them through. When they reached the lobby, he disengaged the alarm, dug in his breast pocket, and handed the bill back to Bonnie, insisting that he didn't like bribes any better than he liked drug dealers. But he acquiesced and took it back when she signed it with a black sharpie she dug from her purse, telling him it was a gift.

Bonnie gave the old ex-con a big smile as she dropped the pen back into her purse, and he took a step back, momentarily dazzled, lifting his hand in farewell as she slipped out the entrance into the dark street beyond. Finn knew how he felt, and he trailed after the girl who had brought him nothing but a pain in his ass and fire in his heart since the moment he'd met her.

They walked quickly but approached the parking lot warily, trying to remain in the shadows, not knowing what they would find. What they found was chaos. Chaos could be good because it provided cover, but from what he could tell, nobody was being allowed to leave. Something major was going down, and Finn doubted the bust was about Jagger. This was big time—big drugs, big players. Verani's was a hot spot for more than the music, late hours, and food, apparently, just like the Escalade driver had hinted. It wouldn't be re-opening anytime soon, and Bonnie and Finn wouldn't be getting to Bear's car anytime soon either.

"What time is it?" Finn asked Bonnie. He couldn't see the face of his watch, and she was the only one with a phone. His throwaway model was in the Charger, and the phone he'd started the trip with was in the Blazer—the first ride they'd had to abandon. He cursed.

"Three. It's three o'clock in the morning," she answered. "We're going to have to leave the car, aren't we?" As usual, she was taking it in stride.

Finn looked at her soberly.

"That convenience store, the one where we got gas?" he said. Bonnie nodded. "It was a Greyhound stop. I saw the logo in the window. How do you feel about taking the bus?"

21
Imaginary Numbers

IT IS NOW believed that Bonnie Rae Shelby and ex-convict, Infinity James Clyde, are driving the black, 2012, Dodge Charger that belongs to Malcolm "Bear" Johnson, Miss Shelby's long-time bodyguard, and victim of a convenience store shooting yesterday. Mr. Johnson has been upgraded from critical to serious condition, though police say he is still not able to communicate or answer questions at this time.

Allegedly, Shelby and Clyde fled the scene of an accident in the small town of Guymon, Oklahoma, earlier this morning, but a witness to the accident took down their license plate number and later verified that a man and woman matching the description of the couple in question, were indeed driving the vehicle.

In addition, a rental car loaned to Mr. Clyde on February 26, and not returned as contracted, has now been reported as stolen by the rental car company, adding to the growing list of charges being leveled against the ex-con, and possibly Bonnie Rae Shelby, as well.

∞

THE BUS WAS only half full, if that, and we slid into two seats about two-thirds back on the left-hand side. We hadn't even had to wait. The bus rumbled in ten minutes after we purchased our tickets from the tired cashier, who happily took cash and didn't ask for ID, though she told us to have it ready when we boarded, along with our tickets. For the first time in my life, I was thankful that my name was Bonita, and my license said so. Finn's name was pretty memorable, but we bought his ticket under Finn Clyde, figuring nobody would recognize the name Finn anyway, seeing as every news report shouted out his full name, complete with his middle name, like he was John Wilkes Booth, Lee Harvey Oswald, or John Wayne Gacy. It was four in the morning, and the tired bus driver took our tickets, ripped off the top portion without a comment or a second glance at the tickets or at us.

I wore the glasses I'd purchased at Walmart—one of the only things I still had from the second Walmart shopping spree, besides my makeup—and Finn had snagged two ball caps sporting the telecommunications logo of the business we'd traipsed through with the surprisingly helpful janitor. He'd had a change of heart when he'd seen the small tattoo on Finn's hand. Finn said it was a symbol of the scumbag brotherhood—another prison tattoo, easily recognizable by other ex-convicts.

He might have been less helpful if he'd seen Finn take the hats from the shelf, but Finn had stuffed them in his jacket and informed me on our walk back to the convenience store that if we got caught with the hats on, the company would be thrilled with the free publicity.

With the hat and glasses, I felt fairly safe, but the moment Finn dropped into his seat beside me, I found his hand. My bravado was gone, as was the adrenaline from the stage. The euphoria from having Finn's eyes on me, from his hungry mouth pressed to mine, from running from the police, all of it had worn off. We stayed silent, hands clasped, until the Greyhound pulled away from the convenience store and rumbled out onto the freeway, taking us away from yet another fiasco.

I was scared again, reality almost too much to take at the moment. I'd had too many of these moments, teetering between disbelief and elation at the twists and turns our days had taken, and I felt more alive than I'd ever felt before, but reality could be a trip.

We were running out of time. We needed to get to LA. We needed to make our grand statement. And then it would all go away. It would be over. But that's not why I was scared. When we reached LA, when we openly contradicted the media craze, would we be over too? And how many cars were we going to abandon on the way? What the hell were we doing?

"What the hell are we doing?" Finn sighed next to me, his words mirroring my thoughts so exactly I jerked, staring up at him. And then I started to laugh. A few people turned toward us, and Finn cursed and pushed me down on his lap, and I pressed my face into his thigh until I could control the semi-hysterical giggles.

Finn bent his head over me, and rested it against the seat in front of him, his upper body at a forty-five degree angle above my head where it lay in his lap, creating a dark, triangular cocoon where we could converse without being overheard.

"Why did you do that, Bonnie? Why did you sing? Are you so hungry for attention that you couldn't resist?" His voice was soft, but confused, like he didn't get me at all. My bubbling laughter fizzled immediately, tamped down by the gulf that separated me from his understanding. I wanted that understanding. I desperately needed it. Without it, he was lost to me.

"I wanted to sing to you," I said. "I needed to tell you how I feel. I needed for you to believe me. And you listen best when I sing."

"But it was foolish. And you know it."

I felt tears prick my eyes at his censure. He'd been angry with me all night. And I didn't know why. "I thought you liked it. You . . . you kissed me."

"I kissed you because it was beautiful and you make me feel . . ." he bit out, his voice a harsh whisper. "You make me feel . . . crazy things. Desperate things. Impossible things. You make me feel. And feeling that much is irresistible sometimes. You are irresistible sometimes."

I reached up and touched his face. I couldn't see his expression, and I wanted to smooth away his displeasure. My fingertips crept along the ridge of his nose and smoothed the furrow between his brows, and danced down the line of his jaw.

"That's why I sing, Finn," I whispered. "It makes me feel. It's so real. And so raw. And it's the only thing in my life that *is* real anymore. Except you. Although sometimes I think you're imaginary." My thoughts ran back to the conversation I'd had with myself about what was real in the bathroom at the little park, the six hundred pound woman weighing heavily in my thoughts.

"Did you know that in mathematics they determined what was real by what was not imaginary?" Finn's voice was just a soft rumble beneath my fingertips that had found his lips

"What?"

"When mathematicians came up with imaginary numbers, accepted them, defined them, they had to come up with a name for everything that wasn't imaginary. Everything that wasn't an imaginary number from that point on became a 'real' number."

"What's an imaginary number?"

"The square root of negative one is an imaginary number."

"Is that all?"

"Any number that was once the square root of a negative number becomes an imaginary number. Square root of -4 becomes 2i, square root of -100 becomes 10i."

"Is infinity an imaginary number?"

"No."

"Is it a real number?"

"No. It isn't a number at all. It's a concept of endlessness, unreachableness."

"I knew it. See? You *are* just a figment of my imagination."

Finn laughed, a quiet chuckle that didn't travel farther than my ears. "A real number is just a value that represents a quantity on a continuous line. But that doesn't mean it shows the *value* of something real. Almost any number that you can think of is a real number. Whole numbers, rational numbers, irrational numbers."

"And infinity can't be measured." I thought I understood.

"Yeah." Finn grasped my fingers that played against his lips. "There is no point that marks infinity."

"But it still exists."

"It exists, but it isn't real," Finn countered, obviously enjoying the word play.

"I hate math," I said. But I smiled and he leaned down and kissed me, forgiving me, making me love math. Very much.

"Math is beautiful," he murmured.

"Math isn't real," I argued, just for the sake of arguing.

"It isn't always tangible, but some of the best things in life aren't tangible. Love isn't tangible. Neither is patience. Neither is kindness or forgiveness or any one of the other virtues people talk about," he said.

"I've been looking for what's real for the last few years," I confessed wistfully, the sound child-like, even to my own ears. "But reality is usually ugly. Beauty? That's harder to pin down. It's like a sunset. It's beautiful, it makes you feel something. And that's real. But the feeling only lasts as long as the sunset. It's so fleeting. So it's easy to believe it isn't real." I sighed, wondering if I was making any sense.

"Fame and fortune seem like that. Like they can't be real. And then suddenly they are. You are . . . rich and famous. But you don't *feel* any different. So it doesn't feel real. So you keep looking. And before long … it becomes so easy to just give in to the ugly. Because it's everywhere you look. So you take from it what pleasure there is to take. Because there *is* pleasure in it. And it's real," I insisted again.

"But the pleasure gets harder and harder to find, and you have to dig deeper and deeper into the crap, so deep you're covered in it, and you get coated in the ugly." I felt despair rising in my chest, and

Finn seemed to sense it because he kissed my forehead and then my eyelids and then my lips once more, demanding that I pause, just for a moment.

"I get it, Bonnie Rae," Finn said, holding my gaze. "You think I don't get that? Prison is full of all that is truly ugly. I was surrounded by it for five years. I think sometimes I'll never be able to scrub off the stench."

"What I feel for you, Finn? It's not like anything I've felt before. It's better than real. So maybe the challenge in life is not letting what is *real* convince us that that is all there is."

Finn didn't respond, and I didn't know if I'd gotten through to him. But I needed him to believe me, and the turbulence in my chest had me peering up at him, entreating him to hear.

"Maybe I'll stop looking for real," I whispered, just making out his eyes as he stared down into my face, his features softly illuminated by the hushed light of the moon that bathed the world streaming past the bus windows. "Maybe I'll stop looking for real, now that I've found Infinity."

∞

THE BUS STOPPED in Gallup, New Mexico, about two hours into the trip, but we stayed on the bus. When the bus resumed the journey, we slept for a while, the little sleep we'd gotten over the last week, along with the soothing hum of the bus making it easy to drop off. We kept our hats pulled low over our faces, and Finn traded me seats so he could lean against the window, and I could lean against him.

When the bus made a stop in Flagstaff, Arizona, about three hours later, and halfway into the trip, we stayed in our seats again, deciding that the less attention we drew to ourselves getting on and off, the better. While we waited for the journey to continue, I dug through my bag until I found the Sharpie I'd used to sign the janitor's one hundred dollar bill.

"Who carries a marker in their purse?" Finn shook his head.

"Tools of my trade, Clyde. I never leave home without one."

"Please don't start signing autographs on this bus, Bonnie Rae. We still have hours to go, and it's broad daylight. No concerts, no signings, no entertaining the troops." There were a handful of soldiers on the bus, which I had pointed out to Finn, telling him about my work with the USO.

"Hold your horses, Infinity," I teased. "Give me your right hand."

Finn did as I asked, crossing his hand over his body so I could hold it in mine. I pulled the lid off the fine-tip marker with my teeth, and very carefully, added a dot to his tattoo. There were still four dots comprising the "cage"—but instead of one man in the cage, now there were two. Two dots, that is.

Finn looked at my handiwork and then looked at me, his eyebrows raised in question.

"You aren't alone anymore. Neither am I. We may still be in a cage . . . and I know that's my fault. But we're together." I felt a lump rise in my throat and looked away. Damn my feminine emotions.

"Do you know that two is an untouchable number too?" Finn said after several long minutes, his eyes on his hand.

"It is?"

He nodded slowly and traced the dots which now numbered six. "And six is what is known as a perfect number. The sum of its divisors—one, two, and three—all add up to six. The product of its divisors are also six."

"So what you're telling me, then, is together we are perfect and untouchable?"

Finn's eyes shot to mine, and the yearning in his face made me long to be anywhere but where we were. I leaned in and pressed my lips to his, needing his mouth, even if only for a heartbeat. I pulled away immediately, not wanting to draw the eyes of the other passengers.

Finn took the Sharpie from my hand and turned my right arm so my palm was facing up. Then, on my inner wrist, he drew the sign for infinity, a slumbering black eight, about an inch long.

"I'm guessing you've always been perfect and untouchable. But now you're mine. And I'm not giving you up," Finn said quietly, but his expression was fierce. It sounded to me like he was trying to convince himself.

∞

ALMOST ELEVEN HOURS from the time we ditched Albuquerque, the bus came to a squeaking, shaking, gasping halt outside a huge casino right on Fremont Street, the epicenter of old, downtown Las Vegas, north of the strip. Fremont Street was still glitzy and neon encrusted, but she was showing a little tear in the fishnets, and her pancake makeup didn't hide her age.

The bus made two more stops, and Finn bribed a little, Hispanic woman on the seat in front of us, in broken Spanish and hand gestures, to buy herself and us water and sandwiches and to keep the considerable change. We hadn't gotten off the bus a single time in the whole trip, even using the onboard bathroom (ugh!), and I was stiff and shaky-legged as I descended the steps of the bus. I was used to taking buses, but my tour bus was a far cry from the Greyhound that smelled like exhaust, stale cigarettes, and too many people. And we were going to have to get back on another bus to get to LA, a fact that made me groan inwardly and think of the millions of dollars I had made in the last few years with angry longing.

We immediately purchased bus tickets to Los Angeles, fearful of not making it now that we were so close. We were in Vegas. We were here. The original destination. Now, we had just a little bit farther to go, and maybe the craziness would end.

The bus we were on was heading in another direction, but there was a bus to LA at eight o'clock that night. It was three o'clock now. And I needed a dress worthy of the Oscars and a tux worthy of Infinity Clyde. Tall orders when I was trying to keep a low profile, wearing dusty jeans, a ball cap, and granny glasses. Finn had combed his hair with his fingers and tied it back again, the miles and the travel making him look none the worse for wear. In fact, he just looked like Finn—big, blond, and beautiful. It made me want to smile and cry simultaneously.

Finn caught my expression and cuffed my chin. "What?"

"I'm feeling especially Hank Shelby-ish at the moment, Clyde. Mean and ugly. I need a miracle makeover, and I don't think I can pull one out of a Wally bag."

"We've come this far, Bonnie Rae. We can find a dress in a party town like Vegas with our hands tied behind our backs. We have five hours, and we're in walking distance of everything. Don't cry, Hank. We'll find you a pretty dress." He winked at me, and I gave him a smile, but Finn had no idea what he was getting into. I decided not to even try to explain.

I hadn't been to the Oscars before, but I'd been to the Grammys and the CMAs, and it was flash bulbs, air-brushed people, glowing skin, million dollar necklaces, and designer dresses. I would have Finn on my arm, which was better than any diamond bracelet, but I needed to sell a story, a love story, *our* love story, and I couldn't do it if I looked like I was hanging on by a thread . . . or wearing threads.

I couldn't walk into a store and throw around my celebrity status—even if I could, I didn't have the funds to buy a designer dress. That meant I had to find a store that had a decent selection. I cringed at the thought of going to the Oscars in a sparkly cocktail dress, like I'd just been asked to the Homecoming dance. I knew what I needed, and I didn't know if I was going to be able to find it, and if I found it, it had to fit perfectly. Finn's tuxedo had to fit him perfectly too, which might be an even harder proposition. Finn wasn't built like the average guy, and though I was secretly thrilled that he wasn't, it made our mission all the more difficult.

I didn't want to wander up and down the streets. I was too tired for that. Finn and I found a couple of chairs in the hotel lobby, and I started googling dress shops like a mad woman. I eliminated all dress warehouses because I figured we would need a little more help than a warehouse could provide, and then I nixed hotel boutiques because they were too pricey and too intimate. I was wearing red cowboy boots and a black tank top beneath my fluffy pink coat, and I would draw way too much attention.

I stifled the urge to cry again. I felt hideous, and Google wasn't helping. I needed a woman's referral. I needed to ask questions. Somehow, I didn't think any of the women at the nickel slots behind us would be able to help me.

I looked around desperately, and my eyes landed on the concierge desk. A slight man with glossy, swept-back hair, a dapper bowtie, and an impeccable suit was busy polishing the counter in front of him. I told Finn to sit tight, and I walked toward the fussy little man, hoping he loved fashion and hated gossip. I almost laughed. There was no such thing. Gossip was the lifeblood of the fashion world. They were as inseparable as Bonnie and Clyde. My stylist knew everything about everyone. And she made sure I knew it too. I had often wondered what she told people about me.

He saw me coming, and he eyed my stupid ball cap briefly. I yanked it off and ran my hands over my flattened, hat hair. Damn. I left the glasses on though. Vanity would get me nowhere.

I set my purse on the counter, and his eyes widened a little. The buttery, yellow leather screamed expensive, and he met my gaze with a tad more approval. His nametag claimed his name was Pierre. I was sure it wasn't—but then again, my name was really Bonita.

"I need a dress. Think Oscar-worthy. Sleek, full-length, no bling, size four. And I need it today. Now. I also need a suit that will fit my friend over there without alterations," I drawled, the Tennessee more noticeable than ever. It was like that when I got nervous.

Pierre's eyes widened even farther as he looked beyond my

shoulder to where Finn was sitting.

"You mean Thor?" he gasped.

I laughed. Finn did look like Thor. "Yeah. Thor."

"What's your budget, sweetie?" he said conspiratorially. Oh, yes. This man could help me.

"Two thousand for the dress. A thousand for the suit. Another five hundred for shoes, socks, underthings, everything. I'll throw in another couple hundred for jewels, obviously fake, but they need to look real. And I need discreet."

Pierre pursed his lips and tapped them with a manicured finger. Then he picked up his phone and punched in a number. He repeated my list of demands, even the part about Thor, and asked, "Can you do it?"

He listened for a few seconds and said, "I'll send them your way."

22

Mutually Exclusive

THE 2012 BLACK Charger owned by Malcolm "Bear" Johnson was recovered in Albuquerque, New Mexico, last night during a drug raid on a popular, local nightclub called Verani's. Local law enforcement and DEA coordinated the sting in the early morning hours, detaining everyone inside the club. People in the club report seeing Bonnie Rae and an unidentified male believed to be ex-con, Infinity James Clyde, who for a time, was believed to have possibly abducted the singer. Interestingly enough, the songstress turns twenty-two today. Fans of the singer have been sending messages on social media, wishing her a safe return and many birthdays to come, but doubts about her innocence are mounting. Club-goers claim Bonnie Rae Shelby actually sang to them before the bust went down. A bartender on duty claims Bonnie Rae was clearly at the club to purchase drugs, though it isn't clear at this time why the singer and her companion were not apprehended by police. Police sources say there were some vehicles reported stolen in the area around the time of the raid, and that it is likely the pair have stolen yet another vehicle in their attempt to evade capture.

Ms. Raena Shelby has put out yet another statement that her granddaughter is being held against her will, and that she believes Mr. Johnson was attacked by Shelby's captor or captors, when Mr. Johnson didn't provide sufficient ransom for her release. When *pressed for more information on ransom demands, Ms. Raena Shelby claimed she could not comment further.*

∞

PIERRE TURNED OUT to be a Godsend—albeit a slightly expensive one. He took the $200 I slipped him with a whisk of his hand and without a blink of his eye. But when I mentioned needing a room for an hour to freshen up, he gave us two keycards for the indoor pool, which had restrooms and showers, and he didn't charge me. I almost wept. Every girl knows you can't go dress shopping with hat hair and old makeup. It would be like trying to run a marathon in cowboy boots—you were screwed before you even started. Finn was nervous about being separated, even for a shower, but after seeing the mostly empty pool area and restrooms, he caved. Forty-five minutes later, still dressed in our old clothes, but with clean skin, hair, and teeth, and fresh makeup for me, I think we both felt a whole lot better.

We were directed down the street several blocks to a wedding chapel with a giant, stained-glass window and a mural of Elvis as an angel painted along one side. A man dressed like Little Richard was playing the piano, and a wedding was in session as we made our way past the room designated for nuptials to a long hallway. Pierre had insisted the hallway led to a set of stairs that would take us to Vegas's best kept secret—a wedding boutique that was so fabulous (his word, not mine) that only the locals were aware of it, and only the most well-connected locals, at that.

We clomped down the stairs until we reached the bottom. An unremarkable door with a little gold plaque above it greeted us with the word *Monique's*. *Monique's* had a nice ring. Not as nice as Vera Wang . . . but we were in Vegas, and Vegas was more about cash than class, and I was a hillbilly, so I didn't know what I was getting picky about.

We pushed through the door and were greeted by creamy neutrals and soft lighting. It smelled like vanilla and leather. Expensive but approachable.

Monique was a tiny woman with a beehive she'd borrowed from another decade. She paired the beehive with all black—slim black trousers and a fitted black shirt covered by an equally fitted black vest. She wore men's dress shoes—white with black toes and heels, and no jewelry besides the horn rims she paired with deep red lipstick. Her style was the love child of Amy Winehouse and Sammy Davis Jr.—and it worked. I expected a thick, fake, French accent, but instead she greeted us with a smile and a twang as thick as my own. I felt like hugging her and breaking into a Loretta Lynn tune, but I restrained myself.

With a few questions she took charge, sending Finn away with a man who was as large as she was small, as furry as she was sleek, and nearly as impressed with Finn as I was. I hoped he was safe. Finn shot me a nervous glance before he disappeared behind an ornate partition. And then Monique started pulling dresses with the speed and focus of a squirrel storing nuts, mumbling as she did, eyeing me through narrowed eyes magnified by her giant glasses.

The first few were beautiful, but the sparkle and the fluff didn't quite mesh with the boyish cut of my hair—and I looked a bit like Ken's little brother trying to moonlight as Barbie. I'd done my best to glam it up with slicked back hair, dark eyes, and glossy lips, but it wasn't enough, and I told Monique my opinion regretfully, pointing to my shorn strands. She tsked and brushed my fears away.

"It's a pixie cut. And it's sexy. Nobody ever thought Tinker Bell looked like a boy. Why do you think all those lost boys stayed lost? Tinker Bell is a succulent little morsel, and so are you, Sunshine. We just have to find the right combination."

She changed tactics after that, though, and when she helped me slip a slinky swath of white satin over my head, she stepped back with a satisfied smirk on her face, her eyes running from the top of my head to my bare toes.

"Tell me you don't love it," she said, triumphant.

She moved away so that I was alone in the mirror. I stared at my reflection with pleasure. The neckline of the silky white slip dress hung from thin straps, kissing my breasts, and skimming the hollows and swells of my body all the way to the floor, pooling the slightest bit at my feet. It almost looked like French lingerie, something a 1930s movie star would wear with fuzzy-toed, high-heeled bedroom slippers. I turned, admiring the way the drape left my back exposed, long and smooth from the nape of my neck to below my waist, the most revealing part of the dress. I felt both provocative and demure, like a virginal bride on her wedding night. It was perfect.

I faced the mirror again, trying not to run my hands over the silky fall of white. I was afraid I would ruin it or smudge it, and I didn't want to risk it. I had to have it. This was the dress I wanted to wear. This was the dress I wanted Finn to see me in.

And then, like my thoughts had conjured him, he was there, reflected in the mirror, standing several feet behind me, his hands shoved into the pockets of his slim black trousers—the fitted, black suit coat, pristine white dress shirt, and black tie making him look like someone I'd never met. The only thing that was the same was his smooth hair, still pulled back at his nape. Monique approached him and started fussing with his lapels, but his eyes were on me, wide and unblinking. He didn't smile, didn't wink. He just looked.

I felt hot, but I shivered. I grew faint and then flushed. And my breath felt trapped in my lungs. I stared back at Finn staring at me, unmoving. Monique glanced up into Finn's face, waiting for him to answer her. She'd asked him something, but he hadn't heard. Her voice trailed off, and she glanced at me, and then back at him. And then she fanned herself as if she, too, was flushed.

"Good, Lord," she breathed. "I hope you two have booked the chapel."

Booked the chapel?

The wedding chapel.

I realized what she was saying the same time Finn must have, because his blue eyes darkened, and his throat worked, but he didn't look away.

"I'll just grab a few things I think you'll need—shoes so the dress doesn't drag, maybe some earrings. No other jewelry . . . except for a ring, of course," Monique suggested dryly, and she flew off with fluttering hands, like a blackbird with a nest on her head.

We didn't watch her go. We were too busy drinking each other in.

"Would you?" Finn said.

I turned away from the mirror, from our framed reflections, and faced him. He stood maybe six feet away, but he made no move to close the distance. I tipped my head, not daring to believe, and watched his lips move around the words as he tried again.

"If I asked you. Would you?"

His face was taut with emotion, and he'd taken his hands from his pockets, the moment too intense for casual posture. They were clenched at his sides, and I stared at them, at the six dots on his right hand. Six dots. Six days. I'd known him for eight, loved him for six. And I wanted to love him for a million more. My eyes left his hands and found his face. He looked terrified.

"Yes," I said, not sure why we were speaking so softly. Words that meant so much should be bellowed, shouted, screamed, so they could echo and reverberate. Maybe it was fear that stole our voices—fear that loud words would scare away our courage. And maybe it was reverence for the hovering promise that arced between us like static, snapping and crackling in the vanilla-scented air.

"Yes," I said again, more firmly. And I smiled. The smile threatened to split my face in two, but I couldn't contain it. I watched the terror in Finn's face ease, and the tension in his jaw relax into a smile that tried to match my own. And he threw back his head and laughed, the jubilance laced with incredulous relief and a touch of disbelief too. He clasped his hands over his head and turned in a circle like he didn't know what to do next.

"Are you gonna kiss me, Clyde?" I said softly. "'Cause I'm

thinkin' that would be appropriate."

My back was suddenly against the mirror, my feet dangling above the floor, his arms wrapped around my waist, his mouth pressed to mine. I yanked at his hair, loosening the band, and I smiled against his lips as his hair created a curtain around our faces. He kissed me soundly, a performance worthy of his thousand dollar suit, and then kissed me again, though we didn't raise the curtain for the encore.

∞

IT WAS SURPRISINGLY easy. Stunningly easy. Effortless. Monique's wasn't just a boutique—it was a full service wedding center—rings, ceremonies, flowers, photography, all in an hour. With one call, Monique had us in a limo, which took us to the license bureau, where we walked inside, presented ID, signed our names, paid the $60 license fee, and were out again without a blood test, a long wait, or even an autograph request. Monique had taken care of that too. The woman seemed to know exactly who I was and had made sure we were brought in a side entrance and whisked back out again, and the bureau clerk didn't seem surprised to see us or give two cents if our faces were in the tabloids. It was Vegas, I reminded myself. I had the feeling Monique and her contacts had seen it all. The limo then hurried us back to the chapel, where we were squeezed into a fifteen minute window between previously booked appointments.

I didn't want Elvis at my wedding. I loved him, but not that much. Little Richard was out too. No music. No fake flowers. No walks down the aisle on the arm of a dead rock 'n' roll icon. Instead, we were escorted to a little room with an actual minister and a row of tiny candles, and side by side, in a couple of words, we said we would. *Richer and poorer*—Finn flinched at that like he didn't like that he was the latter. *In sickness and in health*—it was my turn to wince. I knew Finn thought I was a little crazy. My gran thought I was a lot crazy. Or maybe that was just how she liked to make me feel. And finally the words '"Til death do us part"—and we looked at each other then, knowing exactly how death could part us from the ones we love.

"I do," I said.

"I do," he said.

All done.

They provided a witness, we exchanged simple rings—I wouldn't have been surprised if our fingers turned green beneath our cheap bands, but as long as Finn wasn't turning green, I couldn't care less. Monique threw in the slim, gold bands with the $500 I paid for the rush wedding package, and the $3,800 I laid down for our fancy duds, which included everything from our underwear to the diamonds in my ears, along with a few extra pieces of silk and lace that Monique was sure I would need, and which I gladly agreed to.

I added a tip for her and another $100 tip for Pierre. They had both saved—and made—my day. If we ever made it out of the mess we were in, Monique was going to be my new go-to girl for dresses. I was good to people who were good to me, and I told her as much. Plus, I was going to be hiring my own people from now on. Gran would not be calling any more shots, starting today, starting now, starting with the man who I'd just pledged to love all the days of my life.

He was sober and serious, silently observing it all, like the process was an elaborate equation he hadn't yet solved, but when he said "I do," I believed him. And when I said, "I do," I meant it with all my heart. And considering that my heart had swollen in size, filling my chest so I could hardly breathe, that was saying something. I was surprised I wasn't floating, the sensation of helium in my head was so pronounced that I clung to Finn's hand to hold me down.

We posed for some pictures, but made them use a disposable camera, which we took with us, not eager to see our wedding pictures splashed everywhere before we even made it to LA. It was our secret, our moment, and we would tell the world when and if we felt like it.

We retreated to the boutique and changed our clothes, though I kept on the lace panties and pulled on the matching bra. We relinquished our finery to Monique, who packaged it carefully in garment bags that were constructed like padded cells, complete with reinforced compartments and straight jackets. We walked out of the boutique three hours after we had arrived, bags over our shoulders, rings on our fingers, and a five hour bus ride before us. No romantic honeymoon for Bonnie and Clyde.

We stopped at a deli, and Finn bought us sandwiches and cupcakes with frothy white icing and sprinkles, the closest thing we would get to wedding cake on our big day. When Finn stuck a thick candle in mine, I started in surprise.

"Did you steal that from the ceremony?" I asked, laughter making me wheeze.

"Yeah. I did. I grabbed it and snapped it off at the top and shoved it in my pocket in case I didn't have the chance to buy birthday candles." His mouth twisted in a small grin. "I think I got hot wax on my tuxedo pants." The smile faded, and he leaned forward and kissed my lips gently. "Happy Birthday, Bonnie."

"I forgot," I said with wonder. And I had. The last time I'd thought about my birthday was before Finn pulled off the highway in that dumpy little town and rocked my world behind a run-down café that had seen much better days, but never a better make-out session.

"No more hard birthdays. Only happy anniversaries. Deal?" Finn entreated sweetly.

I swallowed the lump in my throat and licked at the frosting around my giant candle. It had been the best birthday I'd ever had—the best day I'd ever had, no contest. I sent a little love note skyward, hoping Minnie could forgive me for making new memories on our day.

"Deal," I said, my eyes holding Finn's.

"You wanna shake on that, Bonnie Rae Clyde?" He grinned

widely at my new moniker.

    I laughed and nodded, extending the hand that wore his ring. Gran was going to crap her pants. I laughed even harder. Yes, indeed. It had been a very good birthday.

23
Axis of Reflection

THEY BOARDED THE bus without hassle or second glances. Finn made Bonnie put her hat back on and her glasses too. She was beautiful enough to receive second looks for that reason alone, and the more they could play down her looks, the easier it would be to keep her identity hidden. The bus departed right on time, and Finn breathed a little easier, knowing they would be in LA, even with another stop, in roughly five hours.

He had felt a slight but ever-increasing drum beat of trepidation since they'd left St. Louis, the pitfalls and problems at every turn creating a sense of unavoidable disaster that even the ring on his finger could not completely drown out. He was happier than he'd ever been, and he was more terrified than he'd ever been. He was madly in love, yet he hardly recognized himself. And he should have known the final stretch would go no smoother than the rest of the journey had.

Forty-five minutes outside of Vegas, the bus broke down. It started to cough and shimmy, and the bus driver babied it along to the closest exit, which fortunately was not in the middle of nowhere, though Primm, Nevada was the strangest town Finn had ever seen, plopped down like a tiny island in the middle of the desert—an island so small it made Vegas seem like a continent. A strip mall that was built to look like an old western town, several hotels, and a roller coaster that ran between manufactured rock mountains were the main attractions, and in the darkness, he felt a little like Pinocchio visiting the island where all the boys turned into donkeys. What was it called? His mom had read Pinocchio to him and Fish when they were little, and it had struck a chord in him. Fish loved the story and asked for it every night, but Finn wasn't as entranced. He related a little too closely to poor Jiminy Cricket trying to keep Pinocchio in line.

Pleasure Island. The answer popped into his head. That was it. The island that bewitched boys and turned them into asses. He hoped Vegas hadn't done the same to him. Initially the driver asked the passengers to stay seated and remain on the bus, but after a half hour of conferring with his supervisors, he informed the passengers that another bus was being sent to their location to take them to Los Angeles. The driver gave them an hour and reiterated that the journey would resume on the new bus at ten thirty, and to please be prompt so they wouldn't be left behind. He gave them a quick tour-guide style run-down of the available restaurants and sites to see in Primm, including a huge Buffalo shaped pool at Buffalo Bills Hotel, and the roller coaster that Finn was suddenly determined to ride. But when the bus driver mentioned that the bullet riddled car of the infamous outlaws, Bonnie and Clyde, was on display at Whiskey Pete's Hotel and Casino, he and Bonnie looked at each other in wide-eyed wonder.

Finn had started to laugh, almost choking on his disbelief.

"Now that, Infinity, is a sign," Bonnie drawled, and immediately scowled. "William's sign is still in Bear's car. I've got to get it back. If I only come out of this trip with one souvenir, that's the one I want. A cardboard sign and a big, blond husband. That's all I ask."

He and Bonnie waited as the seats emptied around them before they disembarked. Bonnie joked that they could tell the tabloids they had spent their honeymoon in Primm riding the roller coaster, but Finn was pretty sure that like him, her thoughts were narrowed in on the car. When they climbed off the bus, they headed, without a word, in the direction of Whiskey Pete's and the "death car."

It was a pale, yellowy-grey Ford V8—a color that only made the bullet holes more glaring—and it looked as if someone had driven it right off a gangster movie set. They couldn't touch it or look inside. It was enclosed behind a glass wall on every side, just sitting on the plush carpeting outside the main cashier cage. A sign made to look like it was blood spattered and bullet riddled claimed that the car was "The Authentic Death Car of Bonnie and Clyde."

"Those two don't look much like Bonnie and Clyde," Bonnie slipped her hand in his and nodded toward the two mannequins posed, gangster-style, beside the car inside the glass barricade. The mannequins were holding automatic weapons and looking very little like the two lovers from the pictures in the little book Bonnie had bought. The mannequins looked like they belonged on the streets of Chicago in the roaring twenties, not driving through the dust bowl during the Great Depression

"On May 23, 1934, law officers killed Bonnie and Clyde in a roadblock ambush, piercing their car with more than one hundred bullets," Bonnie read from the plaque in front of the display. She knew all of that—they both did—but she still seemed awed by it—especially now that they were looking at the actual car where the two had died.

"It was almost eighty years ago," Bonnie whispered, her gaze trained on the driver's side door, which seemed to have the highest concentration of bullet holes.

The account he and Bonnie had read said there were fifty-four bullet holes in Bonnie Parker, and even one through her face. Finn didn't like that. He also didn't like how people had gathered to gawk at the bloody ambush site before the gun smoke had even left the air. And before the police could run them off, people were trying to claim souvenirs, cutting pieces from the clothing of the two lovers who had yet to be taken away and still sat, slumped and filled with lead, in the front seat of the Ford. One person had tried to cut off Clyde's ear, another had wanted his finger. Someone had gotten away with locks of Bonnie's hair and a piece of her blood-soaked dress.

Couldn't they have just killed Clyde? Nobody could ever prove that Bonnie had hurt anyone. She was just in love with a piece of shit. They'd taken pictures of Bonnie Parker in the morgue, naked. He didn't like that either, and felt a flash of outrage that in death, the world got to see her bare breasts which were full and unmarked, youthful. No bullet holes to see, but they'd still taken pictures. People just loved pictures.

"Let's get a picture," Bonnie insisted, proving his point, and pulled out the disposable camera from their shotgun wedding.

"Bonnie Rae," Finn warned, but she was already looking around for someone who could take their picture. An Asian couple strolled by, and Bonnie waved the camera in the man's face, apparently the universal sign for "Can you take my picture?" The man instantly smiled and nodded agreeably, taking the camera from Bonnie's hand, though Finn suspected he didn't speak any English. Which was probably good. Safe.

Finn stood behind Bonnie, his arms folded around her, and he posed obediently for the picture. He was sure she was beaming, but he didn't smile. The car behind him gave him the creeps, and he could only imagine what the tabloids would do if they ever got their hands on a picture like that. His unease rose another notch, and he hurried Bonnie out of the casino and back into the darkness, away from the ghosts of another couple who'd finally run out of luck.

It seemed only fitting that their roller coaster journey should include an actual roller coaster ride, and when Bonnie protested, telling him that she got a little motion sick, he promised her he would distract her. He wanted to distract himself. Not from what he'd just done or the promises he had made, but from the fear of what was to come. The roller coaster promised flight, speed, and a suspension of time. And he wanted all of those things. Her proximity would taunt him all the way to Los Angeles—sitting by her, his ring on her finger, lust in his veins, and not a damn thing he could do about it.

So they stood in the line, keeping their faces averted, their eyes on each other, and waited to ride the roller coaster. They sat on the very back row—Finn had plotted exactly where they needed to be in the line to slip into the last car, and when the coaster began to collect speed, he pulled Bonnie's face to his, and kissed and cradled her through the loops and turns, ignoring the ride and the wind whipping around them, his lips and tongue mimicking the climb and plunge of the ride, the pounding of the rails echoing the pounding in his chest, the squealing of the brakes on the final stretch reminding him that the ride was over, for now, and another was just beginning.

∞

THIS JUST IN. We have confirmation that Bonnie Rae Shelby and Infinity James Clyde were spotted in Las Vegas on Saturday, and that a marriage license was issued for one Bonita Rae Shelby and Infinity James Clyde, putting to rest speculation that the singer was an unwilling accomplice in the crime spree that spreads across the US. It's not surprising that Bonnie Rae Shelby's album and download sales have hit record-breaking levels as people are tuning into this story. Reports of sightings of Infinity Clyde and Bonnie Rae Shelby have started to pour in from literally all over the country. Everyone is transfixed with this story, and no one seems to know what to believe. Is this a case of a beautiful young superstar being kidnapped and held against her will? Or is this a scenario where a captive falls for her captor?

∞

BONNIE'S EYES WERE wide and trusting, watching him. Studying him. For all her sass and her salt, she could be very sweet. Very tender. Very serious. She was perfectly still, abnormally so, and there was a flush to her cheeks that hadn't been there before. He could see her pulse. It thrummed wildly, and somehow that settled his own nerves, knowing she was afraid. She shouldn't be afraid. He would take care of her.

He walked toward her but stopped two feet in front of her, suddenly not eager to rush. Miraculously, a new bus had arrived in Primm, and they had boarded her without incident. In fact, the final four hours of their trip had gone seamlessly, contradicting Finn's rising certainty that they would never make it to LA. But it had been the longest four hours of his life. He and Bonnie had both been vibrating with the rumbling bus the entire way there, adrenaline, lust and eager anticipation making the final stretch of their journey almost unbearable.

There had been no police waiting at the end of their journey, no Bonnie and Clyde style ambush outside the venerable hotel. Bonnie had called ahead, giving the concierge the name Bear had instructed her to give. Their cab was directed to a special entrance, and a doorman was waiting to escort them in a private elevator to the top floor. He hadn't blinked or looked twice at either of them, his face as expressionless as a royal guard, and he took their garment bags with the utmost care and even bowed as Bonnie tipped him with a practiced hand. And then he'd left them in their suite, the most opulent rooms Finn had ever seen, and closed the double doors quietly behind him. They'd each taken a minute to freshen up in separate, luxurious bathrooms, and amazingly enough, Bonnie had finished before him and now stood in the center of the room as if she stood in the center of a stage, waiting for the music to begin.

It was after three o'clock in the morning, in a suite in a very famous hotel, the balcony doors slightly open to welcome in perfumed air to brush their fevered skin, and they were alone. Finally. Two feet apart and about ten feet from a huge, beautiful bed. Finn reached for Bonnie's hand and twisted the little band that circled her finger.

"What are you thinking about?" he asked, the question almost inaudible it was so soft.

Her eyes rose from their hands and held his, a small smile lifting one corner of her mouth. Then she stepped forward and stood on her tiptoes placing her cheek to his, smooth against rough, and he kissed her neck, making her shiver.

"Mirrors," she said in his ear.

"Mirrors?" he asked.

"Reflections," she said.

Finn lifted his head, raising his eyes to the ceiling above the entire pedestaled sleeping area, to the mirrors that made the ceiling a reflection of the room below. He'd noticed them immediately when they'd walked into the well-appointed room. He was sure Bear hadn't known about that feature when he'd booked the room for the two of them. He was quite sure he'd booked the suite because there was a fold out bed in the private sitting area and a door in between. It was a room fit for a rock star or a princess, or someone who was a little bit of both.

"Remember what I told you about mirrors? How sometimes it's hard to look at my own reflection?" Bonnie asked.

"Yeah." Finn caught his own gaze in the overhead mirrors as if he were looking down on himself. Bonnie lifted her eyes as well, and they stared at each other, at their upturned faces and clasped hands.

"When you're with me, beside me, in front of a mirror, I don't feel that way. When I'm standing next to you, I know exactly who I am. I don't see Minnie. I don't lose myself in memories of her. I just see us."

Bonnie stopped as if she couldn't continue, and he saw her chest lift and release, a steadying inhale and exhale, before she finished. "At the boutique, I saw you standing behind me, beside me, and I felt whole. Not a piece, not a half, not a part. Whole."

It was her turn to twist the ring on his finger. "So now . . . I'm thinking about mirrors. And watching you make love to me." And she looked away from his reflection above her head and met his gaze, and Finn had to close his eyes and concentrate, committing himself to care so that he didn't toss her bodily onto the bed and ruin the only first time they would ever have. He must have worn an intensely focused expression because Bonnie smoothed the groove between his scowling brows with her fingertips.

"You aren't thinking about numbers are you?" She spoke only inches from his lips, and he closed the brief distance so he could feel her smile in the curve of the kiss, teasing him, and he left his eyes closed and enjoyed the sensation of the barely-there touch of her mouth.

"I'm thinking about subtraction," he murmured, moving his face gently from side to side so that his lips brushed hers softly, back and forth.

"You are?" he could hear the smile again and nipped at it with his teeth.

"Yes. I am." His hands slid up beneath her shirt, the silk of her skin warm against his flattened palms. She caught her breath, and Finn paused, waiting for her to release it, the flutter of air tickling his tongue when she did. Then he moved his hands higher and pushed her tank top up and over her head. He didn't open his eyes, but he took her lips again, his hands spanning the smooth length of her back as he kissed her, open-mouthed.

He slid his hands from her back to her hips, to the waist band of her jeans and found the button, releasing it and pushing it aside as he unzipped them. He slid her jeans around her hips and felt her shift, sending them down her legs and pooling at their feet.

"See? Subtraction," he whispered.

"I think I like math," she breathed, and she stepped fully against him, away from her clothes, away from the dainty pile of lace he had fingered sightlessly, only to discard because he longed for what was beneath.

"It's beautiful, isn't it?" he murmured, and opened his eyes slowly, unable to resist any longer, filling his vision with dark eyes and parted lips, with rosy skin and slender shoulders. His eyes clung to the hollow at the base of her throat before he drank in the rise and fall of her breasts, of her belly, the softness and the slope of her hips and her thighs, and he fell to his knees before her, pressing his mouth to the curve of her stomach, wrapping his arms around her trembling legs.

Her hands gripped his hair and splayed across his back, pulling his shirt from his shoulders, briefly separating his mouth from her skin as she tugged it over his head, and then she was on her knees as well, as if her legs wouldn't hold her. And so Finn held her, rising to his feet as he swept her up and laid her on the pale duvet that made her look like a fallen angel languishing on a cloud. And she opened her body to him, entreating him to lay with her. And he humbly obeyed.

Above their heads, the mirrors bore silent witness of a man and his wife engaged in the pulse and pull of passion, in the warmth and weight of wanting, in the falling away of fear and forever to a moment so ripe with the present, with now, with need, with never let me go, that there was no before, no after, no tomorrow or yesterday.

And it was perfect and untouchable.

∞

A FEW FEATHERS had escaped from the duvet and Finn pinched them between his fingers, setting them gently on my head.

"I'm making you look like an angel," he said sleepily.

"An angel who has been rolling in the hay."

"In the feathers," Finn corrected.

"The feathers," I amended. "An angel who has been rolling in the feathers all night long." Which wasn't far from the truth. Which was why I couldn't keep my eyes open. "Whenever I think of angels, I think of Minnie. And now, I think of Fish too."

"Fish wasn't an angel."

"He's your angel. Your guardian angel," I whispered. "And Minnie's mine. They brought us together, Finn. I'm sure of it. You and me? We couldn't have happened without divine intervention, and you know it."

Finn sighed, but it was more a chuckle than a groan, and I smiled sleepily with him.

"If I weren't so tired, I would make myself a headdress and a little costume out of those feathers and dance for you. I didn't get the chance in Vegas. And I promised Minnie."

"You promised Minnie you would dance for me?"

"Ha," I yawned the word. "I promised Minnie we would dance topless in Vegas." I was drifting off, the feel of Finn's fingers making circles on my bare back, so soothing I could no longer stay awake.

"Bonnie Rae?"

"Hmm?"

"There will be no topless dancing in Vegas, baby."

"Yes, there will be, Huckleberry, my handsome husband. But you can be the only one in the audience, okay?"

"Deal," he murmured.

And I burrowed my head into his chest and fell asleep, wondering how I'd ever fallen asleep without him.

And I dreamed of mirrors and angels.

∞

THE CARNIVAL CAME *every year. It traveled through the Appalachians to small communities like Grassley, offering cheap entertainment and spun sugar to ease the summer doldrums. We looked forward to it like Christmas. The operators—we called them carnies—were usually as toothless and filthy as the worst hillbilly stereotype, but we didn't mind as long as they came and brought the carnival with them. I got motion sick, but Minnie loved the rides, so I endured the spinning tilt-a-whirl and the rocking boat for Minnie's sake, and though the mirrors always scared Minnie a little, she didn't complain when I insisted on spending an hour in the fun house.*

I was mesmerized by the fun house—the mirrors morphing me into someone different with each angle. A giant, a dwarf, a stick, or something worse. I would grow dizzy and a little disoriented looking at all the ways my body and face could be stretched and contorted, but it was funny, and Minnie and I would howl with laughter as we made our way through.

When Minnie lost her hair, and I shaved my head in support, it was August, we were fifteen, and the carnival was in town. Minnie was too nauseated for the rides, which was a relief to me, but she still wanted to go to the fun house. We bought a caramel apple and a bag of cotton candy that neither of us ate, as well as a couple of brightly colored bandanas to tie over our smooth heads so we wouldn't "scare" the carnies—we thought we were so funny—and made our way into the ramshackle house of mirrors. It creaked as we walked through, and for the first time I felt the uneasy prickle of a hundred distorted images staring back at me and Minnie, as if we were surrounded by the very worst of ourselves, our fears, our faults, our ugliest features, in living incarnations.

"This is a depressing place," Minnie said softly.

"Yeah. It is." I said. I tried to poke fun at one of my reflections to scare away the gloom, but my humor fell flat, and we moved on quickly. Toward the final hallway, we found an attraction that hadn't been there in previous years. Or maybe in other years we were more innocent and less observant, more eager to run to the next delight. Whatever the reason, as we neared the exit we were caught between two giant mirrors that faced each other, reflecting the image between them back and forth ad infinitum.

We had dressed alike as we often did, or as often as cheap clothing and Goodwill bags would allow. We had on pale colored shorts and plain pink T's, our heads covered with the fluorescent green bandanas we'd purchased, and flip flops on our feet. I was browner and a little heavier than Minnie—the chemo made her more susceptible to sunburn and killed her appetite, but other than that, we were still identical.

Minnie and I stared at the rows of twins that had no end, one behind another in smaller and smaller replicas of the original. Bonnie and Minnie forever . . . and ever and ever. I reached for Minnie's hand, and all our reflections joined hands as well, making the hair rise on my neck. Maybe it should have been comforting, the thought of the two of us going on forever, but it wasn't.

"There are twins, triplets, quadruplets, quintuplets, right? But what do you call that?" Minnie said, her eyes glued to the mirror in front of us.

"Scary as hell," I answered.

"Yeah. It is. It's freaky. Let's go." Minnie let go of my hand and stepped out of the frame. She was closer to the exit, and she turned and hurried out into the sunlight that beat down beyond the flaps that covered the makeshift door. And I was alone between the mirrors. All by myself, into eternity. I spun, trying to find an angle that made the phenomenon disappear. Instead, all the Bonnies spun with me, looking for a way out.

The echoing mirror image was no longer scary. It was terrifying.

24
Impossible Event

WE ARE LIVE at the red carpet at the Academy Awards, and we've seen everyone who is anyone make their way into the Kodak Theater for tonight's big awards show. The dresses have been breathtaking, the stars stunning, but the big news tonight was the shocking attendance of country singer, Bonnie Rae Shelby, and her new husband, Infinity James Clyde.

About twenty minutes ago we received word that Bonnie Rae Shelby had just arrived at the theater. Some of our viewers might not be aware that Bonnie Rae was nominated for the Best Original Song category for "Machine," the title track from last summer's blockbuster movie of the same name. We all knew she had been nominated, but in light of recent events, no one expected her to be here.

The news started spreading through the assembled press, and the cameras were all trained on her, as she and Infinity Clyde, the ex-convict rumored at one time to have actually kidnapped Bonnie Rae Shelby, made their way to the entrance of the theater.

The whole nation has been riveted on this story. The young singer apparently walked off the stage at a concert just over a week ago, and her inner circle started putting out the story that she had disappeared. Her manager even claimed there had been a ransom demand. Then tonight, to see her walking the red carpet, glowing like a new bride, looking absolutely stunning and quite changed with a new hair color and style, was jaw dropping, to say the least. She and Clyde made a striking pair, and most people can see from the images captured tonight, America's sweetheart is all grown up

When asked where she's been and if she was aware of the national attention she'd been garnering, Bonnie Rae simply laughed, shook her head like it was all ridiculous, and then proceeded to smile and wave to the crowd all the while holding tightly to her new husband's hand. As for Infinity Clyde, the man whom so many wanted to hate, he stayed by her side, a hand at her back, and didn't answer any questions, as the two of them traversed the famed carpet.

The questions being directed at attendees before the surprising arrival of Bonnie Rae Shelby had all been about which designer an actress was wearing, or trivial questions about nerves or excitement over a nomination. When Bonnie and her infamous Clyde walked the carpet, those questions changed dramatically. We had fashion reporters and entertainment correspondents shouting questions about abduction and shot-gun weddings.

Regardless of the questions being asked, the only question that Bonnie answered was a question about her dress, an elegant white sheath that complemented her skin and figure beautifully. She informed the reporter that the dress she was wearing was her wedding dress. This drew quite a reaction from all those who heard her response, and more questions were raised, at which point Bonnie introduced Infinity Clyde as "her husband, Finn."

The folks here tonight saw entertainment history in the making. The two newlyweds seemed very intent on one another, and though it is customary for attendees to pose for some pictures separately, the two did not do so, declining requests for such shots as they made their way through the throng. As a result, every shot taken has them with their arms around each other or holding hands, and it is quite apparent that the rumors of kidnapping are fiction. You can bet when word spread to news affiliates about the appearance of this wanted couple at the Academy Awards, law enforcement must have been scratching their heads, along with Bonnie Rae's own management team, who has continuously floated rumors of ransom requests and tried to squash reports of crime sprees. The couple we saw tonight told a very different story.

Unlike most celebrities, these two were not escorted by a publicist. They exited their limo just like other attendees and walked hand in hand through security and up onto the carpet. They were a last minute arrival, which usually means less press time, since everyone is in a hurry to get into their seats, doors are getting ready to close, and people are being directed away from the event because it's about to start. Most of your biggest celebrities come right at the end, like Bonnie Rae did, just to avoid waiting a long time for the show to begin inside. But I can guarantee, regardless of their arrival time, Bonnie Rae Shelby and Infinity Clyde will be getting all the press coverage tonight.

∞

I WAS CONVINCED we'd done it.

We'd gone to the Oscars together, dressed in our wedding clothes, as Finn had called them. And the response had been perfect. Cameras flashed, and every camera and all the attention was riveted on us. I almost felt bad for the people who got there at the same time, because they were ignored, and Hollywood stars don't spend hours getting glamorous, starving for days so they aren't bloated, picking out the perfect dress, only to be upstaged by a hillbilly and an ex-con.

I certainly hadn't meant to upstage. I had just wanted everyone to see Finn and to acknowledge him. Not Infinity James Clyde the ex-convict. Not Infinity Clyde, the villain who stole America's country bumpkin, but beautiful, smart, innocent, Finn Clyde. My Finn.

And I was pretty sure they had. The women had gaped. The men had paled in comparison, and because I was with him, I felt like the most beautiful woman in the room.

The truth of it made me giggle. We'd been up all night, so we'd slept all day, and we'd had to rush a little to get ready. I got ready for the Oscars in an hour. I was sure that was also a record. I was bathed and shaved, moisturized and perfumed, made up and done up with very little fanfare. But even without a team of people making me look like a movie star, I felt amazing. And because I felt amazing, maybe I looked amazing. Finn certainly did. He looked so handsome that I had wondered how I would make it to the theatre and keep my dress on.

However, resisting the urge to seduce my husband in the limo didn't turn out to be as difficult as I thought it would be. Finn was tense and ill at ease, and the closer we got to the venue, the more nervous we both became. Finn was vibrating, his left knee shaking up and down as I pressed my hand to his thigh and promised him it would be okay. He'd just looked at me and told me I was beautiful, but he didn't relax.

"When this is over, we're going to go back to the Bordeaux. We're going to stay there for a week. Maybe two. I've already reserved our room, indefinitely. They know where to bill me. And we are going to have a true honeymoon. We're going to make plans, make love, and make bacon."

"Make bacon?"

"I'm hungry." I shrugged. "When was the last time we ate?"

"Yesterday, in Las Vegas."

"Holy cow! I'm a terrible wife. A man like you can't go that long without nourishment. I'm used to starving. Gran watched every damn bite I put in my mouth."

"All right then. We'll order bacon and eggs and a pile of potatoes. We'll eat when we're done tonight. We'll celebrate. And I promise you can eat as much as you want, whenever you want, and I won't mind."

I laughed, and Finn took a fortifying breath, and with meat on my mind and a man on my arm, Finn and I had stepped out of the limo and taken on the red carpet.

I didn't win the Oscar and I was relieved. I made sure I was snuggled into Finn when the camera panned to me as my name was read, and I had smiled brightly and given America a little thumbs up. But I had been thrilled when the award went to someone else. I'd probably clapped a little too enthusiastically, but had I won I was liable to go up on stage and say something I would have regretted—something that wouldn't have played well in the media. Something like, "I love Jesus and I love singin', so I'm thankful for the voice He gave me to sing this song. But I hate all you fake-assed people with your plastic boobs and messed up priorities." And then I would have looked into the camera and said. "And yes, Gran. I'm talkin' to you."

And my drawl would have made them all think I didn't have a brain in my head, and people would have laughed at me, and Finn would have said "Bonnie Rae," in that voice he used when he wasn't sure if he wanted to laugh at me, love me, or lose me. So it was good that I didn't win.

Finn and I slipped out of our seats after that, and I called for our limo to return for us. We'd done what we needed to do, and it was time to eat bacon at the Bordeaux.

∞

THE LIGHTS FLASHED behind us. Then there were lights in front of us, and lights to the side of us too. Not flashbulbs any longer, but blue lights, spinning. And the sirens wailed.

The window between the driver and the back of the limo slid down, and the driver informed us in a few panicked words that he was pulling over. We were only two blocks from the Kodak Theatre. They'd been waiting for us to come out—that much was obvious. Maybe they thought we were armed and dangerous and wanted to get us away from the crowds. Had Gran created this mess? And why did they want us at all? We'd carried out our plan to show the world we were together. But apparently the police had gotten the breaking news bulletin from E Buzz.

Finn looked at me as if he'd known it was coming. And he kissed me, quickly, almost desperately, as the limo came to a stop at the side of the road. I kissed him back frantically, and clung to him, wondering momentarily if there was still a way out, as if we could outrun the police that now surrounded us. There were police cars everywhere.

"It was worth it, Bonnie. Every second. It was worth it." His voice was soft, and his eyes were grim, and I flinched as we heard a voice demand over a loudspeaker:

"Step out of the vehicle with your hands in the air."

"We're going to do exactly what they are telling us to do, Bonnie Rae. We'll clear this up, and it'll be over."

"I'm so sorry, Finn! I'm so sorry! All of this is my fault."

"Step out of the car with your hands in the air!" The voice over the loudspeaker came again, adamant.

Finn opened his door, lifted his hands, and climbed out of the car. I couldn't see exactly what happened next but beyond the opened door I could see guns drawn and cops creating a bit of a perimeter around us.

It was like we were the true Bonnie and Clyde, in our own ambush, and my heart raced at the memory of the bullet-ridden car.

I stepped out behind him, since I was closer to his door than my own. I saw him being pushed to the ground, even as I registered that the same thing was happening to me. My heel caught in the back of my dress, and I felt a tug and something tear as I faltered and lost my ensnared shoe. I fell hard and found myself face first on the ground, my hands wrenched behind me, and I lifted my head, spitting at the gravel that had found its way into my mouth. My dress would be ruined—the dress I had wanted to cherish, the dress I'd been afraid to touch for fear of messing it up. It's funny the things you think about when you're being handcuffed.

My face stung, and I shook my head, trying to shake off the dirt and bits of debris that clung to my face. I felt something wet slide down my forehead and drip down the left side of my face and realized my head was bleeding. I struggled to see Finn through the legs of the officers surrounding me and found him, head lifted, straining to see me too. His eyes met mine, and I saw his mouth move around my name. I couldn't hear him though his head was only ten feet from my own. But I held his gaze for as long as possible, needing the contact in whatever form it took.

Hands slid up my body, between my legs, over my arms, patting up and down, and I shuddered and flinched and had to look away, the pat down all the more personal and invasive because I was sore in the way new brides are sore, tender in the way women are tender, and the hands that moved over me now were a rude parody of something that had brought me so much pleasure only hours before. I shivered, the damp of the evening seeping through the thin material and clinging to my bare arms, making me feel even more exposed. And then I was pulled to my feet and led toward a police car, away from Finn.

"What the hell is going on? Why is she being arrested?" I heard Finn shout, his calm completely abandoned, and then he was gone, shoved into the back of another police car, the doors unceremoniously shut on his outraged voice.

25

Restricted Domain

BREAKING NEWS: INFINITY James Clyde and Bonnie Rae Shelby, seen earlier tonight at the Academy Awards in an appearance that shocked the nation and rallied law enforcement, were detained after the Awards and brought separately to the LA County jail. Onlookers claim the newlyweds were in their limo, only blocks from the Kodak Theater, when they were surrounded by police and again, bodily detained and handcuffed. No charges have been filed yet, although warrants are said to be forthcoming. It is believed that Clyde will indeed be charged with kidnapping, though that seems difficult to substantiate, given what we saw earlier tonight. It is also likely that he will face attempted murder charges and car theft, in addition to several more related charges. We have no word on what, if anything, Bonnie Rae Shelby will be charged with, but she, too, has been detained and is currently at the LA County Jail.

∞

HE'D BEEN THROUGH it before. He knew what to expect. But they'd arrested Bonnie too, and taken her someplace else. She would be feeling as scared and humiliated as he'd felt the first time, and there wasn't a damn thing he could do to save her from it. Her face had been bleeding, and her dress was torn. He'd seen her fall as his face was forced into the dirt. And the sight of her wide eyes, trying to meet his as they patted her down had made him want to howl with fury.

When he'd been booked into jail the first time, he'd been terrified, but he had also been in shock, the shock numbing him to the humiliation of the fingerprinting, the mug shots, the strip search, and eventually, the bars that closed behind him. Eighteen years old wasn't very old at all, and mostly he'd wanted to cry like the child he was.

He'd been arrested at the hospital, his brother on a gurney beside him. He hadn't known where else to go. He'd driven to the hospital with Fish laying across his lap, not breathing. Not blinking. Blood everywhere. And he'd run through the emergency room doors soaked in it, yelling for help. They'd rushed Fish inside, but he was dead. And there was no saving the dead. Then the police had been called. His mom had been called too. And when they'd arrived, Finn had told them everything that had happened, his voice dull and emotionless. And they arrested him. His mother had been left with one dead child while another had been taken away.

He didn't blame her for staying with Fish. She couldn't come with him anyway. He'd been eighteen years old for all of three days—legally old enough to be charged as an adult, questioned without his parents present, and old enough to go to prison.

This time around they didn't book him right away. Apparently, he was only being detained. Arrest warrants were on their way, according to the detective who brought him a glass of water and placed a yellow notepad and a pen on the table, cuffing his hands in front of him so he could write.

"You have the right to remain silent and to refuse to answer any questions. Whatever you say can and will be used against you in a court of law." But Finn didn't want to remain silent. He was going to talk and talk and talk. He was going to tell them every damn thing they wanted to hear and a few they didn't. They had put him into a holding cell for an hour when they'd first arrived—ostensibly so he could calm down. It was cold, the size of a bathroom, nobody there but him. It felt weird to be completely alone. He had been with Bonnie almost every second of the day since he'd found her singing in the park in the middle of the night and had known he never wanted to be apart from her again.

"You have the right to an attorney. If you can't afford one, one will be appointed to you." He couldn't afford one. But Bonnie could. And that was more important anyway. He hoped she'd been able to make a call, and Bear and her grandmother had come swooping in to whisk her away. They hadn't given him a phone call. He'd kind of lost that privilege when he'd lost his temper when they'd put Bonnie in the back of a police car. It didn't matter anyway. He wasn't going to call anyone.

"Do you understand your rights as I have explained them to you?"

Finn understood. And he didn't have much faith that understanding them would help him at all. Somewhere between Massachusetts and LA, his world had been turned upside down and shaken, loosening the change from his pockets, scrambling his brains, and leaving him dizzy, dazed and disoriented.

"Name?"

"Infinity James Clyde." The detective knew his name. It was on the paper right in front of him. But he asked it with a note of incredulity in his voice, like he couldn't believe what he was reading.

There was a raise of the eyebrows and the slightest smirk, which Finn ignored. I have a stupid name, douche. Grow up, he thought. But he didn't say what he was thinking out loud.

"And why do you think you're here, Mr. Clyde?"

Finn stared stonily at the man across the table from him. He'd introduced himself as Detective Kelly, "I honestly don't know, Detective."

Another smirk.

"Says here you're wanted for kidnapping, extortion, theft, grand theft, assault, and attempted murder. That ring any bells?"

Finn stared at the detective in stunned stupefaction. He kept waiting for the punch line, but there was none forthcoming.

"What did you say?" he asked, his voice a hoarse whisper.

"Kidnapping, extortion, theft, assault, grand theft, and attempted murder," the detective rattled off once more.

He didn't understand any of it, except the kidnapping part, which was easily explainable. He focused on the most horrifying first. He tried to keep his voice steady, but the blood had been pounding in his veins since they'd dragged Bonnie Rae off like she was trash, and his outrage returned with a heady rush. With every question his voice increased in volume.

"Who did I attempt to murder? What the hell is grand theft? Who did I extort, and who did I assault? I'd really like to know."

"Cut the crap, kid. Grand theft auto." The detective sighed wearily. It was one o'clock in the morning on Monday, and he looked wilted and worn thin, a man just doing his job, but the detective would be going home to his own bed, and Finn would be going back to a cell. Finn reined in his frustration and tried to focus on the task at hand.

"Okay. One by one. Whose car did I steal?" he asked. "I can't exactly defend myself if I don't know what I supposedly did."

"You didn't return a rental car—but that's not the big one. We're awaiting a warrant for the attempted murder of Malcolm Johnson and the theft of his car."

"I don't know who you're talking about! I don't know what you're talking about!" Finn shook his head in denial, staring at the detective who was looking back at him like he was ready to be done with the interview.

"You don't know Malcolm Johnson—called Bear Johnson by everyone close to him? Bonnie Rae Shelby's bodyguard? You didn't drive his car across several states and abandon it when you thought you were going to be apprehended?"

"Bear?" Finn felt the earth shift, and the room grew dim for a moment, like his brain had checked out, needing a break from the Twilight Zone.

"Oh, you do know him?" the detective asked with feigned interest.

"Is he okay?" The unreturned messages and the unanswered texts suddenly made sense. And he and Bonnie had been too wrapped up in each other to worry. They'd been too intent on just moving forward, on making it.

"You said attempted murder. Is he all right?" Finn demanded again. Bonnie would be finding out the same way he was. And she would be devastated.

"He's going to recover. That's all I can tell you."

"What happened?"

"We don't have any surveillance footage but we think we have a pretty good idea. You see, some ex-con arranged a meeting with Mr. Johnson at a gas station just outside of St. Louis. Maybe Mr. Johnson thought he was coming to get the girl, maybe it was something else. Instead, the ex-con proceeded to shoot Mr. Johnson, who was at the pump filling up his tank with his iPod blaring. He didn't hear the guy coming up behind him. He was shot in the back and left for dead while the suspect drove away in his car. But you know that."

Finn was shaking his head emphatically. "No! Bear wasn't driving his car. He was driving my rental car. We switched in St. Louis, at my dad's house. He was going to turn it back in in Nashville. I called the rental place and told them it would be returned by four o'clock on Thursday."

"Well, it never was because you took Mr. Johnson's Charger and left your rental sitting at the pump."

"Bear was driving that rental car. Bonnie and I were already headed in the opposite direction. Bear knew we had his car. How stupid would I have to be to leave my rental car sitting there after I tried to kill someone!"

The detective raised his eyebrows and looked down at the pages he held in his hand.

"How about we start at the beginning–when you left Massachusetts. Okay? You give me a timeline of where you were, when. I want specifics. When you're done, I'll look at your timeline, I'll see if there's corroborating evidence to substantiate your story, and we will go from there." He pushed the pad of paper and pen closer to Finn and stood.

"We're waiting for the warrants to come in. Then we will book you. You'll see a judge sometime tomorrow or the next day for your arraignment hearing and after that you'll be extradited to St. Louis—but I'll be back when you're finished with your statement." He turned to go.

"When will I know what's happening to my wife?"

Detective Kelly halted and turned. Then he shoved his hands in his pockets and tipped his head.

"Your wife. Yeah. I bet that'll last long. She's still in interview, far as I know. She has a temper, that one. And a big mouth too. Another spoiled celebrity . . . we seem to book a new one every month. But it's looking like she's going to be released."

Finn felt faint with relief and laid his head down on the notepad, smelling the clean, papery smell, and wishing he could fill the pages with numbers instead of words—numbers that would continue to grow and expand, unending, breaking down the walls that held him, creating a force field around him. The thought gave him an idea. He lifted his head and looked at the empty page, contemplating the numbers that documented his journey from a bridge in Boston to a cell in Los Angeles.

"I'm sure she'll come see you as soon as she can," the detective added, interrupting Finn's train of thought. Then the detective started to laugh. "Or not."

∞

WHEN THE WARRANT came down from the Missouri DA, the lead agency in the case, Finn was officially booked into the LA County Jail.

Fingerprints, mug shots, medical checks, strip search.

He'd been through them before. Many times. In prison it's a common occurrence. Yet, as they took his clothes and put them in a sack, and then told him to stand up naked and stretch his arms and legs out, it wasn't any easier to endure. As they told him to stick out his tongue, bend back his ears, tilt his head, wiggle his fingers and toes, lift his arms and legs he cringed and bore down on the indignation that rose in his throat. All he could think about was Bonnie. The thought of her being put through the humiliating process made him angry and desperate, and when he was instructed to bend and spread he couldn't do it.

He didn't respond the way he should have. He got agitated, he didn't cooperate, he shoved the officer conducting the search, and he was immediately pushed to the floor and left without his clothes for an hour before they conducted the search again, a little more forcefully than before. This time he contained himself, and he was given a jumpsuit and rubber shoes and left in the holding cell once more.

26
Significant Digits

FINN HAD SPENT the rest of the night and the entire day bouncing between holding and the various booking procedures necessary to process a new inmate. The rest of the day he'd spent waiting for this interview with the detective who had instructed him to write his statement. His arraignment hearing had been moved to first thing Tuesday morning, which meant more waiting. He hadn't had any word about Bonnie. If she was out, he wouldn't be able to see her until after the hearing anyway, but when Detective Kelly walked into the interview room, a thick file in his hands, and dropped into the seat across from Finn, Finn welcomed the first words out of his mouth.

"Your wife's been released, and you're still on the hook for a bunch of shit. How do you like them apples?"

Finn felt a sinking in his chest that belied his deliberately blank expression. Bonnie had been released. He would focus on that and ignore the rest of what the detective had to say. He looked down at his hand, at the five dots that made up the man in the cage. The sixth dot, the one Bonnie had added to represent herself, was fading. Another day or two, and it would be gone.

"And really, Mr. Clyde. Are you trying to be a wise ass?"

Finn brought his attention back to the detective who was eyeing him with exasperation.

Finn maintained his neutral expression and waited for the detective to clarify exactly what he meant by "wise ass." He'd spent hours writing his full statement the night before, and he'd taken it very seriously. After all, his life sorta depended on it.

"This statement is twenty, hand-written pages long." Detective Kelly scowled.

"It's a detailed account," Finn replied, but his mouth twitched a little.

"Yeah. Detailed. Did you enjoy making up license plate numbers and exit numbers?"

"Did you check the license plate numbers and exit numbers?" Finn asked.

"Now, why in the hell would I do that?"

"Because they validate my timeline."

"I see. And did you take note of all these things as you drove?" the detective asked, his lips pursed doubtfully.

"Depends on what you mean by taking notes. I didn't write them down, if that's what you mean. Even if I had, I didn't have them when I wrote my statement, did I? The guy who kept staring at my ass during the strip search will verify that."

Anger flickered over the detective's face at Finn's insolence.

"So you're telling me that you just remembered all these numbers?"

"I'm good with numbers."

The memory of the last time he'd said that very same line echoed in his head. He'd told Cavaro as much before he'd been beaten up and tattooed with playing cards. He hoped the result here would be different. The detective turned pages again.

"You pulled over on February 28th to assist a motorist with the West Virginia license plate 5BI-662." Detective Kelly raised his eyes from the page and shook his head like it was highly doubtful.

"That's right."

"You wanna explain to me how you remember that little detail?"

"It's a game I play. I convert letters to their corresponding alphabetical number. So 5BI would be 529. 529 is a perfect square. So is 662. So the license plate had two perfect squares." Finn shrugged. "That's how I remembered it."

"So why didn't you just remember the 529 662 part? How could you remember which numbers were changed from letters? How did you remember 5BI?"

It wasn't a bad question, and Finn could have told him then that he had a photographic memory—which he did when it came to anything numerically related, but instead he pointed to the page.

"The guy driving the maroon van was named Bill Isakson—BI. And Bonnie was the one looking for license plates from different states. She had a song for every state. She'd been looking for West Virginia."

"Okay. Fine. Two perfect squares and a guy named Bill Isakson."

"It wasn't his car. It was his daughter's car. But it shouldn't take too much digging to verify now that you have the license plate to work with."

"And you two just made a habit of helping stranded motorists and hitchhikers around every turn? A couple of do-gooders?"

"I wouldn't have helped any of them. Bonnie's the do-gooder," Finn answered.

"Oh, I see. And you just wanted to do Bonnie?" the detective asked.

Finn felt his anger whiz and ricochet around in his head, like he'd released an untied balloon. He took several deep breaths, letting the anger expend itself. Then he looked at the smirking detective and waited. He knew all cops weren't dicks. But this one was trying to ruffle him. He knew the game. When he didn't comment, the detective moved on.

"I actually called this Shayna Harris you refer to. She hasn't returned my call. You say she gave you her number in case you were ever in need of anything. And you memorized it. Kind of creepy, Mr.

Clyde. Let me guess, another perfect square?"

"No. Her phone number is prime."

"Prime?"

"A prime number. You know. Only divisible by itself and one?"

"And her phone number is a prime?"

"Yes. 3,541,541 is a prime number."

The detective read the number from the sheet. "704-354-1541. How did you remember the area code?"

"It's three digits. It wasn't especially hard to remember." The microwave clock at Shayna's house had said 7:04 when he'd walked through the kitchen to retrieve the boots she'd given him and found her thank you note with her number inside propped against the laces. He'd left Cincinnati in pursuit of Bonnie and his orange Blazer that evening at 7:04 pm, according to the clock in his rental car.

704 had been the number for the day. He usually discovered there was one—a number that kept reappearing everywhere he looked. It had carried over into the next day too, and the next. He'd spent seventy dollars and four cents filling up Bear's car and buying two sub sandwiches and several bottles of water at the convenience store in Pacific. William's initials, G.O.D, were also 704—G is the seventh letter of the alphabet, D is the fourth. And finally, 704 was their room number at the Bordeaux Hotel, which he'd considered a good omen.

"I checked. 704 is a North Carolina area code." The detective threw this irrelevant piece of information out like he was really onto something.

"Okay."

"But you say Shayna Harris lives in Portsmouth, Ohio."

"She does. You'll have to ask Shayna about her phone number, but her husband's parents live in North Carolina."

The detective harrumphed and turned back to the beginning.

"The old man who pulled your car out of the ditch in Ohio . . ."

"His license was CAD 159," Finn said, not waiting for the detective to finish the question. "Change the letters to numbers and you have 3.14159—the first six digits of pi."

"The deputy who saw you running in Freedom and asked for your name?"

"His badge number was 112—three consecutive numbers in the Fibonacci Sequence. The clock on his dash said 11:23—four consecutive numbers in the sequence."

One by one, they went through the numbers on Finn's statement, exit numbers and mile markers and license plates and road signs—numbers that Finn hadn't consciously tried to remember, but numbers that might save him. Again. The detective grew more and more astonished and less and less skeptical as they talked, until all at once, he stood from the table and walked out of the room without a word, Finn's twenty page statement in his hands. A few minutes later, Finn was escorted back to his cell where he waited once more, trying not to contemplate the number of times he'd thought about Bonnie and the infinite ways that he missed her.

∞

BONNIE WASN'T AT his arraignment hearing. But her gran was. Raena Shelby was fine-boned like Bonnie, with the same high cheek bones and square jaw—that square Shelby chin Bonnie had mournfully told him about when she'd cried about her resemblance to Hank.

When he saw her, Finn had known immediately who she was, even though her hair was a store-bought red, her eyes a pale blue, and her skin several shades lighter than Bonnie's. Bonnie had those dark eyes and that golden skin that made her look perpetually warm and sun-kissed. This woman wasn't sun-kissed. She was unsmiling and stern, and kept glancing over at Finn like he was filth and they were on an episode of *Law and Order*.

She sat in the back with a man Finn assumed was her lawyer, and they whispered back and forth. He wanted to catch her eye and spit, letting her know exactly what he thought of her, but instead, he kept his face blank and his stare hard and continually twisted his wedding ring until she was the one who looked away and didn't look back.

It was a small victory and provided little comfort. The fact remained that Bonnie wasn't there. And he wasn't the only one who took note of her absence. The room was thick with reporters, although cameras were not allowed in. The media frenzy hadn't lost any of its fervor.

The arraignment hearing wasn't much more than a swift procedural stamp. Finn waited for his turn longer than he stood before the judge. No defense was offered during arraignment. It was all business. Charges were read, Finn pled not guilty, and an attorney was appointed to him. He would not be talking to the police from there on out, and his new, albeit temporary until he was extradited, attorney promised to meet with him later in the day. He would be brought to Missouri within the week unless he waived extradition. He wouldn't be waiving it. What was the point?

∞

"YOU HAVE A visitor."

Finn wasn't surprised. He'd been expecting his new lawyer. But he wasn't led to an interview room. He was led down a long line of stools, sparsely populated by inmates who faced a glass partition and talked to their visitors through phones on the other side. His heart leaped in his throat, and he tamped down the urge to surge forward, expecting Bonnie to be waiting across the glass. Instead, her grandmother sat there, her elegant hand wrapped around the receiver of the phone, her mouth set in a thin line, waiting for him to pick up the receiver on his side and speak with her.

He considered refusing to see her. But his curiosity won out, and he slid onto the stool and grasped the phone in his manacled hands, holding it to his ear as he waited for her to speak. He didn't ask for Bonnie, he didn't ask her what she wanted. He just waited.

She considered him briefly and then said, "Aren't you wondering why you're still being charged, while Bonnie has been released?"

He didn't respond.

"I mean, if you two were together . . . wouldn't she be guilty too?"

Finn wasn't sure what the purpose of this visit was, but Raena Shelby—Gran—obviously was. Gran didn't fit her at all. Gran sounded like a woman with gray permed hair and little bifocals.

"Police believe you drew Bear in with promises to turn Bonnie over to him. And maybe you really did plan to exchange Bonnie for the cash. But Bonnie had pulled a fast one on you and escaped in your Blazer. Which is why you had to rent the car, which is why, when Bear showed up without the money, you shot him."

"What money?" Finn broke his silence, incredulous.

"The $500,000 you demanded."

Finn just stared, dumfounded once more.

"I withdrew the money two days before you shot Bear." Raena Shelby was studying him as she spoke, as if gauging the effectiveness of her story.

"Why are you here?" Finn asked, his head spinning, his heart in his throat. He'd never asked for a damn dime.

She ignored him, continuing on like an attorney in cross examination.

"The reason you're being charged, and Bonnie isn't, is because the police have a very clear picture of what really happened. It's not hard to figure out." She paused, waiting to make sure he was hanging on her words. Her blue eyes were icy, and her hand tightened on the phone.

"You found Bonnie wandering around Boston. Suicidal and lost. And instead of taking her to a hospital or calling the police, you took her across the country."

For the first time, Finn felt a twinge of guilt.

"You recognized her. You saw dollar signs. And you took her." Raena Shelby's eyes narrowed, and she sneered disdainfully. "There's evidence that she tried to get away from you. She took your Blazer to escape, which is why you had to rent a car. And all of this was right around the time Bear was shot."

Finn didn't allow himself to respond. He gritted his teeth and waited her out, knowing it didn't matter what he said to defend himself. She had written the narrative, and she was delivering her lines like a seasoned actress.

"There is also evidence that she is not mentally stable. Bonnie Rae isn't well. She was diagnosed with bi-polar disorder. She's supposed to be taking medicine. Did you know that Finn?" She asked the question curiously and said his first name like she was suddenly his friend.

Finn wanted to hang up the phone. He wanted to signal to the guard that he was done. He wanted to break the glass and strangle the self-satisfied woman who sat across from him, attempting to reduce the last week of his life—the best week of his life—to rubble.

"I thought for sure she was dead when I saw her hair strewn around the dressing room. She had a nervous breakdown. That's what these last two weeks have been—one big nervous breakdown. She's not well, Finn. You don't really want a girl like that, do you? Oh, I can see how you might get distracted by her beauty. And her talent. And her money, most of all. She's rich. That's got to be irresistible to a man like you."

A man like you. Irresistible. Finn fought the urge to throw up. Bonnie Rae *was* irresistible. What had he told her? *You make me feel. And feeling that much is irresistible sometimes. You are irresistible sometimes."*

She shot a glance down at the ring he wore on his finger and met his eyes once more.

"She doesn't want to see you. Now that she's been released and has had some time to think, she just wants to put it all behind her.

The marriage will be annulled, obviously. It's being taken care of."

She waited for him to respond, and when he didn't, a flash of frustration tightened her lips.

"You thought you were being so smart, didn't you? You thought marriage would save you." Raena laughed, and Finn caught a brief hint of Bonnie's wide, curving grin in her grandmother's expression. But there was no sunshine or joy in the smile—making the resemblance shallow and false.

"None of it was real, Finn. You married a girl who is hungry for attention and totally incapable of taking care of herself at this point. It was an imaginary love affair that was never going to survive the week. It wasn't real," she repeated, adamant.

"You never got the money you asked for. But we'll give it to you—all of it. You're going to need it to defend yourself. And who knows? I just got word that Bear's regained consciousness. So maybe you'll get off. And maybe you'll have some money left to start over. And in exchange for $500,000, you will never speak to Bonnie again. You won't give interviews, you won't write a tell-all book, and you'll take off that wedding ring."

Finn laid the phone down abruptly and stood from his chair. He signaled to the guard, who motioned him forward, and without another look at Raena Shelby, he walked away.

27

Major Arc

WE HAVE BREAKING news that Hank Shelby, the brother of singing sensation Bonnie Rae Shelby, has just been arrested in Nashville for the attempted murder of Malcolm "Bear" Johnson. Hank Shelby has been in and out of rehab, and has most recently been living in his grandmother's home in Nashville.

It is believed that Shelby followed Bear Johnson from Nashville to St. Louis on February 28 and reportedly shot Malcolm Johnson at a St. Louis gas station. Police have issued a statement that Hank Shelby was behind a $500,000 ransom demand, and that all charges against Infinity James Clyde have been dropped, and he will be released from the LA County Jail within the hour.

Bonnie Rae Shelby, arrested alongside her husband, Infinity Clyde, was released from LA County Jail Monday evening, and there has been no statement from her or from her lawyers regarding the arrest, her release, or her involvement in the ongoing investigation which, again, is now being focused on Hank Shelby, Bonnie Rae Shelby's older brother.

∞

HE WAS FREE. At eight am Wednesday morning, he was called into interview and Detective Kelly informed him, with very little apology, that the entire case against him had fallen apart. The DA in Missouri had contacted them and told them all charges had been dropped against him. According to the detective, Finn's numbers had added up to a whole lot of reasonable doubt, but most importantly, Bear Johnson had been cogent enough to talk to police, and he had corroborated Finn's story.

It had taken a few hours for the paperwork to be processed. Then they'd given Finn his property—his suit and his wallet, along with his shiny black shoes—and he'd signed a bunch of forms. To his surprise, his dad had come and was waiting for him in the reception area. Apparently he'd been waiting inside for hours. Neither of them were prepared for the crowd outside.

"Mr. Clyde, have you talked to your wife?"

"Is Bonnie Rae here, Finn?"

"How does it feel to be cleared of all charges?"

"Are you going to press charges of your own?"

"What do you think about reports that Bonnie's brother was behind the attempted murder?"

"Does your wife have a drug habit like her brother?"

"We've heard rumors of an annulment—can you comment on that?"

"Why isn't Bonnie here, Mr. Clyde?"

Rapid-fire questions came from every direction, and there were microphones in Finn's face and cameras surrounding him.

It was like the Academy Awards on crack. He was jostled and bumped, and the questions became more persistent as his dad took his arm, and they made their way to a grey sedan in the parking lot.

"I have nothing to say," Finn kept repeating, shaking his head and plowing through the assembled reporters and onlookers, moving with determination until he reached the car.

"What happens next for Bonnie and Clyde?" someone shouted right in his ear.

Finn halted, the question reverberating in his head, ricocheting off blank walls and bare floors like he was alone in an empty room, instead of in the middle of an impromptu press conference. He lifted his face to the midday sun, sun that was too bright for early March. It was the kind of day that made people keep coming back to California. You couldn't help but forgive her for the fog and the rain when she stood in all her glory, sunshine pouring down on you, making you forget you were ever cold or alone. Like Bonnie. Bonnie was just like that.

Finn took a deep breath and closed his eyes against the rays. And he stood, hands over his eyes, waiting for the grief to ebb.

"Mr. Clyde? Are you all right?" someone asked.

"What happens next for Bonnie and Clyde?" the same reporter repeated, clearly aware that her question had affected him.

"Bonnie and Clyde died a long time ago," Finn said, and pulled the door of his father's rental car open, managing to create just enough space to wedge himself through the opening. His dad did the same, started the car, and they inched their way out of the parking lot, until they were finally clear of the media circus.

∞

"IS THAT ALL you have?" his dad asked after they'd been driving aimlessly for a while. His dad was sure they were being followed, and he was probably right. So they just drove.

"What?"

"Your clothes. You're wearing a tux. Is that all you have?" Jason Clyde pointed to his suit.

Finn pulled at the hanging curl of his bowtie, still wrapped around his neck and held in place by the collar. It came free easily, and he wadded it up and stuck it in his pocket with his wallet. He had his wallet. That was something, he supposed.

"Yeah. This is it." Everything else he owned was either in the

Blazer or scattered across several states. Everything except the stuff in room 704 at the Bordeaux Hotel—his leather jacket along with the boots Shayna had given him, his jeans and the T-shirt Bonnie had purchased for him in Oklahoma. His shaving kit and toothbrush were there too. And Bonnie's things—her red boots and her puffy pink coat. He was sure all of it had been gathered up by housekeeping. Maybe the maid had kept it, and maybe it was all being auctioned on eBay at that very moment.

"So you married that girl?" His dad kept looking at the ring on Finn's finger. He should take it off. It was over. An imaginary love affair. But he didn't want to. Not yet.

"Yeah. I did."

"Where is she?"

"Gone—I don't know, Dad."

His dad looked at him, his brow creased, one hand on the wheel, one hand rubbing his chin, the way he did when he was trying to unravel something incredibly elusive. It was a look Finn knew well, a look he understood, a look he hadn't seen in years. He and his father had talked since his release, but that was all. He was still tall and thin, and he had always rounded his shoulders, stooping slightly, as if the weight of his brain had bowed his back. He had bright blue eyes and thinning brown hair. Finn had the same bright blue eyes—Fish had had them too—but they'd inherited their Norse blondness from their mother's side of the family—and probably their brawn as well, considering his mom's father and her brother both looked like Vikings.

"Why are you here, Dad?" Finn asked.

His father's hand fell from his chin and joined the other hand on the wheel.

"Bonnie called me. She thought you might need me. I thought you might need me."

Finn nodded once, ignoring the way his heart leaped at the sound of her name. She had cared enough to call his father. "I've needed you before now."

"Yes. I know. But I didn't have any answers. Not then. This time . . . I thought I might."

"Oh yeah?" Finn laughed, but it sounded more like a sob, and he turned and stared blindly out the window at the palm trees and green bushes and businesses that hugged the streets they wandered.

"I have the Blazer back in St. Louis. I thought about driving it here, thinking you might want it right away. But it would have taken me too long to get here—and I wanted to be here when you were released. I flew in this morning and came straight here. I've just been waiting for you to be processed."

"So you came to take me back to St. Louis?" Finn reached for the button to roll the window down. He couldn't breathe.

"Yes. If that's what you want."

Finn's eyebrows shot up. "If that's what I want?" He laughed again, the same rattling sob that he didn't recognize. It hurt coming out of his chest, and he placed a hand on his heart to make it stop. "When have I ever gotten what I wanted, Dad? I can't think of a single, damn time."

He had wanted Bonnie. He had wanted her more than anything else. And he'd gotten her for a few precious days. For one perfect night. But she wasn't his anymore. She really never had been, if he was being honest with himself. But he'd wanted her. He'd wanted her so badly.

"Why?" His dad looked from the road to Finn's face and back again.

"Why? Why what, Dad?" He threw up his hands and brought them down heavily on the dashboard. His wedding ring caught the light and he swore.

"Why don't you ever get anything you want?" Jason Clyde's brow was wrinkled in confusion, and Finn was reminded just how irritating his dad could be. So simple, yet so intelligent. So focused, yet so unaware. So smart and yet so damn dumb.

"Because I keep chasing after things . . . after people . . . I keep chasing the wrong things," Finn finished ineptly, throwing his hands up in frustration.

"So you want the wrong things?"

"This isn't a goddamn paradox, Dad! This isn't math. This is my life. I'm talking about people I love. And there is no magic formula or unknown number that can make the equation work. "

"You're right, Finn. But to people like you and me, everything is a paradox. We overthink everything. It's what we're good at. But sometimes the answer is very simple. Both in math, and in life."

"Really? And what is the answer, Dad? I am in love with a woman who is as gone to me as Fish is. That doesn't seem simple at all."

"Are you sure?"

"Her grandmother paid me a visit. Told me Bonnie didn't want to see me, that the whole thing was a huge mistake. Marriage over. Call it temporary insanity. She said Bonnie's sick. She said the last two weeks were evidence of a nervous breakdown. She even offered me money to go away and stay away."

Jason Clyde frowned. "I talked to Bonnie. She didn't seem crazy."

"Oh, she's crazy." Finn tried to laugh and couldn't, it hurt too damn much. So he continued on. "She's crazy . . . but not in a bad way. In the best way. She's impulsive and unpredictable. And she's sad." Finn gritted his teeth against the ache in his chest, thinking about the way she'd looked that night on the bridge, her face tear-stained and her hair in ragged blonde spikes. It was amazing to him she was as sane as she was, considering the family she was raised in.

"But in spite of that sadness, she still laughs. She still loves. She's kind and way too generous for her own good." He shook his head helplessly. "She's also completely impossible, and I want to wring her neck half the time."

"That's not bipolar. That's just a complicated woman. She sounds like your mom."

"Yeah." Finn's smile was pained. "She's a little like Fish too."

"And that's hard for you. Because you're afraid she'll end up like Fish. You're afraid you'll lose your other half, just like you did before."

"So I'm afraid? That's the simple answer?" Finn said, exasperated.

"Yes." His father nodded. 'Yes. That's the simple answer."

Finn felt the anger burst in his chest like a bomb had gone off—a ticking time bomb, set and counting down since the day his dad had moved far, far away from his family, from his sons who had needed him.

"I need to get out, Dad."

"Finn—"

"I need to get out, Dad!" Finn shouted, his hand on the door handle.

Jason Clyde pulled into the parking lot of a Chinese Restaurant with a quick squeal of tires and a tap on his brakes, and Finn was out before the car was completely stopped.

His father followed him, the doors to the grey rental hanging open, the car parked haphazardly, chiming insistently that the key was still in the ignition. It reminded him of the morning he'd kissed Bonnie in the Motel 6 parking lot, angry, frustrated, confused—already in love and unable to find a rational explanation for it. The memory made his legs weak, and he walked to the curb and sat abruptly.

His father sat beside him, leaving a few feet between them, but he reached out and touched Finn's shoulder tentatively.

"Finn. You're scared. Scared doesn't mean weak. You're not weak. Don't misunderstand. You're one of the strongest people I've ever known. You're loyal. You're steady. And I am in awe of you, son."

Finn wanted to shake his father off, but he held himself still, waiting.

"I am in awe of you," his father said again, emphatically, and Finn fought the rising flood inside of him with all his strength, feeling the cracks that raced and widened, threatening to break him open.

"But you are afraid, Finn. And as long as you're afraid, you won't ever get what you want. Take it from someone who has been afraid his entire life." His dad's voice broke. "You're afraid of being like me. You're afraid of losing yourself in the numbers, of not being there for the people who need you. You're afraid of being who you are . . . and you're afraid that who you are isn't enough."

Finn flinched, panting at the effort it took to keep his defenses in place. He wanted to bury his head in his hands, but his dad wasn't through chipping away, though he did so softly, sympathetically, his hand never leaving Finn's shoulder.

"You're afraid you love Bonnie too much. You're afraid that she'll tell you to go, the way your mother told me to go. From the moment I married your mom, I was afraid of losing her. I fed that fear with the focus of a true mathematician. Mind over matter, they say. So when she told me she wanted a divorce, I wasn't even surprised. I was almost relieved that I didn't have to be afraid anymore." Jason Clyde smiled sadly. "And if I know you, Infinity, you've been expecting this result from day one. You've been anticipating the end from the beginning."

His father was quiet beside him for several long seconds, as if he were deliberating whether to say anymore.

"And you're probably afraid she'll be like Fisher, constantly getting you in trouble. And from what I can see, you might have reason to fear, in that regard."

Finn's dad wasn't trying to be funny—he was deadly serious—which was what made his final statement hilarious, and Finn found himself laughing weakly as the remains of his fury receded—the flood of truth deafening and devastating, but mercifully quick and surprisingly liberating.

"If we're being honest, that's one of the things I like best about her," Finn confessed. "It's one of the things I loved about Fish, even though I pretended to hate it. I never felt more alive, more conscious, than I did with Fish. Not until Bonnie."

"So what do you want, Finn?"

"I want to run far away and never look back. I want to lose myself in formulas and equations and patterns and numbers and never resurface. I never want to see my face on a magazine or a television show again. And I sure as hell don't want to go back to jail."

His dad's jaw slackened in surprise.

"But I want Bonnie more. I want her more than all of those things put together."

"So what are you going to do?"

"I'm going to hope and pray that she still believes in Bonnie and Clyde."

∞

THE CHARGES AGAINST Finn had been dropped. I'd been in contact with my attorney non-stop since I'd been released, and I knew Tuesday night that he was going to be released. I called his dad. I told him Finn needed him, and I asked him to come to LA. Turns out I didn't need to. He was already on his way.

I could have shown up at Finn's arraignment and made a big scene for the reporters who had gathered just to see the spectacle unfold. I could have gone to the jail and waited until they released him, and we could have embraced and made a joint statement to the cameras. But I hadn't. And I knew what some people might make of that. I knew what Finn might make of that. And that scared me.

But Gran had been right about one thing. I didn't wish my life on Finn, even if I loved him so much I couldn't imagine life without him. And because I loved him, I was going to give him the opportunity to walk away, if that's what he wanted to do. Gran told me Clyde wouldn't come. She told me he was only after one thing. Then she'd proceeded to tell me three. I told Gran he could have all of those things—sex, money, and attention—and that I would give him all of those things as often as he wanted them. Happily. For the rest of my life. And I told her to get used to it, because I was married to him, no pre-nup, no conditions, and she'd better be nice or he might divorce me and sue me for every last dime. Then where would she be?

She told me she had talked to Clyde and he just wanted out. He just wanted his life back. She told me if I loved him, I wouldn't want this kind of life for him.

I laughed at that. I laughed so I wouldn't consider the truth in what she said, and then I slapped back.

"Oh, yeah, Gran? That's interesting. So what you're telling me is if *you* loved *me*, you wouldn't want this kind of life for me?"

Gran had stared at me and then made a huffy sound like I was impossible, and she was "through trying to reason with me."

That's when I got good and mad. And that's when I told my grandmother that I loved her. I told her I was sorry for the way I left. And I told her I forgave her for the things she'd done that caused me to run. I told her she would get a lovely percentage of everything I made every year for the rest of her life. A finder's fee, so to speak. She could also keep her house, her car, and whatever she'd stuffed in her mattress and in her panty drawer. I was guessing it was substantial.

And then I told her she was done. I had meant what I said when I said it the first time, ten days before. She was fired.

Then I called my attorney. Again. I'd had a few little chats with him since being released from the LA County jail on Monday night. And with him on speaker and Gran listening, I outlined Gran's retirement package.

I fired the accounting firm which had handled my finances since the day I had won the million dollar recording contract on *Nashville Forever*. They were Gran's employees. Not mine. I threatened to sue them for what they had allowed to happen. I had been cut off of my own accounts, put in a dire situation, and they would meet with me and my new accountant—recommended by a recovering Bear—when I returned from LA, giving me a full accounting of my finances, how my money had been invested, handled, and where the money had been spent over the last six years. They would do this or charges would be filed. I thought Finn would be proud of me.

My attorney assured me I would win. If there had been any fraud, embezzlement, or gross mismanagement, Gran could go to jail. Gran listened to this little tidbit stonily. I told her sweetly that jail wasn't so bad. After all, it had been her fault that I'd gone to jail, now hadn't it? She had created a firestorm that had become a manhunt and a media free-for-all. For what? For attention? For sales? So she could control me?

It was at that point that I informed her, with my attorney listening, that she would not get a dime of her retirement package until my $500,000 was back in the bank, and until my accounts were all in my name and my name alone, with Finn listed as beneficiary if something were to happen to me.

That's when she laughed. And then she disconnected my conference call with my lawyer.

"Why do you think I got the $500,000 out of the bank in the first place, Bonnie Rae? It was ransom money! Finn Clyde contacted me last Wednesday and demanded $500,000 for your release." I must have flinched because she made a sympathetic sound like I was five years old.

I stared into her eyes and tried to remind myself that the coldhearted, manipulating woman I was looking at wasn't all she was. There was more to her than that, just like Bonnie, just like Clyde . . . but for the life of me, I couldn't see it anymore. And I wasn't going to let her see how her words ripped me up. I wasn't going to let her see that part of me believed her.

"He never got it. But I told him it was still his if he left quietly. You'll thank me for this, Bonnie. When your head's clear and you're back on your medication, you'll thank me. That boy's trash," she soothed.

"You can't pay him to stay away from me, Gran. If Finn wants an annulment, that's up to him. And he can have the money—he earned it. But it's my money, and you aren't in any position to make contracts with my money. I believe my attorney would agree. Should we call him back?"

Gran became enraged at that point, and I had to threaten her with my red cowboy boot raised over my head and the crazy Bonnie look on my face, to convince her to back off. Then I demanded her wallet, took her new "company card," the card reserved for my staff, the card that Bear had used to secure my hotel room, and the only one that hadn't been closed, and I told her to leave. She had a plane ticket and her passport to use as ID to get back home, along with whatever cash was in her bra. Plus, she had my meds in her purse, the pills she was so convinced I needed. She could pop a few of those to help her through the coming days. I wasn't too worried about her.

And then I waited for Finn.

28
Point of symmetry

FINN HAD STUCK his room key in his wallet when they left for the Academy Awards. Even then, with Bonnie's hand on his arm, with her cheeks still flushed from the kiss he'd pressed against her neck, with the scent of her on his lips, he'd been afraid they wouldn't come back. His dad was right. He'd expected the worst, he'd mentally planned for it.

In the limo she'd talked about spending two weeks at the Bordeaux. She told him it would be a true honeymoon. Making plans and making bacon, she'd said. They wouldn't go anywhere—except maybe shopping. But not at Walmart. Not again. He'd told her he didn't care where they went shopping, as long as she kept the red boots and wore them often. Even if she wore nothing else. She told him she would wear them every day for the rest of her life if it made him happy. And secretly, maybe even subconsciously, he hadn't believed her. He had known it was going to end.

His dad had taken him to the hotel and told Finn that he was a phone call away. Finn hadn't been stopped or questioned as he'd walked into the posh entrance and headed directly for the elevator. Hope bloomed when his key took him straight to the penthouse floor.

Fear was a hard habit to break, and hope hurt, but it hurt in a way that promised a happy ending. So he stood, outside the door of

INFINITY + ONE

the room he and Bonnie had occupied—Room 704—and waited a full five minutes, feeling the pain of that hope, not wanting to exchange it for the pain of despair. Then he took a deep breath and stuck the key into the slot. When the locks disengaged with a sleek buzz, his heart hitched, and he pushed the handle down and opened the door.

Bedding was piled on the floor, like housekeeping was in the middle of a thorough clean. The TV was on, blaring, and Finn searched the space, walking farther into the suite, climbing the platform that housed the huge bed beneath a ceiling of mirrors. He'd watched Bonnie in those mirrors, worshipped her. Even as she'd slept, feathers in her hair, he hadn't been able to take his eyes away from her face, from the way she'd looked curled next to him, from the image of them together in that way. Perfect, untouchable.

There was no sign of Bonnie. She hadn't called out when he entered the room or come running to see who was there. The euphoria of a working keycard plummeted and pooled like tar in his belly. He felt sick. He walked to the TV, needing to silence it, to soak up what was left of them in the space, and he saw himself, wearing the tux he now wore. He was smiling down at Bonnie and she was beaming up at him like they weren't surrounded by flashing cameras and shocked faces. They'd made their statement, all right. He could see the stunned fascination wherever he looked. Bonnie had waved and glowed, laughed and blown kisses to fans who were seated in makeshift bleachers in designated areas for a small number of diehard stargazers.

The screen split, showing the continuing footage from the awards, as well as the news anchor seated on the Entertainment Buzz set, wearing a sleeveless top that showed off her toned arms and her fake tan. She was talking into the camera with the practiced sobriety and professional cadence of a serious journalist, and as the picture on the screen morphed from footage of him and Bonnie Rae into an old black and white photo of Bonnie and Clyde, she began to tell their story, as if it were breaking news and hadn't happened 85 years before.

Bonnie Parker met Clyde Barrow in Texas, in January of 1930. It was the height of the depression and people were poor, desperate, and hopeless, and Bonnie Parker and Clyde Barrow were no exception. Clyde was twenty years old, Bonnie, nineteen, and though neither had much to offer the other, they became inseparable . . .

Clyde listened, unable to look away, to turn it off. He listened as the reporter compared them to the outlaw couple, twisting their story until it was almost unrecognizable. He listened until the reporter shook her head sadly and asked, *"What happened to Bonnie Rae Shelby?"*

Then he couldn't take anymore. Maybe because he didn't *know* what had happened to her. He didn't know where she was, and he didn't know where to go looking. How was he going to find her? He switched off the TV with a violent shove and turned to leave. He was striding toward the door when he thought he heard the sound of water running. He stopped abruptly, suspended between the fear of being caught in a place he shouldn't be and the hope that finally he was in exactly the right place at the right time. It was the shower. And in that instant he became a believer. God's voice did sound like rushing water.

Finn walked toward the huge bathroom with the heart-shaped, sunken tub and the giant, glass walk-in shower. When he neared the door he heard her, and he smiled, even as his chest ached at the sound. Crying. She was crying in the shower. Again. And Finn found himself laughing through the tears that were suddenly streaming down his own face.

The door wasn't locked. Thank God. Or thank Fish—his guardian angel. Somehow he thought Fish might be the one unlocking bathroom doors for his brother. Naked girls were Fish's favorite thing. He turned the handle and silently asked Fish to please remain outside if he was still lurking around. He needed to hold his wife without an audience.

He shrugged out of his suit jacket and tossed it on the vanity as he pulled open the shower door and stepped under the spray fully-clothed, taking Bonnie into his arms before she even had time to react. She jerked and pulled back, even as she realized it was him.

"Finn? Oh, Finn," she cried, falling against him, holding him tightly and looking up into his face in disbelief. He pushed her streaming hair out of her eyes even as his own dripped heavily down his back.

"Bonnie. You aren't fooling anybody crying in the shower, baby. The water hides your tears, but it doesn't hide the sound, and I don't want you to cry anymore." He kissed her as the water soaked through his shirt, plastering the white cotton to his skin, seeping into the black suit pants, and soaking the shoes that had cost way more than Bonnie's ring. She still wore it, and he kissed that too, frantically. And she cried harder.

"I didn't think you were coming back." She sobbed into his chest, and Finn held her tightly, letting the cascading water wash away the words. He almost hadn't come back, and the thought made his legs weak and his heart quake. He held Bonnie closer, burying his face in her neck and letting his hands stroke the naked length of her body, needing to reassure himself that she was still his. Bonnie was suddenly as frantic as he was, pulling at the buttons of his shirt, trying to peel it off his chest, as if she needed to feel his skin the way he could feel hers. His shirt fell to the shower floor with a heavy, wet slap.

"Your grandmother told me you didn't want to see me again, Bonnie."

Bonnie closed her eyes and her hands stilled, her face crumpling with his words. She shook her head emphatically. "No. That's not true. That's never been true! Not for one second since I met you. I knew exactly what I was doing when I married you. I was just hoping, just praying, that you knew what you were doing."

Bonnie reached for him, laying her palms against his face, tipping her chin up so she could hold his gaze, even as water streamed through her hair down her cheeks. Finn kissed her mouth again, not able to help himself. Her lips trembled beneath his, and he tasted her slick heat and the salty, sweet mix of tears and tender words.

"She told me none of it was real," he whispered against her lips.

"But . . . didn't we decide that we don't want real?" she replied, her mouth never leaving his.

"Yeah. We did," Finn breathed, "but I'll take real too. And I'll take imaginary, and I'll take it all, Bonnie." And he wanted to take it all, he wanted to sink into her and let the endless supply of hot water beat down on their bodies, and for a moment he was sidetracked by her lips and her skin and the swell of her breasts and the way she felt beneath his hands. He wanted it all, but Bonnie—though her hands and mouth were as busy as his—had not stopped crying. It was as if she couldn't believe he was there. As if she still couldn't believe he'd come back.

"I wanted to come find you," Bonnie said, her mouth against his skin, her voice as urgent as her hands. "But I had to let you choose. I thought you might have decided this was all too much. My family, my brother, my life. I hurt you, Finn. So much. It's all my fault. All of it. Bear getting hurt, you getting thrown in jail and accused of things you didn't do. Even the things Hank did. The things Gran did. I put it into motion."

"Shh. No, Bonnie. You can't take responsibility for their greed. Greed put this whole thing in motion, and you have your faults, but greed isn't one of them," Finn soothed. "But none of that would have kept me away."

He captured her hands in his, bracing them against the shower wall so he wouldn't be distracted by her touch, and he laid his forehead against hers, trying to find the right words—the words he needed to say, and the words she needed to hear, so she wouldn't spend her whole life wondering about the way he felt and why he'd come back.

"I love you, Bonnie. So much that I hurt with it. And I hate it, and I love it, and I want it to go away, and I want it to stay forever. And I am terrible at this!" He laughed in frustration. "I feel like I'm asking Bear to have sex with me. Damn, that must have been awful."

"It was," she choked out, half-laughing, half-crying. He stole a kiss then, but didn't release her hands though her body swayed into his, and she protested sweetly.

"This thing we have, it hurts," he continued. "But the pain is almost sweet because it means *you* happened. *We* happened. And I can't regret that, no matter how little or how long I get to tag along with you and pretend that I don't hate having people recognize me or take my picture or having people whisper about my record—"

"Your record?"

"My criminal record, Bonnie. Nothing platinum there. I'm an ex-con, and instead of starting over and building a new life where I can put it behind me, I'm building a new life where it will *never* be behind me, and for you, it's worth it. It's easy math."

"You'd do that for me?"

"No. I'm doing it for me," he confessed.

"I like a selfish man," she said, her face splitting into the smile he loved so much, and Finn felt a tidal wave coming, growing in his chest, and he released her wrists so that he could cradle her face in his hands.

"What's Infinity plus one?" she whispered and kissed his unsmiling mouth, and he answered her from his heart and not his head.

"It's not infinity after all. It's not even two. It's one, Bonnie Rae. Didn't you tell me? You and me? We're two halves of a whole. We're one," and he pulled her up and into him, the steam making a thick fog around their bodies, reminiscent of the night they met on the bridge. The night Bonnie met Clyde. And Finn realized something then. That was the night they both jumped. The night they both let go. The night they both fell.

And that was the biggest paradox of all.

Epilogue

End Behavior

I HAD PULLED all the bedding off the huge white bed and made a pile in the middle of the floor because I couldn't face the mirrors. While I'd waited for Finn to come back to me, I'd slept on the pile, far away from my lonely reflection and the bed where Finn had held me and loved me like he would never let me go.

Finn carried everything back, making the bed neatly, making me laugh at his fussiness. I tended to destroy a room faster than a tornado—something Minnie had hated, and something I pledged to work on so that my fastidious husband had one less thing to tolerate in his life with me. And I would make sure we had maids. Lots of them.

"They're just going to get all messed up again," I pointed out. "You're a powerful lover, Clyde. It will all just end up on the floor again. Just like the first time."

Finn laughed and blushed, just like I'd intended, and I tackled him, toppling him into the center of the fluffed pillows and the straightened duvet. And then we talked about what came next.

Vegas was out. Nashville was out. My brother was going to be on trial for attempted murder in St. Louis, and as much as I longed to be far away from anything concerning my family, Finn and I would both be involved in the trial. Hank had gotten desperate. He had a drug habit and he owed money to some very scary people. When I came up missing, and rumors started to abound that I was in the company of an ex-convict, Hank saw an opportunity to capitalize on it. It wasn't hard. He was living with Gran and knew everything that was happening as it happened. He sent Gran a ransom demand, pretending he was Finn, and arranged a drop off location and a time—Thursday afternoon. But then I'd contacted Bear. Hank got nervous that Bear was going to bring me back before he could get his hands on the money. So he watched Bear's house. When Bear took off Thursday morning for St. Louis, Hank had followed him. When Bear left Finn's father's house in Finn's rental car, without me, Hank had followed him to the gas station, and he'd shot him—shot him in the back so Bear wouldn't interfere, so Hank could collect the ransom that afternoon, and so everyone would think Finn had done it. Hank had been stupid though. He hadn't made sure Bear was dead, and he'd quickly searched the car Bear was driving, stepping over Bear's body to get there. Bear had seen Hank's snakeskin boots, the ones I had given him for Christmas a couple of years before, and he'd known who shot him, even as he lost consciousness. If I had gone back to Nashville with Bear, odds were Hank would have shot me too. And the sad thing was, it wasn't hard for me to believe. Because it wasn't hard to believe, I didn't grieve for him, not the way a sister should grieve for her brother. Hank had never been mine in anything but name, and pretending differently didn't change it.

But there were other reasons to settle in St. Louis. Finn's father had begged Finn to consider going to work for a St. Louis think tank closely associated with the math department at Washington University. It would mean time with his dad and a chance to put his genius to work. He was my Clyde—but there was enough Infinity to go around, and I could share. According to Finn's father, the math community was a small one, and it didn't care about socio-economic status, ethnicity, or even a prison record. If you could do the math—if you loved math—you were welcomed.

St. Louis was only four hours from Nashville, my record label, and my career, which Finn insisted I had to take ownership of. He said I was too brilliant and too destructive to sit still. I needed to be singing. It was what I was born to do. That, and love him. And this time, I couldn't argue with Infinity.

∞

HE WAS ASLEEP now, relaxed and loose, one big arm under his head, one thrown across my body. We hadn't left the suite at all in two days. Food was brought in, clean sheets too, and we were officially holed up. Not because we had to be, but because we wanted to be. And right now, I didn't want to sleep. I was too happy. I wanted to burrow into Finn, but I was restless, and I knew I would wake him up, so I slid out from under his arm and tiptoed to the sitting room and flipped on the television. It had kept me company while I'd waited for Finn, but we hadn't watched it since. I had needed it to drown out the conversation in my head and the fear that he wasn't coming back, and it was on way too loud.

I rushed to lower the volume but halted when I saw a familiar face fill the screen. And this time it wasn't my own. And it wasn't Finn's either, thankfully. It was Shayna's, and Katy sat at her side smiling shyly into the camera, a cute flowered hat on her head.

The camera cut away to a different scene almost immediately, and I realized I'd missed the point of Shayna's appearance. Another interview, probably pre-recorded, between an older man and a boy and one of the E-Buzz reporters began. The old man told the reporter how "Bonnie and Clyde" had stopped when no when else would. He explained how we had followed him to make sure he and his grandson made it home safely, and he got a little choked up when he relayed that I had given his grandson money to help with repairs on his daughter's van, unbeknownst to him. It was Ben and his grandfather!

My mouth fell open in amazement as another interview, this one apparently live, began.

"So you're telling us that Bonnie and Clyde picked you up when you were hitchhiking?" the pretty blonde correspondent asked the afroed man with the grizzly beard and the oversized army coat.

"Yes, ma'am they did. And they treated me kind. They sure did. Miss Bonnie gave me food, and Mr. Infinity gave me his boots." The camera panned down to his feet where, sure enough, William was displaying Finn's old boots like they were the best gift he'd ever received.

"I was naked and you clothed me, I was sick and you visited me, I was in prison and you came to me.' Then the righteous will answer him, saying, 'Lord, when did we see you hungry and feed you, or thirsty and give you drink? And when did we see you a stranger and welcome you, or naked and clothe you?"

I shrieked with laughter when William pulled the microphone from the reporter's hand and got right up into the camera, preaching his favorite sermon with a voice worthy of a packed hall. He finished his scripture with a thrust of his dirty finger into the lens.

"And the King will answer them, 'Truly, I say to you, as you did it to one of the least of these my brothers, you did it to me!'" William's eyes were fierce on the lens as the reporter managed to retrieve her microphone.

"Thank you, William. Well, you heard it here, folks. Reports have been coming in from people who say they were helped or assisted or enriched by the cross-country flight of Bonnie and Clyde, ever since all charges were dropped and the two were released, separately, from LA County jail."

"Praise the Lord for their release! God protects his servants!" William could be heard shouting in the background. Then his face filled the screen once more, blocking out the young reporter who had completely lost control of the situation.

"Miss Bonnie? If you is watchin', listen up. I had a dream last night. A girl named Minnie and a boy named Fish—looked just like you and Mr. Infinity—they told me they is saving you two a big room in the Grand Hotel, but no hurry. You've got Infinity, and they've got

each other. And Fish says, 'Who's the genius now?'"

The feed was cut and a commercial for a new season of *Nashville Forever* flashed across the screen, but I was too stunned to move.

"Bonnie Rae?"

Finn was standing behind me, his face lined with sleep, his body gloriously uncovered. He'd said my name, but his eyes were fixed on the TV—his expression incredulous.

I threw back my head and laughed. I could have danced around and said "I told you so," but I didn't. What William had just said was unbelievable. Impossible even. But, then again, he'd really said it all with a message on a little cardboard sign.

I believe in Bonnie and Clyde.

∞

BEAR RECOVERED AND eventually got his car back, though I had already bought him a new one. As promised, he received a substantial raise and hazard pay, which he thought was funny, but Finn said was only fair, considering I was an accident waiting to happen. We also retrieved our belongings from the backseat, along with that cardboard sign I would have hated to part with.

I had it matted and framed, and it hangs in our house in St. Louis on a wall filled with pictures from the disposable camera Monique gave us on our wedding day. There are pictures of us at the wedding chapel in Vegas and standing beside the "Death Car" riddled with bullets in Primm. I even framed magazine clippings of us on the red carpet at the Academy Awards, along with copies of our mug shots because they made me laugh, and Finn hated them. I told him we were jailbirds and lovebirds, and it was funny. And he was the one who'd said, "Sometimes funny is all you've got."

But we had a great deal more than funny, and I never wanted to take it for granted. That's why, in the center of it all, I framed an enlarged, black and white photo of the original Bonnie and Clyde, arms around each other, standing against the backdrop of desperate times. And I framed Bonnie Parker's words so I wouldn't forget our own incredible journey and the vows that Finn and I had made. It was Bonnie's version of 'til death do us part.

"The road was so dimly lighted.
There were no highway signs to guide.
But they made up their minds,
If all roads were blind,
They wouldn't give up 'til they died."

And I planned on living a long, long time.

The End

Author's Notes and Acknowledgements

I THINK EVERY book is harder to write than the last. It's a lonely occupation, the pressure increases, the expectations rise, and each time I know full well how much work it's going to require, which is intimidating in itself. But I can't think of anything else I would rather do. I love writing books that readers can sink their teeth into. I love learning new things, discovering hidden meaning, and falling in love with a whole new set of characters. But as lonely as writing can be, I couldn't do it alone and need to acknowledge and thank some folks.

First off, I am not a mathematician. I had to read and study extensively to even begin to understand how someone like Finn thinks. Luckily for me, my mother IS a mathematician. She read *Infinity + One* before anyone else and made sure there wasn't any fuzzy math, so to speak. I am so grateful for her insights and her brilliance; the book is dedicated to her because without her, there wouldn't be a book.

I'd also like to thank my go-to guy, Andrew Espinoza, retired police sergeant, for patiently talking me through legalities and police procedures and helping me navigate so many unknown areas. I took creative license here and there, and any mistakes or elaborations are my own. Andy has answered my questions on my last three novels, and I am so grateful for his expertise.

Special thanks to Tamara Debbaut, who has proven to be an invaluable personal assistant. In addition, a big thank you goes to Vilma Gonzalez for her superb organizational skills, her friendship, and her professionalism. To Karey White, a great author and editor, thank you for making *Infinity + One* sparkle. And, as always, I don't know what I'd do without Julie Titus of JT formatting. She is my right hand in all my formatting needs and has become a valued friend. To the team at Dystel and Goderich, specifically Jane and Lauren, thank you for everything. To Rebecca Berto of Berto designs, thank you for the beautiful cover, you do fabulous work! Finally, thank you Lamine Kacimi for your management of my website. You have made my life so much easier.

To my beta readers on this project: Alice Landwehr, Emma Corcoran, Cristina Suarez-Munoz, Michelle Cunningham, Shannon McPherson and Vilma Gonzalez, big thanks, ladies. Beta reading is a hard job and an often thankless one. It takes courage to tell an author she stinks. *wink, wink*

To so many readers, bloggers, and authors out there who have welcomed me so kindly and who make this all possible, thank you from the bottom of my heart. I could start naming names, but would leave someone out, and would hate to do that. You all have my sincere and humble gratitude for your support with this new book and with past projects. Words just don't suffice. Thank you.

The lyrics of the folk songs I included in *Infinity + One* are all public domain as well as the poetry written by Bonnie Parker—"Suicide Sal" and "The Story of Bonnie and Clyde,"—and no copyright infringement was intended. The song, "Infinity + One," that Bonnie sang in the Albuquerque night club is a song I wrote for the book. The lyrics to "Machine" were written by Paul Travis and permission was granted to use his song in this story.

To my husband, Travis Harmon, and to my children – Paul, Hannah, Claire and Sam – thank you, my loves. Thank you for sharing me and putting up with me.

To my parents, siblings, in-laws, and friends – thank you for your support and for your enthusiasm.

And always, all gratitude for Jesus who pilots me.

About the Author

AMY HARMON IS a USA Today and New York Times Bestselling author. Amy knew at an early age that writing was something she wanted to do, and she divided her time between writing songs and stories as she grew. Having grown up in the middle of wheat fields without a television, with only her books and her siblings to entertain her, she developed a strong sense of what made a good story. Her books are now being published in several countries, truly a dream come true for a little country girl from Levan, Utah. Amy Harmon has written five novels - the USA Today Bestsellers, *Making Faces* and *Running Barefoot*, as well as *Slow Dance in Purgatory*, *Prom Night in Purgatory*, and the New York Times Bestseller, *A Different Blue*.

For more information about Amy and her books, visit:

http://www.authoramyharmon.com/
https://www.facebook.com/authoramyharmon
http://www.goodreads.com/author/show/5829056.Amy_Harmon
https://twitter.com/aharmon_author

Printed in Great Britain
by Amazon